For Lisa

THE SHADOWLESS

by
Christopher D. Schmitz

Stay in the light!

The Affliction Cycle

Special Offer:

Get the Shadowless prequel novella, *The Dark Veil Opens,* from Christopher D. Schmitz FOR FREE

More details found at the end of this book. Subscribers who sign up for his no-spam newsletter get free books, exclusive content, and more!

https://www.subscribepage.com/shadowless

© 2021 by Christopher D. Schmitz

All rights reserved. No part of this book may be reproduced, stored in a retrieval system, or transmitted in any form or by any means without the prior written permission of the publishers, except by a reviewer who may quote brief passages in a review to be printed in a newspaper, magazine, or journal.

The final approval for this literary material is granted by the author.

PUBLISHED BY TREESHAKER BOOKS
please visit:
http://www.authorchristopherdschmitz.com

For my KIDS...

Just in case I never told you, there really *were* MONSTERS in your closets.

THE SHADOWLESS

Prologue

Doctor Raymond Lems awoke with a gasp and sat up. Pain riddled his body. It forced him to drop back upon the collapsible stretcher where he found himself laying. His torso felt like someone stabbed him with burning pokers. Raymond touched his hand to his chest and looked at it with groggy eyes. *Blood.*

With great effort he lifted his head enough to glimpse his chest. Raymond cried out as he peeled away the blood-soaked gauze. *Bullet holes—and why can't I hear anything?* He could only feel an empty rattle in his throat as he screamed—tinnitus drowned out all sounds. Shock rang in his ears, drowning out everything else.

Where in the Hell am I? What happened—this is all General Braff's fault. I'm certain of it!

Raymond didn't recognize the room, though it looked familiar... these were the same color schemes company designers painted at his research lab; supposedly they calmed people. He growled. Raymond had quit the lab after finding they had begun secret experiments on children and the disabled.

Wiping away a hot tear, he tried to piece everything together, but he couldn't remember anything that had happened since meeting up with Agent Scofield at that crappy diner. "Why can't I remember?" he barely heard his voice as the ringing in his ears lessened.

He knew why he couldn't remember, but he refused to entertain such a notion. If he had become a carrier—if those *things* had controlled his body—then all hope was lost.

Even though Raymond wasn't a medical physician, he was still a doctor, and as such he recognized many of the haphazardly strewn medical supplies upon on the table next to him. A bag of blood hung on a rack; it fed into his IV and kept him from bleeding out. *Why did they leave me here? Where are the doctors and nurses?*

A second bag of fluid hung nearby—this one contained a mix with morphine in it, but it hadn't been injected yet. Shakily, Raymond pinched the catheter and rammed it into a vein. It only took a few tries. After a few seconds, the pain relaxed enough that his ears began operating again; his body fought back against the trauma and shock.

He looked over his body again, assessing the swelling and purple bruises. Some kind of noise blurped in the hallway as he looked over the bullet wound.

Who in the Hell shot me? Raymond wondered as he scanned his surroundings with fresh eyes. *And who puts a gunshot victim in a supply room?* He groaned and crawled off the bed before staggering across the linoleum. He knew the answer: *someone with no intention of coming back.*

The research scientist yanked the intravenous lines from his arms and pushed open the door where the swelling sounds of chaos greeted him. Yellow lights flashed everywhere in the hall, bathing everything with pulsating amber. Warning sirens shrieked in time with klaxon lights. Inhuman screams echoed from a nearby stairwell sounding like some kind of portal to the underworld he'd often joked that his and Swaggart's madcap research would open.

Raymond stumbled across the hall and found a door with a familiar nameplate. He scowled, but opened the entrance to General Roderick Braff's office and locked it behind him.

"Where are you, Swaggart?" Raymond limped across the hallway and towards the broken window at the far side of the room wondering where his friend had gone. Blood leaked from his oversaturated bandages and he felt light headed.

Shards of glass crunched underfoot as he meandered past the general's ornate, wooden desk. A bittersweet odor tugged at his nose. The doctor grabbed clumsily at the smoldering cigar that lay on the desktop.

With shaky fingers, Raymond barely succeeded in placing the smoking husk between his lips by the time he got to the busted window pane. He peeked out at the commotion. A herd of bodies sprinted across the far slope, heading up the hillside in a herd panic. Dread filled the researcher's gut with hot regret. It all made sense: the blackout, the gunshots, the sirens. *The entities have broken free from their containment units in the basement.*

He looked at the ground and noticed an empty shoe abandoned upon the tangle of broken, bloody glass. Raymond couldn't be certain, but he thought it could be Braff's brand. It made him happy to think that someone had finally thrown that bastard through a second story window. He just wished it could have been there to see it.

Raymond looked back towards the mountainside. The peaks stood in stark contrast to the eerie light glowing behind them. Then, something brilliant flashed and all the light on Earth went out.

PART I.

BLOODGUILT

1,291 Days Post Extinction-Day

1

Michelle ignored the gentle hum of fluorescent panels; their ever-present whir assured them of protection like some kind of 60-cycle Holy Spirit. She looked across the room at her older brother and the priest. "I hope Ricky won't be too much trouble, Father."

She and the Father Ackley both looked at Ricky.

Ricky folded and tucked his tattered paperback into his belt. Her big brother took that old book everywhere he went; *1001 Jokes and Puns* was a kind of security blanket that he'd carried with him for years—even since before they'd arrived at the facility.

Fidgeting with one of the priest's origami models, Ricky squinted against the sterile, mechanical light.

Despite having Down syndrome, Ricky possessed a certain, keen intelligence. His sister recognized it, even if she was biased. He always concentrated on something new and exciting.

Father asked, "How long have you known me, Michelle?"

"Ever since arriving here on E-day... about three years, now."

"Have I ever let you down?"

She sighed. "No."

Father put a hand on her diminutive shoulder. The feisty woman didn't protest his attempt to comfort her. He was one of only a few who could get away with it. Ever conscious of her size, she typically interpreted such acts as condescension.

"I've got this," Father insisted. "He won't be any problem at all."

They both glanced over at Ricky. The gentle giant slowly and methodically unfolded the paper toys, noting exactly how they went together. He struggled through the first couple of folds and then lost his way. Ricky turned to his sister. Worry creased his face and he feared he'd broken one of Father's figurines.

"Don't worry," Father reassured him. "I can put them back together, and I'll even show you how to fold your own. Is there something you want to make?"

Ricky's demeanor brightened, and he turned back to the papers. "I like ducks," he said. "Let's make a whole flock."

Father smiled at him and nodded. He turned to Michelle and repeated, "Don't worry. You need this break. Before you know it, you're going to be busier than you'd have ever imagined."

"Fine," she huffed, flooding her voice with begrudged resignation that belied how badly she wanted to stretch her legs in the miles of maze-like tunnels below the mountain. The complex had been their home ever since Extinction-day: the day mankind nearly died out. "But I'm going to find some of those supplies we talked about. I'm sure that there's got to be a cache of prenatal vitamins in the facility somewhere... Lord knows we've got everything else stockpiled."

"I'm sure you will find them," Father assured her. That's what he did; it was why people trusted him to lead. "Oh, one more thing I want to warn you about," he said, making sure he had her attention. "There is a man, a recluse of sorts... people have spotted him in the halls from time to time.

Nobody knows his real story; why he's a recluse remains a mystery."

She met his gaze. "'The Hermit of the Halls?' I've heard of him from the others… only rumors, really. I think I saw him once, a long time ago. What about him?"

"Just… stay away from him," he asked, but he looked at her sternly enough that it felt more like a direct order. "You have no idea how important you are to this community. What if medical problems arise over the next trimester?"

Michelle downplayed his warning. She understood her role in Earth's remaining population.

Shrugging off the warning, she honestly hadn't thought about the stranger in years—but now that he'd mentioned it, Michelle felt distracted by all manner of what-if scenarios.

As one of the community members with limited access codes for the secure areas, like the infirmary and medical storage, she had recognized signs that another person had accessed locked places from time to time. Nobody could ever explain the odd things she noticed when asked and she suddenly wondered if this "hermit" had some kind of high-level security clearance.

Outside of the remnant, he was the only other human left alive on the planet and why he wandered the corridors instead of joining the community proved a great mystery. Michelle bobbed her head in absentminded agreement before she turned to leave Father's office. She smiled at Ricky who waved goodbye.

"Michelle?" The priest knew she hadn't paid him any mind.

She met his gaze this time.

"I mean it. Don't go stepping into any shadows."

Michelle nodded, understanding his inference.

Illumination panels on the facility walls and ceilings made the notion impossible in a literal sense. "I'll be careful.

I promise." She shouldered her canvas backpack and left Father's office.

Crossing the main community square, she waved to Janet and flashed a lackadaisical smile before exiting the central hub of the main residential zone.

The only female resident with any military experience, Janet often assisted Michelle in medical procedures. She had received enough cursory training in the army to make her an asset.

Janet fired back with an inquisitive look as the diminutive doctor headed towards the cloistered community's primary exit. Michelle said nothing as she walked past; she'd kept her brief vacation quiet, coveting her calm before the storm began and she was tied to the delivery room.

Michelle entered the endless miles of well-lit, manmade tunnels some unknown third party had the foresight to construct before the apocalypse began.

Swag shuddered and woke under the artificial brightness of the UV lights. He floundered and sucked air as he blinked rapidly, finally coming back to full consciousness. In a fresh panic he wiped the saline crust from his eyes.

It must be time to increase the dosage, he recognized with a racing heart. He'd begun to dream again—something he absolutely had to avoid. *A familiar dream—that reoccurring one from when I was a kid! The monster under my bed... waiting for me to fall asleep as it whispered in the dark. A demon voice like drums whispering to more of its own kind.*

He shivered and shook his head—at least it was just a stupid kiddie-nightmare and not the real thing. *That* he had seen in person.

Reaching for his pocket he noticed his supply had run low. Drugs helped Swag rest... they kept away the dreams. He'd used them for such a long while now that he barely remembered the last time he dreamed—not since before the E-day tragedy. No more dreams... *no more nightmares.*

Even if his mind occasionally ruminated over nostalgic memories, he never truly slept, so this momentary dip into a dream cycle surprised him. Usually his exhausted brain relived the good old days as if his mind replayed home movies—like that time Raymond purchased a cheesy wedding cake for them to celebrate the anniversary of their first big breakthrough in the lab... the day they'd implanted a rat with the mysterious parasite they'd discovered. *"Well, it's unlikely either of us will ever marry at this rate," he had laughed by the time their third anniversary arrived.* Swag shook away the ethereal image of better times long since gone.

He would need to restock his pharmaceutical cache before nighttime... not that any person ever knew when dusk really fell.

With a stiff groan, he rolled to his side and climbed to his feet. He'd laid all night curled up against an air recycler that vibrated slightly, but emitted its subtle warmth. Swag glanced at the *Ark I* nameplate above the machinery and sighed, closing his eyes to block out the ever-present electric luminaries. He was glad for the safety they provided, but their sterile light burnt his itchy eyes and ground a bone-weary tiredness into his soul.

Swag didn't want to open his eyes until his tear ducts lubricated them enough to tolerate the recycled air. His mind drifted in the darkness and replayed scenes from that cursed night. He opened his lids early and rubbed the remaining, crusty particles from the edges.

Three years had passed since this all started, but the darkness began long before E-day, for him anyways. The evil creatures found him long before the containment system failed at the lab and the Eidolon Commission initiated E-day protocols.

He shambled down the corridor and squinted against the light panels that ensured a minimum brightness threshold. Any area where humans might venture within the miles of tunnels that twisted through Ark I had them.

Swag wandered adrift for an hour, meandering through the endless halls which looped through the guts of the mountain like intestines of some giant, earthen-beast. The thin air tickled his throat and made him cough.

He sniffed and took gauge of its quality. Every day since the last, it seemed to grow in quality; the available oxygen supply was on the rise.

Swag descended a sloped ramp and wandered near an intersection of paths. One corridor that terminated at an exterior hatch had fallen black. Its electric light banks no longer operated.

As he stared at the blackness, Swag's heartbeat thumped in his ears. Ethereal voices called his name from the shadows. Swag's eyelids fluttered. He turned and fled from the dark spot—only a few such places existed within the Ark. Any of them might contain the *things… the entities.*

Finally calming down, his ears picked up the whirring servos of a repair drone before he saw it. Two tripod automatons buzzed around a corner and zipped past him on motorized wheels. They plunged into the darkness of the hallway where Swag knew no human dared go. He watched curiously as the service bots followed their programming. They dismantled the next furthest set of light panels and removed their light tubes, pirating them for some other luminary that had failed elsewhere in the Ark: likely in some neighborhood closer to the population.

Swag shook his head. He'd seen inside the storage rooms and knew the backup supplies of light tubes stacked thirty feet tall. They would never run out of bulbs.

"Droids are buggy," Swag muttered, quoting Hank Chu, the man who had programmed the robotic maintenance units during the Ark's original construction. His voice echoed in the empty hall.

The whole place had gone together so quickly that occasional glitches were expected—despite the level of Hank's genius.

Swag grimaced at the sound of his own voice. He wondered how long it had been since he'd last spoken words aloud? Months probably. Swag had begun feeling a little like those automated repair units. The units tootled cheerfully at each other and ferried the scavenged parts away. He shrugged and resumed his regular voyage towards the medical storage room.

Michelle crept up on Percy and Gordon as they each pulled heavy, rubberized environmental suits over their bodies. They noticed her when she got near and nodded to acknowledge her presence.

"Taking a walk, Doctor?" Percy grinned, looking down at her. He slid on the gummy, galosh-style crampons. They fit over their boots with inserted LEDs built into the clear rubber. "Gotta get in some R and R before the babies arrive."

Percy and Gordon, two of the military men among the remnant, stood significantly taller than Michelle's optimistic four-foot eight. At least soldiers were usually disciplined enough to keep any condescension from their voices.

She frowned momentarily. Michelle knew she looked more like a child than an adult. She glanced forlornly at her waist; her condition went beyond the mere proportions of her body, she knew.

"It looks like you guys are doing the same?" she shot them an inquisitive look. "Taking a walk, that is."

The whole community had been mobilized in the months since Father discovered new environmental data on the local sensors. Their recent findings proved encouraging: perhaps things were not as hopeless as they'd originally seemed for the species.

"We've gotta clean the dust out of the ports on sensor sixteen again. A windstorm jammed it all up for the second time this week," Gordon said matter-of-factly.

Fascinated by the equipment, Michelle watched them finish dressing in some kind of hybrid hazmat-spacesuits. The men assisted each other as they locked on the clunky helmets.

Shoulder mounts held four steel rods that supported a metal halo where light fixtures hung at overlapping angles to provide an illuminated circle of protection around the workers.

Percy and Gordon turned the knobs on hip-mounted bottles. They fed oxygen into their containment suits. "Switch on," Gordon's deep voice came from the tiny, shoulder mount speaker.

They safety locked their switches and the light rings blazed brilliantly. Gordon pressurized the compartment that adjoined to the exit doorway.

"Don't lock us out!" Percy teased the doctor as his partner opened the hatch and the two men stepped through. A moment later, they walked well beyond the safety of the Ark and into the barren countryside.

Michelle watched them go, not sure if she should be jealous of their ability to exit the facility or terrified on their behalf.

#

Purgatory, Swag thought as he paced slowly. *If that was a real thing, that's what this seems like—paying the price of penance.* He grimaced as his thoughts touched the religious. *But Evangelicals didn't believe in purgatory, either.*

He spat and mused over his name. *Jimmy Swaggart.* His hyper religious parents saddled him with the unfortunate moniker at birth and he'd endured Armageddon to finally be free of it. The scientist frowned, unsure it had been a good trade.

Swag sighed. *Not penance. Not atonement... those were religious concepts—debt collection? Due penalty?* Old feelings of guilt trickled back into his heart before he could harden it against them. He wasn't prepared to entertain such philosophical thoughts and so early in the morning. Swag looked for any available distraction.

A broken drone slumped near the wall. Its servos had spooled out to the max so that it appeared to slouch. Painted in red block lettering on the shoulder area, the number seventeen identified it. Apparently, Seventeen's peers had pirated components off of its body. Swag felt a certain pity for the machine.

"I miss the doing," Swag confessed to his robotic confidant. "I miss knowing that I was useful, you know? Of course you do; you're a robot—your purpose is the reason for your existence." He stared at the empty battery compartment.

"You know what I miss? A proper toilet." He stared at the machine's dead camera. It had slouched to about eye level for him; they normally stood a little over six feet. Surely the machine wouldn't understand the differences between the composting latrine system that fed the botanical systems and the flush variety. "Proper toilets... I'd happily endure another apocalypse if we could have them back. I don't know what Hank was thinking." He chuckled awkwardly. *Maybe I have been away from people too long*; he recognized he'd slipped well past eccentricity, although conversation skills had never been a strong suit for him.

Swag wished for the old days again... before E-day, before office politics, before he'd ever heard of Franklin Cuthbert and his prestigious science team.

Human voices echoed down the hall. Swag took his leave of Seventeen and hurried down the corridor, stopping at a hatch sealed with a numeric lock. At the distant bend, a trio of workers from the community rounded the edged and caught sight of Swag just as he finished keying a code into the lock mechanism.

A large man carried a battery. Two others flanked him: a woman with a satchel and a very thin man with glasses. Glasses stutter stepped when their eyes met his. Swag pushed his way through before any of them could call out. The door locked behind him.

Heart racing, Swag couldn't tell if he felt exhilaration, fear, or guilt. The humans approached in the hall, likely speculating about the recluse's past. Swag could only hear muffled words as they paused outside the locked portal.

He dreaded the possibility of a knock and held his breath. No knock came, and the group returned to whatever errand they'd come on.

Swag exhaled and scanned the room. He was in the infirmary. One of many such stations, this one, like the others, had been staged for some kind of procedure. He wasn't a medical doctor, but one of the remnant must have possessed some physician's training, at least.

Catching sight of himself in the mirror Swag stared at the scruffy, unkempt man looking back at him. He felt suddenly tempted to shave and comb his hair. Obviously, his momentary break-down with the machine was some kind of subconscious cry for help by a fragile psyche—perhaps he ought to make himself presentable, walk up to the first human he could find, and introduce himself?

And say what, he argued. *Oh, Jane? Lovely to meet you—maybe you heard of me? I'm the guy who destroyed the planet!* Swag blew a sarcastic raspberry. *Just lie. Obviously.*

He shrugged, knowing he could grab a toiletries kit in the adjoining room and clean up to look like a proper gentleman if he so chose.

Swag shook his head and banished the thought. He rarely won arguments with himself. Swag looked for a way to placate his mind, to distract himself from any real self-talk.

He turned away from the mirror and spotted the cedar box on a ledge nearest the door. Swag snorted mischievously and flipped the cigar humidor upside down, exposing the letters J.B. that were engraved into the underside, just as he had done on his last six visits. Whoever staged the room must have thought someone played a game with him or her.

Swag turned and exited through a rear door. Keying in the code again—Hank's master code—he walked into the connecting medical storage bay.

The room yawned wide and rows of steel, utilitarian racks stood perched throughout the chamber like giant dominoes. Swag knew what he wanted and exactly where to find it. He passed the toiletries without a second thought and drew nearer the familiar location.

He cast a glance at some of the empty racks in the distance. Not everything had been placed in its proper spot before the world ended. Swag knew the missing supplies were likely on site somewhere, buried deep within the underground warehouses full of provisions.

The addict arrived and stood near a tall, steel rack he'd raided before. Swag opened the container of vacuum sealed drugs and tore free a packet of generic prazosin.

Swag clutched the pouch of drugs in his fist. If there was one thing he could not endure, it was dreaming. He would have rather entertained those three workers in the hall as guests for tea than let his haunted dreams—the dark *memories*—catch up to him.

He glanced at the clock on a distant wall. It took him most of the day to get to the drug cache and was not too early for a dose. He stuffed a handful of pills into his mouth and opened the door back into the hallway. The capsules stuck in his throat and he swallowed hard, noticing that Seventeen had disappeared.

2

Swag felt the shadow fall over his face and startled awake! No, not a shadow, he realized as he opened his eyes: just something in between he and the light.

He licked his cracked lips and looked into the face of the young girl who examined him intently. Sitting upright, Swag suddenly felt very self-conscious.

She stuck her hand out and introduced herself. "My name's Michelle."

Swag shook her outstretched hand slowly and arched his brows. The playful look on her face reinforced the appearance of her youth. He scanned her up and down wondering how a child had wandered away from the remnant. "Swag," he responded to her introduction.

Michelle tilted her head and watched as Swag stumbled to his feet. He looked disheveled and ill-kept, although his clothes did not look nearly as ratty as expected for the last homeless man in existence.

She suspected he had some kind of access to a laundry facility and used it on occasion. He wasn't emaciated either, so he must've also had access to food stores. His health was fine—he was just shaggy. Michelle shrugged and smirked at the nomad.

Swag met her gaze and felt immediately embarrassed, even though her scrutiny didn't indicate any condescension. "Are you lost? Where are your parents?"

Michelle sighed and rolled her eyes and backed off in a huff. "Yup." She turned as if leaving. "You're just like everyone else, after all."

"What do you mean?" Swag called after her, concerned he'd blown the first real conversation he'd had with another human in three years. He scowled, and his innate problem-solving nature bristled. Swag didn't know what he'd said that was wrong, but he desperately wanted to correct it.

Michelle turned back and stared at him with intense eyes—experienced eyes.

Swag suddenly understood. Her face wasn't quite like a teenager's and her eyes owned far more experience than any child.

She dumped several years' worth of pent up ire on him. "I'm not just some little girl, you know!"

He raised his hands in surrender. "Okay. Okay, I understand."

Not leaving and not relaxing, she glared at him with a set jaw and fumed.

"Okay. I don't understand." He held his breath. *So much for reintegrating back into society*, he thought.

Michelle glared a few seconds longer and finally exhaled. She smoothed her hair and looked at him again, this time with softer eyes. "Let's start over," she said measuredly. "I'm Michelle."

He saw her age, now. Something in her commanding tone allowed her to take control of a situation in a way that no child could.

"I'm Swag," he said again. His hands hung at his side since she hadn't offered a handshake this time. He bowed slightly, instead.

Michelle stifled a single laugh. "Well that was pretty awkward," she chuckled. "How about we skip the formal introductions and take a walk? I think you can help me."

Swag scanned the bright corridors. "Where are you going?" He stutter stepped and caught up to her; she'd already started to walk in the opposite direction he'd expected... away from the community.

"Pishon." She scanned a laminated map card as she walked ahead.

"The far garden?" Catching up to her was not hard. Michelle's short legs didn't allow her that much speed.

"Yeah. I want to do a little sightseeing before my schedule gets slammed."

"But there are *shadows* in the garden!"

Michelle looked at Swag intrepidly. "Don't worry. I'll protect you. Mankind coexisted with the darkness for millennia. I'm sure I can handle a visit to a garden."

Swag swallowed and kept step with her. A few silent moments passed, and the momentary fear was forgotten. Finally, he beckoned her to follow him. Michelle put her map away.

"So what's your *real* name," Michelle asked.

"Why does that matter?"

"Curiosity," she said. "I just want to know."

He mulled over the opportunity to lower the oldest of his defenses. He bit his lip and finally admitted, "Doctor Jimmy Swaggart."

Michelle laughed. "I didn't know we were going to get fancy with titles." She stopped and bowed to him. "Doctor." She grinned, "How come you go by Jimmy instead of James? Wouldn't that sound more formal?"

"No." He scowled with faked the bluster, just glad she'd laughed at something other than his burdensome name. "I don't go by either."

She held up her hands in surrender to his imitation outrage. "Swag it is. But if I knew we were bringing professional credentials into it..." she reintroduced herself with a curtsey and a fake southern accent. "Doctor Michelle Taggert."

Swag looked at her skeptically. "Doctor?"

"As if pieces of paper mean anything in this world anymore," she stated sarcastically. "But yes. And I'm just grateful I'll never have to repay all those student loans. Thank you, apocalypse."

"Doctor of what?"

She started walking again as they conversed. "Obstetrics. How about you?"

Swag laughed. "Nothing quite so useful!"

Michelle laughed, "You must be a psychologist?"

He shook his head. "Even less useful, still. I have a PhD in Quantum Mechanics and specialize in Zenotian Para-Existential Fields."

"Totally useless," she agreed. "If we still had money I'd bet that you just made that up. That's gotta be a fake thing."

Swag shrugged. "It almost is. I pioneered the original research on Zenotian Para-Existential Fields, but the whole thing was mostly classified by the government—so it's not like it could ever prove it's a thing, anyways. I'd lose your bet."

"So, make your case, then. What is it?"

"We derived the field from research into the Quantum Zeno Effect." He saw the excitement in her eyes glaze over.

"Who's *we*?" She jumped at the chance to divert him away from the hard science of his work.

Swag frowned. "Raymond. He's my… he was my best friend before all of… this." He waved to indicate the miles of subterranean tubes that made up Ark I.

"You two were very close?"

Swag wordlessly worked his mouth for a second. The complexity of their relationship hit him in waves. Finally, he bit his lip and nodded.

"We discovered Zenotian para-existentiality in my garage during college. We were something like prodigies." He glanced at her tiny frame. "But what about you? Some kind of child phenom like Doogie Howser?"

Michelle rolled her eyes. "You have no idea how many times I've been called that."

"How old are you, then?"

"Twenty-six," Michelle said matter-of-factly—an adult, though not old enough to have watched the original television series' broadcast. She pointed to her face and then waved her finger around at the rest of her body. "Turner's syndrome. I'm a chromosome short of the full Monty, but hey, it keeps me looking young and fresh, right? Even if it means I need a stepladder to wash the dishes."

He smiled sympathetically. Swag knew what it was like to be overlooked for his accomplishments. He'd honestly lost track of his own age, but he knew he was somewhere in his early thirties.

She flashed him a salacious grin. "Of course," she continued in her sardonic tone, "why any guy would intentionally avoid a 'Beach Boys scenario' is beyond me."

"Beach Boys?"

"You know. Two girls for every guy?"

Swag responded with an ignorant look.

"You really don't know much about the remnant, do you? Of the three hundred and thirteen souls left, one hundred ninety are female."

He nodded with sudden understanding, finally catching her reference.

"It's kinda why I'm out here. I had to get away from all the baby-making. I feel a little useless as one of the few humans left on Earth that can't contribute to the repopulation efforts."

Swag narrowed his gaze.

She shrugged in response and reiterated. "Turner's syndrome."

"Repopulation?"

"Yeah. We voted. Breeding moratorium is reversed—it's become something of a duty to the species, now. Data indicates the oxygen levels outside might be in recovery. I mean, if projections are right, the atmosphere won't be breathable for almost two decades but it's time to start planning for a future. Mankind's not done, yet."

"I guess I never really considered there would even be a moratorium. I mean, Ark I is supposed to have enough supplies to last a hundred-thousand people for almost two decades with standard rationing."

"I *knew* it!" Michelle accused. "I knew you had more information than you let on; only a few people know about the stockpiled supplies. *Who are you?* Who were you before E-day?"

Swag grimaced, tight-lipped. Something about Michelle had made him forget to play his cards as close to the vest as usual. He looked into her eyes and his voice almost wavered as he spoke. "Whoever I was… I'm not him anymore, so it's not important."

She stared at him and Swag knew Michelle wouldn't give up on learning his secrets.

"There's a machinery pool up this way," he changed the subject.

They rounded the corner and Swag quickly passed the turn-off to the dark hallway, refusing to look at it. Michelle stopped in her steps and stared into the deep, unfamiliar black. Swag walked back and stood next to her. She stared into the inky murk, transfixed by the corridor's seeming vastness.

Swag inched closer. "Michelle?" The closer he crept, the clearer he heard the otherworldly whispers speaking to him with some indecipherable language of the dark. He knew only he could hear it. Prior to E-day, the gibbering echoes had begun calling to him, threatening his mind with overwhelming madness.

He put a hand on Michelle's shoulder. His touch startled her from the trance and she recoiled, almost falling into his arms. She shook her head clear and stepped back.

"Where does it go?" she asked.

"It's a maintenance shaft for the solar collection fields. It eventually leads up to the surface. The service bots use it pretty regularly."

Michelle nodded, regaining her composure. "We were headed to the machine pool?"

"Straight this way," Swag pointed ahead. They drew nearer to a corrugated, sliding door which opened by crawling into the ceiling and revealed a shocked teenager.

Swag locked eyes with the skinny, young man he'd seen the previous day. The startled youth stood next to the repaired and operational drone, Seventeen.

"Edward!" Michelle exclaimed. "What are you doing out here?"

Edward did a double take when he spotted Michelle. He reluctantly averted his distrustful gaze from Swag. "Repairing this machine... well, experimenting is a better word. I didn't want to mess up a perfectly functional unit."

The teenager waved a tablet computer in front of them. Cables connecting the droid to his touchscreen unit swung freely. "I was able to get it into slave mode."

He looked at her with a twinge of worry on his face; Edward's eyes flitted to the raggedy Swag. "You're okay here?"

Michelle nodded. "This is Swag," she introduced him.

Edward nodded an apprehensive greeting. Swag responded in kind.

"He's helping me get to Pishon."

"Does Father know you're here?"

She glared at Edward. Michelle didn't say a word, but stared him down. Edward wilted beneath her gaze.

"Okay. I'm sorry; I didn't mean to insinuate that you're a child or something."

"Well, don't forget it," she snapped. Her cheeks flushed with rage. "And you should know better. I'm, like, way older than you are."

Edward nodded. "The others have a cache of supplies they want me to bring back. I figured Seventeen could be of assistance." He bobbed apologetically. "You do know, though, that you're on the wrong path if you're heading to Pishon?"

"I know," Michelle stated matter-of-factly.

"Then… good luck, I suppose," Edward said as he ducked sheepishly through the door.

Once he'd gotten out of sight, Michelle pulled out her map and shot Swag a demanding look. "So are you going to tell me why we're off the trail to the garden?" Anger simmered on the edge of her voice.

"It's a long way to Pishon," he stated. "It would go much faster with a transport." They walked over to the collection of electric, golf-cart style vehicles.

"We don't have any of the keys for them," she insisted. "We tried these a long while back."

Swag walked over to the electronically sealed lockbox and keyed in a combination. The box clicked and opened. He grabbed a key and sat in the driver's seat. She stared at him, incredulous.

"Well? Get in. It's a long walk, otherwise."

Michelle approached the machine.

"You better let me drive. I'm not sure you have a license for this thing."

She narrowed her eyes at him. "Ha. Ha," she said sarcastically.

Swag turned the key, glad that his humor hadn't gone back to robot Seventeen levels.

#

"Have you been to any of the gardens, yet?"

Michelle shook her head. "No. They are all so far away. This is my first time out of the central core, really."

Swag nodded. He had been there several times, but not for a long time. He'd been almost everywhere in the Ark over the last few years except where he risked finding others.

His mind drew up the memory of his last visit to the main barracks. He'd left just as the remnant began a census in the hours following closure of the Ark doors.

The memory of those doors locking shut against those who needed safety resurfaced and twisted Swag's gut. He stiffened and refused to entertain the memories, opting instead for small talk.

As the electric cart jostled above a gentle rise, Swag pointed to the large indicator painted on the wall which read "Pishon." On the other side of the massive opening the garden stretched out before them. It might have once been a sports stadium which had grown over with jungle-like greenery.

"There are three other gardens: the Gihon, Tigris, and Euphrates." An immense geodesic biosphere spanned high overhead as they cleared the main aperture. A thin, pale sky hung beyond the angular panes; natural sunlight had a qualitatively different kind of light as it fell through the glassy barrier and fed the mature flora. Deeper within the green zones, darkness dwelled below leafy canopies, hiding patches of terrain from the sun.

The little cart zipped around paved paths that were protected by banks of vertically tilted luminaries that protected the path against potential shade. Swag slowed the cart near a huge, automated aquaponics setup. A network of pipes dripped with controlled flows all over the garden beds and plant life spilled over the edges. Immediately behind them they heard the writhing of fish as they splashed through the narrow water trenches between holding pools.

Swag continued the tour as Michelle took a deep breath of air. "The gardens play a critical part in the operation of the air recyclers. They supplement the system with a supply of fresh, natural air when it can't draw enough from the damaged atmosphere."

"Uh-huh. And you just happened to know all this because of your secret, irrelevant past?"

"I know some things," Swag admitted coyly.

She stared at him and arched eyebrows, demanding more.

Swag thought up a lie and he thought it up quick. "I was in charge of installing some of the Ark's mechanical systems."

Michelle cocked her head and shot him a look of disbelief. "You have a PhD in Quantum Mechanics, but you worked as a glorified air conditioning specialist?"

"Yes," he lied again, digging in deeper, suddenly terrified at the idea of Michelle learning the truth. "I've known lots of people with Masters' degrees who ended up managing Steak and Shakes or selling insurance in the suburbs… you know the drill—college loans."

She shook her head but let it go, obviously not buying it entirely. "So, you've visited all of the gardens, then?"

"Every one," Swag said quietly. Though each was named for a river near the mythic Garden of Eden, none of his pilgrimages had brought any kind of respite to his guilt-ridden soul.

Swag watched her examine the aquaponics arrangement. Mist from the water dispensers cast tiny prisms all around her. Rainbow light splashed off of alabaster skin that hadn't seen the sun in years.

Under the natural light, Swag noticed a deep kind of beauty within her. She was short; her body had never—

would never—mature in the same way as other women, but beauty never care for things so trivial as genetics. He allowed himself a momentary smile and felt suddenly self-conscious about his grizzled, untamed mane.

Beauty was inherent in all life... except his. Guilt bubbled up deep within. Swag knew what he'd done—the role he played in E-day. He took a few steps backwards. "I think... I think I should go." His voice faltered ever so slightly and he started off on foot. "You can keep the cart."

"Wait! What?"

"I'm not really a good guy. It might not be safe to be around me."

She strode towards him with uncanny speed and jabbed a finger into his chest. "Hey! You're not going anywhere, Doctor Swaggart."

He tried to backpedal and ignore her. She gave him a shove, proving herself fierce well beyond her size.

"Listen to me. You pull your head out of that sad-sack you call an ass and man up! This world is not a safe place *and it never was.* I don't need your phony excuses or poor-me attitude; you're not protecting anybody here but yourself. If you want to wuss out and go hide in the hallways for the rest of your life be my guest, but don't you dare blame *me* for your self-loathing. Deal with it—and don't ever treat me like a little girl who needs saving! I take care of myself."

Swag stood straight and barely dared to breathe as Michelle huffed, puffed, and blew his miserable little house down. He nodded, perhaps more fearful of her anger than of confronting his deep-seated remorse.

"Now get in the driver's seat. The only place you're going is around Pishon while you show me the rest of this garden—and you're going to act like this whole thing never happened. Got it?"

He nodded, slid into the vehicle, and complied.

###

Standing on the edge of the entryway, an amber light strobed in warning while Swag and Michelle overlooked the massive garden.

"The gate's going to close soon," he explained. "Automated safety measures. They close at dusk every night and can't be cycled again until internal sensors register enough ambient light to make the garden passably safe." He pointed back to the lights on the main path. "Those trail lights don't always connect to each other—anyone caught inside a light bubble could be trapped until daylight… stuck standing in place so that your own shadow can't connect to the greater darkness. If you accidentally moved too close you might allow the… entities… to claim you."

Michelle nodded as she looked at him with a glimmer of disappointment. "I'd hoped to watch a sunset."

Thin-lipped, Swag gritted his teeth. Before the doors could close, he walked to a wall-mounted control panel near the inside of the door and punched in an override command. The warning signal quit, and the duo slumped against the vehicle. They slid to the ground inside the lighted hallway and faced the darkening horizon from their protected perch.

As Michelle and Swag leaned against the cart, the sky beyond the dome turned pallid orange and faded into a kind of pastel magenta. The diluted atmosphere lessened the amount of scattered light along the spectral wavelengths making the sunset's colors faded compared to their pre-E-day hues. As the sky grew darker, the roads through the dome glowed even brighter by comparison.

"I know it's not what it used to be," she said, "but it's still nice to see the sky… an actual sunset." Several minutes later, the stars shone visible in the black sky. They glowed more brilliantly through a broken atmosphere that shielded less solar radiation than since she'd seen it last.

"I don't quite know if I like it," Michelle finally said. "It's still beautiful, but somehow… colder."

Swag produced a couple blankets from the trunk of the cart and rolled them out on the floor so they could lie down comfortably. They needed no top blankets; geothermal heat in the Ark's floors kept them comfortable enough, aside from the unyielding firmness of the concrete.

As he laid there staring at the stars, Swag's hand touched the pouch of pills stashed in his pocket. He glanced over at Michelle. She didn't appear tired at all—her starry eyes still full of wonder as she watched the sky.

The day full of human interaction had fatigued his mind beyond what he was accustomed to. He dared not dream, but he didn't want Michelle to think that he was a junky, either. Swag hadn't truly valued anything in a long time; this sudden relationship had taken him by surprise.

He glanced at Michelle and bit his lip; she'd stretched out and propped her head up to watch the sky beyond the giant fish-bowl that covered Pishon. His gut twisted and he realized this new friendship might be the most valuable thing in his life.

Swag weighed the risks; they were too great to pop his nighttime pills in front of Michelle. The doctor was too keen to let him medicate without any explanation. He needed to invent an excuse to get away and take them in secret, but his sluggish, tired mind responded too slowly to the request. He'd already begun drifting towards sleep.

His mind cycled through excuses when Michelle broke the silence.

"Hey Swag? I've got a burning question for you. I think I've finally figured it all out."

His mind ratcheted tight, even if he couldn't shake his body back awake.

"You're the jack-wagon who keeps flipping my cigar box upside down, aren't you?"

He grinned sleepily. "I've got a perfectly good reason," he mumbled with a drowsy croak.

"Which is?"

"Let's just say you don't know everything." Swag touched the lump in his pocket one more time before slipping into deep sleep and accidentally dreaming. He remembered the first few links in the chain of events leading to E-day. He remembered six years ago.

3

"Really, Swag?" Raymond asked as he mindlessly spun on the squeaky office chair they'd pulled from a dumpster together during freshman year.

"For real. It's going down in two hours," Swag explained to his partner.

"Well, this explains the censorship." Raymond kicked his feet onto Swag's desk. "And where the heck is Jessica?"

"I sent her home. I'd hate to subject her to scrutiny... or watch us burn out hot and fast." Swag scowled and knocked his friend's feet off his desk. "But I am sure the censorship has nothing to do with your conspiracy theories and the secret Swollen Eyeball society or whatever."

"Hey!" Raymond pointed a finger at his friend in jest, "Don't bring Invader Zim into this—how dare you mock the greatest cartoon to ever exist."

"I'm just saying that the censorship, or whatever is happening on campus, doesn't mean that the government has any plans to weaponize my research."

"*Our* research," Raymond reminded him. "That's right. I know I don't do much around here except brew coffee and microwave the hot pockets, but I still expect to share credit on the paper when we publish."

"As long as *you* write it. I can't conjugate a verb to save my life."

"That's fine. I learned how to conjugate from your mother," Raymond teased as he kicked back away from the desk on the rickety, wheeled chair. It screeched as it glided across the two-car garage that was their laboratory. "How would *you* explain it, then? How come we could never get a spot located on the campus to continue our research?"

Swag leaned back against the second-hand desk laden with notes and stacks of composition pads. "Oh, that part is easy. Either the powers that be can't stand our sunny personalities, or they have too hard of a time accepting our premise—or maybe they are too scared to look at the empirical data—think of what it implies about their presuppositions and the nature of the universe. But I'm sure it's the personalities."

Raymond waved it off. "Or maybe they just couldn't stand to see the name Jimmy Swaggart listed anywhere in their *science* facility brochures."

Grimacing, Swag straightened his piles of notes. "I don't know. I only know that we've been blacklisted from all the major journals. Something in our research triggered some kind of government response."

An alarm chirped, and Raymond sat up and checked his messages. "Oh crap. They're early."

Swag flew into motion. "Put on a tie, Raymond. We're about to entertain presidential advisors and a military panel."

Raymond struggled with his hand-me-down necktie. "You seemed so nonchalant a minute ago."

"It wasn't real a minute ago! Now that they're here, it's like someone kicked open Schrodinger's box." Swag bustled about their makeshift research space trying to somehow make it more presentable.

"It's really got you worked up, hasn't it?"

"It's my chance, Raymond: the opportunity for someone to finally take my work—our work—seriously."

"So what if some bureaucrats think our work is good or not. They don't know much about metaphysics anyway. I mean, I get the desire for funding—but, for Pete's sake, we're operating out of a glorified garage. It'll never get more impressive than this."

Swag pulled a neatly folded letter from his back pocket and handed it to Raymond. "Fine. Fine. Tell me if I'm overreacting. This is the letter they sent a week ago."

As he unfolded the embossed paper Raymond rolled his eyes at his friend. "Jeez, man. Maybe if you didn't always play things so close to the vest I wouldn't be such a conspiracy theorist."

Raymond scanned it quickly. He dropped the letter, sprang to his feet, and tucked his shirt in.

"It's that bad?" Swag asked.

Raymond fidgeted a moment more with his tie and then started arranging the tables and cleaning anything he could. "You didn't recognize any names on that panel?"

Swag returned a blank stare.

"No names at all?"

"I keep pretty busy here with the research. Maybe I should follow current events more—subscribe to People or watch TMZ?"

"*Franklin Cuthbert doesn't ring any bells?* The guy's a billionaire," Raymond exclaimed. "And Tom Holland is the presidential Science Czar!"

Swag shrugged. "Oops. I guess I didn't pay any attention when the new administration made appointments a few years ago."

They continued a frenzied tidy wave and stepped very cautiously as they approached the far quadrant of the laboratory. Lines of tape marked boundaries on the floor. "Warning," had been written on them in black marker. They always kept this quarter fastidiously clean and left proper clearance around the emergency generator. A bank of UV lights hanging overhead blazed brilliantly; they lit up a workspace shrouded by a protective curtain of clear plastic.

Just as they began checking pressure ratings against normal safety regulations, someone knocked on the garage door. Swag and Raymond traded worried glances and then opened the side door to grant the six-person team access to their cramped research space.

Swag's heart fell slightly when he noticed the first four persons through the door cast disapproving glances around the place. His nervousness remained, but without the optimistic infusion of adrenaline. He suddenly felt he was going to vomit, and then a familiar face stepped through the door. Swag recognized Franklin Cuthbert's face—even though he hadn't connected the face to the name until minutes ago.

The billionaire, who he'd only seen on magazine covers, looked affable enough. His eyes sparkled with enthusiasm as he scanned the room. A man with a stern face flanked him; he wore a military uniform and tightly cropped salt-and-pepper hair, but his eyes did nothing to discourage the young scientist. The duo seemed like a rare sort, as if they saw the world as it really was with all pretention stripped away.

Raymond practically cowered in the corner as the team meandered through, taking initial looks at whatever they could. The military officer cleared his throat and interjected some decorum, introducing himself as General Roderick Braff. He shook hands with Swag and Raymond.

"I'm sure you're at least somewhat familiar with Franklin Cuthbert and Tom Holland?"

Swag bowed briefly. "Yes, quite so," he stretched the truth.

Cuthbert shook hands in turn. "I'm quite excited to see what you've been working on. The initial research looks unbelievable!"

Holland scoffed. "Of course it does! It's not really science—paranormal research is a fluff pseudo-science reserved for crackpots and reality television."

Swag held up a hand and stifled the most powerful government regulator in the country. "Except that, if you read the paper—and I'm assuming you're only here because you read it—then you know that there is some solid science backing up what we're doing. I also assume you're here because I'm onto something big and that you're the ones responsible for stonewalling me from the major science journals."

Braff grinned at what he assumed was an uncommon display of backbone from the otherwise mundane seeming scientist.

Feeling a little defensive, Swag fixed his gaze on Holland. "And it's not *paranormal science*. I didn't watch horror movies as a kid; my crazy mother thought *all movies* corrupted the soul. She thought I'd go to hell if I watched Star Wars, scary movies, or read Harry Potter. Heck, even My Little Pony was off-limits in her house. I didn't grow up with any occult fascination or the desire to commune with ghosts, which we certain agree don't exist—I stumbled onto my discovery quite accidentally. Ladies and gentlemen, this is not pseudo-science; it is pure metaphysics."

Raymond projected a quick slideshow onto the flat screen and cycled the images while Swag gave them a dumbed-down version of the science and mechanics behind the discovery. Holland rolled his eyes through the entire presentation, though the rest of them gave it a thorough analysis.

Cuthbert nodded enthusiastically. "So, what you're saying is that you've discovered an empirical link between the supernatural and the natural? You've scientifically proven the possibility of angels and demons and ghosts—like they're some kind of life form on a different dimensional plane within string theory?"

Chuckling, Swag shook his head. "No. I merely discovered a way to observe new fields of existence we hadn't yet been able to observe. While we have found new types of life forms, calling them angels or demons is way out of line… and quite seriously, our research begins to explain away many of those kinds of corporate myths." He nodded to Raymond who advanced another slide.

The team of observers stared intently at the image. None could quite understand exactly what they were seeing.

"It's a kind of adapted photo created with a modified hyperspectral imaging device," Swag informed them. The slug like creature's image was rendered in transparent, colored pixels; waves of shifting color effused around its edges. "I say 'adapted' because normal human senses are too limited and incapable of detecting these life forms. We did our best to convert them to something our eyesight could interpret. We call these life forms 'entities.'"

They stared for a few moments longer. "These things live among us?" Braff's gruff voice sounded almost reverent.

Swag glanced at his partner.

"Let's show them," Raymond suggested.

The entire demeanor of the observation team shifted to one of excitement and enthusiasm as the scientists flung back the plastic drapery and beckoned them closer. At the center of the restricted quadrant an aquarium had been hooked up to a network of cobbled-together machines and sensors. A white lab rat exercised on his wheel inside the enclosure. A steel and glass cylinder sat nearest the habitat where its transparent portals glowed with an eerie light.

"Ladies and gentlemen," Raymond introduced with his best ring-master voice, "Meet Little Satan."

Swag rolled his eyes.

"That's an odd name," Cuthbert grinned.

"Not the rat," Swag corrected. "The rat's name is Horton. Raymond nicknamed the entity we captured. Little Satan is the creature in the vial." He certainly had their attention.

"Wait," a Latino gentleman in a business suit interrupted. "You've gone beyond observation and have begun *interacting* with these... entities?"

Swag nodded. "Yes. I touched on it in my paper."

The visitor made the sign of the cross and mumbled something about Holy Mother Mary. "I'm the lawyer," he stated, clearly worried. "The science portion was lost on me."

Shrugging, Swag returned to his presentation. He wheeled a number of flat-screen displays into different places surrounding the workspace and repositioned the EMF sensors to ensure the readings were most accurate.

A baseline reading spiked and jumped in an erratic pattern as the sensor picked up data from the glowing cylinder. The rat's biorhythmic pattern scrawled across the screen, steady and subdued. While Swag setup the safety equipment, Raymond explained.

"The entities can exist either in free flow in our environment or they can tether themselves to living things, using them as their host."

"Like demonic possession," the lawyer whispered, followed by very quiet mumbling in his native tongue.

Raymond continued, ignoring him. "We call the parasitic state when an entity attaches 'affliction.' Entities have the ability to move and operate freely only under a minimum threshold of light, as mentioned in the research packet. Basically, they can't move if there is light—unless they have a host—think of it like astronauts in space needing a shuttle to dwell in, transport them, etcetera. The natural realm is not their home environment."

"And these readings?" Holland pointed to the screen's erratic display.

"Those are the current ones coming from Little Satan. It does that when we hold him under light for long periods of time."

Swag stepped in, guessing that Holland recognized the type of data on the screen. "I believe the entities are intelligent. At the very least," he indicated the spiking line, "they give data consistent with emotions." Swag traced the zig-zagging lines with a finger. "For instance, anger. Rage."

Returning to the table, Swag picked up the illuminated vial and clipped on an attachment that gave it a feeding tube so that the rat could drink the fluid. He affixed it to the side of the cage, flipped the light switch off, and stepped back.

"Horton hasn't had water for a while, so it should only be a moment."

The mammal scurried over and began eagerly drinking. A couple of slurps deep and the rat turned and watched through the walls of its enclosure as if looking for something in particular. It did nothing but stare, although the angry readings seemed to hop over to the rat's biometrics while the tube's sensor flat-lined.

Tension mounted for a few moments under the rat's baleful gaze. Swag stepped closer, holding another tiny cage and another animal; Horton bristled. As Swag attached the second unit with a one-way door, the tribunal held its collective breath while a second, control rat found its way through the connection.

Little Satan, controlling Horton, shrieked violently. Its otherworldly screech startled the secondary rat as it entered his proximity. The afflicted rodent leapt onto the docile invader and tore him to shreds, leaving only a bloody smear of fur and viscera upon the cedar shavings. With its red-stained muzzle, the possessed rat turned and resumed its hateful glare towards the scientists.

Tense silence followed.

"My God," General Braff whispered to Raymond. "Where did you capture this thing at?"

"Just outside a local preschool," Raymond whispered back.

"As you can see," Swag said, "there's certainly a need to learn more about these entities... and not just for the curiosity of science, but also for our own defense."

The six ranking observers immediately began talking over each other, agreeing and disagreeing on points. Raymond joined Swag who leaned against a desk.

Cuthbert broke away from the arguers. "Gentlemen, consider yourselves fully funded. Whatever you need! This might be the most significant discovery ever made."

Buzzing with excitement, Swag asked, "Does this mean that I can finally publish my findings?"

The room quieted. Henry Winger, a prominent sociologist, stepped forward. "No. And I'm not sure when—or if—that will ever be possible." He stole a look back to the quadrant where Little Satan stared at them, occasionally stamping his tiny feet. "The mass panic that this kind of discovery could trigger in the general populace might very well upset the balance of our culture."

"Well," Raymond huffed, "let it. Who cares if it's upsetting? People have a basic right to knowledge."

Winger shook his head. "Maybe you know something of metaphysics, Doctor Lems, but cultural-environmental models have real-time implications. If mass hysteria breaks down our government, or swings the economy even a few points to disrupt the norms, then the rules of the playing field change significantly."

Raymond returned a curious look.

"Let's say we tell the world and people go nuts, they buy up 'apocalypse supplies' in a panic only slightly worse than the laughable Y2K computer scare several decades ago. A violent swing of the economy could jeopardize the source of your funding, even if no other negative outcomes affect you." He pointed to Cuthbert.

Raymond swallowed and nodded. *Too much* transparency endangered their livelihood. If they wanted funding, they had to play by the rules.

Franklin Cuthbert clapped Swag and Raymond on each shoulder. "I look forward to following your work." The committee began exiting, single file.

General Braff, the last to go, stopped at the door. "Gentlemen, pack your things. You're going to get a much, much bigger lab."

#

Swag jumped as that darker world of memory faded and gave way to the bright illumination of Ark I. He felt the gentle warmth of Michelle's hand resting on his arm as she shook him awake.

He gasped deep gulps of thin, recycled air as he emerged back from the dream state like a diver underwater too long. Swag realized his entire body had gone tense and stiff. He struggled to relax his muscles as he regained full control of his faculties, taking back control of his mind from the unrelenting memories of the buildup to E-day.

His hand instinctively felt for the comforting lump of pills in his pocket. Michelle watched him grab his thigh, but said nothing.

"You seemed like you were having night terrors," she diagnosed.

Swag nodded and sat up, still recovering. Michelle slouched next to him.

She said, "Sometimes my brother gets like that, too. Ricky has… he feels things intensely."

"Was Ricky there when the riots started? At ground zero when Joshua Brady, if we can really call him that, rampaged through the main facility?"

She shook her head, although she vaguely knew what he was talking about. If mankind endured, Joshua Brady's name would live in infamy, not just as a serial killer executed by the state, but as one of the key pieces in humanity's collapse.

Michelle sighed. "No. But sometimes Ricky lets his mind gets carried away, even though he didn't actually see the worst of the horrors on that day... he saw enough. There was this girl—a sweet girl. She died right in his arms after telling us how to get to shelter... Ricky seemed like he grew up more than ever that day."

Swag nodded and said nothing. He didn't want to accidentally trivialize the intimate thing she'd just told him.

"What time is it?" He yawned, not feeling well rested.

Michelle checked her wristwatch. "Very early, still." She left the statement open ended, not sure if he'd hoped to go back to sleep for a few more hours.

Swag blinked the extra moisture away from his eyes. Still tired, he wasn't prepared to return to his memories again. "Tell me about Ricky," he said, instead.

Smiling, she took the bait and gushed about her big brother: how he'd been her self-appointed guardian since grade-school, about his love for animals—most of which now appeared to be extinct except for his origami representations, and finally about the strain that raising two children with chromosomal defects had put on her parents' marriage.

"Ricky got an extra chromosome, and I got one too few." Michelle bit her lip. "I'm pretty sure that my parents would have never made it to the Ark, but maybe their lives wouldn't have been filled with such problems if everything had just worked out the way nature was supposed to. Nature can be a cruel thing."

Swag puffed a breath of air and whistled ironically. "Yeah. If only things worked out the way they're supposed to." His mind reeled back to studies on Heisenberg's

Uncertainty Principle. "I'm just not sure that anything is ever actually guaranteed, except maybe Murphy's Law."

Michelle smirked. "Used to be we could count on death and taxes... but there aren't any taxes in the remnant," she hinted, trying to sway his opinion.

Swag merely nodded. He recognized she tried to steer the conversation towards his solitude. "How long are you away from the community for? I assume you'll want to go back now that you've had a chance to tour the garden?"

"I'd also hoped to do a little exploring." She retrieved a list from her pocket. "I've got some supplies that I think would be very useful."

Glancing at the list he asked, "You need prenatal vitamins? Why not get them from medical storage?"

She slapped his shoulder. "See, I *knew* you're the guy messing with my cigars." She continued, "We're doing the best that we can with diet control and regular supplements for the pregnant women, but we don't have any actual prenatal vitamins. There's a huge, empty rack where they are supposed to be stored, but they never got shelved by whoever set this whole facility up."

Swag nodded; he'd seen the empty shelves. "I think I can help with that. They're probably inside the storage areas off of C-12."

Michelle looked at him skeptically. "We can't get into the C-12 pod. It's locked shut, except for the service droids that occasionally go there, but the hatch opens and closes too quickly for humans. It's been too risky for our scouts to explore—besides who knows what's beyond the doors?"

"Is that why the skinny kid—"

"Edward."

"Is that why Edward is trying to reprogram Seventeen?"

"That's probably a part of it."

He tapped his chin thoughtfully. "I can get us into C-12. It's not even a dangerous place, except that it's where the loading docks were. I'm sure it was automatically locked down because it's a place where hull integrity could be more easily compromised. It would've been something the designer might've thought of." He almost dropped Hank's name and demonstrated too much intimate knowledge.

She stood and motioned with her hand. "Lead the way."

Swag slid into the driver's seat of the electric cart. Michelle skootched in beside him and gave him an appreciative look.

The doctor pushed her agenda a little further. "The remnant would certainly be better off with someone around who had your skillset."

He didn't take her up on an open door for that conversation. Swag stared ahead and drove.

"Well, you're certainly a man of many surprises," she continued. "And wild beard-growing skills: you would certainly win the new World Record if you returned to civilization."

Swag bobbed his bearded head with amusement, letting his facial hair sway. He drove but didn't need to consult a map. He pointed the machine in the right direction: towards C-12.

4

"I disagree!" Michelle exclaimed as her host piloted the vehicle through the long, bright corridors. "All genres of music have a certain kind of natural, innate beauty."

"That's not how this game works," Swag said. "If you could pick a type of music to prohibit from Ark I, what would it be? You have to pick one, too."

She scrunched up her nose. "You really think all country music is that vile?"

"I stand by my original answer," Swag said. He nodded to the unfolding hallways indicating that they were drawing close.

"Alright. Fine. Bagpipe music. I can't hear them without thinking about funerals."

Swag placed a hand over his heart in mock offense. "What, no Danny Boy?"

"Don't tell me, you like the pipes?"

"Not really. But my father actually played them, a little. He tried to get me into it even; maybe that's why I accept your answer. No bagpipes in the new world!" He stared into space for a moment and remembered his childhood. "Yeah. We're better off without em."

An awkward pause hung between them. "We're almost there," Swag interjected. "Just around the next tunnel."

They arrived at the immense door of the locked pod. It was large enough to drive a train through. The hydraulic blast door's horizontal seal split the Krylon block lettering which read "C-12."

Swag pulled the cart right up to the hatch and swung his legs out of the transport. Michelle watched from her seat as Swag walked towards the mechanical access for the automated drones. On the wall nearby a keypad glowed; he checked the readouts as a safety precaution and then pushed some buttons. The enormous door clicked, groaned, and then the two halves separated and slid apart with hydraulic ease.

He walked back grinning victoriously.

"You really do know your stuff."

Shrugging nonchalantly, he piloted the car forward through the doors.

"Why don't you come back with me after we're done here?"

Swag shot her an apprehensive look. "I'm just... not ready."

Her scrutinizing eyes pierced him to the quick. Swag kept his gaze dead ahead, refusing to meet her gaze.

"You're a pretty hard case, Mister Swaggart. Not very logical."

He frowned at the accusation.

"If you hate the remnant, you shouldn't be helping me. If you were crazy, we wouldn't have had all those scintillating conversations. If you were afflicted, I'd be dead already."

"It's none of those things," Swag sighed. "It's just... I've done things..."

"So we're back to this guilt and pity thing again? You know you'd be in a better position to atone, or whatever the heck you need, if you were around actual people. If it's purgatory you're after, there're plenty of chances to feel depressed while still being useful. On the upside—if you're looking for more ways to be miserable, one of the guys in the barracks has a guitar and only remembers old Shania Twain covers."

Swag parked the vehicle. He drummed his fingers on the steering wheel for a few seconds. "I'll think about it," he promised as they explored the zone.

The pod spread open before them. Its long, wide tunnel ended in a loading hatch on the edge of the facility. Heavy doors towered on both sides of the hall; each led to storage compartments that held unmarked and undistributed supplies.

"One of these must have your prenatal vitamins in them," he said, heading towards the furthest one. "We'll have to start somewhere."

Michelle followed him to the access. A nearby, discarded hand jack sat haphazardly parked, abandoned many years ago. The entry slid open at the push of a large button. A domed roof carved from rock hung high above where the overhead ventilation ducts creaked softly with the intermittent vibration of the air circulators. Rows and rows of stacked crates filled the immense, warehouse-sized room.

Swag began a search for any kind of manifest that might list the contents of the unsorted boxes. Picking up a stray crowbar from near a quiet forklift, Michelle began breaking into a huge crate which stood nearly twice her height.

The dried wood protested as the nails started to give way. She yelled and cursed at the wooden panel, prying with all her might, until the side popped off with one final heave.

Toppling onto her rear, she dropped the crowbar and slid to the floor ungracefully as the crate's side split open and spilled water bottles with affixed packets of flavored electrolyte powder. Bottles bounced and rolled across the cement floor with dull, thudding sounds.

Swag jogged over to check on her, holding the manifest. As he offered a hand to help her up he suddenly froze like a deer caught in headlights.

"We've got to go. Now!" He snatched the crowbar up and looked around the room. Swag held the tool like a defensive weapon.

As soon as Michelle stood she saw what frightened him.

A dead body leaned slouched and crumpled against the wall nearest the door's interior controls. It had shriveled and desiccated like an unwrapped mummy. Even at this distance she could see the controls had been destroyed and busted open, wires hung out of the breach in a nest of cut and bare connections.

"We must have walked right past him without noticing."

He tugged her along as quickly as he could make her move. As they got closer, they saw an old, bloody handprint had dried to a rusty brown on the wall above the controls. The body wore military BDUs. His useless sidearm lay beside him with the action locked open; the magazine had been spent—apparently on the door panel.

Where the man's husk rested against the wall, one faded, ruddy-brown word was painted in the victim's blood. The single word could barely be made out through the streaks where gravity had misshaped the three-letter warning. *"RAT."*

Just as they neared the corpse Michelle shook free from Swag's grip. She stood entranced by the cadaver for a moment and read the tarnished nametag affixed to the soldier's uniform. "Roderick Braff."

Swag regained his footing and stepped back to Michelle. "Don't touch the body," he urged, understanding he couldn't make her come with until her curiosity was sated. He stood by her for a tense moment as she analyzed the remains.

Old bloodstains marked the floor near the lifeless form. "It looks like he bled to death, here. Alone." She saw the recognition on her companion's face.

Swag nodded. His body language urged haste. "I last saw him on E-day, just before the Exodus."

Michelle looked at him quizzically and understood his expression. "You knew him?"

Clamming up at the fear of over-sharing, he shrugged.

"Was he a good man?"

"He…" Swag trailed off. "He tried to be."

She looked at him suspiciously. "How much do you know about what happened at E-day?"

"Not much," he lied, refusing to look anywhere but the open door a few steps beyond them.

Swag took her hand and tugged her towards the door. She reluctantly followed him out and he slapped the exterior control button as soon as they'd cleared the aperture; it slammed shut and Swag hurried over to the cart.

He tossed the manifest onto the dash—mainly to prove that they'd never have any need to open that door again. Flipping up the seat, he found the tool kit. While rummaging through it he stated, "I don't think that it's a good sign if he somehow made it inside the Ark. He was outside when the doors closed."

Still pretty certain that he hadn't fully leveled with her, she glared at Swag while he procured a can of aerosol marking paint. Michelle pried, "You got awfully freaked out for not knowing much about what—who—we saw in there."

Swag walked over to the door as he shook the can. "I know less than you think I do. It's nothing to worry about, really—just irrational fears and paranoia. But we shouldn't ever open this door again for safety reasons. There is too much we don't know and too much at stake if we open it again."

He tried to steer any conversation back to the original subject. He waved the shipping manifest. "Give me just a second and we'll check the next room for vitamins and supplies."

In fluorescent spray-paint he scrawled "CONTAMINATED" across the gateway. Swag led the way to the next storage bay and ignored the gnawing warning in the pit of his stomach as a faint, drum-like whisper called to him from the edges of his consciousness.

"There you are," Swag mumbled at the crate stamped with the QSM letters and logo. He'd walked through the aisles, frequently checking over his shoulder until the recent nervousness in his gut subsided. "Hank would've been glad to know that you actually made it here." He patted the box and left it behind to check the lading bill of the next nearest container. Swag smiled.

"Over here," he called from behind a box wall in the maze of wooden containers. "I found a whole crate of prenatal vitamins."

Michelle joined him as they looked over the packing slip stapled to the side of the massive carton. "This looks good; it's more than enough for a community even five times our size." She stared at the enormity of the wooden box. "Let's see if we can find a dolly or something to bring these back with us."

"I've got an idea. Give me five minutes." Swag jogged back to the vehicle. He wrinkled his nose as he hit the hallway. Hours had passed since he'd marked the door but the cloying, aerosol odor still hung heavily in the thin air. The air recyclers seemed less efficient here—like they were sucking though a straw with a pinhole.

Rummaging through the supplies again, he found a length of steel cable. Swag backed the electric cart up against the derelict hand truck and attached it to the rear of the cart.

He walked back to the pilot's seat when a sudden wave of loneliness hit him. He'd only been gone a few minutes, but he already hated the familiar sense of absence he'd been immersed in over the last several years.

Despite his sudden, urgent impulse to return to his companion, Swag paused after entering the cargo bay. He stepped out and closed the door behind him to help quell the sense of disquiet still unsettling his nerves since finding Braff. Swag thought about the general dying at that doorway and shuddered. He pushed the thoughts out of mind and resumed the short trip. Turning the train around, he drove backwards and pushed the truck ahead of him.

Backing the contraption in towards Michelle's position was no easy task, and his eagerness to reunite with his only living friend made him hasty and sloppy. He finally got the makeshift trailer into a position where it could be used to jack up the crate and haul it from the holding berth in C-12.

Joining Michelle where she slumped against a box and waited patiently for him, he noticed her drowsy eyes. Swag leaned close and stole a peek at her wristwatch; it had gotten late, even if the overhead luminaries tried to deny the fact.

Michelle handed him the crowbar. "Seven crates down the line," she said with a sleepy grin.

Her odd request intrigued him enough that he walked to her container and checked the label. It was a filled with bedding supplies. Swag smiled, finally feeling his own fatigue, and cracked the tall, wooden face off of the container.

Michelle meandered over to him and stared into the crate as if it held Aztec gold. She reached as high as she could and started tugging. A six-foot stack of plush blankets spilled out and onto the floor. "Exactly what I wanted!" She flopped down onto the cushioning and thrashed until she'd made herself a nest.

Swag joined her in the blanket pile, keeping just enough distance to remain polite. He immediately felt exhaustion set in. Barely able to keep his eyes open, his hands brushed against his pocket and then retracted. He didn't want to *look* like an addict—moreover; he didn't want to *be an addict* anymore.

Fear welled up inside of him. Despite the bravado of all his self-talk, he had begun to care about Michelle's opinion. *Perhaps human relationships are worth the trade-off? Worth the obligation of dreaming?*

Knowing he was mere seconds from passing out, he tucked his hands under his head so that he couldn't reach for the pills again. *Maybe the dreaming is worth it... but what about when she goes back to the remnant?*

Swag's breath came in shallow, gravelly draws. In two breaths he'd be asleep—and he'd have to remember.

"Swag?" Michelle's exhausted voice drawled.

"Hmm?" One breath left.

"Will you come with me tomorrow... when I go back?"

"Ask me tomorrow," he slurred, taking one final, rattling lungful. His eyes rolled back and started REM. Swag dreamed. He remembered... Hank Chu, the genius who'd built Ark I, and General Braff of the Eidolon Commission. His mind replayed the time Hank insisted they replace the circuit boards with QSM's surge protected model as soon as possible. The momentary reverie soured and turned, as it always did, back to the carnage of E-day.

#

The hateful presence awoke and wrapped shadowy tendrils through the animal's mind, shaking the tiny creature from its deep torpor. The rat stretched and shook, coming back to some semblance of life, stimulated by the sheer willpower of the alien presence.

A tangy, metallic odor in the air alerted the vermin of the aerosol flavor. That the creature's senses operated at all was odd; it had lived long past any normal life expectancy. The rat felt an unknown thing in its mind—the passenger—as it compelled its body forward, urged it ahead.

The white rodent crawled slowly, barely more than a shamble upon old joints that had long since lost all cartilage and synovial fluid, but pain no longer mattered to the creature. The passenger forced it to transcend such ailments. It sniffed out the body of the dead human; long had it lain here. The man smelled familiar, even though his odor was incredibly faint. Maybe the body was edible, but the rat was not compelled to eat—the hunger that consumed the animal was entirely other-worldly.

Reeling back, its senses detected something else: water. The rat was dry, like old bones, and it felt as if its stomach had turned to dust. It located the trove of plastic water bottles and gnawed through the sidewall of a container. Precious water leaked all over the floor.

The rodent rolled in the pooling fluid, soaking in as much of it as possible, even gorging itself on water until it retched much of it back into the puddle. With beady, red eyes the rat examined the body of the dead human and with lightning quick speed it darted up the cadaver.

Thoroughly drenched, the animal launched itself into the nest of bare and damaged wires. Writhing around within the knot of hot and neutral leads, the rat flapped its dripping, wet tail and body against the circuits. Electricity poured through the tiny body, zapping it with painful energy as it momentarily completed circuits.

The rat squeaked tiny shrieks of agony and rage. Connections popped and sparked; smoke sizzled from the burning, vermin flesh.

Deep inside of section C-12 the hydraulic doors marked "CONTAMINATED" cracked apart. They'd moved barely an inch, but it was open, and it was enough.

5

Neither Swag nor Raymond recognized any faces in the small crowd. Neither had ever served in the military, so they had difficulty telling which cluster of brass, pins, and colorful flair outranked the next. The only certain thing was that they all ranked highly, they'd been invited, and that skepticism was their default belief.

General Braff cleared his throat to get their attention. His colorful pins might have appeared less numerous than others, but he clearly controlled this crowd. If they'd all crashed on a desert island as boys in some hypothetical Lord of the Flies scenario, Braff would obviously emerge as de-facto leader.

He nodded to the two scientists at the front of the spotless laboratory Franklin Cuthbert had furnished them with. "Take it away, boys."

Swag nervously returned his nod. "Thank you, ladies and gentlemen." He stared around the room awkwardly. "While I'm not entirely certain about the reason for this demonstration—the General tells me it's all quite classified—we're aware that you've each been briefed on the nature of our experiments. Please bear in mind that this is an entirely *new* field of science; please don't judge us for any rough edges. We're pioneers, not public speakers."

A wheel squeaked at the back of the room and a bubbly blonde lab assistant pushed a cart towards the front of the room where they stood. Atop the cart, Horton scampered around his enclosure, sniffing at the fresh bedding in each corner. Another enclosure with a connecting tube linked to it.

"Thank you, Jessica," Swag said.

She bowed and backed away with a smile. Her eyes gleamed a little when they moved to Raymond. She'd been with the two scientists since her college days, almost like some kind of science groupie. Neither of the guys had ever made a pass at her, even if she'd hinted that it would have been welcome. Without knowing it, she'd almost split the friends' bond early on until Swag and Raymond made a pact that made dating her off-limits.

Jessica had always been the most composed of their trio. She nodded at the assembly and then left the cart before returning to watch at the back of the room. The gazes of several men in the audience followed her with their eyes.

Swag indicated the rat. "This is Horton. He's about to demonstrate just how dangerous the entities can be. As you've read in your packets, the entities natural habitat is in a state of total darkness." He pointed to the five flat panel readouts with fluctuating statistics. A footnote readout cited the page number in the binders where the science team hypothesized either deep-space or subterranean origins in prehistory.

"These three panels show the life signatures and biorhythm stats of our three rats: Horton, Jazmine, and Edmund. Edmund is there at the back of the room, providing a control statistic for real-time comparison."

Swag pointed, and the military panel turned their heads. Jessica stood next to their control subject and waved.

The three animals' displays showed nearly identical vital signs. "If you watch the displays you can see that these are ordinary animals, each similar to the other. Just normal lab rats. My colleague, Doctor Raymond Lems, will demonstrate the affliction process: when an entity takes over a living host."

He pointed at the other two panels. A display labeled Entity B showed a different set of vitals from the other, featuring a spiking set of lines like a brainwave scan. The other readout, labeled Little Satan, drew a nearly flat line that skittered slightly as if it desperately tried to break out into wild peaks and valleys. The line maintained the flat-lining course with tense blips indicating duress.

"Little Satan's containment unit has been under UV saturation. You can tell from his EMF readings that it has put him into an agitated but restrained state."

Raymond positioned a sensor that faced the cage and hooked up the canister labeled Entity B. He dropped a dark and thick material over Horton's cage, draping it in darkness. A few moments passed, and Entity B's readings and Horton's normalized with each other, forming a symbiotic bond.

Swag nodded to him and Raymond yanked the cloth away. Horton meandered through his cage with very little effect.

"Horton has currently entered an afflicted state," Swag explained. "We've learned that all entities are not equal in strength and ability. Although it seems that most of them can be lulled into a docile state over time and even the docile ones can be put into agitation as well."

A hand rose. "Your rat doesn't seem to be affected much at all."

"This is a new finding that didn't make it into the notes, but we assumed that you'd want to know. Creatures can be afflicted by multiple entities. And they can fall under several effects. For instance, Horton is currently displaying brainwave data that one might associate with severe depression. In a moment, we will demonstrate the violent thralls of affliction that you came to see."

Raymond set up the drinking device and the panel watched with rapt interest as Horton sipped from it. The rat's readings went wild, as did Little Satan's and Entity B's.

"Little Satan's agitation has also rubbed off onto Entity B," he pointed out while the other rat, Jazmine, cowered in the corner furthest from the barrier that protected her from her frenzied peer.

Horton crashed into the side so violently that the enclosure shifted on the table. Several panel members stiffened in surprise.

"It's okay," Swag cautioned. "It's the same kind of glass they protect the Pope with. Short of an RPG round, we will be fine."

Horton ran erratic circles and shrieked with alien rage. Raymond pulled the external, sliding tab and opened the cage divider. The afflicted rodent tore madly through the tunnel and leapt upon his victim, tearing poor Jazmine to pieces with reckless abandon.

The expressions on the panel ran the gamut from horrified to intrigued. The little beast seethed and stared at the audience, shaking and stamping about like they'd shot the rodent up with super-charged PCP.

Another hand rose. "The entity caused Horton to experience the symptoms listed on page eight, but this seems much worse than indicated in the paper?" The short, redheaded questioner looked like her hair bun might've been wound too tight.

"Correct," Swag said. "Under aggravated conditions entities can induce dementia-like rage."

"So, these things can give people nightmares or erratic thinking, but if you rile it up, it might turn you into a slobbering, super-powered psycho?"

"That pretty much sums it up, yes."

"Interesting." The redheaded tapped her pursed lips, lost in rapt thought. "Most interesting, indeed."

Raymond shot the lady an askew look.

Swag caught his eye and shook his head *no* with a barely noticeable gesture, silently begging him to behave and not provoke their superiors. He knew well that Raymond's aversion to enlistment went well beyond any mere apathy towards the military. It bordered on antagonism at times.

"How many entities can your rat be afflicted by at once?"

"We're unsure at the moment, but we think that, at some point, the stress would tear poor Horton apart."

She nodded.

Several faces in the gathering remained perfectly placid, even unimpressed. Swag's heart beat under their scrutiny of their poker faces and Raymond turned away so that his scowl wouldn't be noticed—but Swag could feel the ire wafting off of him at the implication that the entities could have any sort of military uses.

Swag fielded another question as Raymond turned and faced the cage. He locked eyes with the afflicted rat and the rodent leapt for him, crashing into the cage repeatedly and with such violence that it shook the entire table and silenced the men and women in the room.

Raymond turned away, hoping that it would calm the creature if he broke eye contact. The shrieking animal caromed off the side wall and broke the lock of the secured lid on Jazmine's side of the enclosure.

Swag and Raymond both leapt for the cage as the military personnel simultaneously jumped to their feet. They were too late! The rat burst from its restraints and sprang onto Raymond's face, biting as if it could somehow gnaw its way inside of the scientist.

After a moment, the rat fell harmlessly to the ground where it scampered away near Jessica. She scooped up the docile animal as Raymond whirled around, eyes glowing baleful and red. He punched Swag in the midsection and sent him soaring across the room. Jessica screamed, and the military panel scrambled for defensible positions behind desks and overturned tables.

"He's afflicted!" Swag screamed through the blood trickling down his nose.

Raymond charged towards the nearest bench and knocked it over, knocking back the two officers cowering behind it. He turned towards the door and narrowed his gaze.

"Don't let him escape!" Braff yelled.

The general pulled his sidearm, but Raymond grabbed him by the throat and used him as a shield against the other armed military. They held their fire as Braff choked and gurgled, trying to scream an order for them to open fire.

Raymond kicked equipment over and flung heavy appliances at his enemies with his free hand. Swag dove under a desk which flew at him like a shuriken. He slid to a stop near the experimental apparatuses he and Raymond had worked on since before arriving in their new facility. Swag snatched the armload of devices and ducked behind the table just before the body of a doomed corporal slammed into the steel framework; the officer crumpled lifelessly to the floor where Swag crouched only seconds prior.

Activating a softball-sized unit, Swag tossed the contraption towards his afflicted friend where it clattered to the floor emitting an interpolating noise. Electromagnetic and sonic waves whined and pulsed.

Raymond dropped General Braff and fell to his knees along with any other officers within a fifteen-foot radius of the device. The nausea forced some of them to wretch and induced vertigo in the others. Raymond emptied the contents of his stomach all across the floor in a long, grotesque splatter just before he passed out completely.

Swag sprang to his feet immediately after the timed device switched off. In one hand he held an EMF reader and in the other was a cylindrical device with several gauges and LEDs; a nose-end on the top made it look like a high-tech butane torch.

The scientist paced alongside the puddle of sick with his EMF device. "The entities are contained in the vomit. Nobody touch it."

Braff choked a raspy retort as he rubbed his throat. "As if that was any of our first impulses."

Swag pointed his collection device at the puke and held the button until the LEDs turned color and began to flash. "This machine will put these guys back into containment."

Braff traded a glance with the red-haired woman. She nodded. The twinkle in her eye perhaps belied the severe look that seemed otherwise permanently affixed to her face.

"Soon as you're done with that, kid, we need to have a serious conversation about you joining the Eidolon Commission."

"What's the Eidolon Commission?"

The woman glanced down at the unconscious scientist who had attacked them. "A paramilitary organization funded by Cuthbert. We're the men and women who are going to save the world."

###

Father closed his journal and pressed pause as Edward stepped into his office with an armload of books.

He set the technical manuals down on the desk and caught a glimpse of the journal's contents. Edward said nothing, but spied some kind of timeline the old preacher had drawn in the pages.

"Don't stop what you're doing on my account," he urged, trying to get an angle on the old recording that held his community leader so enthralled.

"Are you sure? It's pretty boring stuff," Father deflected.

The youth waved a copy of *Radio Frequency Communications Principles NAVEDTRA 14189* in front of him and raised an eyebrow. "Try me."

Father chuckled and kicked Edward a wheeled office chair. "Okay—but don't say that I didn't warn you." He pushed play and resumed the debate between two parties at their respective podiums.

"Oh hey," Edward recognized, "It's that POF nut-job! His fifteen minutes of fame came suspiciously right at the end, don't you think?"

Father put a finger over his lips to shush the teen. "I think he may have been on to something, though." Ever since entering the Ark the priest spent his free hours trying to unravel the mysterious cause of the apocalyptic event.

Angry voices shouted over each other on the low-resolution television recording. It had obviously been filmed for some kind of low-circulation cable access channel. A digital overlay of the gaunt speaker in an outdated business suit labeled him as *Reverend Michael Severson, Pillar of Fire Church—Denver*. "I don't know why you're even worked up! We believe in the same thing!"

The camera panned in jerky fashion over to the other man, a pudgy and balding thirty-something. *"Rev." Jethro Diggleton, former MMA fighter—Clarksville*. "You can say whatever you want, and I don't care, but I'm not going to let you say the kind of," a string of profane audio had been bleeped out by the television censors, "that you've been saying without resistance."

"Which part do you agree with, then—the evidence I present that shows a clear pattern of supernatural activity increasing every so many hundred years, or my disdain for pretend ministers who try and wield the Word of God like a weapon rather than a salve for the hurt and lost?"

"You shut your mouth! You want a fight? I'll fight you right now!" Diggleton slammed a fist onto the podium.

"I'm sure you know that's not my style, though I wonder how much I'd really have to fear," Severson retorted. "If your supposed 'MMA' skills are as real as your degree-mill diploma and internet ordination then I've got little to fear."

Diggleton puffed out his lower lip and stiffened before slamming his podium down and yelling, "Let's do this, then! You can't just disrespect me—*that's like disrespecting God Himself!*"

Severson looked to the moderator who chimed in with a reminder that Diggleton was expected to control himself, as agreed upon before filming the debate. A producer with an earpiece stepped onstage and escorted the fuming man back to his place. The microphones barely caught him muttering about his willingness to fistfight the moderator, too.

"Can we get back on topic, now?" the moderator pleaded. "Similarities between eschatology, world religions, and western nationalism."

"I assume that *Mister* Diggleton has no opposition to my belief in the literal existence of the supernatural world and the presence of demonic beings in our midst?"

Another string of bleeped out expletives. "You'd better believe I can disagree. Your whole set of beliefs is wrong—"

"Enlighten me."

"Well, for one thing, it's way too close to those nut-job scientologists and their Dianetic system of Thetans and crap. Plus, your hyper-spiritual rhetoric is way too restrictive—it inhibits the freedom God gave us and expected us to walk out."

"Exactly how much grace and freedom are we talking here?" Severson slipped the camera a wry grin as if he had something planned.

The chubby, bellicose arguer glared at him. "Freedom enough to ignore someone who won't outwardly admit that the USA is God's chosen people and that every Muslim, Hindu, and pagan is under the direct control of the demonic forces that, *yes*, we both believe in."

"I was going to guess you were drawing the line at committing adultery, tax evasion, drunken and disorderly conduct, and child abuse. Oh, and fraud should be in the mix, too, according to my friends in Tennessee who are familiar with your organization and personal reputation."

Another flurry of bleeped curses and Diggleton flew across the stage and struck Severson in the face before the production crew could wrestle the larger man off the theologian. The video switched to a test pattern.

"Wow," admitted Edward. "I never thought theological debates could be so… spirited."

"Trust me," Father said, tapping his journal with his pen. "That was anything but a theological discussion."

Edward stood to leave.

"I've got more," Father offered, retrieving another video disc.

"More Diggleton versus Severson?"

Father laughed at the ridiculousness of it. "Diggleton? No. I'm actually more interested in the data Severson was looking into." He read the disc's label. "This is a recording of when Severson was laughed off of Dateline. That was about five years pre-E-day."

Edward held his hands up in surrender. "No thanks. I've got some computer code I wanted to study."

The older man chuckled at the teenager's excuse. "Suit yourself."

###

On limping legs, the haggard rodent explored an empty hallway of section C-12. Barren and cold, the large hallway promised nothing except more open ground and thin air. The animal had no avenue of escape.

Silently, a service droid accessed the bay as it made its way through on an automated mission. The robotic tripod planted itself near a wall and extended a ratcheting appendage. Disconnecting the wall panel, the mechanical unit set to work changing out a rubberized seal on an airtight length of ducting which had tripped a fault circuit.

Unimportant to the machine, the rat scurried over and clambered up the metallic service unit. Seconds later, the rodent slipped into the network of ducts that cycled the air through Ark I and headed instinctively for the comfort of darkness—for the corridor where the lights had gone out.

Its sensitive nose pointed it in the direction of where the freshest air flowed and extended its senses. It had been so many years since it last fed. Still, hunger barely registered in its tiny brain—only its dark purpose. An overwhelming sense of hatred drove it forward. The beast within the vermin lived and lusted only for revenge.

It caught a familiar scent in the recycled air: people. Not just the odor of humans—one specific person registered in its mind. The creature scampered into the blackness. At last, the dark presence would find vengeance.

6

Swag double checked the cables he'd rigged up to the back of the electric cart and slid a toe underneath the pallet-jack's teeth to make sure he still had clearance all the way around. Crossing his fingers and hoping for the best, he hopped into the driver's seat and gently pushed the accelerator pedal.

Nothing happened at first and he gave Michelle a nervous grin. Slowly the tethered machine lurched ahead with the load in tow and it cleared the door to the C-12 pod.

Michelle jumped out and jogged ahead to activate the main doors. The massive hydraulic opening parted as Swag drew near. He piloted the craft through and Michelle slipped back into the passenger seat; the short train picked up momentum and sped forward as they entered the network of long straightaways.

Despite the long, deep sleep they'd both gotten within the plush pile of cushioning, Michelle yawned long and loud. She shook her head and roared away the drowsiness.

"I could really use some coffee. That's the first thing I'm going to do when we get to the community." She trailed off, waiting for his response.

He only nodded.

"You really are bad with people, you know; that was an easy place for you to say, 'Why yes, Michelle,'" she impersonated his voice, "'I'd be delighted to get a coffee and hang out with the only living survivors of planet Earth.'"

Swag stifled a laugh. "You know, your bedside manner's sure gone to crap since the apocalypse, doctor."

"Well maybe I never had any to begin with," she huffed as Swag braked, slowing the cart to a stop. "Hey! What's going on? I didn't really mean to turn you off—I just hoped you had an answer about staying with the community." Worry crept into her voice.

Stepping out of the cart, Swag merely grinned. "I don't want to go to your community looking like a caveman," he said and then turned to punch in his access code at the medical bay door. "I ought to stop and shave, at least. I'll be right back in a few minutes."

Michelle cocked her head inquisitively. She watched him go. Just before the doors slid shut she saw him pause in front of the wooden cigar box. He flipped the humidor upside down and then went on his way. Michelle rolled her eyes; she scowled despite her antagonized amusement and waited for him to reemerge.

After several long minutes she ran out of patience and crawled out of her seat to go find Swag. The first thing Michelle did after stepping inside the medical bay was flip the humidor back right-side up. She wandered for a few moments in search of her lost driver; Michelle heard movement in the scrub room.

She could barely see over the ledge and through the window. Michelle blushed as she caught sight of him from the back; he pulled up a pair of pants and still bore water drops on his naked back from what must have been a hasty shower. Her cheeks flushed momentarily—just because she could not bear children did not mean that she was not a woman.

Swag turned, and Michelle panicked and ducked, suddenly very grateful for her diminutive height. She back tracked all the way to the entry when the scrub room's door opened, and Swag stepped out wearing a fresh set of scrubs.

Michelle whirled around and pretended as if she'd just come into the medical bay. "Oh. Uh, I just came in looking for you. You took a little longer than I expected."

As he finished towel drying his long hair, a clean-shaven Swag asked, "So am I presentable? I found a change of clothes, too."

She looked him up and down and tried her best not to blush. Underneath all of the wild facial hair and dishevelment he'd actually been quite handsome. "You look perfectly fine."

He sighed away the anxiety resting in his gut. "Alright, then. Let's get these vitamins to the colony."

Michelle nodded and spun on her heels, suddenly more nervous about his company than when he looked like some kind of Paleolithic throwback. She walked back towards the vehicle and Swag followed. He discreetly flipped the humidor again as they walked out the door.

A few minutes later Swag coaxed enough speed out of the cart that they coasted through the corridors at a decent clip. After a long stretch of silence he grumbled, "I hate road trips… especially with no radio."

"At least we won't be arguing over what station to listen to."

"True… but we could argue over what station we *would have* listened to."

"Okay," she said. "I'll count to three and we'll both say what kind of radio we'd turn it to."

Swag nodded.

"One. Two. Three."

"Talk radio," Swag exclaimed while Michelle kept her mouth shut. "Hey! You cheated."

"Yeah, but at least I don't like talk radio, you weirdo."

He shrugged. "Whatever." They rode another length of hallway in silence. Swag awkwardly broke it. "So, what brought you to Ark I?"

"Oh, you know," she said sarcastically and leveled her hands as if she was having a difficult time weighing her options. "It was either this or die at the end of the world." She chuckled, "I'm sure that's not what you meant."

"No. It's exactly what I meant," he exclaimed sarcastically. "I'm only here because of all the great perks they offered in the seminar... you know, the one where they try to get me to sign me up for an Ark I timeshare. I did get free tickets to Disneyland. But I can only use them in February."

"Very funny," she smirked. "I was actually a practicing OB in Nashville up until E-day. My parents had passed only recently, and Ricky had been staying with family in Colorado. He didn't like going very far from where he grew up and so when my aunt offered to move into my folk's house after the accident and take care of Ricky... it seemed like a perfect solution."

She shrugged. "And then the news started talking about government sponsored ghost-busters and demon possessions..."

"Affliction by entities," Swag corrected her.

"Whatever," she responded. "I call it like I see it. When the Joshua Video went viral and hit the news Ricky was freaking out. He was so scared... he begged me to come and visit." Michelle shrugged. "He's my family. I got on the very next flight to Denver. How we got inside the Ark is more a story of luck than—"

"Ahhrgh!" Swag screamed as if he'd been electrocuted. He slammed on the breaks and yanked the wheel to one side, swerving hard; the makeshift trailer jackknifed and slipped, spilling the load to its side. The crate broke open on the floor and scattered the contents all across the hallway. Shaking the light panels with the impact of the collapsing box, a bank of luminaries flickered for a few seconds before dimming permanently, emitting an electrical buzzing noise.

Michelle nearly ejected from the cab, even at the low speed. She whirled around to check on Swag. He sat stiff and blanched white with fear.

"What is it?" she demanded.

His voice trembled. "I thought I saw a rat," he said, almost in a whisper.

"That's impossible," she said. "There aren't any rats anymore; at least that's what the sensors suggest. There definitely aren't any in the Ark."

"You—you don't understand. It was *the* rat. My rat."

She looked at him skeptically.

Swag got out of the seat. "You don't believe me? It's over here." He stalked off towards the nearby junction and stepped around the corner.

Michelle hesitated for a moment, unsure if she should follow him or give him space. She decided to follow him and found him on his knees, covering his ears and staring into the dark tunnel they had passed two days earlier. He mumbled something unintelligible.

She approached him cautiously. "Swag? Swag, are you okay?"

"The rat. It's not over," he whispered.

"It wasn't real," she promised, suspecting that some kind of psychological stress from returning to civilization might have gotten to his mind. She nudged him… nothing. When his silence grew awkward she tried to levy the heaviness with humor. "Look around. It's most definitely over."

"I shouldn't be with you. I shouldn't go near anyone."

"Back to this again? I get it. You've got a guilt complex. You survived when others didn't. But you've got to work past it. There is no remorse in living."

"No. It's not that… I'm just… I'm a bad man."

"No. You're a stupid man."

Swag blinked in surprise.

"You heard me: stupid. There's only about three hundred remaining humans that we know of. I know everybody's story in the colony. But more than anyone's past, I know the future: I know that we need each and every person if the human race is to survive. The remnant colony includes a murderer, two thieves, and even a former lawyer."

He reeled dumbstruck by her argument. After a tense minute of silence he nodded and asked, "Is that true? You guys really kept the lawyer?"

"Well, not many ambulances to chase here, are there? Now let's go."

Swag stood on shaky legs and wiped the tears from his eyes. They got back to the vehicle and assessed the damage. The crate's corners were split apart. On their own, there was no way they could get it back together and mount the box back onto the pallet jack.

"I'm sorry," Swag said dejectedly. "I don't know how we can get the supplies back in one trip, now."

"Yeah. It's a tough world," she said unsympathetically, accepting his apology but not his self-loathing. "You messed something up. So fix it."

Swag stared at the mess for a few moments. He didn't take her stern edge as insulting, but rather as a challenge to overcome.

"I've got it," he said as he began unhooking the tethered wheel-jack. "Get in. I've got an idea." After a few minutes they arrived back at the motor pool where they first commandeered the cart. Swag grabbed a few industrial sized laundry carts from the back of the storage area and tied them together; he then connected them to the cart.

Michelle smiled at him with a certain kind of adulation… glad he'd pushed through whatever emotional baggage held him down. He'd overcome the problem at hand like only she believed he could.

After only a few minutes more they neared the pile of scattered vitamin packets. A pair of automated drones had already begun working on repairs to the damaged light panel from the collision.

Stopping the train near the jack, Swag hopped out. "I hope it's not too much to ask you to help clean up the mess, but would you?"

"Of course I'll help you." She grinned, and they got to work.

The doors to the main promenade slid open as the electric cart arrived at the colony. A collection of people that had gathered there stood and watched Swag and Michelle's approach with the supplies in tow.

Stopping the cart inside the main receiving area, Ricky ran up and threw a big hug around his sister. Bending way down, he nearly scooped her up like a child.

Two serious looking men flanked an older black man who showed the early stages of salt-and-pepper forming at his temples. They apprehensively approached Swag as he exited the lead cart. He couldn't be sure, but Swag guessed that they were former military by their demeanor.

Swag took a deep breath and stood a note taller. The air quality was better in the populated section; ventilators dispersed the heaviest concentration of oxygen in the central community. He spotted Ricky spinning around Michelle playfully, and then stepped forward to shake the black man's hand in greeting.

"Sam Ackley. Everyone here calls me Father," he introduced himself. "Do you have a name?"

"Swaggart, people call me Swag." The irony swept over him. *Nobody calls him anything, anymore; except for Michelle, he hadn't spoken to anyone in years.*

"Like Jimmy Swaggart, the preacher?"

He sighed. Even at the end of the world he couldn't escape the burden his parents had saddled him with. "Yes. But Please—I never had much time for men like him."

Father nodded knowingly. "Depending on exactly what you mean, neither did I… Swag."

Michelle came over, towing Ricky by the hand. The big guy looked away bashfully. "Ricky, this is my friend Swag."

Ricky stuck his hand out wordlessly, even though he looked in the opposite direction, refusing to make eye contact.

Swag shook Ricky's hand. "It's nice to meet you," he said. "Your sister talks a lot about you."

Ricky's infectious smile lit up the area. "She says you were lonely out in the hallways, so you moved here."

Swag caught Father's half-grin. "That about sums it up," he replied.

"But Edward says you're crazy," Ricky continued. Michelle gasped like a mortified parent. "I've never met a crazy person before. Do you want to hear a joke? Do crazy people like jokes?"

Michelle stifled a laugh and covered her mouth as Swag shot her a glance, searching for guidance. "Trust me. You want to hear it," she said.

"I'd love to hear your joke," Swag said.

"I wasn't going to get a brain transplant…" Ricky fidgeted for a moment. "But…" His words faltered and, so he pulled a heavily worn and rolled up book from his waistband and flipped it open to his joke from sheer memory. "I wasn't going to get a brain transplant, but then I changed my mind."

Swag couldn't help but chuckle. "That's a very good joke."

Ricky lit up again and looked directly at the newcomer. "I can tell you more later," he said, flipping through the booklet. Behind him, Michelle mouthed the words *He likes puns*. Swag nodded and smiled in response.

Father stood by and observed Swag's response to Ricky.

"Do you want to see it?" Ricky asked, tentatively offering Swag his cherished book. "But you've got to be careful. My dad gave it to me; he was a very funny man… the funniest man ever."

Swag choked up a little at the offering. He cradled the book in his hands and flipped a couple pages, not really reading. "I can see he must have been. This is a very fine book, my friend." He handed it back to Ricky who held it close to his body.

"Maybe you could make our new friend a paper duck, like I showed you yesterday?" Father asked.

Ricky nodded and set to work folding and coloring on the nearby floor. The distraction allowed them a few minutes for private conversation.

"I've seen you in the hallways," Father said. "I don't know your story—" he held up his hand stopping Swag from trying to interject and give him any information. "I'm sure I'll get your story sooner rather than later. While I'm fascinated by your sudden desire to join the community, and intrigued by the incredible risks Michelle must have taken to establish contact," he glanced sidelong at Michelle where she wilted sheepishly, "I do want to be upfront with you and establish how this all works."

Swag nodded. "I can appreciate that."

"In the three years since we came to the Ark we've formed a very tight-knit group, and it may take some work for you to establish yourself within that framework. I hope that you are up to the task? Michelle seems to think that you have something important to offer." He looked at the cart. "More important than the vitamins we've been looking for or the ability to hotwire an electric cart."

"Do you have any suggestions?"

"Don't expect things to move too quickly. Work hard—if you don't work, you don't eat; only three of us have the access codes to the storage facilities and only I have the code to access the central operations room. We've got to maintain a clear chain of command somehow," he explained. "My final advice is to always either tell the truth or to say nothing."

Michelle joined them. She wore a look of amazement, "I've never seen Ricky open up to anybody like that before. He doesn't let many people touch that book, either—it takes a lot of trust from him."

Father nodded, concurring with her observation.

"Should we find him some sleeping quarters and introduce him to the remnant?" she probed.

Father motioned one of the men over and gave him the task of finding some appropriate housing. The way he phrased his words seemed to imply his status as a probationary member of the colony. "I'll make an announcement about our guest at dinner tonight and we can set up a distribution list for the women who need those vitamins. We do thank you for helping Michelle locate her supplies." He turned to Michelle, "Were you able to visit the gardens like you had hoped?"

She nodded vigorously. "Yes. Swag showed me all through the Pishon. He really does know the facility better than anyone else here."

Father nodded and raised an eyebrow at the newcomer, unsure if Swag's knowledge was due to his solitary roaming or if it somehow went beyond that. "That's good to know. Tell me Mister Swaggart, did you know the four gardens are named after the rivers in the Garden of Eden?"

"It would actually be *Doctor* Swaggart, but please just call me Swag. And I actually *did* know that. But I don't have much use for religion... I never really have." His face fell as he suddenly realized that 'Father' was likely a religious honorific.

Michelle stifled a giggle.

Swag looked from Father to her. His face asked the question instead of his words.

She nodded and explained. "Father was a priest."

"Don't worry, Swag," Father said. "We've got plenty of spare shoes in storage in case you put your *other* foot in your mouth, too. And I'm still a priest," he told Michelle. "I just stopped wearing the collar because I want everyone to know that I'm a member of the human race, still, with all the duties and obligations that come with that."

Michelle accepted that answer and waved back to the man who motioned for them to follow. "It looks like your room is ready."

"We'll chat later and figure out where you fit best into the community," Father promised, dismissing him to see to his new dwelling.

Swag followed Michelle and whispered, "Is he the only priest here? Because if he is, that basically makes him the Pope, doesn't it?"

She smirked, wondering if he was correct.

"Wait!" Ricky called out. He rushed up and gave Swag an origami duck he'd folded. The edges were cross-hatched where he'd folded and refolded the lines making multiple attempts to get it just right. "I made this for you. It's a very special duck—more special than the rest I make."

Swag nodded. "It's a very nice duck. Thank you." He held it up and admired it. Words crisscrossed the paper which had once been a page inside Ricky's prized book.

Michelle raised an eyebrow at the gesture which she recognized as extreme for her disabled brother.

"Let's make it as special as possible, then. The most special duck in the world." Swag unfolded it just slightly and wrote something inside the folds.

"Is it another joke?" Ricky asked while Swag wrote.

"No," Swag replied. "Just something else that is special to me." He slid the duck into his pocket. "I'll put the most special duck in the world someplace important in my room to show it off."

He grinned wide and broad. "I'll save you a seat at dinner," Ricky promised.

Swag nodded and followed his escort to his new quarters. Something about Ricky warmed the coldness that had weighed so long upon his heart.

7

Father coughed and spat out the cupful of water he'd just filled at the public water terminal in the center of the public square. The priest hacked up a wad of phlegm and tried to clear his pallet. The water had suddenly turned undrinkably salty.

He glared at his cup before turning to look for help with the malfunctioning unit. Father signaled Janet who walked nearby. She was the closest citizen with a military background—even if it wasn't in an active combat role. Father kept a mental inventory of every person's skillset and background for exactly this sort of situation. He spilled the remainder of his cup down the drain.

"Yes, Father?" Janet walked over.

With his soured lips puckered he asked, "Can you escort Debra to the service station? There is some kind of problem with the main water recyclers. The pumps on the aqueduct seem like they are working fine, but the filtration system must be down. We've got nothing but salt water here and I know she's got experience with industrial plumbing systems."

Early in their stay Father had given her the schematics for the water plant because of previous life experience. He'd done as much with several others in order to establish a chain of command in dealing with a wide variety of problems that might result from mechanical failures. His eyes spotted

Janet's holstered sidearm and he thought, *or societal breakdowns.*

Janet's eyes widened in fear, but she held it in check. "The service station?"

Father nodded grimly. It was one of the few places inside Ark I that had no light. "I need someone who knows how to help her suit up in a light harness."

The soldier nodded and then left to find Debra.

Another nearby woman, Jennifer, attempted to drink at the nearby fountain. She spat it back and gagged. Jennifer turned incredulously to Father. "Salt water?"

He waived her off. "Yes, yes. I'm seeing to it."

#

Swag stared at the duty board and looked for work, but he kept thinking of Ricky.

Since his arrival he had spent much of his time with Ricky who he discovered had a lot more going on than bad jokes and origami. Ricky had always wanted to be an archaeologist and loved maps; he'd plotted several imaginary adventures on old National Geographic inserts. Swag had even spent several hours with him drawing large maps of Ark I and labeling the important things like airlocks and the gardens.

It was hard not to focus on Ricky when he so enthusiastically expressed his devotion. Several of the females in the community had also let their eyes linger, of course, and some of the men found new reasons to puff out their chests in his presence as if declaring ownership like the extinct silverback gorillas might have done. It was safe to say that Swag hadn't yet figured out his place within remnant.

In the two days that passed since arriving, Swag had learned exactly zero new names in the colony... besides Father and Ricky. After an introduction at the community supper, nearly every person made personal introductions. He simply didn't possess the storage space for that much immediate data. Swag spent much of the last two days trying to avoid eye contact or find ways to avoid using personal names in conversation; he dreaded the thought that the others expected him to remember their names.

Swag barely even recognized Edward, the skinny tech who'd gotten Seventeen operating again. But even that feat required a pneumonic device Swag made up by stressing the sound of the Es in Seventeen.

He frowned—everyone else had to learn only one name, he was expected to suddenly know over three hundred. Swag sighed as he stared at the duties board posted in the center of the main, public promenade.

The large whiteboard listed standard tasks that community members could perform in order to earn the listed number of credits. Each person, unless he or she specialized in some field, like Michelle, was required to perform so many credits worth of work each week unless there were special circumstances. Like Father had said, "If you don't work you don't eat."

Swag rubbed his chin with a sigh. Metaphysics wasn't exactly in high demand in such an austere culture.

Michelle cleared her throat behind him.

Startled, he turned and spotted her. "You're like a tiny ninja." He recoiled in mock fear as she struck a vague martial-arts pose.

"How long have you been here?"

Swag rubbed his brow and tried to calculate the time. He balked at the question.

"Well, you were staring at the board when I walked by a half hour ago."

"I'm just trying to find my place," he admitted. "I'm not really sure how or where I belong." He nodded to the older, stern-faced woman sitting with crossed legs at a nearby table. She seemed to glare at Swag. "I don't think she likes me," he said in a hushed tone.

"Oh, Jennifer doesn't like anyone. Between you and me, it's a medical condition, but we don't have the right equipment to operate and, so she's had to live with a stick up her butt all this time. She'll be fine, but my prognosis isn't good for everyone around her."

"Well, it's not just her," Swag sighed.

Michelle nodded solemnly. "You're probably right about some of it, anyway."

Swag gave her an awkward look. "Hey. You're supposed to tell me I'm just imagining it or something like that."

She shrugged. "I probably should have asked you about this earlier, but we've got to get on the same page."

"What do you mean?"

"The stuff that you can do," she said. "You have access to parts of the facility that others don't. You've got a story that I don't know—well, you let me learn little pieces of it, but I don't really know what you are okay with me sharing. It's not my story to tell, and you're not very transparent about it all."

He stared at her for a second, unsure of how to respond.

"Like, I know you've got secrets, Swag. But you do such a terrible job at hiding them."

"Secrets?" he tried to play dumb. But even *he* wasn't convinced by the sound of his own voice.

Michelle gave him a knowing look. "I know you have some kind of advanced clearance level that Father doesn't know about—a level higher than his, in fact. I know you've got deeper connections to E-day than you let on. And I know you've got some kind of drug addiction."

Swag refused to look at her. His mind reeled, and his mouth tried to latch on to some kind of denial or rationalization. None came to mind.

"Listen. I don't need you to defend yourself to me." She had his attention. "Your secrets are fine—they belong to you unless you want others to help you shoulder the load. That's not why I'm here—I don't want to force you to open up before you're ready."

"Then why? Why are we even talking about this?"

"Because I don't want to lie to Father."

Swag looked confused. "Lie?"

"He wants to know more about you and I don't know how much you want me to share. We never really talked about that—and so I haven't said anything. But listen, you've got to talk to him... Do you trust me?"

He only stared at Michelle. Unsure if he meant it or not, Swag knew he could answer only one way. "Yes," he said.

"Good. I hope you mean that. Please believe me when I say that you can trust Father."

Swag looked hesitant.

"I'd even trust him with Ricky," she said.

Swag seemed to melt at how much confidence she placed in the man. He nodded. "Okay. I'll have a chat with him later today."

"Good. Trust is the only currency we have left."

She began to walk away when Swag caught her. "But I want you to be there," he said.

Michelle looked at him like a deer in headlights. She hadn't expected so much so soon. She nodded an affirmation and then departed.

The scientist knew exactly what it was he needed to say to the old priest. That knowledge didn't put him any more at ease. He watched Michelle go. Swag felt like he was always watching women walk away. *Maybe coming here wasn't for the best.* Whenever other people got involved things always fell apart; interpersonal contact was always difficult for him.

As soon as Michelle turned the corner, Swag sucked in a big gulp of air and realized he'd been holding his breath. He turned back to the board and let his mind wander again, wishing he knew his way around human relationships as well as he did this facility.

His thoughts drifted. He'd had friends before. They were only alive now in his memories.

###

Swag and Raymond kept trading incredulous glances as they sipped their respective drinks, obviously out of their element. A small television in the corner of the bar played a newscast that the two men pretended to watch raptly. The Dateline anchor actually folded a tinfoil hat and put it on to openly mock the guest, Reverend Michael Severson, as he accused him of being a superstitious fear monger.

"Whatcha guys watchin?" Jessica bounced in between her two men and signaled the bartender.

"Oh, nothing," Raymond laughed. "Just saw this friend of Swag's parents on the screen."

Swag grimaced and shook his head.

Their vivacious blonde laughed, but both knew she probably didn't fully understand the joke. Swag's hyper-religious parents weren't common knowledge.

Unlike the two stiff scientists, Jessica had spent plenty of time in drinking establishments and easily sucked their attention away from the television. She pounded back two shots before slowing to something milder in order to stretch out the buzz without knocking her off the barstool. Neither of the men had seen her eyes sparkle quite like this before.

Of course, neither of them had ever been much of a socialite, and Jessica was a few years closer to her college partying days than either of them and they somewhat envied her for possessing pretty enough looks that enabled her to have enjoyed a nightlife. Both scientists locked eyes on their assistant and each silently lamented his part for the pact they'd swore to uphold regarding the bubbly blonde. Her flaxen hair glowed pink under the neon bar lights, further teasing them for such a foolish decision.

Jessica dipped her finger in Raymond's drink and then licked her finger almost suggestively. She did likewise to

Swag's drink and giggled while flagging down the bartender. "Hey Reggie? Can we get some *real* drinks down here for my boys? Two Scotches. Top shelf."

The middle-aged man behind the counter nodded and reached for some fresh glasses and winked.

"God. It's been forever since I've been out like this," she said giddily and slid the two Old Fashioned glasses to her counterparts. "I've missed this!"

Swag and Raymond gave her hesitant looks as they sniffed their replacement drinks. "You don't think I can just stick with my Long Island Ice Tea?" Raymond asked as he took a sip and scrunched his face.

Jessica raised her eyebrows to the fresh glass Reggie had delivered indicating he should take a sip—which he did. She lightly touched her hand to the bottom of his glass and then lifted, forcing her friend to chug a huge gulp.

Swag chuckled, and Jessica turned to glance at him. He snatched up the whiskey and took a swig before she could force him. The trio laughed and then shared a toast to celebrate their first day working as employees of Franklin Cuthbert and a newly formed division of his research labs called the Eidolon Commission.

"To Cuthbert," Swag raised his glass.

"To Cuthbert's money, you mean?" Jessica corrected.

"No," Raymond said. "He didn't do anything but inherit some cash. We did all the work. *To us!*"

The threesome nodded and smiled. "To us." Their glasses clinked, and Jessica watched to make sure each took a drink, so they could equally share in the joys and miseries of her stupor.

Swag licked his lips. "I think I could drink that more often," he commented.

Raymond pointed to a framed photo on the wall nearby among several other pieces of flair decorating the walls. "Is that you?"

She gave him a sheepish shrug and feigned embarrassment. A middle-school teen dressed in a lab coat struck a goofy pose for her cameraman; a white rat with pink eyes sat perched on her shoulder. "Yes," she groaned the admission, "my parents own this bar and another one down the road a few blocks."

Raymond and Swag both pushed past her and ignored her mortified pleas not to look at the photo. Swag asked, "Was this your pet?"

"Yeah," she laughed, "His name was Fuzzynugget—I let my sister name him."

They shared a moment—and lost it a second later when an inebriated man and a pair of his friends sauntered too close. Each man scanned Jessica with eyes gleaming lasciviously. Swag recognized the one as Sergeant Darren Scofield, one of Braff's employees.

"Are these guys bothering you?" Scofield's friend asked jokingly.

The scientists clammed up. The situation leapt straight out of a brat pack movie and completely blindsided them.

"No. I'm fine," she said and turned a disinterested shoulder, trying to shut the man down. He merely stared at her back side.

"Let me buy you a drink at least," he offered, clearly irked at being rebuffed. The man rubbed his stubbled, square jaw and dimpled chin as he tried to figure out why his classically handsome face hadn't stolen the girl away from the nerds in the corner.

Jessica barely spared him only a moment. "No thanks. I'm not thirsty." She wouldn't even turn to face him.

"You haven't even given me a second to introduce myself," he put a thick hand on Jessica's shoulder and turned her to face him as he slurred his words.

Jessica's eyes widened as the man broke clear social protocol. Everyone nearby tensed. Swag balled his fists and

Reggie stiffened, hedging towards a Louisville Slugger he kept under the bar.

Scofield dropped a hand on the man and pulled him back. His friend feistily tried to free himself from the sergeant's grip, but one look into Scofield's intense eyes made him relent. Scofield shoved his friend towards the open seating on the other side of the tavern and tipped his head. "Sorry about my friend." He eyed the blonde and winked. "There aren't many men around these parts worth the attention of a girl like you—mostly just boys like that one. But if you were ever interested in real men, I'm sure you'll come say hello." He gave her one more inviting look before escorting his drunk friend across the bar.

The next several minutes passed awkwardly as the trio of scientists noticed the soldiers drinking and watching them from across the room. A disquiet unsettled their celebratory mood.

Finally Raymond made his decision. "Well, I think it's getting late for me," he checked the clock on his phone.

"Same here," the others agreed, feeling Scofield's eyes follow them out the door.

The bar didn't lay in a busy part of the city, though it was close enough to their place of employment to have been a logical watering hole for them to meet at—that, plus the promise of discount drinks because of Jessica's connections.

"You really handled that creep well," Raymond complimented as they left the building.

"Yeah," she chuckled. "I'm a city girl. That wasn't my first rodeo with guys like him."

Her friends escorted her to the bus stop. Swag and Raymond had each parked adjacent.

"You know," Swag mentioned as he pressed his thumb to the scanner and unlocked his car door, "you could get one of these company cars for yourself, too. It's part of Cuthbert's benefit package if you want it."

"What did I just get done saying?" she grinned.

Flabbergasted, both men shrugged.

"I'm a *city girl*." She pointed drunkenly to her bus stop a few yards away. "The bus pretty much goes everywhere that I need to be."

Swag walked towards Father's office. He'd steeled his guts with the intention to tell the priest everything.

Father looked up from his desk where he had a thick binder laid open that traced water lines, valve positions, and electronic shut-offs for the central water source. Much like a barracks setup, individual living quarters did not have separate plumbing lines and the community relied on the main water distributor for its daily supply.

As neat and orderly as the one side of the desk was with the schematics and documents, the other was littered haphazardly with an opened bible, commentaries, notes, and other scribblings. None of the religious materials overlapped or even touched the civic documents.

He wondered at how well Father compartmentalized his life's duties. They had that in common, except that Swag had begun to fail at his ability to maintain the separation without the prazosin.

Swag raised an eyebrow at a sticky note with a hand-scrawled scripture affixed to Father's pencil holder. *God is light; in him there is no darkness. If we claim to have fellowship with Him and yet walk in the darkness, we lie and do not live out the truth.* Swag knew the reference—his mother had been very devout and she had often quoted this particular epistle.

Father looked up at Swag. "Do you need something?"

Swag tried to push away the whelming thoughts of his upbringing. His feet had frozen in place like they'd been in dipped in cement. He suddenly balked as his resolve fled—his and Father's eyes met, and he guessed that the priest already knew everything, knew he'd been part of the Eidolon Commission, guessed his real identity, and had him pegged as murderer of the human race. Swag's heart raced. *Why did I ever come to the community in the first place?* He silently chastised himself and then he remembered the tiny, stern-willed doctor who any man would find it difficult to say "no" to.

Father broke the gaze and flipped open a different binder. His demeanor changed like he'd closed one compartment and opened another. "I'm glad you're here, Swag," he said.

With the gaze broken Swag's guts halted mid-freefall and he found himself able to finally move again. He moved about the man's office and tried to act as normal as possible to cover up such an awkward encounter. Swag swallowed and tried not to think about his secret yearning for a dose of prazosin to take the edge off and get out of his own head.

"I see that you haven't signed up for any jobs just yet. That's okay. I have a job for you." Father turned the book over to face Swag. He watched the newcomer's reaction to the opened pages.

Swag's eyes narrowed. "The main doors? You want me to go to the Ark's primary entrance? There's nothing there."

"I need one of these things," Father flipped the page to a schematic showing an Electro Magnetic Frequency detector. There were a number of them built into the entryway systems; they scanned new arrivals in order to make sure that guests were fully human before the system allowed any person admittance. They helped prevent any carriers—the afflicted—from accessing the Ark when it had taken in survivors.

"Can you get me one?"

Swag stared at the page and then nodded. He had to prove himself useful in the community, though an EMF was a pretty useless item in the absence of any entity threats. He flipped a page back and forth. "I can get one, I'm sure, but I don't think that it will do much good without a power source."

"We've got plenty of batteries in storage," Father said.

Swag finally looked up and realized the priest had been watching him carefully. Clamming up, Swag guessed he was being tested somehow. His heart tightened in his chest and any intention of coming clean to the priest suddenly fled. "I'll get started on it right away," he said, turning on his heel.

Father watched him go, tight-lipped. "Be careful. Nobody's been over there in a long time."

Swag nodded on his way out, but refused to make eye contact and reveal too much. He headed towards the electric cart and looked through the emergency supplies to make sure that the standard tool kit was complete. Confident that he had everything he would need to pull the EMF reader out of its housing he looked up and jumped back, startled.

Michelle and Ricky stood nearby. Ricky waved, and Michelle raised an inquisitive eyebrow.

Swag shook his head, barely discernible. "Father sent me on a mission to retrieve a piece of equipment."

Ricky leaned forward. "I like equipment."

Michelle and Swag both looked at each other and laughed. Ricky obviously wanted to spend time with Swag.

"I'd invite you along, but it's just gonna be work. Not so much fun, Ricky."

"I wish I was more helpful," Ricky said. Swag knew Ricky well enough to understand that he genuinely did want to contribute.

Swag shot Michelle a sidelong glance.

"What?" She asked like cautious mother.

"It's just a quick job," Swag said. "I probably *could* use an extra set of hands and lifting heavy stuff isn't much of a special skillset."

She furrowed her brow slightly. "It's not dangerous in any way?"

"Father asked me to go," Swag stated.

"It's not *dangerous*," Michelle reiterated, "*in any* way?"

Swag shrugged. "Probably not."

She glowered at Swag.

"We'll be careful, Michelle," Ricky insisted. "Don't turn into Mom."

She turned her gaze onto Ricky who seemed to wilt beneath its heat. Finally, she relented, dangerously aware that she *had* in fact become her mother. "Okay. But you guys be careful."

They both nodded and crawled into the cart. "It's a quick job," Swag told her. "It won't be more than a couple hours, and most of that will be driving to the font gate."

She raised an eyebrow, but didn't say anything more.

#

Swag steered the cart through the final bend and then coasted into the main receiving area just inside the main doors of Ark I. The massive doors stretched seventy-five meters across and the concaved roof sloped down to meet the broad aperture that stretched ten meters tall. Banks and banks of lights covered the ceiling panels casting their rays downward.

Dust and debris covered the ground. Nobody had been here in ages—not since E-day, when the gates closed for good, sealing the survivors inside.

As the vehicle rolled to a stop Swag looked beyond the corral-like kiosks where the EMF sensors were located and spotted several mummified bodies, parts, and old, ochre blood stains at the door where the gate had closed. The cold, unfeeling hydraulic doors didn't stop for any man... not when the wolves were at the gate.

Swag glowered at the souvenirs left by the dark day. He hadn't actually been here when it happened, but he remembered where he was. The tragedy had been dark enough that Swag hadn't visited this part of the facility since *before* E-day happened.

The cart came to a stop adjacent to one of the entry booths so that they had easy access to tools.

Swag looked overhead. Many of the light panels flickered on and off. The area had succumbed to a number of glitches and diagnostic problems in the three years since anyone had been here.

Looking across the rows of retention corrals, Swag thought about enforcing some safety guidelines. Blocking the access to Ark I from the outside word, every person had to pass through an enclosure booth with an EMF scanner. If the scan read positive, the booth locked shut and the floor opened, jettisoning the infected person into a large tube that dumped him or her into a ravine down the mountainside.

Swag looked at the flashing lights on the ceiling. Certain spots nearly strobed like a disco ball. The Ark's designer was good, but not infallible, and Swag knew of a number of glitches in the system. He used a touchscreen console and his master code to access the override systems and lock the floor systems in place. Swag didn't want to take any chances, like being accidentally flushed down the mountainside by a malfunctioning sensor.

"What are you doing?" Ricky asked, gripping his tightly rolled joke book in his hands. He looked at the flickering ceiling nervously.

"Just making it a little safer for us to work here," Swag said. He took out the tool kit and began opening up an access panel with a screwdriver.

Ricky wandered the main bay for a few minutes before returning. "This is the one I walked through," he told Swag. Ricky walked into the slightly dim booth. When he entered, the motion detector sensed his presence and lit the side panels, brightly illuminating the corral. The doors slid shut, detaining him momentarily. The scanners hummed for a split second, and then the doors opened again.

"I was so scared back then," Ricky insisted. "I'm much braver now."

Swag smiled. "I believe you. But I've never been real brave, myself," he admitted.

"That's easy," Ricky said, joining Swag by his side. "Just think of the stuff that scares you," he told his friend.

"Okay. I'm thinking about it."

"Now just do that stuff."

Swag chuckled as if he should have known that.

"It's okay to be brave and scared at the same time," Ricky insisted, fidgeting with a pile of loose screws his friend had removed.

"Ricky?"

His ears perked up and he looked at Swag.

"You just might be the world's foremost philosopher and thinker," Swag said.

Ricky squinted at Swag. "Are you making fun of me?"

Swag shook his head. "You know what? I'm really not. You're dropping truth bombs that are blowing my mind right now. Keep it coming." He smiled.

Ricky smiled, believing his friend.

"I just might nominate you for president," Swag insisted.

"We don't do it like that," Ricky smiled. "But you can still nominate me if you want."

Swag winked at him and removed the access panel on the metallic plinth between two corral pens. He disconnected a few leads and unseated the heavy EMF sensor. The unit was roughly the size, shape, and weight of a heavy automobile battery.

Ricky helped him hoist it out and set it on the ground. The big man stood and then took a step backwards, into the doorway of the corral.

The door slammed shut, knocking Ricky backwards into the booth. Beneath him the ground clicked and groaned as the hatch tried to open and dump its prisoner into the void.

Ricky screamed, and Swag sprang into action, grabbing the control panel. "Hang on, buddy! I'll get you out!"

"I don't want to die! It's gonna drop me through the floor and make me go outside," he wailed.

"No it won't," Swag promised. "I turned that part off."

The sensor pod emitted an electronic blat when it tried again to take the EMF reading from a sensor that wasn't connected. Gears ground again as the locked floor panels tried to disengage. A ripple of electronic errors cascaded and lights in the bay blacked out.

Ricky shrieked. "I don't like the dark!" He pounded on the door, "I don't like the dark. I don't like the dark," he repeated like a mantra.

Seconds later, the emergency lights came on, providing pockets of light. Swag stepped into one of them and kept working on the digital menus. Nothing worked.

"I've got you—I'll get you out, Ricky!"

"Please hurry," he whimpered.

Swag yanked the tow strap out of the electric cart and looped it through a handle on the door. He leapt into the cart and gunned the engine, getting as much speed as possible before hitting the end of the rope and jarring the door and the vehicle.

The door didn't budge. Swag backed up and tried again. Still nothing.

"Hurry!" Ricky yelled.

Swag backed the rear bumper all the way up until the door touched. He leaned over the steering wheel and clenched every muscle in his body as the strap ratcheted tight and yanked the cart sideways, tearing the bumper free.

Already half turned around, Swag looked at the detention corral and saw the door had also broken free. Ricky squeezed and pushed his way through the opening and rushed over.

He clapped Swag in a big hug. "I don't like the dark," he whispered.

With the door's electronic connection broken the lights flickered and came back to life.

"It's alright, buddy," Swag assured him. "I've got you."

Ricky wiped his tear-streaked cheeks and climbed into the passenger seat.

"Let's get back to home."

Ricky looked at him, his breathing had mostly returned to normal. "Aren't you forgetting something?" He pointed a thumb back to the EMF sensor.

Janet walked through the boxy, maze-like grid of housing units and knocked on the door to Debra's apartment. The door slid open.

Debra stared at Janet with confused eyes. "Did I forget I was supposed to be somewhere?"

Janet shook her head. "No, Father sent me to grab you. There's a problem with the water systems so he's calling on you to troubleshoot it and effect the repairs. The promenade's only got salt water right now, for some odd reason."

Grimacing she grumbled, "Never shouldda told him about my past work experience." Debra slumped her shoulders and stated the obvious, "We've got to down below." Reluctance bled into her voice.

Janet nodded slowly. "I've already gotten a light-suit ready," she said. "It shouldn't take too long to get ready… just gather the tools you think you might need."

Debra sighed. "You really think we'll have to go into the dark?"

Shrugging, Janet asked, "It's just a little darkness—what could go wrong?"

They looked at each other and laughed nervously. Each one faking it for the other. They knew.

6

Swag pulled the cart back into the central hub of the community, the Promenade, he'd heard some of the men and women call it. Ricky crawled out of the vehicle and began walking back to his quarters.

Michelle met him after only a few steps. "How was that, Ricky? Did anything exciting happen?"

He shrugged. "Not really." Ricky turned and kept walking.

Swag raised his eyebrows at his friend. He'd thought the experience might've rattled him enough to warrant some tale he'd want to share.

Michelle turned to Swag who hoisted the bulky sensor out of the electric transport. "What does Father want with this thing, anyway?"

Swag grimaced. "Heck if I know." He leaned slightly to one side as he walked stiff-legged, carrying the heavy equipment on one side. Looking up, he met Father's gaze on the other side of the main court.

If Father had access to video recordings at the main gate, then he might've watched and tried to spot him on the feed. Swag knew he wouldn't be anywhere on film—he remembered where he was on that day.

He bit his lip and hoped that retrieving the EMF sensor hadn't been some kind of test to verify Swag's partly-fabricated story. There were a few others in the community who hadn't come through the main gate, like a woman named Janessa. Swag only recently learned it—and luckily, *she* hadn't remembered *him*. He couldn't forget her face. Swag let her into the ark during the panic of E-day, right before Jason…

A pulsing sound like drums began to echo deep within his ears. Swag didn't want to dwell on Jason's fate. He shook his head and exhaled; the drums stopped.

Michelle shot Swag an askew look. "Something on your mind? You look like you zoned out for a moment."

Swag nodded slowly, glancing again towards Father who stood outside his office door. He felt pretty certain that the jig was up. If he didn't level with Father now, he might regret it later.

"I think I've got to chat with Father."

She looked at him seriously. "The talk?"

He bobbed his head reluctantly.

"Do you still want me to be there?"

Swag half-shrugged, half nodded. Nothing seemed certain to him anymore.

"Okay, but I'm going to go check on Ricky quick. He seemed like he had quite a scare in front of the main gates."

Swag looked down at his friend. "You were watching?" He imagined how tense she must've been during Ricky's debacle with the corral.

She didn't hint at any anger and this time *she* shrugged. "It's one of the few places with lots of cameras, so of course we were watching… Father and I… and Jack: Father's second-in command. He's kind of a vice-president."

He tried to play the situation off as less serious than it had been and lighten the mood. "Don't you mean Vice-Pope?"

She smiled. "You read my mind. I'll be back in a few minutes."

Swag watched her go. He set the heavy EMF sensor down on the floor, and then walked unencumbered the rest of the way to Father's office where the leader had retreated seconds earlier.

Debra followed Janet down the vertical shaft and into the sub-deck below the remnant community. She clutched the heavy satchel laden with mechanical tools and took care not to drop them onto her escort below.

Janet's brow had already begun sweating from the extra work required to hold onto the shoulder-mounted light harness. It had been disconnected from the environmental suit but even so, the bulky contraption remained heavy.

The women descended hand over hand until they arrived at the tunnels leading to a variety of mechanical rooms for the different systems that operated Ark I's primary infrastructure items. A steady, droning hum weaved through the air; the sub-floor's mechanical systems operated below a layer of noise-dampening material that kept the machinery out of mind.

Janet asked, "You know where you're going?"

Nodding reluctantly Debra led the way to the wing housing the water, sewer, and waste systems. "Funny, I never really thought I'd have to do any of this kind of maintenance work again." She sucked in her breath as they arrived at the edge of the door and stared inside the black room.

Debra gulped. "I never thought I'd see darkness again, either."

Janet looked at Debra apologetically. Debra nodded and confirmed her resolve.

"Do you have any idea what the problem could be?" Janet asked as she began assembling the contraption and attaching the battery pack.

"No idea. There's no way to tell without seeing the system first."

Janet clipped the battery pack to Debra's belt and put the rigging on her shoulders. She adjusted it for the service worker's comfort and switched the unit on. Bright lights lit and formed a ring of illumination around her. Janet moved a hand all around and over Debra's head in order to make sure there were no unlit spots. "Okay. Are you ready?"

Debra huffed and tensed her gut. "As ready as I'll ever be." She grabbed her tools and stepped into the dark room.

Steeling himself for an uncomfortable conversation, Swag exhaled, trying to expel all his nervousness through his mouth. About to lay it all on the line, he rapped on the door to Father's quarters. Located nearest the central operations room, Father resided at the main hub where he had the most immediate access to both the facility's systems and to his people.

"It's open," the voice replied.

Swag sighed one more time, ducked his head, and plowed onward. He gently closed the door behind. "Do you have a few minutes?"

Father smiled knowingly. "I have time for *you*." He closed a dog-eared journal and slid it to the side.

Swag cocked his head as he caught a glimpse of the pages' contents. They were filled with hand-drawn arcane sigils and signs—the sort his parents had been ever wary of spotting in their hyper-religious zeal to avoid everything from pentagrams to yin-yang signs. The drums tried starting again and Swag exhaled a terse breath to silence them.

Seating himself directly across from Father's desk, Swag stared blankly at the wall of books behind the remnant leader, wondering exactly how to begin. The shelves mostly held technical manuals for Ark I, but many were also journals and pleasure reading. At least the one lying on the desk, the one he'd closed, looked like a private diary.

"Did you come here to tell me something specific, or just stare at my books?"

"Michelle says that I can trust you," Swag began. His voice verged on cracking.

"I'd like to think that."

Swag fidgeted a moment longer. "How did you come to be in the Ark? I mean, why *you*? What got you in here on E-day?"

Father explained that he'd received a panicked phone call just days prior the veritable end of the world from his brother in law. "He wouldn't say what it was regarding—*he couldn't*, he told me. But my genius little brother Hank said I had to meet him immediately."

Swag almost flinched at the name. The gesture wasn't lost on Father.

"I didn't know that it would be the last time I ever saw him. That was shortly after the Joshua video went viral and the whole planet went nuts. I didn't realize Hank was in so deep with the government—and with the Eidolon Commission—until I'd arrived at the address. I mean, I knew he worked for Franklin Cuthbert, but I didn't connect the dots that the Cuthbert Research Center was the home base for the Eidolon Commission until my rental car's GPS brought me to the parking lot. I got here just as the riots began. Hank had given me an access code for the doors to the Ark and said he was on his way."

Swag nodded. Most of the residents of Ark I amounted to being in the right place at the right time. Father's presence was more intentional than that.

Father grimaced at the dark memory. "I opened the main doors with his code and watched everyone that survived walk through the sensor units at the gates. There are only a few here that I didn't see come through." He held Swag's gaze. "Where is my EMF unit, anyway?"

Swag nodded his head towards the door. "In the courtyard."

"You couldn't bring it all the way over?"

He shrugged. "I kind of figured it was all a test anyway."

The priest flashed a lop-sided grin and half-shrugged.

"Well? Did I pass?"

"We'll see." Father leveled his eyes at him. "What is it that you want to add? Fill in my missing blanks. Why didn't I see you enter on E-day?"

"Michelle doesn't know much more about me than you do. I've never really been an open book." He spilled his guts and shared everything that Michelle would have known by observation over the last week. "I don't know how much you really know about the Eidolon Commission. Heck, I don't know how much *even I* really knew about it, but I was a part of it; I worked in… research." He tried to downplay his direct involvement at least—surely Father had figured out that he was somehow connected to Hank and perhaps the Ark project. Swag's guts twisted, and he hoped he wouldn't need to implicate himself quite so deeply in the death of his planet.

Someone knocked on the door.

Debra's breaths came in nervous, short bursts as she wandered through the banks of large control panels. Her light circle gave her plenty of light to see by, but she could feel the darkness pressing in around her as if it possessed physical weight.

In the distance, she spotted a steady red light on a bank of blinking green LEDs. She approached and read the engraved emblem below the light. Sure enough, there was a fault in the water recycling systems.

She pulled a schematic out of her satchel and traced the circuit route to a nearby panel and looked the unit over. Debra traced electrical lines with her finger until she came to a network of fuses. A glass-tube fuse the size of a common AA battery sat cockeyed in its junction near the floor.

"Curious," Debra muttered to herself. "How did you come unseated?"

Crouching down, she pushed the cylinder back into place where it snapped firm. Her ears picked up a gentle hum as the recycling filters began processing the water to drinkable-safe standards.

Her eyes caught movement in the corner of her eyes. She spotted the white rat just as it scurried up her leg. Debra's screams echoed in the distance and then cut short.

Janet stood in the lit hallway beyond the dangerous dark.

Beyond the threshold Janet called out, "Debra?"

Nothing.

"Debra, are you there?" Still only silence.

Janet drew her sidearm and peeked inside the room as far as she dared. She heard footsteps approaching and called out again. "Debra! Answer me."

Suddenly the woman leapt from the darkness. Wild-eyed and snarling, Debra tried to wrestle the gun from Janet. Three shots went off as the afflicted Debra overpowered her escort.

The first two bullets ripped holes open in Debra's chest. A third round lodged in Janet's midsection.

Janet collapsed in a gory heap and Debra fingered the bullet holes leaking blood in spurts below her collarbone. She turned her attention to the vertical access shaft. With superhuman speed she darted up the tunnel and into the center of the human community.

###

"Come in," Father responded to the rap at his door without breaking eye contact with Swag.

Michelle stepped inside. Ricky followed close behind, barely watching where he was going as he admired his newest origami creation.

"I made this for you!" Ricky said, seeing Swag.

He gratefully accepted it. "Thank you, Ricky. I'll put it with my collection," he said. Together, with Ricky, they'd made quite a menagerie, creating a little paper zoo at the edges of Swag's new apartment.

Michelle asked, "What did I miss?"

Father turned to Swag and stated, "Swag was just about to tell me how he knew my brother-in-law, Hank Chu."

"Yes. I did know Hank." The mental circuits finally clicked in Swag's mind as he connected the dots between Father Sam, Hank Chu, and General Braff. "He was a good guy, and it wouldn't surprise me to know that he was looking out for his family—even though I didn't know he had any siblings."

Father nodded. "So tell me exactly what kind of research work you did for the EC?" he asked. "There's a difference between studying computer models and working with... *them*. Did you work on the entities?"

Swag slowly nodded yes.

As if to punctuate the admission, a blood curdling shriek split the air outside of Father's office. He and Swag sprang to their feet in an instant. Ricky recoiled in fear and curled up near the far edge of the wall. "Stay right there! Keep out of sight," Michelle ordered her brother as she followed the other two.

Bursting through the door they found chaos in the promenade. Scrambling citizens tried to flee the screeching woman as she flailed and screamed. Jennifer's hand leaked blood in a thick pool all across the floor where her attacker had bitten her. Debra lay twitching on the floor nearby, bleeding out from the two bullet wounds in her chest.

Jennifer's screaming, frenzied seizure suddenly stopped. She turned and locked eyes with Swag; her jaw seemed to disjoint as she howled with an otherworldly roar.

The afflicted woman raked her long fingernails across her face, dragging them down her body and cutting jagged lines through the skin, drawing long rivulets of blood. She whirled and sprinted unbelievably fast towards the edge of the crowd.

"She's afflicted!" Swag yelled. "Don't let her bite you! Entities are transmitted through body fluids! No blood! No Spit!"

At the word "entity" the people panicked even more, fleeing Jennifer with as wide a berth as possible. A loud wail came from Father's dorm as Ricky stood in the doorway; every part of him had frozen in fear except his voice.

Jennifer stopped her charge and stood to listen like a predator hearing the cries of young prey. She locked her wicked, contracted eyes on Ricky and seemed to see right through him with tiny, red-wreathed pupils that let only the most miniscule amount of light. She turned and snarled at the crowd before locking eyes on Swag. She leveled an accusatory index finger at him; her eyes burned with baleful fire.

With jittery movements she clacked her teeth as if testing out their strength. Jennifer cocked her head and spoke in an otherworldly voice several octaves lower than possible. "I've taken everything from you once previous, Doctor Swaggart. Before this is over, I will do it again."

Gordon and Percy, both soldiers, broke off from the pack. Hurling taunts at the possessed woman, they baited the demoniac with their close proximity. She gave chase and suddenly sprinted after them.

The two men, the remnant's best defenders, dashed inside a storage compartment. As the woman hurled herself inside like an enraged beast the door slammed shut like a panic room. Before Swag or Father could get to the door to see what happened through a tiny viewport, shrieks of anguish and terror drowned any other sounds.

First, men's cries—the sound of scuffling. And then a woman's screams. Suddenly all fell silent.

Swag arrived first and peeked through. He moved aside, looking as if he might puke. Father looked through and turned away, ashen-faced. He slid against the wall, trying to hold it together. The rear door had been opened from within and Gordon, possessed by the afflicting entity, had escaped. Jennifer's demon made the jump to him before forcing its new host to bludgeon the poor woman who laid in a broken heap.

Not wasting a second, Swag barked orders. "You've got to seal this area off right away. Now—you've got to seal it outside of the community!"

"How do you know so much about the entities?" one person demanded from their safety in the crowd.

"Yeah!" another accused. "I think the new guy brought the demon with!"

"Entity," Swag corrected, but his voice was drowned out by the clamoring crowd.

"We hadn't seen an affliction since E-day, and now, what, two days after he arrives we have one!"

"Please!" Swag hollered. "I'm an expert. This was my field of study before the world fell in the crapper!"

"Expert? Expert in getting us killed, maybe!"

Michelle jumped up on a chair. Her booming voice commanded more attention than her tiny frame seemed capable of, but people listened nonetheless. "Listen up, he's an expert! I know it, and Father knows it—now do as he says."

The people looked to Father for verification. He nodded his head curtly and the people leapt into action, sealing doors, and attempting to barricade any potential access points.

Swag grabbed Father by the arm and pulled him aside. "I'm sorry I didn't fully level with you before, but there isn't time, now—and God do I wish there was. I've got to know, though, how much did those military men know?"

"What do you mean?"

"I mean clearances, codes, vital information. That kind of stuff."

Father gave him a skeptical look.

"You don't get it. Everything Jennifer *knew*, and everything Gordon *knows*—both memories and skills—the entity now has access to."

9

"Gordon doesn't know all that much," Father reassured them. He'd called the community together at the central area in the interest of keeping a strong, united force against any possible attack.

Swag glanced around at the remaining three hundred and ten humans. He disagreed with Father's tactics and didn't think it wise to put the entire remnant of humanity in the same location where an entity could easily access them all. But Swag wasn't in charge and this entity wasn't the same afflicted beast that the EC had accidentally created during the Pandora project.

Familial bunches of people gathered within the greater whole. Each cluster had between one and four women and a male who tried to assure them of their security. Many women showed signs of pregnancy. Swag looked for Michelle. Her face had set with stern resolve in the midst of the crisis—she had no man—she could not bear a child. Two distinct pairs of women comforted each other, faces streaked with tears: Gordon and Percy's wives.

Aside from the greater gathering in the main promenade, Father held a private briefing with his most skilled people as the rest of the colony milled about nearby, feeling safer simply because of the proximity. Swag had been summoned, too, still not quite sure which group he belonged in, if any.

Edward nodded as the outsider joined him—the young man did not have any women to comfort. He was easily the youngest resident.

The community grew restless as their options grew fewer and Swag could feel the heat of their glares on his back. He knew their thoughts. *It was happening all again*; Swag had screwed everything up and doomed the species... for a second time.

"What is the worst-case scenario," Andrew, one of the four former military guards asked. With the disappearance of Janet, only he and Bart remained of the military now that Gordon was roaming the passageways, afflicted.

"Extinction," Father said. "Every scenario, if it goes poorly, could result in the ultimate end of mankind."

A serious looking man with silver temples and slicked hair nodded. Jack, they'd called him. Swag recognized him as one of Edward's escorts when he'd been spotted a week ago, just before meeting Michelle.

"So we have no good options." He tapped his thumb against his chin thoughtfully. "Is there a reason that we haven't asked for advice directly from our resident expert on the topic?"

All eyes turned to Swag who'd refrained from giving input since Gordon fled. He stumbled over his words, "I'm sorry. I just didn't know if it was my place to speak up. My advice might not be very popular, especially given my relative newness."

He looked at Michelle on the other side of the advisory circle that had formed nearest Father. She nodded to him in support.

"The answer probably sounds too simple. While I agree with all of the other suggestions like shifts of watchers and closing off doors to limit access, none of those things address the problem: Gordon is controlled by an entity that wants to destroy humanity. This enemy is locked inside with all of us. Eventually he *will* get us unless..."

Jack probed, "Unless?"

Swag did a double-take. He thought it had been obvious. "We've got to kill Gordon."

A few colony members within earshot gasped audibly. Swag could feel that hateful stare returning to his backside as muttering voices rippled the news of his advice through the remnant.

Everyone looked to Father. Father nodded resolutely. "It is the only logical course of action for preservation." He nodded very subtly to Swag as if to thank him for voicing the only real solution, however distasteful. Father didn't want to come across as its chief advocate.

An uncomfortable silence hung over the group for a few seconds.

"And then what. What comes after," Jack asked. "If we are going to take a man's life, we ought to have some kind of angle—I mean, killing Gordon won't ultimately get rid of the entity, will it?"

Swag nodded slowly, uneasily. "No. It won't. We will have to quarantine the body in the end. We could drag the body outside, or push it into the section of tunnels where the lights have failed, or just leave him in that area and make a no-go zone. It really depends on where the body falls and how much bodily fluids are spilled when... when we..."

"Shoot him?" Jack asked.

Swag nodded. "Assuming that's our method. Yes," he sighed.

The silence returned.

"Andrew and Bart each have firearms," Father stated. "Swag, you're the expert. I assume you can accompany them on this task? Given your background, is there any significant danger should *you* become afflicted?"

Everyone looked at him.

Swag closed his eyes. His mind relived the times he'd seen this order handed down by the Eidolon Commission—and the few times necessity had actually forced him into the field. Swag also knew that he owed it to humanity to stop the next E-day before it happened.

"Yes... I'll go. I don't really know enough for the entity to bother with me." he lied. Michelle glared at him sidelong.

Father turned abruptly. "We've got little time to waste."

Edward cleared his throat. "I'd like to accompany them," he said loudly.

Father's hardened resolve softened. "You're very brave, Edward. But you're still a teenager." he grasped for an excuse.

The young man narrowed his eyes. His skinny body huffed, "Aren't you forgetting that Bible you often talk about: don't let anyone look down on you for your young age? The Apostle Paul says that."

"First Timothy, Four Twelve," Father confirmed. "I'm sorry, Edward. It's not a matter of your age as much as limiting our risk and sending out the most qualified and experienced people."

Even Swag felt like the response was mere lip service—but he agreed with Father's decision. He glanced at the teen and sympathized. Edward would remain the youngest person in Ark I for at least the next three or four months; his age gap put him in a difficult position. None of the three assassins being sent were overly keen on the assignment, but that was the sort of reaction brought on by experience.

Edward crossed his arms and stomped away angrily. Father shrugged as if the youth's response had perfectly demonstrated his point. "I have the firearms locked away," he nodded to the three men appointed to the mission. "Give me a moment to retrieve one."

Those with military training always kept a sidearm handy while on duty, but luckily Gordon had been unarmed when the creature took him. This particular mission mandated increased firepower.

Before he stepped too far away, Father pulled Andrew and Bart aside and spoke with them in hushed tones. Swag couldn't hear him, but he knew by the tense glances sent his way exactly what Father instructed them to do should the entity jump from Gordon to Swag.

###

Andrew and Bart each carried a full-auto rifle as they wandered the halls with Swag in tow. The two soldiers seemed anxious. Both had left loved ones behind and likely had vivid memories of E-day.

For different reasons Swag felt jittery. He left the handgun holstered at his hip to avoid any mishaps. He'd never been entirely comfortable wielding lethal power.

A lack of firearms didn't stop you from nearly killing off your entire species, last time, his self-talk accused.

Swag pushed the critical thought to the back of his mind. "It's going to take us another hour or so to get to the nearest motor pool."

Bart nodded and shifted the weapon from his tattoo sleeved arms to a shoulder. "They've got something in there that seats us all, right?"

The scientist glanced at Bart's ink and thought it ironic. Tattooed in faded black lines were tribal patterns with skulls and other demonic imagery worthy of a heavy metal album cover. He shrugged and ignored the poor choice of body art given the present state of the world.

"I'm certain of it," Swag said, a little out of breath. He wished again that he'd had the foresight to have swapped out for a different electric cart prior to joining the remnant. They might have still had enough power in the batteries if he'd exercised a little more foresight. As it was now, the cart was charging in the colony's main promenade.

Neither of his two companions seemed tired by the brisk pace they kept. They'd remained active in all their time in the Ark and their physiques benefited for it.

After another two kilometers they slowed their advance to a crawl. All three knew that they drew near a hub of corridors where many junctions veered off. What raised their nerves, however, was the black hall: the tunnel with no lights.

With practiced, military maneuvers, Andrew and Bart covered each other and cleared the corners as they rounded them slowly and cautiously. They moved silently.

Swag brought up the rear, gun now in hand; he barely breathed, and his head swam in the limited oxygen. It took a great deal of his concentration to keep from shaking as the adrenaline rattled between his nerves like a pinball.

They paused and hung near the wall as they approached the dark passage. Andrew signaled to them with his hands. Swag thought he might have seen those gestures in an old Chuck Norris movie, but he wasn't certain. He understood the gist: they were going to cover it as a single unit; if ever there was someplace they expected the entity to drive its host, it was under the cover of darkness, and this hallway was the only location where that was possible outside of the gardens or the deserted utility chambers.

Andrew silently cautioned Swag about muzzle control, tapping the barrel of the .45 auto in the scientist's hands. Neither he nor Bart seemed excited about taking a potential slug in the back. Swag nodded that he understood, and Andrew fingered a rhythmic three-count.

The trio leapt into the front of the dark opening. They stared into the blackness for a full minute, watching, examining, and waiting for Gordon to leap from the shadows and kill them all. But nothing happened.

Blood pounded in Swag's ears. The foreign whispers weaved their way through Swag's thoughts and he broke into a cold sweat. He nearly resorted to prayer as he looked into the dark and expected death to reach back and snatch him up like a scene from a horror movie.

"Whew," Bart exhaled, still keeping his eyes on the unknown, although he lowered his muzzle slightly. "I was sure that's where we'd find him."

Andrew gave a signal with his pointer finger and they backed away from the tunnel, continuing onward, but still covering the threatening tunnel as if it were the veritable mouth to Hell itself. "Let's get on with it. Swag, how much further?"

"Not much," he shook off the thrall that the darkness had instilled him with. "Just up ahead a little ways."

Bart covered the rear while Andrew watched over the straightaway. Swag ran ahead and opened the door to the massive hangar. "There should be one parked somewhere in the rear."

His two escorts jogged to catch up, not wanting him to rummage through the area without someone watching his blindside. Just because they weren't tight with the newcomer didn't mean they wanted any harm to befall him.

#

Edward kept a safe following distance from the trio Father sent out to kill Gordon. He'd easily caught up to them a half hour after they'd departed by riding on Seventeen. Just above one of the wheels on the unit's tripod legs he'd mounted a pair of foot pegs so that he could easily tag along.

His heart caught in his throat for a moment when he got too close to Andrew, Bart, and Swag. They'd stopped abruptly, and Edward was sure that they'd picked up the sound of Seventeen's electric servos as they spun the gear-driven wheels.

Edward dismounted and peeked around a long, turning bend. He could just barely see them preparing to leap out and face some unseen threat in the distance.

Both his mind and heart raced as he tried to come up with a plan on the fly. In mere seconds they could come face to face with Gordon. He ground his teeth; the primary reason Edward wanted to go along wasn't some morbid desire for death and conflict but because Gordon was a friend and he wanted to do his best to save him if at possible. But now—now with only seconds to spare Gordon could be gunned down!

Uncertainty froze him. *Father was right!* His youth meant he had no experience to draw off of and he watched helplessly as the kill squad jumped in front of the junction with the black tunnel.

He thawed slightly after the first few seconds passed with no gunfire. A few seconds more went by and he chided himself for such self-deprecation. *You're here because you need to do something,* he insisted. *Father doesn't know everything... You've got skills. You can be useful here.*

The forward team moved onward after a pause and Edward reactivated Seventeen, closing the distance very slowly. He didn't want to creep up on them too quickly and be seen.

Hearing faint voices ahead, Edward stopped in front of the darkness. He glanced to the right, thinking that he saw movement. *Nonsense... they cleared this area already!* He stared directly into the face of the blackness. He couldn't pick out anything except for silky, smooth void. He scolded himself again for such childish jitters and turned his attention back to the trail of the hunters.

There it was again! Clear movement in the corner of his vision where the rod photoreceptors of his eyes picked out a humanoid form in the dim light. He turned just in time to see Gordon throw off a bolt of black cloth and charge at him.

Edward barely had enough time to compose the blood curdling scream that escaped his lips.

#

No sooner did they move an assortment of tool boxes and equipment in order to clear a path to the electric carts than they heard the shriek of terror echoing from the hallway. Hands immediately grabbed the handles of their weapons.

Andrew and Bart took defensive positions near the door and peeked beyond. Swag crept between them and stuck his head out. Impulsively he raised his gun and yelled, "It's Gordon!"

Swag fired two shots in quick succession as Andrew and Bart stepped past the threshold with guns brandished high. Swag's shots went wide, and Gordon raised his hands in surrender, yelling back at them and trailing a length of dark fabric.

"Don't shoot! Don't shoot!"

Bart pushed Swag's gun aside, so he wouldn't accidentally shoot their friend.

Keeping plenty of distance between them, Andrew demanded. "Stay right there where we can see you!"

"What happened to me?" Gordon called back, putting a hand to the side of his head and shrugging off the body-wrap which clearly confused the wearer.

His left ear had been ripped from his body and bled all down his side. He could barely stay standing with the blood loss from that injury and a variety of other wounds. "The last thing I remember is Percy and I trying to lock Jennifer in the cleaning room… the next thing I know, I'm fighting off Edward and I'm way out here in the halls!"

Andrew looked to Swag for answers. "You're the expert," he insisted.

Swag nodded. "That sounds consistent with how an entity switches bodies."

Bart whispered, "Would an entity know how to fool us?"

Shrugging, Swag said, "It depends on the entity. They can learn with degrees of intelligence. Some are more devious than others."

"And you can tell the difference if you examine him?" Bart sounded hopeful.

Grimacing, Swag bobbed his head. "Do either of you have a flashlight?"

Both of them gave him screwy looks. "When have we ever needed a flashlight in the Ark?"

Swag sighed. "Well, we do now." He handed his sidearm to Andrew. "Just in case." Trying to act brave, he walked up to Gordon where he tottered on his feet.

"Look into my eyes," Swag insisted. "Okay. Good. Don't move your head, but just your eyes; now stare directly into the brightest part of the light over my right shoulder." He watched the wounded soldier's pupils contract into tiny points.

"He's good," Swag announced.

The trio helped the teetering Gordon onto his back while Andrew cursed. "This means Edward disobeyed Father. Things just got more complicated."

Swag nodded, fully understanding the reluctance to kill anyone, let alone someone who was barely more than a child. He tapped Bart on the shoulder. "Help me get that four-seater out. We've got to get him back to the community before he loses any more blood and update Father."

Bart nodded. "I just hope that the thing hasn't decided to race us back to the community." The worried look on his face inspired them both to work faster.

###

Father and Jack sprang to their feet when they heard the distinct squeak of wheels on the smoothly surfaced floors. Father gave the nod and Jack activated the door. Air seals hissed slightly and opened; they'd taken no chances and internally sealed all of the hatches granting access to the promenade.

An electric cart piloted by Swag peeled around the corner. It pulled right into the midst of the community as the gates closed automatically behind.

People recognized Gordon who lay bloody and immobilized on the short flatbed at the vehicles rear. Panic immediately swept through the population. Even Father recoiled slightly at the thought.

"Whoa!" Swag leapt from the machine and tried to calm the people down. "It's just Gordon! He's not afflicted anymore."

The crowd remained apprehensive—especially given the source of the information—and gave the cart a wider berth than normal. Even Gordon's wives remained at a distance.

"Then where's the demon?" a voice cried out.

Wanting an answer to that very question, Father approached Swag.

"Can we get some assistance?" Andrew yelled from the back, keeping Gordon's upper body elevated. None moved an inch.

"We need bandages, a sewing kit, blood, and an I.V. right now!"

Still no movement.

"Oh for God's sake," Michelle burst through the crowd, pushing bodies almost twice her size out of the way. "What a bunch of babies," she spat. Michelle pointed at an individual nearest her. "Joan. Get those supplies he requested." The tone of her voice didn't leave room for any disagreement.

"What happened?" Father asked Swag quietly as Joan hurried to a nearby storage room.

Swag frowned and kept his voice down. "Edward followed us. Or at least he tried to—we never saw him, but Edward found Gordon first. The entity jumped him... took him... and then they disappeared."

Father bit his lip and ran his fingers through his tightly knit hair, nearly pulling it out. He couldn't hide the trepidation creeping onto his face and, so he made sure not to turn to the crowd. "This is bad," he managed to whisper.

Suddenly understanding that there was more to the problem than Edward's youth, he asked, "How is it worse than Gordon?"

Exhaling tensely, he confided, "Edward has a very broad skillset. If you hadn't noticed, he was able to hack a service drone. He's the one we turn to when we need to know how something works." Father grimaced; he'd always tried to keep the boy away from dangerous responsibilities because of his high value—though he knew the teen had always assumed it was due to some kind of ageism. "He's read most of those service manuals in my office cover to cover and while many of us can follow the schematics or gain an understanding of mechanics, he has a natural, uncanny understanding of those things."

Swag matched his grimace—figuring he likely hacked a door to escape the remnant in the first place. "This is bad."

As if on cue, the entire facility fell silent… suddenly plunged into total darkness.

10

A maddening cacophony of screams filled the black void as darkness blanketed the colony. None reached Swag's ears more urgently then Ricky's low wail.

Several seconds into the outage, the emergency backups turned on, flooding the promenade with the light. A collective gasp ran through the crowd which quelled only slightly. Shadows were still a foreign sight and the flood lights only cast brilliant halos of protection enveloping huge swaths of floor while leaving ominous dark spots.

Michelle tried to comfort her brother who clutched his old book in one hand and a rolled-up, handmade map in his other. He still howled with fear, inconsolable. Swag found him quickly.

"Ricky! Ricky, look," he unrolled the map they'd drawn together and pointed to the gardens. "There's always light at the gardens—at least for part of the day. See, it can never stay dark for long."

Ricky still whimpered, but calmed considerably.

Michelle looked at him and mouthed her words, "Thank you."

Something in Father's eyes beckoned him and so Swag joined the leader. Jack, the priest's second in charge, also joined them.

"Do you feel that?" Father asked with his hand outstretched.

Jack gave him an askew look. "No. what?"

Swag chimed in, "The problem is that you don't feel *anything*. The air has stopped circulating."

Father nodded. "But those lights' batteries will die before we run out of oxygen."

"It's the demon," Jack recognized. "We need to breath and we'll have to open the doors in order to do that."

"How long?" Swag asked urgently.

"I don't know," Father replied. "I could go into the operations center and check the diagnostics, but if I open that door and the creature gets in, he might gain total access to the entire facility. At least, for now, he's trapped in Edward's body and won't be able to let in more entities and finish what started at E-day." He said it with the conviction of a man who had actually been there and seen its horrors.

"This will not be the end of us," Father insisted. "We can always migrate into the gardens if we cannot eliminate the threat."

"Are you mad!" Swag blurted. "When the darkness comes every night we will have to face the entities."

Father glared at him coolly. "You have such little faith."

"I have *complete faith*! This thing will find a way—and even if you set up an armed perimeter, what if this entity just kills its host and floats its way through the dark. What stops it from taking control of *you,* father?"

He guffawed at the notion. "These things cannot possess me. Not *everyone* is susceptible to your demons."

"So what? You're somehow immune or biologically resistant?" Swag's mind scrambled—it could be possible. He'd seen cases of it during his work with the Eidolon Commission. Raymond and Jessica were on the verge of a breakthrough in that very field before it all fell apart.

"Call it what you like. But I'm secure in my faith—and that protects me."

"You need a little more science and a little less fairy tale."

Jack pursed his lips and took a step back.

Swag shook his head incredulously. "And what, should we all sit back and believe that some Flying Spaghetti Monster will protect us all and move to the gardens based on your say-so?"

Quietly, Father said, "No. I'm sure that you know that's not how this works, Mister Swaggart. And that's not at all what I am suggesting. I'm merely listing options and stating facts."

"Even if they are not at all empirical."

Father nodded and conceded that point. "True enough, although nobody feared the existence of demonic entities until some overzealous scientist found the empirical links and proved their existence."

Swag's neck blushed. He knew the leader somehow suspected his involvement.

Father continued. "Faith is the substance of things hoped for and the conviction of things not yet seen," he quoted a familiar scripture passage. "Don't you see it? Faith and evidence are not exclusive. They are partners."

Swag swallowed hard. "So, we need a plan that we can believe in?"

Father nodded.

Jack finally exhaled as the tension broke. "Is there any way we can somehow capture or imprison this thing? If we can save Edward, all the better, but the old US government used to do it all the time... it was all over the news right at the end of things. There's got to be a way."

"The Eidolon Commission did that," Father specified, staring at Swag. "If only we had one of those men, maybe an expert—even one of the men who originally pioneered the creation of the technology used to capture and hold these beings."

Swag met his eyes. "You knew all along?"

"The notes Hank left here were copious, but I'd hoped that you would admit it on your own."

Jack looked at Swag accusingly.

Nodding, Swag admitted it. "I'm the man who discovered these things existed in the first place. I also invented the capture technology." His voice wavered, and he felt like he might vomit at any moment. "*My discoveries led to the destruction of the planet.*"

"You're responsible!" Jack spat. "And now you've brought damnation on us... again!"

Father put a hand on the confessor and gave Jack a warning look. "I don't strongly believe in coincidence. You're not to blame for this mess, Swag. Whatever part you may have played on E-day is in the past. I believe you were sent here to help save us, even if some of us might think differently."

Swag looked at the older man through new eyes. It had been so long since he'd thought of himself as an agent of hope.

The priest leaned closer. "I know there is not any of the capture equipment within the Ark. That was one of the first things I searched for in Central Control's files when we arrived on E-day; all of the capture equipment was stored onsite down the mountain at Eidolon Commission Headquarters—I think they anticipated things were going to go poorly during operation Pandora. But *you invented the technology*. Can you recreate it?"

For a moment, Swag's face brightened. "I could. Everything we would need—the raw materials—would be somewhere inside Ark I. It really is that big and well stocked." His face fell, "But it would take months in order to make a working model and we don't have that sort of time."

Jack grew excited at the possibility. "Maybe a mission to the ECHQ? Could that be done?"

"I'm not sure where the equipment would be," Father admitted. "All hell broke loose that day and even if our files listed their location, they might not be there. The whole place might've been destroyed, even. It would also be tight on oxygen supply. I can speculate where they would have been, however. Maybe if we sent along a spare oxygen tank?"

"No," Swag interrupted. "The equipment was destroyed by..." he trailed off. "All the GB's are gone."

"GB's?" Jack asked, confused.

"Gadarene Baconators," Swag stroked his face, unsure if he should laugh or cry. "It's so stupid," he almost grinned. "Something Raymond—a friend of mine—made up."

"Entity capture devices," Father confirmed. "BCnTR. Being Capture and Temporary Restraint. I read about them in some of the binders in my office. And incidentally, I wish I could have met Raymond. I think I would appreciate his humor." He said aside to the bewildered Jack, "The Gadarene demoniac is a story from the Bible. Christ cast a legion of demons out from the man and they went into a herd of pigs. Baconator. Ha."

Swag shook his head and enjoyed the momentary mirth when it suddenly came to him. "Wait! There is one unit left. I just remembered: I always kept a prototype locked inside my car! It's not an actual GB, but it *could* save Edward!"

"Can we get to the equipment?"

"I believe I can."

Father nodded. "Then we've got to set it up." He glanced at the nearest battery-operated light. "Immediately."

Swag nodded and turned to leave. He paused for a moment as he digested his thoughts. "You're placing an awful lot of faith in me. I'm still an atheist, you know."

Father grinned. His beliefs weren't impacted at all by Swag's narrow set of labels. "Your science will prove my faith. Make my faith—my belief in a hope not yet actualized—into a reality. Make my faith empirical, Swag.

Give me evidence of the things I believe in. Bring back your prototype."

#

Swag nodded to Bart who finished rechecking his weapons. Andrew and Gordon did the same; the latter was on his feet, but barely, after Michelle stitched his wound. Even now she forced a pouch of fruity electrolyte solution into his hand to keep him upright and functioning. Father brought them up to speed on the plan.

"I don't like it," he heard Michelle say.

Andrew replied, "Someone's got to stay here with eyes on the community in case Edward comes back—we need someone with judicious aim."

Gordon nodded hastily. "It's all good, Doc. I have to go so Andrew can stay—he'll be a better defender than I am at this point—but at least I can be an extra gun in the tunnels."

"Exactly—and that's the most likely place an attack would come from since we're locking the doors! You'll be susceptible to attack."

The wounded soldier shrugged. "I guess, if the entity jumps into me again Bart or Swag will put me down and trap the entity; that will be the end of our problems. Besides, I'd never even know it, right Swaggart?"

Swag nodded somberly and put a hand on Michelle's shoulder. "We'll take the electric cart, so we can make all due speed."

A nervous buzz ran through the crowd as Swag and his team prepared to head out immediately. The general sense of dread hung heavy in the air. All that anxiety focused firmly on Swag, Bart, and Gordon.

With people in motion to accomplish the task, Father stood tall and tried to give the people hope, despite the circumstances. "Brothers and sisters! This is not our end—many of you have known, for lack of a better word, our friend Swag as the Hermit of the Halls. Only recently he came to us, and just in time. You see, he was a member of the Eidolon Commission before E-day happened."

A murmur spread through the people. It might have been good cheer, then again, it might have been a grassroots movement to lynch him as a war criminal; humanity might die but they could at least take a token amount of vengeance first.

Father raised his hands to beg their silence. "I know. Some of wonder about his involvement in humanity's extinction. Maybe he could have done something to prevent this—but we can't get caught up in what might have been. There isn't time for that. He *can* do something *now*. Swag has access to the capture equipment that the EC used against the supernatural beings before everything hit the proverbial fan."

The murmur rose again: definitely excitement.

"However.... He will need to leave Ark I in order to retrieve it." He looked across the room and to the lights which appeared slightly dimmer. "He will go immediately, with an escort."

Gordon and Bart's wives rushed to them to say hasty goodbyes. Gordon's wives were especially disturbed by him leaving again so soon after injury. Swag watched them with a pang of yearning. A twinge of regret pulsed ulcerically in his gut.

He turned to find Michelle and Ricky standing next to him. He recognized that same painful farewell painted on Michelle's face; Ricky's tear-stained cheeks were flush with such sadness that they overshadowed hers.

"Do you need our map?" Ricky asked, offering it to him.

"No," Swag said, almost choking up at his friend's grief for the departure. "Thank you, but I know the way."

Ricky suddenly leaned in for a bear-hug and quoted his favorite book. "What does a nosey pepper do? Get jalapeno business," he said flatly. "I don't really like spicy food." He didn't release the hug, and so Michelle took Swag's hand.

"What do you call a fake noodle? An impasta." Ricky's voice broke; he said it as a goodbye.

Swag interjected his own, "What do you call an alligator in a vest?"

"An investigator?"

"Yes, Ricky. Goodbye."

Michelle squeezed Swag's hand and released it as Ricky let him go. She locked eyes with him as they separated paths. "Make sure you come back to us."

"I will do my best." Swag signaled to his accomplices. They quickly loaded into the electric cart and departed.

Donning the air-tight environmental suit, Swag looked to Bart for confirmation that he was wearing it correctly. Bart nodded, "You're doing fine, doc."

Swag glanced at Gordon who laid on the cart's flatbed. Propped up against the cab he faced the tunnel with his gun laid across his lap in case they needed defense. Neither had to say it; Gordon might fade away before Swag returned.

Bart fitted the helmet onto the neck connector and locked it into place. Clipping the hip-mounted air canister onto the belt, he turned on the air flow.

Breathing deep, Swag noticed that he felt almost giddy, stronger. The oxygen quality was high from the concentrated bottle.

"You've got a good long while on that tank," Bart said, fitting the other hip with a bulky battery. He latched the bracing hardware to the shoulder mounts and connected the power. Bright, enclosed lights lit up from the bracketed halo providing Swag with a mobile light shield; a small set of brilliant LEDs shone behind to send a beam directly vertical where the ring of light banks abutted. He was surrounded by light even more brilliant than the emergency backups that dotted the hallway leading to the airlock.

"Here's your HUD," Bart pushed a button on Swag's helmet and a heads-up display showed on the inside corner of his helmet giving him critical data like oxygen supply and battery life.

Swag tucked a small battery pack and its connectors into his belt alongside a multi-tool. He clamped the alligator clips onto the belt so that they wouldn't catch and nodded awkwardly in the head-mounted contraption. "I'm ready."

Bart nodded curtly as if to salute him for his bravery. "You're sure it has to be *you*?"

"Yes. It was EC protocol. All ranking members' vehicles had bullet-proof glass and thumbprint scanners for door locks. Franklin Cuthbert was a real security fascist." Swag assumed that Bart might have been able to break into his car, provided he could find it, but something in the scientist's gut demanded that he go. This mission had become a personal one.

Opening the first aperture to the air-lock, Bart waved him through. "Good luck. Be safe."

Nodding felt too awkward in the suit and so Swag gave him a thumbs-up and stepped through. The door clanked shut resolutely and he peered out the small, glassine porthole and into the old world-gone-by.

Aside from the murky quality of the air, everything else looked exactly as Swag imagined it would. A weather blasted golf-style cart lay busted nearby; frayed rubber ringed the rims where its tires should have been. White-washed bones of the men and women who'd tried to access the back door on E-day remained strewn between the cart and the hatch they'd hoped would give them access the bunker.

He steadied himself for a moment, inhaling deeply, and then pushed open the portal and stepped outside for the first time in three years. Gravel crunched under his feet in the valley-like crevasse that spilled into a trail leading away from the mountainside. He looked back as he closed the door and read the faded, stenciled letters identifying the door as Ark I, door number thirteen.

Lucky me, he thought. But Swag didn't believe in luck any more than he believed in the tooth fairy or the God his parents had tried so vainly to force upon him.

Protected by the halo which provided him ample light, he began his journey down the steep slope. He spotted a number of other service doors mounted nearby alongside the steep rock face. Each led to different service corridors inside Ark I.

The downward trail flattened for a bit and the scientist spotted a couple steel-posts with yellow caution signs indicating a sheer drop into a ravine beyond. Swag thought it best to keep his distance and step lightly.

He chuckled for a moment, but only because laughter was so wildly inappropriate for the moment that he was compelled to it. *Here it is: the end of the world,* he mused, *and I'm stepping outside for a leisurely stroll.*

11

Swag stumbled over the rocky terrain which sloped downward at a sharp and steady grade. Since E-day most of the surface resembled the blasted, parched surface of an alien world.

The weight of the battery on one hip and the tank on the other tired him quickly. He silently chided himself for not spending the last three years lifting weights instead of sulking. It certainly would have served him better.

Darkness had fallen already, not that it mattered much in the grand scheme. The mission was too important to hold off on—and the suits were still mandatory. In this environment, cloud cover could boil quickly and so thick that it mimicked nightfall; it sometimes lasted for days. Post-apocalyptic weather was not to be trifled with.

Swag glanced at the pedometer on his helmet's HUD and noted his distance. "Just passing one K now," he stated into his radio. The total trip might take an hour and a half; Swag estimated his car sat about two kilometers from Ark I.

"Roger that," Bart replied. "All clear here."

Swag swallowed dryly. The suit felt hot, even though the air temp was incredibly cold outside, and the walk had been all downhill so far. Stress likely contributed to that. Swag tried his best not to think about what might exist beyond the brilliant halo that protected him as he walked through the desolate, grey landscape.

He thought instead about how demanding the climb would be on his way back up the mountainside. Swag calculated the time again. *People walk about five klicks per hour, plus a half hour at my car... but the last leg is uphill... two hours tops.*

The grade suddenly took a steep turn upwards where a sand dune formed across the natural trail he followed. His feet plowed through the soft ground and the extra work made his brow sweat. He crested the dune and continued downward, nearly tripping over the suddenly stony earth where the wasteland hardened again and leveled out.

Swag paused to catch his breath, resisting the urge to claw the helmet off his head to get more air. He knew the atmosphere beyond the Ark was too depleted to breathe, but resisting the impulse was difficult.

Momentarily sinking to his knees, he closed his eyes and focused on breathing. He tried to keep himself centered and calm. Swag jerked his head left, thinking he heard voices... *no, just the otherworldly chattering, again.*

He arose as the bright moon peeked over the mountainside behind him. The pale luminary reflected just enough light to glint off the rows of parked automobiles in the distance.

With his target in sight, Swag quickened his pace until he arrived at the graveyard of pitted, entombed vehicles. Windshields appeared cloudy and the paintjobs had been largely scratched to a flat sheen by the sweeping winds that carried silica sand.

Swag located his car and quickly set to work, noting the HUD's reading for battery and oxygen levels. He'd used about a quarter of his power, but had plenty of oxygen; he had plenty of time. *So far, so good*, he thought. He would've crossed his fingers, but he needed them for the task at hand.

As he sank to his knees near the car door, he pulled the screwdriver from his waistband and carefully tried to pry the thumbprint scanner away from the metal skin of the Volkswagen. His hands, made clumsy from the gloves, fumbled the tool and it tumbled between the fine sediment banked up around the vehicle and the locked door. It slid below the frame of the car and into the darkness.

With his stomach tying itself in knots, Swag used his hands to shovel away as much of the fine silt as he could, though the heavy lighting contraption on his head made much of the movement impractical. He'd cleared enough of a path to attempt reaching under and grabbing the screwdriver: if only he could get some light to shine under the chassis for protection he could safely grab it.

Try as he might, he couldn't quite contort his body so that light shone under the car.

Swag bit his lower lip, pushed away the gibbering, otherworldly voices in his mind—hoping more than ever that they were just his imagination—and reached under the frame and frantically felt around in the dark. His hand found the tool and he yanked it back into the light.

He breathed a giddy sigh of relief with the item in hand. Taking care not to drop it again, Swag popped the sensor unit free and pulled it a few centimeters away from the car. Swag used the alligator clips and small battery unit to feed the sensor enough power to activate the locks.

Drawing a sharp breath when he felt the cold, Swag disconnected his left glove, exposing his unprotected digits to the air. He ignored the cautions as his suit shrieked at him; the arm vented oxygen and the HUD's air supply indicator flashed dire warnings.

Swag pressed his thumb to the scanner and the door locks popped up. He hurriedly reconnected the glove and opened his door, silencing the beeping and blinking notices. After raking away a small mound of sediment, Swag pulled the lever and the trunk latch popped free and opened.

Inside the trunk, an assortment of tools and prototypes lay strewn about. Swag unfolded a blanket; a writhing mass of cockroaches scattered as he disturbed their home. Finding the emergency satchel he'd placed there years prior, he slung it over a shoulder and began his journey back.

"I got it," he reported into his radio.

"Roger that." Bart's voice crackled as distance inserted static pops.

Swag glanced at the chrono on his HUD. It had been forty minutes since departure—he'd made good time. The little victory against the clock put a spring in his step; he knew he'd need the extra pep for the climb back up to door thirteen, but the inspiration encouraged him to jog wherever the footing allowed. He couldn't risk falling and tearing the suit.

He huffed and puffed. Swag's lungs burned, but he reminded himself that there was an electric cart waiting for him inside the Ark. Minutes into the run, he "hit the wall," as an old jogger friend had called it. He pushed past the urge to puke inside his suit until he found his stride.

Barely paying attention to his HUD, the burst of scrambled static jolted him out of the zone his mind had fallen into. He looked at his distance log and realized he'd forgotten to check in at the one klick mark.

The white noise burst again, and Swag played with dial at the edge of his helmet's shield to adjust the squelch.

"Man, you really made great time." Bart's voice. "Opening the door, now."

Swag hit his radio. "What are you talking about?"

No response.

"Hello? Hello?" Recognition suddenly set in. "That's not me!" Swag yelled into the communicator as he quickened his pace.

Shrieks suddenly filled the radio waves. Swag sprinted uphill; at his maximum pace, he could arrive in only ten minutes. He tried to call again on the radio, but his lungs burned, and he choked on the words.

He saw the steep climb ahead and knew he'd closed in on the last half-kilometer of the journey. Swag's steps grew clumsy and he staggered on the slope.

A jolt of surprise rippled through Swag. Another human in another unlit enviro-suit stepped into his light halo. Swag could make out the man's features, even at this distance. His eyesight had always been good—even in the dark.

"Gordon? Gordon, why are your lights off?"

No answer. The form approached him, expressionless, although his eyes indicated Swag's worst nightmare. The scientist backpedaled and tried to open his satchel.

"Gordon. Answer me!" His chest heaved with both exertion and terror. His mind filled with cacophonous demonic chattering.

Gordon lunged into motion and Swag yelped, turning to flee. The afflicted soldier grabbed him from behind and flung him into a nearby stony escarpment with superhuman force.

Swag howled in pain. His spine crunched against the rock wall with a wet sound like snapping celery. Worse was the whooshing noise and flickering system alerts all over his HUD. He scrambled to his feet and leapt aside even as Gordon charged and smashed into the rubble where Swag had laid a moment earlier.

In the distance Swag could barely make out the warning-sign marking the edge of the vertical drop. Swag still had a full halo of light, but his forward bulb had been smashed by the impact, dimming the front segment of his protective circle.

He fumbled with the stuck satchel zipper one more time, trying to grab the prototype GB so he could save Gordon—and himself!

The afflicted man turned and roared at Swag. His face contorted into a twisted snarl; Gordon's hands stayed away from the Push To Talk button and didn't transmit any noise. Swag ignored the beeping warning him of the air loss; he fumbled around feeling for a tear in the suit, and tried to calculate the odds of his survival.

The afflicted splayed his arms and sidestepped like a predator stalking prey. He could pounce at any moment.

"Who are you? Leviathan? Mephistopheles, Abbadon, Belphegor?" He rattled off the names of several code-named demons the Eidolon Commission had used in sensitive projects.

Gordon's hand clicked the communicator's PTT. "We are Legion," it hissed.

Swag's heart wilted, and his eyes finally caught sight of the air leak. A thin mist spewed from the air tank at his hip. He looked up just in time to see Legion leap towards him.

Adrenaline coursed through the doomed scientist as he turned and sprinted towards the edge of the sheer cliff which emptied into chasm a half-kilometer below. Gone was the caution he'd exercised earlier.

Swag could feel Legion's pursuit one step behind him… reaching out to grab him. At the last second, with the rocky footing plunging away into nothingness, Swag hooked an arm out and grabbed the steel post where the warning sign hung.

Swinging his body around like a tetherball, Swag's feet flung him around with centripetal motion and he only half-fell over the ledge. His peripheral vision tracked the afflicted Gordon who spun through the air and plummeted out of sight, trying vainly to reach through the ether and choke the life from the scientist.

Swag hacked and coughed on the thinning air as he tried hauling himself back over the ledge, taking care not to snag the battery or the bleeding air tank on his hip. The HUD screamed in his ears; falling oxygen levels neared critical stages.

He clambered to his feet and dashed for door thirteen as best as he was able on limping legs. The HUD blinked red as the air supply reached single digits.

Pounding on the door with all his might, Swag peeked through the thick, transparent pane. An environmental suit lay shredded on the floor. Blood smeared the walls. Swag stood on his toes and clicked his communicator, screaming into it.

"Let me in! Someone unlock this door!"

On his toes he had enough leverage to catch sight of a bloody forearm that bore a black pattern of tattoos. Bart was dead.

Swag hammered his fists over and over, hyperventilating as the air supply bled to two percent... one percent... and then the LED winked out: zero.

"Somebody let me in!" he continued screaming, even though he knew his panicking only consumed his last few breaths that much sooner.

Blackness creeped in at the edge of his vision from oxygen loss and the porthole filled with a familiar face: Edward.

Swag pounded again on the steel hatch and clicked his communicator. "Edward? Edward, let me in!"

Edward turned to fully face him through the window. His eyes were contracted to tiny points, blocking the entry of any light.

"Edward... whose there?" Swag choked.

He slowly picked up the handheld com device. The radio crackled, "Little Satan." He grinned, turned his back, and walked away from the locked door.

Swag's heart sank into his feet and he collapsed, only inches from the air supply of Ark I. His vision turned black as he gasped in the all-too-thin atmosphere beyond the sanctuary.

As his sight faded completely, he uttered a phrase he'd not spoken since long before the break with his ultra-religious parents in his undergrad years. "Oh Lord... Help me?"

Intense terror and regret overwhelmed him in his death throes. He had one vain lungful left before the end and tried to make it count.

"Yea though I walk through the valley of the shadow of death..." He struggled to voice the next few words in the airless environment. "I will... fear no..."

His burning lungs gave up and seized solid. Swag's eyes rolled back into his head and everything went black.

PART II.

BEFORE TOMORROW BURNED

6.5 Months Pre-Extinction-Day

12

The radio announcer rattled off the headlines with a practiced cadence. "...and Uqbah al-Kassab, all members of the so-called Sinister Six. Today marks the anniversary of the Six's attack on a local woman at her college campus. The six students, coined The Sinister Six by the media, consisted of half a dozen international students who live-streamed their attack and rape of an American on social media while shouting Islamic rhetoric and issuing a call to Jihad."

Swag looked up from his work long enough to turn up the radio's volume. He'd almost forgotten about the incident, even though it had happened on the nearby campus when he was still working on his doctorate. The woman had been an adjunct faculty, actually, though he'd never met her. She worked mostly with undergrads in subjects outside of the sciences.

The newscaster continued his report from the other side of the speaker. "The court determined the six young men were not in control of themselves during the time of their crime due to the side effects of a then-new and potent khat and flakka hybrid which had only recently become popular in the United States' Muslim populations—the pharmacological plant's new form tested nearly forty times more powerful than the normal supply. Each of the Six was sentenced to just sixty months, less time served. Because of their severe abuse while behind bars, the federal government began to reevaluate how inmates from Islamic backgrounds are processed for detention—an act that that redefined the landscape of the prison industry.

"Unfortunately, Professor Wanda Ackley, the Six's victim, died of her injuries shortly after the attack."

As the program switched to the BBC world report Swag turned the volume back down to its regular level. He heard the approaching footsteps of his military handler who approached through the hall.

Sergeant Darren Scofield dropped a stack of reports on Swag's desk and glared down his nose at the scientist. He didn't try to hide his condescension for the civilian agents in the Eidolon Commission and had commented on occasion that it ought to be a strictly military operation. The sergeant twirled his keys impatiently as a signal that they needed to depart.

Swag scooped up the disheveled stack of cream-colored hanging folders. "What am I supposed to do with these, *now*?" he grumbled. "I needed them *before* the field test."

"It *is* before the test," Scofield stated matter-of-factly.

Swag merely scowled and rolled his eyes. He tossed the information on his desk where he could scan the data later. He grabbed his satchel and turned the computer off as they left for the test. "How long have we been doing this, now?"

"Nineteen months, Doc."

"And in a year and a half, have I ever done anything by the seat of my pants?"

Scofield shrugged and led the way to their nondescript, black sedan.

Swag shrugged. There were certain things he'd just have to accept about his role in the Eidolon Commission; he knew he was important, but he didn't have ultimate carte blanche—there were many things that went beyond his pay grade. The frustrated scientist watched for his partner on their way to the parking garage.

The Sergeant anticipated his question. "Raymond is already at the site."

"Okay. That makes sense," Swag nodded as he got into the car.

Scofield hefted a large, locked case into the trunk. Minutes later, they merged into traffic and headed to the test site far across town.

Finally arriving at the site, Swag crawled out of the vehicle and took stock of the situation. Run down housing projects towered precariously above chain-link barriers and asphalt basketball courts that were too cracked to dribble on. Curious eyes glanced out of the occasional window, and then quickly looked away—these people weren't snitches and didn't want to seem curious of the military force that had barricaded off a four-block radius.

Raymond stepped out of the huge motorhome which functioned as the EC's mobile headquarters during field operations. He rubbed his stubbly face in frustration as he stretched in the open air.

A corporal glared irkedly at the scientist who failed to shut the door behind him and exposed the interior to scrutiny; specialists fidgeted with surveillance equipment just inside the RV. Another soldier slammed the door shut in Raymond's stead.

Raymond looked up and found Swag. "Glad you could make it."

"You don't look so glad."

"You know me. Just poking the beast and getting chewed on."

Swag shook his head. He knew that Raymond and Braff were frequently at odds with each other.

"He's on the warpath again," Raymond sighed and massaged the tension from his face and neck. "Moreso today than he's been in a while."

"I'm sure he's just stressed." Swag lifted the handle and stepped inside the RV to watch the video monitors. "These tests for the second-generation models are a big deal. Half the recharge rate and far more durability than the original GBs plus ectolumic containment? It's a significant improvement over the prototypes we cobbled together in the old garage."

Raymond shrugged. He couldn't say how he really felt when surrounded by a crew of Braff's men.

A specialist on the communications console flipped a switch and the RV's speaker unit and broadcast Braff's voice from a field command post somewhere nearby. The two scientists scanned the banks of body-camera feeds, trying to discern where Braff might be.

The radio transmission distorted his voice only slightly. "All teams, we've got eyes on the entities. EMF tests confirm entity presence; we are green lights for capture, folks. Standard six-man teams, just like we drilled and performed captures in our pre-GB ops. All non-military personnel," his tone seemed to imply that those persons should know who they are, "should remain safely out of the way and act as observers only. This is a hot military operation."

Raymond scowled. His eyes were glued to the real-time video streams.

"Where's Sanderson?" Swag asked. The screens each displayed tiny digital emblems with the name of the camera operator. "And the rest of them, too? These guys aren't the regular team—except for Anders and Jones."

Swag looked around at the men and women in the surveillance vehicle. He only recognized a few faces, and all of them returned only momentary, blank stares and then returned to their work.

###

Rodriguez, Jones, and Goodthunder moved silently and in tight formation around the corner of the building and crept up the rear stair of the dilapidated apartment complex. They paused at the entry and Rodriguez checked his wrist-mounted EMF device, clocked the strong readings, and nodded to his counterparts.

Using hand signals they counted down and then breached the door. The threesome charged into the hallway where six wild-eyed men stood in surprise.

"Hold it!" Jones hollered.

They stared blankly. Each man was an ethnic minority that was common to the area, but something burning in their eyes alerted the Entity Capture Team members of their afflicted condition. ECTs weren't comprised of weak or fearful people, however.

One awkward second of silence passed and then the men scattered like insects. The largest of them charged the team headlong, bellowing like a madman, while the other five sprinted away.

Goodthunder stepped ahead, dropped to a knee, and brandished a futuristic-looking flashlight. A short-ranged, flickering cone of lasers similar to pointer beams spread from its business end.

The maniac staggered and stumbled forwards, nearly crashing into Goodthunder except that Jones tackled him and rolled the man to his back. "Wha… what happened?" he asked breathily, emerging from a hazy fugue.

Rodriguez stared at the action ahead of him, making sure that the body camera clearly picked up the GB's operation in the field. A shimmering, ethereal smoke hovered for a split-second in the machine's effective field.

Goodthunder thumbed the capture button and sucked the vaporic entity into the device. It chirped with an electronic blat and the LED switched from red to green. Twisting off a rear portion of the device the size of soda can; its plexi window glowed with an amber light as the viscous goo within promised to confine the entity deep within. He quickly attached another before pocketing the containment cell in his hip purse.

Down the hallway they heard more shouting and snarling as Anders, Baker, and Schwartz confronted the others. "Coming back atcha!" Anders yelled.

Two seconds later, four of the remaining afflicted ran back towards Rodriquez's crew. They skidded to a halt and glared at the Entity Capture Team; their eyes burned with intense hate, but they also flickered with malevolent intelligence. The gang of bestial men crashed through an interior door and broke into the nearest apartment. They charged through the empty quarters and smashed headlong through the window, rolling to a stop in the yard.

The ECT was on them immediately and four of them gave chase as Rodriguez and Anders stayed inside to track the seventh EMF signal. As three of the demoniacs went down, one of the afflicted turned a sharp angle and hurried towards the corner of the building. Goodthunder chased him like a pro-bowl linebacker but as soon as his prey hit the wall, he began to spider climb straight upwards with supernatural talent.

Undeterred, Goodthunder dashed ahead, bounced one foot off the eroded brickwork and leapt vertically. He snatched the climber's foot and yanked him back to the broken pavement.

The afflicted snarled and scrambled to his feet. He backhanded the soldier and sent him reeling. Goodthunder spun back around and brandished his BCnTR. As the GB's laser field enveloped the man he stared up towards the rooftop with intense purpose, and then the human collapsed like an empty husk as the entity was pulled the confinement field.

Still inside, the remaining two teammates rushed up the stairs. Careful not to catch the switch-over on camera, Anders dialed his EMF over to a different channel and confirmed his readings on the top-secret tech. "Hermes is a go, General," he spoke aloud, knowing General Braff would make a note of it. None of the Eidolon Commission members in the RV had high enough clearance to understand what the phrase meant.

Rodriguez and Anders kicked open the rooftop access of the building and spotted the source of the altered EMF reading. A stout Latino man stood on the ledge like a king who lorded over a successful battle.

"There you are," the afflicted man said. His voice rumbled with a low and ominous baritone. "You've come to claim a prize and continue our charade?"

Rodriguez and Anders glanced at each other before switching off their audio feeds as the entity spoke—just as they'd been instructed. They brandished their GBs at the ready and rushed towards their quarry.

"I'm not so easily captured. I am a prince!" he screamed as he leapt from the rooftop with supernatural vigor, he slipped out of range of the BCnTRs' beams and plummeted four stories below.

Rodriguez and Anders gasped in shock as the squat Latino landed on the basketball court with seeming grace and fury. The prince stuck his landing and the ground cracked even further, furrowing a man-sized crater; the afflicted one smiled diabolically and turned his eyes upwards to a distant rooftop across the street. He turned his back as the other four ECTs on the ground whirled in a flurry of bewildered profanity and attempted to pursue.

The self-proclaimed prince dashed towards the open end of the alleyway, fully aware that the body cameras would broadcast his escape. He darted towards the giant, sleek motorhome where a burly soldier stepped past the front corner to confront the afflicted.

Sergeant Scofield snapped his sidearm to attention and put two .45 caliber hollow-points through the demoniac's brainpan. The bullets spun the short, middle aged man violently to the ground where his blood and gray-matter spilled across the busted concrete sidewalk.

#

Swag stormed out of the motorhome with Raymond hot on his heels. From their vantage in front of the monitors they watched the afflicted Latino make his mad dash towards them from a third person point of view.

Practically stumbling from the vehicle, they looked up just in time to see Scofield drop the afflicted man before he could escape. Raymond reeled from the deafening bursts of the gunshots. Swag stiffened and stomped towards the sergeant.

"What do you think you're doing!" he levied a finger at Scofield. "You just killed an innocent bystander!"

The sergeant returned a menacing gaze. "There are none innocent, here." He holstered his pistol and started directing traffic. A team of specialists pulled up in a white cargo van and quickly ran into the scene with totes of video and camera equipment along with props and items to stage a scene in case the EC needed to fabricate a story in their defense—it was standard procedure for such operations.

Swag fumed at his counterpart even as a masked man in a disposable biohazard suit dropped safety cones around the corpse's pool of viscera and fluids so that no persons accidentally picked up the entity. "I always carry one of the original entity-capture prototypes! I was right here!" He unclipped the device and wagged it in Scofield's face.

"Listen," the sergeant remained unnervingly calm. "That thing represented a lethal threat, but perhaps even more, it is an invaluable asset. We've invested time and money into these test operations and allowing it to escape could have put the greater population at risk."

It was more his tone of voice than the rationality of his argument which calmed Swag down. Raymond, however, paced nervously behind the scene, letting his emotions boil near the surface.

Baker approached nonchalantly and pointed his cylindrical Gadarene Baconator at the bloody mess of mottled and broken grey tissue and then harvested the entity. Swag swallowed the hard lump in his throat as he watched.

Raymond walked a circuit in the distance, appearing shell shocked by a shooting death in such close proximity. He perked up as Braff strode past, absorbed by the intense conversation on his encrypted sat-phone.

"…Hermes is fully operational, and Project Pandora is fully underway," he stated as Raymond approached from behind. "Of course. These things are resources—tools. Some won't fall under Pandora's jurisdiction so long as they can be plied into use by DHS."

"I knew it!" Raymond shouted accusingly from behind the chief officer. He laid a hand on Braff's shoulder and startled him.

Braff dropped the brick-phone and whirled around, driving a fist into Raymond's jaw and knocking him prone. "Cripes! Ray! Don't go laying hands on a superior officer in a hot-zone like that!" He picked up his phone as the connection on the other end squawked vainly.

"I overheard you," Raymond said with his back on the blacktop. He touched his lip and pulled his bloody fingers away from a split lip. "You're going to weaponize the entities!"

Braff returned a neutral look and offered a hand to help the scientist to his feet. Raymond narrowed his eyes and ignored the general's hand.

"Firstly, civilians are supposed to stay in the motorhome until the 'all clear' is given. Secondly, I don't know what you think you heard, but that's not it—and if it was, that decision's above your security clearance, anyways."

The two traded nasty looks as Swag jogged over. "I've got to get back to you," Braff said into the sat-phone and then severed the line.

"What's going on?" Swag asked, knowing that he would be tasked to play mediator between his peers again. He reached a hand down and hauled Raymond to his feet.

Raymond spat bloody spittle as he stood. "Nothing," he said disdainfully, rubbing his jaw. "Same old, same old. But maybe you want to ask our superior about Project Pandora, or whatever Hermes is."

Braff still glowered at the scientist. "Maybe we ought to chat about eavesdropping on classified intelligence conversations and jumping to conclusions," he narrowed his eyes. "That's the reason black-ops prisons exist."

Swag looked from man to man. The tension snapped and turned into a shouting match, rehashing all the same old arguments, only this time Raymond had a dead body to throw into his philosophical arsenal.

#

Oswald Harrison pushed his glasses up the ridge of his nose the way he did whenever nervousness bested him. His blood ran cold as he watched the top-secret operation unfold on the neighboring streets below. He checked his digital camera and found it still useless.

Thankful for the foresight to bring an older 35mm, he felt more certain than ever of his conspiracy theory: that Cuthbert Industries has developed a kind of directional EMP device that could disable a variety of modern technologies on command similar to cell-phone blockers. *If they'd sold such a technology to the military, it would explain so many things.*

He leaned over the edge of the roofline of the three-story derelict and captured the events in high-resolution glory. He zoomed in on the apprehension of the four men in the battered courtyard, barely having enough angle to make out what the Men-In-Black spooks were doing to the poorer citizens below.

His stomach churned as two more spooks chased a jumper on the rooftop. Oswald popped a handful of antacids when the man survived the jump. An electric chill danced through his fear receptors when the Latino man looked directly at him and grinned. *Did he just wink at me?*

Seconds later, the man lay dead and Oswald had spilled his Tums all over the flat rooftop. He couldn't turn his face away. Keeping the camera pointed at the macabre scene, he continued shuttering as fast as his old, film camera allowed, capturing faces and details of what he presumed would be reported on tonight by the network news as some kind of gang violence.

He focused on the high-ranking brass moving across the courtyard and captured the altercation. The general and a bystander—no—a civilian worker… maybe a consultant— traded harsh words and fists flew. The scuffle grew to three strong as the men screamed at each other.

Oswald zoomed in on the face and got a clear enough shot that a search algorithm might be able to discern the civilian's identity. He smiled; Oswald liked the man's spirit—he obviously didn't like something about the op and didn't fear the high-ranking officer as he spat verbal barbs which couldn't be deciphered at such a distance.

Watching only a moment longer, Oswald looked down and locked eyes with the shooter. The sergeant that murdered the Latino stood in the middle of the street, arms crossed. He stared right at Oswald.

Oswald's spine stiffened; he'd heard of the dark places these sorts of agencies could lock people up in. As fast as

Oswald could, he snatched up his camera and fled towards someplace populated, hoping to throw off any observation drones that might have been dispatched. Scrambling down a dilapidated stairwell that emptied on the far side of the block he fumbled with his phone as it finally powered up again since he'd cleared enough distance from the scene. Making sure it was on a public Wi-Fi channel to help preserve anonymity he shot out a quick message to his contact in Cerberus, an anonymous whistleblower hacktivist team.

Oswald glanced at the roofline watching for drones or snipers—he jumped underneath a storefront's awning. *Satellites—I forgot about satellites!* He quickly purchased a hat inside the thrift store and ditched his jacket. It wasn't paranoia, he understood. Oswald knew that he had really seen more than he was supposed to.

13

"See, you've just got to learn to appreciate his humor," Swag tried to explain the nuanced joke behind the Gadarene Baconator to General Braff as he reclined in the stiff, leather wingback chair.

The officer nodded thoughtfully, bobbing his silver-shot mane, but shrugged. He moved aside the live, Type 91 grenade he'd used as a paperweight; he'd won it off a Japanese officer decades ago. Setting it on the far side of his impressive, walnut desk he unflipped the ornate, wooden humidor. It always rested upside-down on the desk. Braff retrieved a cigar. Gripping it between his teeth, he offered one to the scientist.

Swag shook his head. "No, thank you."

Braff closed the humidor and flipped it again so that the only unvarnished surface faced up and displayed J.B., the carved initials of Braff's son. The general didn't light the Maduro tinted Corona as he often did, even if it broke protocol. Instead, he gnawed on the thing as he worked through his thoughts.

"So you are satisfied with their performance?" the general asked.

"I think they worked exactly as they were designed to, yes."

Braff raised an eyebrow. "You... think there are some improvements that could be made to the GBs?"

Swag shrugged. "Not so much as the capture design work goes. We've really out-performed the parameters of an experimental science field."

"Then you think we haven't pushed the boundaries?"

"Well, of course not—but that's not the part that's got me worried. My thoughts are regarding permanent containment?"

The general nodded and urged him to continue his train of thought. He'd come to respect him enough to know that the scientist's musings often led to golden nuggets.

"I guess I'm waxing philosophical about the morality of it all. I mean, are these entities a part of our natural ecosystem? They certainly seem harmful and dangerous, but what harm might we do to the environment—to the planetary balance—if we permanently remove them from it?"

At that, Braff scowled. "I don't think that's a logical question at all, and not very scientific, if you ask me. I leave the philosophy to the philosophers. These things are quite obviously dangerous, and as far as the science goes: you've never seen humanity undisturbed by the influence of these… things, so you can't draw a real conclusion."

Swag could tell that his superior intentionally avoided using the term "demon."

"We can't speculate that there would be any negative influence if we haven't observed a human community removed from the possibility of affliction. Maybe these things have held back our evolutionary progress since we crawled out of the muck—we can't possibly know." Braff punctuated the statement with a wag of his cigar. "Hooray for the scientific process."

The scientist shrugged and accepted the argument as valid, even if it was far from a silver bullet to dispelling his concerns. "Then what of containment?"

"I agree. I wish we could store more than one entity per GB containment cell, but I think future versions might be able to find a work around on that limitation."

"That's not what has me concerned."

"Do tell."

"Each GB cell takes up a certain amount of physical space and requires a certain amount of maintenance and upkeep in order to operate. If we succeeded in capturing every entity, and let's assume that the lower tier of our projected numbers is the correct one, we're talking about an overwhelming resource burden just to maintain a status quo."

Braff nodded. "That's actually more of a logistics question than a science one," he deflected. "You can be assured, though, that we've got some of our—"

The door swung open and an angry redheaded female stormed through. Donna Loebel's commanding presence froze the room and chased away all nuances of informality.

Waving a nondescript hanging-file folder, the presidential liaison's words dripped with poisonous barbs. "You said you'd take care of this problem," cold forged steel girded her words. "But here I've got reports of new content on that paranoid little twerp's blog page—and every time we shut it down a backup copy pops right back up—hosted in some third world country."

Swag tried to shrink down within his chair, hoping that she wouldn't lock eyes on him. For the most part, he managed to elude her glare. He'd suddenly become a fly on the wall of a room with very powerful players. Seated between the crossfire of two of the six board members of the Eidolon Commission was not a comfortable place.

"Nobody believes that nonsense," Braff countered. "Intel says he's only got a couple of regular visitors anyway." He kept his eyes on Swag, trying to signal to the raging, red woman that they were not alone.

She ignored all his nonverbal cues and levied a finger at him. "Keeping a lid on the operations was *your* job, and now we've got a citizen trying to stir up a panic by leaking information he's somehow gathered on your projects."

"Just another conspiracy theory nut who's trying to get his hit-counter up on the internet," Braff downplayed and nodded to the scientist with a light tone.

She hissed, "He's been communicating with a hacker team called Cerberus and gotten information on Pandora."

Braff's sudden shift in posture sucked the remaining air out of the room. He cleared his throat and indicated Swag with a tilt of his head. "Let me remind you, Mizz Loebel, that Doctor Swaggart does not have clearance on Pandora." His tone turned iron with authority as he flipped the conversation on its rear and shut it down. "Maybe if we all kept ourselves in check, there wouldn't be any possibility of the kinds of security leaks you are laying at my feet."

Donna Loebel blanched and gave him a tight-lipped nod. "We will talk later about remediation," she said flatly.

"Agreed. See my secretary for my next scheduled block. We can brainstorm a creative solution to your problem, I have no doubt."

Loebel turned and departed with more tact than she'd demonstrated with her entry.

Swag looked at Braff like a deer in the headlights and waited for the general to make the first move. He didn't dare ask the question that burned on the tip of his tongue.

Braff sighed. "I'm going to bring you in on Project Pandora eventually," he assured him. "But now is not the best timing. You're just going to have to trust me on that one."

Swag nodded. "And until then?"

"I could use you in the field to oversee another test with the GBs; it's arranged for tomorrow. Give Raymond the day off on this one—I'm obviously trying to eliminate info leaks and so I'm only bringing in a skeleton crew of people I know I can trust—and don't argue this point with me—I've no doubt that you trust him… but Raymond has less loyalty to me. I promise. I'll bring you into the loop as soon as I can."

For once, Raymond was glad to have a day off, even if it had come so abruptly. Swag assured him that he hadn't been fired—at least that allowed Raymond enough peace of mind to try and enjoy it.

He tried to park around back as much as possible to avoid being spotted at the XXX book store just outside the ill-kept highway exit. He hadn't come as a consumer, though, and didn't even know what he'd find at the mysterious address he'd punched into his GPS.

The scientist glanced around uneasily as he entered the adult book store. He nervously looked around. It was still midmorning and the morning regulars looked to be a salty lot. Whoever his mysterious contact was must've known a thing or two about clandestine meetings; social protocol in such seedy places demanded a person keep his or her attention to themselves.

Not letting his gaze linger too long on any one person who shuffled between the various aisles of categorized pornography, Raymond wondered which of these people sent him the message last night. The note was clear: a grainy black and white photograph taken a week ago that showed Raymond arguing with Braff during their most recent field operation. In red sharpie the penned message gave an address, time, date, and the simple note: "He's not telling you everything."

A hand tapped him on the shoulder. "Excuse me sir? I think you dropped your wallet."

Raymond turned to the skinny, weasel-faced man with a receding hairline and too-thin mustache. He held out an old wallet which the scientist did not recognize. "Um. Thank you?"

The man gave Raymond a conspiratorial look and nodded to the sketchy, dimly-lit hall at the back of the facility where locking video booths used to operate. Posted next to the door was a shut-down notice from the county health department citing numerous violations; below that notice a hand-printed piece of notebook paper reading "Keep Out" had been tapped.

Waiting for a reasonable amount of time after the wiry man sneaked through the prohibited door, Raymond turned and ducked inside. He sent up a silent prayer, hoping that this was indeed his contact and that he had not accidentally stumbled into some sort of clandestine, gay sex ring. He bit his lip and searched around for the informant in the shadows.

"Psst!" The man waved to him around the corner of the L-shaped hall where the shadows were darkest.

Raymond walked closer and whispered, "This isn't my wallet."

The man ignored him. "I'm glad you came. You weren't followed, were you? Otherwise things are going to get real awkward really fast in order for me to keep my cover. I'd rather go to jail for public lewdness than wind up in some black-ops detention center for the rest of my life."

"I came alone," Raymond affirmed.

"I won't take long. The less contact I have with you, the safer we both stay."

"Just what are we doing?" Raymond demanded. "And who *are* you?"

The man paused for a moment, as if deciding whether or not he could trust Raymond. "My name is Oswald Harrison—and my life is in danger for the things that I know. I've been investigating the people you work for—the people *you* have no apparent love for."

"General Braff," Raymond spat disdainfully.

"Correct." He paused and then delivered a caveat. "I don't know who I can trust anymore. The government, specifically the Eidolon Commission, has been trying to get to me—trying to silence me."

Raymond eyed him suspiciously; the EC was supposed to be unknown and totally off the books. He'd signed countless nondisclosure agreements to that effect when he and Swag first started. "And you think you can trust *me*?"

"I think you don't like what you see happening whenever you open your eyes and actually look around. I think you're smart enough to smell corruption, government misuse, murder, and probably war crimes against the American people if you objectively look at the EC," Oswald ranted. "I don't *know* that I can trust you. But I've been watching you, well, with the help of Cerberus, and what I've seen doesn't seem to indicate that you're a company man—you're a moral man."

"Cerberus? The hacker group?"

Oswald nodded. "Hacktivist," he corrected. "Can I trust you?"

"I don't really know what you're fighting against. I've got no affection for the General—but is he really… evil?"

"History has shown us exactly what kind of guy General Braff is. He's the sort of person that put Einstein and Feynman to work inventing nuclear weapons. The A-bomb was built on the premise of ending all wars—but murdered millions of innocent men, women, and children in the process. That's the kind of guy General Braff is: a murderer with free range, government funding, and no oversight."

The silence that followed begged for a response. *Can I trust you?* Raymond didn't know what he was agreeing to, but when he weighed his bitterness for Braff against the unknown he felt compelled to answer affirmatively. "I think so. But I don't know how I can help or what you need. I'm not keen on prison, either."

Thrusting a slip of paper into Raymond's hand, Oswald continued hastily. "Meet me at this address tonight. My house got ransacked by government spooks earlier; they got everything—but I have backups. I'll have to retrieve them.

"I don't know that I have all the answers... this thing goes deep... but I know a lot of things I'm not supposed to—things about Pandora and Hermes—even Joshua Brady's real medical records. I probably know more than you do, but maybe you can help fill in the blanks."

"Joshua Brady? The serial killer they put to death a couple weeks ago? And what about Pandora?" his voice was urgent.

"Tonight. I'll give you everything I have, tonight." Oswald clapped him on the shoulder and stepped around him. Seconds later he was gone, leaving Raymond to ponder the encounter in the dark.

"Hey!" the skeezy old woman who ran the place shouted from near the poorly drawn sign. "You can't be back here!"

"Sorry! Sorry," Raymond said, hustling out of the black hallway with sticky floors. He tried to shield his face with his hand as he passed the grumpy-faced troll.

He slipped just close enough to hear her mutter, "pervert," under her breath. And then he was gone.

#

Goodthunder and Anders shook hands with Swag when he stepped inside the large motorhome. They were genuinely glad to see him. The rest of the crew appeared less enthusiastic and looked at him as if he was any other member of the support staff.

Swag didn't hold it against them; they simply didn't know him yet. If he'd had to level with them, he didn't fully trust Rodriguez, Jones, Baker, or Schwartz yet either for those same reasons. The scientist didn't know why the other four members had been reassigned, or where they'd gone, but he knew better than to ask.

The six-person team wore civvies, so they'd be able to blend into the local area with seamless integration. Swag knew that each one carried at least two concealed handguns plus a BCnTR handheld with extra cells.

A stocky monitor jockey approached Swag from the driver's cab. She pushed her glasses tighter and handed him a packet and a headset with attached microphone.

Swag opened the sealed envelope and carefully read the instructions. He promptly dropped them through the shredder, as per protocol and the newer four members of the capture team seemed to suddenly hold him in higher regard now that they realized he was the mission leader today.

"Sir?" asked Rodriguez. The soldier knew better than to salute him. Swag was still only a civilian, even if this was his operation.

Swag checked the monitor banks. The three surveillance techs each shook their heads negatively to indicate that they hadn't yet spotted their contact. Pulling a large photograph from the legal envelope, and six wallet sized prints, the scientist flashed the image to them and distributed the smaller copies for personal reference.

"This is Jill Miendell," he said authoritatively, trying his best to channel Braff's demeanor. "We have multiple surveillance feeds established. Info has come down the pipe that Miendell is afflicted as confirmed by multiple readings on the EMF readers—she could have more than one entity. We're here gathering live information for threat capture and containment. Not only are we testing the GBs against single-multi-affliction, but this is a live test."

"Come again?"

"The area is not cordoned off like we've seen in other missions. There is a risk to civilians—and more than that, we risk being seen. Do not blow your cover."

As the team nodded their understanding Rodriguez slipped a hand up. "I don't mean any offense, but can you tell me why a civilian consultant is in charge of this operation?"

Nervous enough as he already was, Swag pushed that tension deep down in his gut and stared at Rodriguez. "You're not paid to ask questions," he gruffed in his best Braff impersonation. A moment later, he broke character after Goodthunder grinned ear to ear at the un-Swag-like attitude. "Actually, I have no idea why. Maybe Braff wants to give me a deeper role; maybe he's busy with another mission. I really don't know. I only know what my instructions were—and I didn't know I was leading this party until ninety seconds ago."

They nodded, and then filed out the door to get into position. According to the briefing, they might have to wait a while before their target showed herself.

Swag grimaced against the ulceric pain in his gut. He didn't much care for the responsibility that he'd been suddenly handed, but he was determined not to screw it up. He'd been tempted to pray a simple *Lord, please don't let me screw this up*, but consciously rejected the impulse. His childhood training had proved hard to deprogram; old habits died hard, but Swag was a man of reason. He'd get through this, he told himself.

#

Several hours passed uneventfully and with nothing but regular radio checks. The team stuck to the script and remained at their posts until one of the monitor jockeys spotted the target.

"I've got her, Doctor! She's just outside checkpoint three."

Swag relayed the information via headset as he glanced at a monitor. Body cameras on the neighboring screens jostled into motion all around the board. The primary feed showed a bedraggled, middle-aged woman opening a fire door and glancing around furtively. Half a dozen cats escaped through the opening and scampered behind the alley dumpsters.

From inside the mobile base, only half a block from the action, they watched the plain clothes Entity Capture Team move into position. Anders approached the lady as he wandered through the remote alley.

"Excuse me, ma'am?"

She glared at him like a bristling, feral animal and hissed.

"I think I'm lost. I'm looking for the Green Leek Bistro," he said as he moved another step closer, reaching slowly for his GB.

Everything went perfectly according to procedure. And then it didn't.

A burst of garbled static overwhelmed the audio and then all the cameras except for Anders' and Goodthunder's switched to static. Indicator lights on the audio console switched to red on all microphones as they switched off. The mobile HQ went into panic mode as technicians tried vainly to restore services and their chaos drowned out the unfolding conversation between Anders and the afflicted woman.

"Rodriguez?" He called into the headset. No reply.

"Rodriguez! Report in! Jones? Baker? Schwartz?" Their signals were all silent.

"Where are the other four ECTs?" Swag barked.

"I've got them here on GPS," a corporal replied. "No. Wait. They just disappeared!"

Goodthunder sprinted towards Anders as the woman braced herself for a charge. Both men had their GBs out in time. Anders' view screen filled with the woman's girthsome form as she charged straight through the BCnTR's laser capture field and took down the soldier.

"Capture confirmed," the exuberant corporal stated, looking only at his head's up display, and not the terror unfolding on the live-stream. He looked up and his faced paled with sudden horror as the crazed lady beat Anders mercilessly with white-knuckled fists.

Goodthunder's camera shook violently as sprinted towards his unconscious companion in an effort to rescue the downed soldier. As she slipped aside of the GB's energy field with uncanny agility, Swag was out the door as fast as his legs would move, leaving the crews' unanswered questions for orders hanging in the air behind him.

Seconds later, huffing and puffing, the scientist arrived, just in time to distract the afflicted woman. She hissed like a crazed cat and let Goodthunder wriggle out of the precarious position the woman had put him into. Swag's distraction let the soldier slip just far enough away that when she returned her attention back to him her next punch missed and smashed the red brick face of the nearby wall instead of the soldier's neck.

Meeting Goodthunder's gaze Swag pulled a BCnTR from his waistband and charged forward. Combined, the two activated their capture fields and sucked in an entity apiece. The woman crumpled into a pool of her own bodily fluids, falling suddenly weak and disoriented as each GB's indicator switched colored LEDs.

"What? Where am I?" Her pleas went unanswered as Swag and Goodthunder rushed to their fallen comrade.

"What happened?" Goodthunder asked exasperatedly.

"Multiple entities," Swag stated. "I realized it as soon as she powered through the initial capture field. The GBs worked perfectly—we just didn't think of this eventuality—we'd assumed the extraction would cause enough disorientation to counteract that kind of raw rage."

The four defecting teammates trotted onto the scene of the carnage. With hearts like ice, their faces fell only slightly at the sight before them; Goodthunder sank to his knees as he administered first aid.

Swag stood and lanced the crews with a barrage of offensive words as he cussed out the other four men. "Where were you? You deserted your post," he accused, pacing angrily.

The bewildered woman babbled as she leaned against the nearby wall, prattling as if she suffered from dementia. "The voices. The voices are quiet. Where are my voices?" She kept the mantra until she tipped onto her side in complete bewilderment.

"Communications failed. Maybe some kind of interference or EMP," Baker interjected. "How's Anders?" he asked with genuine concern.

"I'm not buying that crap," Swag said sternly. "I want to know!" He stuck a finger into Baker's chest.

Baker glared at the scientist and told him more things with his eyes than his words ever could. One of those things being, *if you don't pull back that finger you'll lose it*. The second silent admission was that they'd been following orders: something else superseded their mission.

Swag pulled his hand back and let it drop. He couldn't do anything except damage his credibility within the ECT by pushing the issue. He frowned and hoped it had more to do with Donna Loebel than with Braff.

The others moved towards Anders to see if they could help in any way. "He's not coming around," Goodthunder reported. "Maybe a coma?" He nodded his head to Swag, "I was next... and she woulda got me, but that crazy S.O.B. came running out of nowhere with a spare GB."

Rodriguez offered the scientist a nod of respect.

Swag returned it and noticed a splotch of blood on the soldier's shoulder. "You get hurt while you guys were incommunicado?"

Rodriguez looked at his shoulder. "Oh yeah. I must've caught myself on some chain-link fencing back there, or something."

Nodding his head, Swag replied, "Yeah. Fencing." He couldn't see any cuts or rips in the fabric. "You should get that looked at."

Raymond turned over the slip of paper one more time in his hands and made absolutely certain that he'd read it correctly. Oswald Harrison's penmanship had been very precise, and he didn't strike Raymond as the type to be late.

Sighing, he tossed back a Zantac and chased it with a slug of his lukewarm coffee... his third lukewarm latte. Raymond knew that he'd have some nasty heartburn if the tiny pill didn't work some gastrointestinal miracle on his behalf. It was far too late to be drinking coffee, but it was the acid reflux that bothered him, not the caffeine.

His cell had been left off and with the battery removed. Raymond didn't know if the government could really spy through mobile phones or if this really even helped but he'd seen people do it in the movies. After trading apologetic shrugs with the late-night barista who could only guess that her lonely customer had been stood up, Raymond tossed back the remainder of his drink and discarded the paper cup.

He glanced one last time at the clock on the opposite wall. Too much time had passed—more than simple oversight could account for.

Nodding his thanks to the brewer, he turned and departed. Raymond had not been stood up. His questions would not be answered—perhaps could never be answered; Oswald Harrison was not coming because it was unlikely he remained still alive.

14

Swag lay in his bed, staring at the red glow of his alarm clock on the nightstand. The display blazed through the darkness, forcing him to stare while robbing the scientist's sleep. Three fifty-two. Not enough time had passed for him to take another sedative, even though the first had done little to alleviate his restlessness.

His mind hadn't been able to let go of the mission. Every time he thought his mind might relax the nearby shadows seemed to shift, jolting him with a spike of fear. Swag knew it was some kind of PTSD thing, and so he shut his eyes tight against distraction—that's when the voices started—like whispers in the night.

He tried music, white noise, humming, but nothing stopped the otherworldly gibbering. It called out in its indecipherable language.

Swag stared at the crimson radiance of the alarm clock for hours, hoping to bore his mind into submission. Even that failed and his brain revolted, asking him the deepest questions of life, dredging up thoughts he'd long-since buried; it reminded him of every regret and questioned every action. His thoughts birthed a growing paranoia. *Why had he carried that spare GB? Did he know the mission would fail, or did he think he needed constant protection from the entities—were those things sentient and out to get him?*

Reaching for the device where it rested on the opposite bedside table, Swag felt more at ease when he held it. He felt more comfortable with it on his person.

Finally, he kicked off his blankets knowing sleep would never come and that the whispers would not let him rest. He figured he might as well be useful.

Swag dialed the nurses' station at the hospital and asked for a status report. Anders remained in a coma. He couldn't be of any service at the hospital but figured he could still find purpose in his office.

After dressing himself, he nearly left the bedroom of his efficiency apartment when he paused and stared into the darkness. An overwhelming terror suddenly caught in his chest and he flicked the light switch on rather than pass through fifteen feet of dark to reach his doorway.

He patted the pocket of his cargo pants to ensure that the BCnTR was there. He'd actually worn those pants specifically because the device would fit in its pockets. *What if I lose it, or if it breaks down?*

Glancing back to a pile of miscellaneous items piled on his table Swag spotted the original capture device prototype from the garage days of his research. He stuffed the first-generation equipment into an old duffel bag and brought it with him.

The halls and parking ramp were both well-lit which helped set his mind at ease. Swag arrived at his company issued car and stared at the thumbprint scanner on the handle-lock. It was one of Franklin Cuthbert's own designs. Swag realized he wasn't the only one with paranoia-level concerns for security.

He popped the latch and tossed the older-model capture tech into the trunk. It would always be there in case his regular GB failed.

After a short commute he found himself finally stumbling into his office. The illumination panels remained well lit.

Everywhere within the ECHQ, modified light panels had been installed to pump out a high enough frequency light wave that the entities could not pass without a host. They hadn't determined sentience, but security measures demanded some kind of barrier in the chance of that eventuality.

He glanced at the containment vials which lined the walls in crystalline, vacuum-sealed tubes and the newer Entity Containment Pods that the current GBs utilized. Swag recognized irony in feeling safe in this room where they'd stored and labeled so many of the captured entities. Each ECP unit was linked via electrodes that kept the prison-bank powered and lit so the beasts remained restrained; the room's ambient light was a failsafe, but Swag knew that nothing in life was truly safe. Even the most routine mission could turn deadly. He'd seen that, too.

Swag sat and began leafing through past research. A bank of monitors replayed old mission files while he watched with tired eyes and looked for patterns, weaknesses, and any kind of data that they'd omitted by accident or intent. He didn't want to get caught off guard again like he did with Anders.

A grainy video cycled in the upper right-hand corner of the screens. He remembered the day: the only ECT fatalities happened on that mission. They'd just missed containing an afflicted man whom they'd cornered on the top floor of an old brownstone. When they caught the frenzied victim with a GB Mark-I, which only induced vomiting, the poor man writhed and retched a vomitus spew out the open window. Its splash infected a pigeon that escaped.

After canvasing the room and ledge in order to ensure the entity had gotten away, the team meandered through the parking lot with their guards lowered. Like a grey, winged bolt, the bird smashed into Sanderlin's face, flapping and plucking an eye out. Seconds later she became a slobbering maniac of rage and death. Before any of her teammates could react, Sanderlin tore Gifford's throat out with her teeth. Everyone knew that Sanderlin and Gifford had been lovers—but she was no longer Sanderlin!

With a face stained by gore, she leapt from the blood-spurting body and tore into Ripley with her fingernails. Anders and Goodthunder had their Mark-Is on her within seconds but Sanderlin vomited onto Ripley who charged ahead and tried to disembowel the hunters a split second later. She moved so fast and neither of them could have reacted in time. But the sniper's bullet was even faster yet; Braff had issued the kill order and activated the fail-safe sharpshooter, determined not to lose another asset.

Swag knew that these were more than creatures of primal nature. They could bear animosity and they had predatory instincts. He watched the film several times, replayed his friends' deaths in slow motion, vainly hoping their loss could help him learn something new.

His eyelids eventually grew heavy and his mind finally allowed some respite, though the whispers continued to haunt him. They disappeared whenever he tried to listen and understand them. The last thing Swag remembered thinking as he finally drifted away was that these things needed to be stopped—even eradicated—no cost was too high to remove such undeniable evil.

#

"Do you ever think that Braff would use the entities if he could… you know, for military purposes?" Raymond leaned up against a research table as his partner stuck his face into an electromagnet scope to watch the being's interaction during a new experiment. Despite the apparent honesty of the question, he kept his tone hushed.

Swag didn't bother replying. They'd gone down this particular avenue, and so many others, as Raymond imagined countless scenarios under which their benefactors would betray them to their illuminati masters or sell them off to any number of shadowy puppet governments. Instead, he glanced up, noted the calculations on the nearby whiteboard, and resumed his work.

"I think my theoretical work could be proven!" he said excitedly.

Raymond sighed. Swag was always excited—pioneering new work was like that. Almost everything felt revolutionary. "This is important," Raymond flatly said of his query.

"*This is important*," Swag sparred back. "I've been working on this for months! And I thought you were working right alongside of me the whole time, but you're obviously engaged in some other kind of investigation at the moment."

"Is it life and death levels of important?" Raymond shot back, squaring up his feet. "Because I'm pretty sure that what I'm seeing *is*."

"*It could be!*" Swag jabbed back. "These protocols could help us track and identify the entities wherever they go on the planet. Don't you remember Sanderlin and Ripley? *This could save lives now.*" He nodded with a sense of enlightened condescension. "Or maybe this is about something else. Maybe you're not miffed at Braff—*maybe it wouldn't matter who it is?*"

"Oh no. It's definitely Braff—and the whole board of directors on the Eidolon Commission."

"Not at all where my mind goes. It seems to me that you might be jealous."

"Of Braff?"

"For the longest time it was you and I, Raymond. And then suddenly we've got a third wheel in the mix and you start getting your panties tied in a knot on a regular basis! You insist on keeping up this constant pissing match with our boss."

"You know what? Fine!" Raymond exploded. "I don't like the General. I think he's an arrogant dick—and yeah, I miss the good old days. I can admit that. But *that is not* what this is about!"

The sudden candor rocked Swag back a half-step. His momentary silence signaled he was open to hearing the next point of Raymond's verbal salvo.

Swag's demeanor let Raymond catch his breath and take the tension down a notch.

"I get that this new research is highly important—even though you know I disagree on its prioritization and that I'd rather be working on sustainable containment methods." He held up his hands in mock surrender—trying to avoid another source of contention between the parties and signaling that he did not plan to revisit that argument. "But I'm concerned with the immediate threats to our safety."

Raymond exhaled and re-centered himself. "You are going to think I'm nuts, but hear me out: it's not a conspiracy theory if it's true. Braff, the EC, the military—only God knows who else—are planning to weaponize the entities. I don't know what their purpose is just yet, but I was on the verge of finding out—on the verge of having proof in my hands."

Swag eyeballed him. "You *almost* had proof. I'm a scientist; I really want to surrender my need for the empirical to have faith in a friend, but I need something more. You know me. That's how I've always been wired."

Sighing, Raymond came clean. "I recently met a man by the name of Oswald Harrison." He dumped the entire story on his friend who politely listened, even smiled at the misinterpreted, clandestine meeting in the dark hallway.

"Did you ask General Braff about him?"

Raymond gave him a stink-eye.

"Shouldn't we ought to at least bring it up to him? We have to do our due diligence. You can't blindly trust strangers."

"No! And you'd better not tell him about this, either!" He rummaged around in his stack of belongings on a nearby table and then slapped down a recent newspaper.

Raymond flipped it open to an article near the back about a suicidal, unstable man who burned down his apartment complex with himself still inside. The summary listed the deceased culprit as Oswald Harrison. "He wasn't insane, Swag. He was eliminated because of what he knew. People who seriously attempt suicide don't make appointments or skip meetings—they conclude all their final arrangements and tie up loose ends before ending their life. And I swear to God, if you tell Braff, I'll be dead within a week, appointments or not!"

Thin-lipped, Swag nodded, and agreed to keep his confidence. Raymond could tell that he still hadn't gotten through to his friend—Swag remained unmoved without evidence.

"I'm sorry. I really am. When I get bent out of shape, I try to work on something that I *can* control—I try and move past whatever bothers me... something like this." He motioned to the large board covered with notes, equations, and theory. "Even despite your focus on other things, I know you're still contributing. The notes you jotted down when I was away on Braff's mission were like a Rosetta stone." He pointed to the whiteboard. "I haven't had this many epiphanies since our early hypotheses for the GBs."

"This handwriting right here?" Raymond indicated the scrawled mathematical equation which spring-boarded his Swag's research past the mental hurdles he'd been mired in for the last month. "I don't know if you ever stopped to really even look at it, Jimmy." Raymond used Swag's first name to inject venom into the statement. "That's not even my handwriting."

As Raymond stormed out in a moody huff, Swag stared at the handwriting on the wall. The notes were indeed foreign—they weren't Raymond's *or* Jessica's. He stared at the shaky script for several long moments until the otherworldly whispers begin their ethereal call for attention.

#

Swag hesitantly entered Braff's office where the General looked up from a report that the science team had submitted earlier that afternoon. "Hey? Do you have a minute?"

Braff nodded and beckoned him towards a seat.

The scientist took a chair and tried to figure out exactly what he wanted to say. He struggled to articulate it and instead made small talk. "Why do you keep your humidor upside down?"

The officer smiled, moved the grenade that usually rested atop it, and flipped it right-side up. Braff offered him a cigar. This time, Swag took it as he glanced at the old photograph of Braff, his teenage son, and Braff's late wife.

"The humidor was a gift from Jason, my son. He made it in his high school woodshop class. It's got a poorly installed hinge, and so it doesn't seal itself quite tightly enough. He didn't have the heart to finish it properly after…" he trailed off for a second, looking at his wife's photo. "Anyway, it was the thought that counts. Maybe the best gift I ever got—and he put a lot of time and energy into it." He closed the ornate box and turned it to get a better look at it. "It only seals like it's supposed to if it's upside down. Besides, I like it better that way, anyhow. It shows off his initials. I'm proud of my son. I'm very much *for* the people who are loyal to me; I care more about *people* than about perfect performance."

Swag nodded thoughtfully. It was a touching story, even if he guessed that the General certainly did have some kind of performance threshold. He wouldn't have kept a crappy humidor if it was made out of an old tissue box.

"In the end, we've gotta keep a tight seal when there's something important at stake. It's like the old sailors' proverb: 'loose lips sink ships.'" Braff sniffed the long Corona. "Neither can I let a leak destroy what I value."

Swag understood he was talking about more than cigars. He nodded with measured precision. "I'm glad that you understand the importance of people. Can we talk about Raymond?"

Braff nodded with a tight-lipped response. He bristled only slightly and let the scientist continue.

"I don't know why you guys are always at each other's throats. I don't get it and I don't care. I don't even want to understand the situation anymore. I just want to know if there's any way that you two will be able to patch things up?"

"I admit that I only kept him on because I knew he was important to you. Your work is critical, and you are a key component to the EC—enough that I decided to fold him in, too, if that's what it took to keep you on board. Cuthbert let me make that decision since I was in direct charge of operations. I recognized early on that he would be a deal breaker for you."

"Am I really such a key component? I hear things just like Raymond does and I'm not stupid, blind, or deaf. I know there is a lot more going on in the EC than you tell the civilian staff. The difference between Raymond and I is that I have sense enough to let you run your side of things with confidence that you'll bring me in on it whenever appropriate."

"You're right," Braff said. "And I can clearly see that you understand what is required of you if I grant you access."

The general slid an ID card across the desk; a neck lanyard trailed behind the laser engraved security card. Swag shot back an inquisitive look.

"I want to bring you in on project Pandora. Your friends, Raymond and Jessica, are still part of the Eidolon Commission, but I can't give them security clearance yet. If you accept, you can't share anything about Pandora with them. The reasons will become evident in time. For now, I need more guys like you working on the project, coming up with answers to tough questions like you did when you refined the BCnTRs. And for what it's worth," Braff pointed to the earlier report, "I was sure that you'd find a breakthrough eventually, with or without that equation one of the boys left you."

"One of the boys?"

"The other scientists," Braff said to the slightly crestfallen Swag, "You're a pioneer and a genius, but this is too big to be left to one or two researchers—and no good science was ever done without peer review."

"How many others are there, and where are they?"

"There is another science team; they are military, and so they think differently. A little cross-pollination can be a good thing. Make an appointment with Scofield. He's been briefed and will bring you to our other facility and then you'll see what I mean."

Slightly confused by the sudden turn of events, Swag stood to depart, and a nervous energy invigorated him. He hadn't realized how much frustration he'd suppressed about the unknown machinations of the EC until he'd been promised access. He felt like a weight had been lifted.

"Oh, and Swag," the general said. "I do promise that I'll do everything I can to mend bridges with Raymond." He nodded to him one final time before making a locking gesture at his lips and then Swag left.

15

Swag trotted down the concrete steps and headed towards the black sedan that waited for him. Scofield arrived precisely on time, as per usual.

"Where are we going?" the scientist inquired when they turned off of the freeway and headed towards the countryside.

"That's top secret." Scofield had lorded that statement over him for as long as he'd known the agent. This time, Swag fired back.

"My clearance has been updated."

Scofield nodded and grinned, well aware of that fact. "We're going to ECHQ," he told him.

"But Headquarters is downtown."

"We're going to the *real* Eidolon Commission Headquarters."

Swag understood. The downtown office never felt like the place a high-level government science station would work out of. It was heaven compared to the old garage, but always felt a little less James Bond than Swag had first imagined any place commissioned by Cuthbert would have been.

They rode the rest of the way in silence. The road rose with continual elevation and it passed through an old, derelict township which had long been abandoned; they crested a hill into the foothills of the mountain range just beyond the ghost town when Swag spotted a facility that looked like a repurposed hospital, except that it had been upgraded with military grade security. A sign above the door labeled it as the Cuthbert Research Center with fire-engine red letters.

Scofield's car crawled to a stop in front of the main entrance. "Good luck, Doctor. Glad you've finally made it to where all the action is."

Swag gave him a measured nod in lieu of the salute he would have offered had Swag been military. He looped his new ID badge around his neck, swung his legs out, and headed inside as Sergeant Scofield left with the car.

A soldier in military fatigues stopped Swag and checked his identification. The doorman skeptically checked over the scientist who he didn't recognize and waived him through to the scanner.

The electronic chip in his badge didn't recognize his credentials on the scanner so it gave a raspberry noise. Swag tried again as the guard drilled him with a suspicious look. The result was the same.

As the soldier approached, hand moving towards his sidearm, General Braff called from the lobby and waived him off. "He's with me, Jones." The general hurried over muttering, "I though Chu said he'd fixed those bugs."

Jones saluted the General and returned to his post.

Swag joined Braff and they toured the facility. It resembled a hospital on the inside with sterile corridors and rooms dedicated to research and science ops, but there were also many restricted, operational areas for the Entity Capture Teams. This was clearly the main base of operations he'd envisioned.

"Tell me about your earlier theoretical work on Cyborg-3," Braff said as they strode forward. "I know long-term containment has always been a concern that you thought I'd put on the backburner. Our resident research team has actually been working on that very problem using some of your earlier notes as a reference."

He bit back any bitterness over having his research farmed out like that; Swag knew that all of it was technically the property of his employers—even if his name was on it.

"Cyborg-3 is just a theoretical model," Swag stated. "It's pure hypothesis, mainly due to ethical issues. We built a functioning prototype of the cyborg system and then upgraded to Cyborg-2 from a human brain donated to science. But it didn't work."

"But Cyborg-1 worked? Tell me about that/"

"It was a cow nicknamed Shiva. It gored someone."

"Yes," Braff chuckled. "I read about that somewhere."

"Entities seem capable of afflicting animals, but there are limitations; they can only hold a small number at once—usually six or less, and so they don't make suitable hosts. That's what Shiva taught us. We know that a human can host a large number of the parasitic creatures—potentially a limitless number... in theory, anyway."

"So living animals are out?"

"Right—for capacity reasons, anyway. Dead creatures—including humans—don't work. Cyborg-2's brain and heart operated perfectly—even though it was brain-dead. We rigged a circulatory system up to a breathing apparatus in a second trial hoping that the blood flow would allow the bonding process that is affliction. That didn't help any. Apparently hosts must be alive for the entities to implant."

They rounded a corner. "Why did you stop pursuing your avenue of research?" Braff asked.

"Ethics." Swag was quick to respond. "It would be a very serious violation to knowingly afflict a person."

"Hmmm..." Braff pondered the statement. "If a condition was temporary and could be immediately reversed at any time, that doesn't sound like a *gross* violation of ethics to me—especially if it were in the service of some great good."

"Well, if you spin it like that," Swag acquiesced, "it doesn't sound like so terrible of a thing. But I'm quite certain that's a legal definition and not a moral one."

Braff put a hand on a heavily reinforced door. "Neither of us are lawyers, philosophers, *or* theologians. I'm a soldier. You're a scientist. Let's leave it to those other people to make decisions on morality. What we are called to do is deal with a threat to our species and learn how to better combat that threat."

Swag swallowed the hard lump in his throat at Braff's forewarning and guessed at what he was about to see. Braff scanned his badge and led the scientist into a viewing gallery, so they observe the experiment happening below.

Standing in the converted surgery theater they watched the writhing, pulsing man who lay strapped to a reinforced gurney. Swag checked his own emotions. He knew he should feel remorse for the man whose spittle bubbled and leaked from behind the Hannibal Lector-style bite mask, but he didn't feel a thing. Perhaps it was the prison uniform he wore, but more likely it was because he wanted the data.

The scientists below pushed past moral and ethical boundaries in their quest for knowledge and something about that inspired Swag. As much as he could empathize with the struggling criminal below, he simply chose not to. After all, that ethical restraint against immoral science was all based upon a set of values and conscience aligned to a god that Swag had rejected for years.

Swag pressed his fingers against the glass and watched as the faceless team of researchers, hidden by their goggled hazmat suits, poured vial after vial of goo upon an open wound on their captive's forearm. He recognized the containers as the ECP storage cells from the newer style Baconators.

"They are afflicting him... purposefully?"

Braff nodded and pointed to the flat panel display where they tracked the number of creatures that attached themselves to the pour soul. Thirty-seven so far. The man shook and contorted as they poured another onto him. Thirty-eight of the ethereal beasts afflicted him; he bellowed with animalistic rage.

Something sinister turned Swag's gut as he watched. Conscious rejection of his morality soured in his core and the faint whispering in his mind pounded in cadence like battle drums. Swag felt suddenly uncomfortable as he watched the doctor empty another ECP onto the victim. Thirty-nine.

The prisoner screamed and snapped a restraint; his freed arm flailed wildly, beating back his tormentors. He burst free and struck a researcher. His savage roundhouse knocked the man clear across the room where he crumped into a limp pile.

Swag suddenly noticed that guards lined the walls. They rushed forward like a baseball team clamoring for a scrum. In small groups, the afflicted one easily overpowered the men who tried to tackle and restrain him even as they used their GBs to siphon the entities out of him, slowly but surely.

The man wriggled free of the men holding him down and leapt over the body-littered floor. Standing upon the dismantled gurney he ripped off the mask and glared hatefully at the men in the gallery before spitting a thick, bile-laced loogie up to the protective glass.

Swag's stomach sank when he recognized the man whose eyes had suddenly turned both lucid with recognition and glassy with fatigue. His face had been all over the news in recent years as he failed appeal after appeal and his time on death row dwindled. A line of fresh guards stormed the room and took down Joshua Brady as he slowly became too powerless to resist them.

General Braff presided over the whole incident with poise and confidence. He clicked a button on the communicator as he tapped the glass and pointed to the sticky spittle only separate from his finger tip by two millimeters. "Be sure to clean this up, too. I'd hate to miss one."

A masked corporal in the room below nodded and saluted before setting to work on the clean-up operations.

"I'd better get down there and debrief the men," Braff said. "And I should probably make sure the science team is okay. I'll be back shortly. In the meanwhile, Doctor Swaggart, welcome to Project Pandora."

Raymond sat on the raggedy, battered couch wearing only his underwear and absentmindedly dipped his spoon into the bowl of cereal. He'd been instructed to stay home today; Swag was out and the powers-that-be apparently didn't trust him enough to run the lab without supervision—even though Raymond was half of the original discovery team from their college days.

Glancing at his mobile phone he scanned the cereal box out of boredom. Jessica was busy with some other errand and wasn't able to respond. Raymond sighed with futility.

He glanced at the crusty couch: a relic from his first dorm that he refused to part with. At least something in his life remained loyal. Raymond grimaced at his Lucky Charms and glared at the happy leprechaun on the box; he knew that Swag wasn't visiting family—that was a lie. He suspected something bigger was going on and nobody had the courage to level with him.

Swag's obfuscation and Raymond's sudden excusal from the lab were punishments for his behavior weeks ago in the slums. If his closest friend lied to meet with EC brass and defend Raymond, that was one thing, but he didn't figure Swag had gone off as his white knight. He'd lost faith that his friend would defend him any longer.

Rumbling on the coffee table, Raymond's cell chirped with an incoming message. He set down the bowl and turned the device over. The number was unfamiliar, and Raymond opened the text string.

This is Cerberus. OH said you would have his info if he disappeared.

Raymond nervously fumbled with his phone. The last thing he wanted to do was anger an anonymous team of hackers who'd proven capable of meddling with stock markets, crashing major websites, and publicly posting CEOs' dirty laundry for the world to see.

He decided the best course of action was to be truthful. *OH never showed up. I have nothing.*

Holding the device in his hands, Raymond paused for a reply. His mind raced with renewed vigor over what might have happened to Oswald Harrison. The adrenaline didn't help put his mind at ease. Raymond waited, but a reply never came.

"You don't have any kids out there that I don't know of, do you?" Braff asked Swag who shook his head no. "I didn't know of any and I never heard you bragging about any romantic conquests." The general suddenly backpedaled as if he'd crossed a line. "I mean, not that I care about which way you lean, or anything. You and Raymond aren't…"

Swag shook his head and chuckled. "I'm not gay. I'm just very committed to my work. When I was in college I decided that I didn't want any distractions like romance or family until I was settled and had made my mark."

Braff squinted in awe. "Good Lord, man. How do you survive?" He laughed. "Don't answer that. I've seen the inside of a barracks on laundry day—I understand."

They shared an awkward laugh and then Braff continued. "It's no secret that I have a son. When you have children, your world-view changes. You want to plan for every eventuality and make their world as safe as possible. Just look at the millions of dollars spent every year on items meant to baby-proof houses. I remember spending money I barely had to lock drawers I never used and jam little plastic plugs in all of our outlets."

He paused for a moment and thought of his family. "I'm bringing you in on the Pandora project, but also on a secondary program called the Ark Contingency—just another failsafe to keep our kids safe. I've got someone I trust like a brother on that one already but it's a *big* project and Hank could always use an outside viewpoint. Pandora, our unlimited entity storage container, is where we plan to lock away all the evils of the world. That one is our primary focus."

Swag smirked and referenced the Greek myth. "You're going to put them all *back inside the box.*"

"And if that all fails, it's worth having a backup plan: a failsafe and last resort. Just up the mountain a little ways is an old nuclear fall-out shelter. It's why Cuthbert picked this location. Calling it a fall-out shelter is an understatement; it's more realistically an underground military base. We've been retrofitting it to meet the needs of the world's changing dangers. Nuclear threats are of less concern nowadays; this generation's cold war is against these… things.

"I *do* have kids, and there's nothing I wouldn't do to make their world safer and better. I'd hook up and torture a thousand Joshua Bradys if I had to in order to protect his world."

Swag replied with a slow, resolute nod. "When can I see this ark?"

Braff picked up a phone and punched in an extension. "I'll make some arrangements."

Someone knocked at the door and Braff checked his wristwatch. "That would-be Doctor Jonas. He's always exactly on time." The general hollered, "Come on in."

A thin man entered. Slightly shorter than average, he looked exactly like every science teacher Swag had ever seen on a television sitcom.

Jonas stuck out his hand to make introductions. "I've read all of your work," he stated matter-of-factly.

Swag nodded measuredly. "You lead the *other* EC science team?"

Jonas nodded curtly. He did not break formality. "I'm part of a military assignment including a few others: Doctors Jindal, Hansen, and Frey."

It was clear to Swag that the other team's men were soldiers first and scientists second. The thought didn't unnerve him, but Raymond would've blown his top had he known.

Scofield pulled up to the front gate in a UTV and beckoned for Swag to get in. "Let's go see the great and powerful Oz."

With Braff on his way to debrief the science team prior to their introduction to Swag they'd figured that might make the perfect opportunity to see secret base.

The chuff-putt sound of the UTV informed the scientist of how much more powerful it's engine was when compared with a golf cart. Scofield grinned and spun the knobby tires in the gravel.

Swag rode shotgun as the vehicle clawed its way up a steep slope. Before long they arrived at a metallic door held aloft by hydraulic arms. The interior bustled with movement; large crates moved back and forth as lifters ferried supplies to the deeper reaches of the facility.

As they got closer to the main hangar, Swag realized that most of the movement was automated. Animatrons did most of the work.

One of the machines was shut down and an Asian man in a mechanic's apron stood up to greet them, setting down the tools and data input device that he'd been holding in his lap. He nodded when he recognized Scofield.

The sergeant skidded to a stop in the loose dirt outside of the gate and shut the engine down. "You busy, Hank?"

"Always!" he called back across the distance. "I've got another buggy droid. I swear it's the tenth time I've reprogrammed this glitchy Disney-Land reject." He closed the gap between them and stuck a hand out to greet Swag. "I'm Hank Chu, lead engineer, programmer, and genius supreme," he joked.

"That's mostly true," Scofield corroborated.

"Swaggart. Doctor Swaggart—my friends call me Swag," he shook the engineer's hand.

"Do you have some time to show him around the Ark?" Scofield asked. "Doctor Swaggart is the scientist who—"

"I know who he is," Hank said. "I've read all his stuff. And I'm surprised it took so long for that knuckleheaded jack-wagon to bring him in on this. Of course I'll make some time to give him the tour."

Swag glanced hesitantly back and forth between Scofield and Chu, as if they'd baited him into some kind of trap.

Hank waived off the tension. "I wouldn't recommend calling him that to his face. The guy has got his own firing squad, you know."

Swag noticed the deep laugh lines in the man's face.

The entire party paused and looked as the glitchy droid started moving and then suddenly ceased, like it suffered from some kind of robotic conniption. They tensed, waiting for a second seizure, but it remained still.

Swag got out and Sergeant Scofield went back down the mountain trail to attend to other business. Hank gave him a brief tour of the oversized loading bay. He pointed out a large, engraved metal plate that labeled it as Ark I.

"There are a number of Ark facilities being installed worldwide. Cuthbert and his rich buddies each pledged to have a number of them operational worldwide by the end of next year. With the flick of a switch the entire system should come online." He snapped his fingers for emphasis.

Meandering through the bay, Swag asked, "How many are operational now?"

"Ark I is the flagship. It all starts here, but the others will piggyback off of our network and their systems will be automatically updated by ours. I only have to program this stuff once that way, thankfully."

The tripod-like loader, identifiable by the painted number seventeen, twitched again.

"There are twelve facilities, each capable of comfortably housing ten thousand—twenty if we ration supplies and double up on the bunks. Some researcher said it takes at least one hundred and fifty people of breeding age in order to continue the species after a post-extinction-level event and something like eight to ten thousand in order to preserve the planet's genetic diversity," he lectured as he walked towards the malfunctioning robot. "I guess Cuthbert is no slouch when it comes to contingencies."

Suddenly, number seventeen lunged forward and snatched Hank into a bear hug. It clamped down and began constricted around the thrashing programmer, crushing him slowly and efficiently. Hank howled in pain; Swag ran up to the machine, trying to decide how he could help.

"Grab the interface!" Hank yelled. "The tablet thing on the ground!"

Swag snatched up the heavy-duty touchscreen. It lit up when he made eye contact with it. "This thing? Its code locked!" He stared at the numeric passcode screen.

"Twenty-seven. Sixteen. Fifteen," he gasped as the thing compressed dangerously around his ribcage.

"Got it!" Swag yelped when the screen cleared to the diagnostics display. He mashed the big yellow button labeled

Initiate total shut down. Seventeen's arms went limp, freeing Hank who collapsed on the floor, gulping for air.

After a moment of coughing and wheezing, Hank crawled to his feet and dusted himself off. After kicking the base of the offending machine with enough force to make his point, but not enough to break his foot, Chu waved Swag forward and they pressed deeper into the complex.

"Come on," he said. "I'll show you to the whole place." Moments later they arrived at a door with a button-style access. Hank tapped in the same code and winked at Swag who raised his eyebrows in realization of that fact.

"It's supposed to be ironic," Hank quipped. "From the twenty-seventh book of the New Testament."

"Revelation sixteen, fifteen. 'Behold, I come as a thief. Blessed is he that watcheth, and keepeth his garments, lest he walk naked, and they see his shame.' Just a little verse about being prepared," Swag responded to the surprised engineer. "My parents were Nazis about religion and were serious end-times enthusiasts. If Tim LaHaye wrote it, it was on their shelf… hardcover *and* paperback."

Hank nodded as he entered the expansive motor-pool. "Mine too," he said as he slid into a seat. Swag slipped in beside him and the electric cart zipped up to a door large enough to let them through.

"Let's go left. I know a storage room where there's a stock of some fifty-year, single-malt Glenfiddich squirreled away. They probably won't notice if *another* bottle goes missing."

#

"Are the inhibitors operational, then?" Tom Holland wore a cautiously optimistic face which Donna Loebel mirrored on the other side of the table. "I know my team was optimistic, but quite honestly I hadn't had the time to read the update prior to this meeting." The presidential science czar had a lot on his plate, and the report was so recent that the omission was understandable.

General Braff nodded, as did Franklin Cuthbert, their chairman. "I oversaw the tests this morning before continuing the work with Brady," Braff assured them. "Our seven special entities can no longer occupy a previously afflicted person—at least not other ones marked by the Hermes protocols. They won't be able to collectively piggyback onto a high-powered host as a way to marshal strength and then resist the capture teams, as they've done before. We've also gained the capability of tracking them anywhere on the planet via Doctor Jindal's work with Hermes; we can even locate our altered units up to two hundred meters below the surface. Within the proper framework, these seven can be bent to our will—within reason—and then later be collected for reuse. We effectively *own* these weapons; they are a part of our arsenal."

The five other members of the board nodded approval.

Henry Winger redirected the conversation back. The sociologist pushed his round glasses towards his face as he scanned his notes. "Have we finally leveraged Doctor Swaggart into our team at ECHQ?"

"Almost," Braff responded. "He's on board and ready to begin doing further research for Pandora, but I wouldn't say he's *fully invested* yet. I haven't divulged any of the EC's Homeland Security components to him. But I'm getting there. I just have to massage a few more wrinkles."

"Wrinkles… like Raymond Lems?"

Braff nodded pointedly. "I'm handling him personally. But until that issue is resolved, we are treating Swaggart like a potential security leak and keeping close tabs on him."

Holland nodded enthusiastically. "Oh good. I've been saying for a while now how a pioneering mind such as Swaggart's is exactly the sort of spark that could catalyze our advanced research team. Just look at what he did over at the

EC's B-site. I assume we will keep that location running too? Perhaps Lems or Hiddleston will head that site up?"

"So the timeline for Pandora?" Guitterez reminded them to stay on task. The lawyer was always a stickler for details.

"Right on schedule." Braff promised. "Even if we experience a few hiccups, I'm pretty sure the golden boy will be able to help us power through them, especially now that he's working on site. A few more months up here and I believe Swag may be ready to help with DHS concerns, even. I've already got a plan for implementation."

The six heads turned when a rap interrupted them.

"Oh good." Braff spotted Scofield waiting patiently in the doorway. He waved him in and handed him a sealed envelope with his mission orders. "You will need to pick up our seven friends. I have a mission for them. Assemble Omega squad and put an ECT on alert. Make sure to borrow some spare Baconators."

A curious unrest curled its tendrils around Raymond's guts and squeezed angrily. The scientist tossed back an early morning Zantac and checked his phone again as he ended his work commute. His mobile's screen remained blank.

The fact that Cerberus had not sent a final message disturbed Raymond. He didn't really want to help and might have previously balked at the request… but *not* being asked also bothered him and he felt like he'd been picked last in gym class. Raymond still knew many things and he had access to all kinds of information.

His pride had been wounded, but more than his wounded pride, the fact that he hadn't received any messages from his best friend in days also hurt him, though he felt more anger than pain over it.

Raymond scowled as he looked around the office. It felt emptier every day for months, now. Not even their peppy coworker, Jessica Hiddleston, was around. According to the entry logs Swag hadn't been on site for days and he hadn't given any updates as to his situation. Raymond furrowed his brow and pushed his emotions through the thunderhead that brewed in his heart.

"Probably having cigars and whiskey with the General," Raymond muttered as he sorted a few forms.

Strolling through their lab, Raymond's footsteps echoed in the empty rooms. He stepped into the room where he'd last chatted with this partner. They'd parted after an argument and the room remained exactly as it had been when he'd left.

He looked at the marker board and the unfamiliar handwriting of the genius "Rosetta stone" equation. Raymond stared at it for another moment, computed it in his mind. The thing was not so revolutionary; looking at it now Raymond realized that it was so perfectly obvious that they'd merely overlooked it up until now—and chiefly for its simplicity.

Raymond knew in his gut that Braff must have a backup science team—probably several of them—working on similar, possibly far more nefarious, projects. Full of resentment, he spun on his heel, ready to find something to work on to distract him when he noticed that something *had* changed in the last few days. Some of the capture cells from the new Baconators had been disconnected from the display racks that lined the wall; a number of older ECPs had gone missing, too.

His guts stirred with a volatile mix of terror, curiosity, betrayal, and concern. Something was definitely amiss, and Raymond had not been kept in the loop!

Raymond scowled; he stormed from the room and thumbed his mobile phone. He disabled all of his traceable signals and then activated the illegal app and ran the dark-web software he'd spent the last few days learning about.

With his signal masked and encrypted he felt confident enough in his anonymity on the network to reach out to his enemy's enemy. He wrote the quick text reply to Cerberus and pressed send.

Oswald Harrison died before he could give me his data. But I think I can still help.

16

"Where the heck *is* everyone?" Jessica commented, trying to distract both Raymond and herself from the unsavory task ahead of them.

Raymond shook his head and shrugged to acknowledge her observation. Most of the staff had been stringent lately. "Most of the brass seems to be away for something. Just some scary aides and the secretary from Hell upstairs in the admin offices doing God knows what." He swallowed the lump in his throat when a bespectacled, middle-aged woman knocked and entered with a clipboard.

"Thank you, Ramona." Raymond took the clipboard and nodded at her departure.

Jessica's eyes asked the question. Raymond didn't answer it.

"Where has Swag been? I know we haven't had many tasks around here lately except for busywork—but still. I know he's been into his office a few times, but it's unlike him to miss work—heck, it's not like him to go *home*."

Raymond glanced guiltily at her, but remained silent.

"Oh. I'm sorry. You guys had some kind of break-up or something?"

"We're not gay, Jessica."

"I know—I know. But you always seemed waaaaay closer than any other guy friends that I've known."

Raymond nodded. "I can accept that." He looked around the room and noted the seven absent BCnTR cells; Raymond and Jessica had already guessed Swag might be working on some kind of independent side-project away from the lab and didn't want anyone to know. "At this point, you might just call it a legal separation."

Jessica nodded and flipped through the pages. She grimaced at the ugly work order. "So what do you think of Ramona?"

"I'm just glad the brass sent out for a temp. I don't think I could carry on a conversation with any of those people in the lobby and still be asked to do what we have to in the lab." Raymond grimaced and wiped the soul-weary lines from his face. They'd been at it for two days now, and it hurt his spirit to continue—but at least Jessica's effervescent personality had mostly weathered the storm.

"I'll go get prepped. You can bring back our next test subject."

Jessica nodded and departed for the lobby while Raymond went to the lab. They'd set it up to resemble a clinic room as much as possible since they were working with live humans. He set up the cameras and sensors to record and double-checked their equipment.

Intentionally afflicting humans with captured entities did not set well with Raymond at all. He saw the logic behind it from a scientific point of view; gathering whatever kind of data they could was necessary—but it was not a pleasant task. It certainly wasn't ethical, especially since they'd lured in this test panel for a "drug and treatment trial" which suggested they might experience vomiting and temporary discomfort yet be compensated accordingly. The dregs had turned up… they seemed more than happy to trade their bodies for coin.

Maybe these people are getting what they deserve, then? Raymond quickly changed his mind when Jessica entered the room with a nine-year-old Latino boy. Even Jessica's face had blanched ashen.

The boy crawled into the exam chair and laid his arms where the restraints would attach. "Strap me in, doc. Mom needs to get some groceries and so I gotta get paid."

"I'm almost there," Braff barked into the handheld radio. He slammed on the brakes and his UTV skidded to a halt outside of the main hangar doors to Ark I.

Swag tossed his walkie to Henry and ran out to meet the general. He slid into the passenger seat. "What's the big emergency?"

Braff stepped on the gas and rocked the scientist back into his seat. "I think it might be best if you saw it with your own eyes. It won't take long."

"Where's Scofield?" Swag expected his usual handler would have chauffeured him rather than the top officer.

"Probably the Bahamas. I didn't ask. He took a few vacation days."

Within minutes, the all-terrain vehicle zipped up to the ECHQ building. He tapped his earpiece to indicate that he was in communication with someone else too and Swag nodded an acknowledgement.

After a short trek, the general led his scientist into a conference room where a number of video screens displayed real-time feeds. It had been set up like a war room. Aides milled about accompanied by Henry Winger, the sociologist from the EC board.

"I apologize for the delay, but I think it's important for Doctor Swaggart to watch the proceedings," General Braff informed the room. "Here's the situation: we have a domestic terrorism alert at the Woodhaven Mall out by the metro suburbs. DHS flagged him for making potentially terroristic threats—something about blowing up the shopping center. One of our contacts did a preliminary reading on him with the EMF readers and determined he reads positive for affliction."

Swag stroked his chin thoughtfully as he glanced from screen to screen on the hastily cobbled together monitor bank. A shaky video cam stream showed an agent rushing towards the exterior of the mall. He asked, "Why aren't you on-site in the mobile BOA?"

"You don't get down to the mall much, do you?" Braff retorted. "That mall's not even in our state."

Swag shrugged sheepishly. "I do most of my shopping online," he muttered quietly and stared at the screen showing a thirty second loop of captured data from an EMF reader. They did reveal readings consistent with affliction.

"That place is packed," Winger stated with awe. He noted a large sign on the jostled feed. "There must be some kind of big holiday celebration going on for Independence Day?"

Swag surreptitiously glanced at his mobile device and checked the date. July fourth. He'd been so preoccupied the last couple of days that he'd totally overlooked the holiday.

Braff grunted. "Leave it to those rag-headed terrorists to target huge population centers during a patriotic celebration."

A generic murmur of assent rumbled through the assembly. Swag raised an eyebrow but kept silent. It didn't follow consistent logic that this was a terrorist act if carried out by an afflicted person who was motivated by an entity.

The General tapped a button on his tablet and one of the screens switched to show a collection of biographical data and photos from the suspect. Khalid al-Kassab had loose ties to several fringe groups in radical Islam. Although his background had no arrests or major red flags, he did attend a stateside college that had been known to produce a few domestic terrorists, including the "Sinister Six," one of which was a blood relation to al-Kassab.

Bursts of static surged from the speaker array. A covert squad of agents reported their positions and actions as they tried to lay eyes on the target and corner him.

"Command, this is Omega Three. I've got eyes on target," a voice stated breathlessly. "Permission to engage?"

The room at ECHQ fell deathly silent. Everyone watched Braff. Braff watched the swelling crowd. In grainy black and white nobody could pick al-Kassab out of the crowd. Swag stared at the video, his eardrums pounded with the whisper-like cadence of those voices at the frayed edges of his consciousness.

Repeating the request, the agent clearly interpreted the silence from command as a communications error. "Permission to take the kill shot?"

Braff sighed. "Negative, Omega Three. Not in this crowd, there is too great a risk."

"Command, this is Omega Three," the voice argued. "Are you sure of that order, sir? Target was seen wearing a bomb-vest. A suicide bomber could do more damage than any stray shot."

The general sighed tersely. It was hard to argue with the logic. "Can you verify the bomb-vest? Do you have eyes on the explosives?"

A new voice broke the line. "Command, this is Omega One. I can verify. Recent receipts on intel suggest it's a ball-bearing loaded vest—lots of projectiles—very high casualty rate in dense crowds."

"Like the kind gathered at the mall," Braff muttered under his breath. "Engage, Omega Three—as long as it's a clean shot."

"Acknowledged."

The screens shook as the other members of the team tried to find closer positions. A shot rang out and a single figure in the crowd collapsed, spewing red mist from the kill-shot. The mass of people exploded in a panic like a cave full of surprised bats.

"Target is down," Omega Three reported.

People bumped and pushed to get away from the violence. After a few seconds, one of the members of Alpha Team got to the body which lay face down near the food court in a pool of blood.

The video showed him clearly. Khalid al-Kassab's skull had fragmented near the rear where an exit wound from a hollow point .308 had burst his skull. Panning the camera down, ECHQ could see the bomb vest, rigged to blow with a depression switch.

Swag had so many questions, but he wasn't certain it was the right time to vocalize them given the state of the room. It had turned into a flurry of activity as people made phone calls to coordinate media spin, order cleanup crews, etc. He heard Braff bark orders and saw people jumping to act.

Why didn't this entity follow the typical patterns? Why didn't it jump out of the body in the blood spray, and why did it use a bomb vest? They hadn't seen any previous activity like this before.

"Can you imagine if that bomb would have gone off in that crowd?" Henry Winger asked.

Braff leveled his eyes on Swag. "Can you imagine if one of these things gets access to someone with nuclear codes, or any kind of biological agent?"

"If this is some kind of new plan, it shows deviation from the entities' nature. This demonstrates a kind of sentient thought," Winger postulated. "If there have been other, similar kinds of attacks, it could establish a pattern. Maybe this is more than just a random, isolated incident."

The screens showed a man snap a photo of the body. Shortly after, Omega One harvested the entity with a Baconator. He detached the containment unit and put a label on it, scrawling *Mephistopheles* on the sticker. Flickering slightly, they switched to a series of stills as directed by Braff. Many images cycled over and over showing that this was no isolated incident.

Winger nodded solemnly. "They're not all violent monsters acting on mere impulse stimuli. Some are methodical and possess an insanely dangerous intelligence. It's not a matter of '*if* they go after a high-profile target,' it's only a matter of '*when*.'"

"Doctor Swaggart?" Jonas, one of Braff's scientists, yanked him from his introspection. Swag had fallen to staring into space as he pondered his questions about the mall shooting.

"Is this something more like you'd envisioned?" Jonas pointed to his corrections on the whiteboard nearby. Large letters labeled the project as a subsystem of Pandora.

Swag nodded, even though he didn't really look at the algorithm. "That's better."

The tests that they'd run on Joshua Brady also weighed heavily on his mind, but as he pitted that moral quandary against the potential mass violence done to innocents, like at the mall, his internal debate became more visceral and less philosophical. Brady's pain could help avert the suffering of thousands, maybe millions, and perhaps this was part of the debt he owed to society. From a logical point of view, "the good of the many outweighed the good of the few or one"; Swag always did love Spock, even if he found the pre-2000s era of Star Trek to be too ordered and sanitary to be believable.

He bit his lip in deep thought again. Swag didn't like the idea of human tests, but there was so much data he still wanted, and those sorts of trials were the only way forward from here. He felt like he was shooting in the dark, trying to figure out why the entity afflicting al-Kassab deviated so much from the patterned behavior. *Unless it's less of an entity issue and merely a human one—something different about al-Kassab, or the circumstances behind his affliction? Maybe it was an intentional infection in order to incite violence... and draw a kill order?*

Sighing, Swag shook off the far-fetched idea. That was the kind of speculation Raymond had been so prone to. *Entities becoming political martyrs was just a bridge too far.*

"Something on your mind, Swaggart?" Jindal asked the far-and-away doctor.

Swag shrugged. "So much... I saw some uncharacteristic activity today—both by people... and more troubling, from an entity, or the afflicted."

Jindal whistled sharply and called out to the rest of the research team, "Think tank, guys!"

Skeptically, Swag cocked his head. He was still very new to the advanced research team.

"It's what we do when we need to combine our mental energies and crowd source a problem." He ushered them into a glass-walled conference room brimming with tattered couches and a vending machine. Jindal bade Swag to sit so they could brainstorm through it. "Just think out loud, and we'll join you."

A few minutes into Swag's monologue about what made him uncomfortable, he suddenly felt very self-conscious. None of the team joined in the discussion. Most of them refused to meet his gaze as he spoke, as if they wouldn't, or couldn't, comment.

Behind them, an officer in battle dress walked through the research lab to the area where they kept a bank of BCnTR cells powered. He set down his duffel bag and attached the charging leads to the cells.

Swag did a double take before trailing off. He recognized him as Omega One from the earlier mission—he must've headed here straight from the mission. "What's he doing?"

"Keeping an entity in confinement," Hansen stated, almost condescendingly.

"Yeah. That's obvious," Swag fired back. "I saw him earlier. But he labeled the ECP... marked it for some purpose. Why?"

The science team only returned blank faces. Frey stood and went to help Omega One who signaled that he needed some assistance. Swag's gut soured with sudden resentment. *Maybe Raymond's not so crazy after all.*

"Really? None of you can tell me anything about what happened with Omega Team? So much for a *think tank*."

"We're military," Jonas reminded him. "Our clearance works differently than civilians'. There are some things that we can't really level with you on—we've gotta stick to the science side."

"If you guys are using these *things* in military operations—we're going to have *big problems*!" Swag turned grumpily and spotted the consternation on Frey's face. She hurriedly waived them over.

For a few moments, Swag hung back, protesting their censure of him with physical distance. When he noticed their terrified faces he discarded the juvenile silent treatment and approached. Clearance or not, they didn't keep the news from him.

Omega One fixed his gaze on Swag as if he hoped he might be some kind of messiah capable of saving them from the grievous error. "We've got a problem." He turned slightly so that Swag could see the seven labeled ECPs. "I don't know how it went wrong. Goodthunder was onsite to supervise the retrieval."

Jonas stated his disagreement with breaking their oath to confidentiality. "Doctor Swaggart isn't cleared for this information." But he did nothing to physically prevent the news-giver.

One of the seven labeled containment cells' LEDs glowed with a different color than the rest. It was empty. "We've lost an entity!"

Swag turned the cylinder and stared at the white file label where someone had scrawled a name in ink: *Little Satan*.

"Little Satan is gone."

Raymond walked into the little lounge in the back of his office building; Ramona had long since departed. He spotted Jessica slouched over the tiny table. A half-emptied bottle of vodka pretended to be a centerpiece.

Bleary-eyed, Jessica struggled to reach an upright and sitting position as Raymond took the seat across from her. "I don't know how much more of this I can take," she admitted.

The scientist nodded. He sympathized with her frustration. Raymond poured himself a few ounces of vodka into a generic foam cup.

"Ya know, I thought you guys were a couple of hot-shot scientists back in college." Jessica wiped a little drool from the edge of her mouth. She laughed through her slurred speech. "Back then I was prepared to sleep with you if that's what it took to get the job as your assistant." She looked around apprehensively. "But I'm not so sure I want any of this anymore." She rubbed the corner of her eye to make sure there were no tears. "I don't think anyone here even knows I have a doctorate too—as if I was gonna stay a research assistant forever." She hung her head disappointedly. "Th'only reason it took so long to get it was cuz I was waiting on one of you two idiots t'finally make a move."

Jessica stumbled to her feet, and then shrugged under the load of her weariness. She kicked her high heels off and collected them as she turned to leave.

Raymond grabbed her hand and held her fast. *Screw the agreement!*

"Maybe I can ask you out to dinner sometime... when you're not drunk?"

She touched his face affectionately. "Oh, Raymond. Maybe if you'd asked before... all *this*." She shook her head and looked away. "I'm sorry."

Raymond could only nod matter-of-factly. His heart still felt too hardened by the human test-trials for him to feel any emotion. "You're leaving. Are you coming back?" he probed.

Jessica paused at the doorway. Finally, she shrugged. "I don't know."

"Let me call you a cab?"

Jessica waved his offer away and started walking.

Raymond bit his lip so hard he nearly drew blood. He fidgeted with his phone, willing it to ring. Finally, he felt the last little spark inside of him die and he dialed Swag's number.

"Hello?" Swag answered, obviously distracted. "Raymond? Oh, thank God. I think I might need some help from you—from someone I can trust." His voice dropped dramatically in volume as he talked to someone else while covering the microphone. "Get off of me. No. I'm leaving, and I don't care what you say! That's ridiculous. There's no way I could be a carrier—look! You can do the test for all I care!"

Raymond knocked back another huge slug of vodka and then paced through the rooms as he spoke to his former best friend. "That's funny, Swag—'someone I can trust?' At least some of us *can be trusted*," he vented.

"What do you mean? You sound angry with me."

"You think I sound angry?" Raymond muttered a string of expletives. "I don't even know you, right now. Do you know the EC is intentionally putting entities into people in order to further their research?"

"How do you know about that? Did Braff increase your clearance?"

"See what I mean!" Raymond fumed. "You *did* know—and they've pulled you deeper into their web. This is unethical, Swag... *on every level!*"

"We can work through this, Raymond. We always do. I've got a huge problem, right now, though, with an escaped entity. Can you come to the other EC lab? I really need someone I can rely on helping me."

"*Another lab?* Are you kidding me? I suppose you lost one of your special seven entities?"

Silence came from Swag's end. "If Braff didn't bring you in on it, then how do you know about the seven?"

Raymond glared at the empty shelf space where seven ECP cells had gone missing. "You're a smart guy. Figure it out."

"Okay. I don't even care about that—but I need you. Please. There's an old facility up the mountain pass on highway four-eighteen. Things are going to get intense."

Raymond severed the line and returned to the lounge. He poured himself a cup of liquor and tossed it back angrily. Wincing and about to pour another, he tossed the foam aside and drank straight from the bottle. He tipped it back and cocked his head when he heard agitated voices coming from the administrative wing of the building. Some of the brass had finally graced them again with their presence.

Setting his bottle down, he turned his ear. He couldn't hear anything specifically, but he recognized Braff's voice, and something inside of Raymond snapped.

#

Swag stared at his phone. Raymond had hung up on him after Swag accidentally spilled a bunch of confidential information—sure his friend could help provide insight, or at least be sworn to secrecy. He still didn't know how Raymond knew that the EC had been testing entity infection on Joshua

Brady. Swag hoped Braff had made good on patching things up with Raymond. Were that not the case, it meant that he'd either caused a security breach or maybe worse if Raymond were in a vindictive mood.

He couldn't think about that right now, though. Swag had to do damage control *here*—and he had to figure something out fast.

"I don't know how you could have lost an entity. These things are practically fail-proof." Swag slid his phone into his pocket. "Besides, I saw you harvest these things at the mall..." He trailed off, searching for Omega One's name.

"Tower," the soldier stated his name. "They weren't all from the mall—there were multiple ops. This one was afflicting some towel-headed computer hacker over at the university. Alim Saleeb: smart kid, they said, but probably working with domestic terrorists."

Swag rolled his eyes. "Of course there were multiple operations." Swag grabbed a GB and pointed it at Tower; the device wouldn't harm humans. "All you have to do is point and click. How hard is that—I mean, I understand that you could be new to the device, but it harvests automatically. Think real hard, is there any chance the entity escaped into someone else, maybe into another bystander? You know that they travel through body fluids or darkness, right?"

"Not these kind," Tower retorted. "Sergeant Scofield told us there are seven that have been—"

"That's enough!" Jonas shouted him down. "Doctor Swaggart *does not have clearance!*"

Swag looked from Tower to Jindal, incredulous. Even Jindal's dark skin had turned ashen. The mortified scientist nodded.

"It's true. There were some modifications by our team. Little Satan, and his six companions, have been locked so that they cannot exit a body without intervention. It has allowed the Eidolon Commission to..."

Jonas yanked Tower's sidearm from the soldier's holster and pointed it at Jindal's head. "Not one more word or I swear to all the gods and cows your ancestors ever worshipped that I will put a bullet through your head."

Jindal raised his hands in surrender. Jonas glared daggers at Swag who also raised his hands under the scrutinizing gaze.

"If the General wants Doctor Swaggart brought up to speed, he will do so directly or will grant him an additional confidentiality variance. The world could be falling apart—but protocol and discipline still sets us apart from the civilians."

Swag could agree with him on principle but now wasn't the time for posturing. "I don't have time for this." He started to leave when Jonas racked the pistol, ejecting the top round, and ensuring that the gun was deadly and ready for any flinch of the hair-trigger.

"You're not going anywhere until each of us have submitted to a full scan to ensure none of us have been hijacked by Little Satan."

"Fine. Scan me—but then *I'm going to find Braff!*"

"You're not going anywhere," Jonas retorted. He used the muzzle to point at the think-tank room, indicating Swag could wait there. "Not until Braff has come and debriefed you. Right now all I see is a walking security breach. Tower? Take Doctor Swaggart's mobile," he ordered.

Nobody jumped to action. "Any of you can join him in detainment if you like."

The soldier and the science team reluctantly followed Jonas's orders.

#

Raymond shouted a string of profanity at the gray-templed general who remained calmly seated, ignoring the flecks of spittle that flew from the outraged scientist. He dutifully nodded along and let his belligerent comrade burn himself out.

"And you can wipe that stupid, smug grin off your face," Raymond pressed.

"I'm not trying to be smug, Raymond. I promised our mutual friend that I'd try and see you in a different light and be as polite as possible. I really do think you are a necessary and vital part of our team."

"Yeah right! A team that doesn't even know the details—like how there's a whole 'nother lab!"

Braff raised an eyebrow.

"And you've got us over here in the slums infecting children and junkies with demons. *Infecting children*, man!"

"Yes," he stated mater-of-factly. "I read some of your preliminary findings. That's how important your data is. I went through it as soon as you uploaded it to the EC server. It's why I came over here so soon."

"Children! You had us put an entity in a child," Raymond spat.

"Yes. And it didn't, or couldn't, afflict the very young ones. That's crucial data!"

Raymond's eyes narrowed to slits. "So what if it didn't take to the kiddies? That's not the point—the point is what you were *willing* to do to them in the name of science!"

"And there were three others whom the entities seemed unable to afflict as well. We've got to find their common denominator, so we can better understand the process and what prevents attachment and affliction." The general fixed him with a very sincere look. "Our work here has just begun. I'd like you to seriously consider heading up this entire testing process—your data is vital! We'd expand the facility, of course, and give you anything you need. A larger staff? A pay raise? What do you want?"

Raymond flung his hands up in the air. "Oh I don't know. Maybe thirty pieces of silver? You want me to keep infecting kids with these things? Why don't you put a down payment on my soul while you're at it?"

General Braff's secretary popped into the room and cut off Raymond's rant. "Sorry to interrupt, General, but you've got an urgent phone call. Omega priority."

Braff's face turned to stone and he nodded to his secretary. "I'm sorry, Raymond, but we'll have to continue this another time. This takes priority."

"Screw you, Roderick; don't bother rescheduling. I quit."

"So be it," the general nodded apologetically.

"I'll send someone by later to conduct an exit interview and express the *absolute* nature of your signed confidentiality agreement. Until then I expect absolute silence from your end."

Raymond fired back with a bunch of choice expletives. He mock-saluted the officer with his middle finger, turned and departed.

"This is Omega One: Corporal Nathaniel Tower, sir. I think you should get back to ECHQ as soon as possible."

Braff asked, "How bad is it, Corporal?"

"Pretty bad, sir. I'm here with the science team. We can't seem to locate Little Satan. We've got a missing entity."

"That sneaky little bugger got out," the general mused. "We've got some contingencies for this, Corporal. I'm on my way." Braff severed the line and barked an order to his secretary. "Call for a car. Now. I've got to get back to headquarters."

His secretary nodded diligently and made the call while her boss dialed another number.

"Scofield?" he confirmed. "I need you to assemble the primary ECT and activate the backups. An entity has somehow escaped a reclamation net. We can't let this get out—put a lid on it ASAP."

"It'll be a problem getting a hold of all of them—at least Goodthunder will be. He skipped debriefing after the Omega missions."

"Was he the man responsible for harvesting Little Satan?" Braff asked.

"Yes," Scofield responded after a momentary pause.

Braff cursed. "If he's gone rogue then Little Satan likely has him. Prep the teams. We'll activate the Hermes protocols as soon as I get back to HQ."

"Isn't that going to…"

"Yeah. I know what Jindal said—it'll probably piss this thing off worse than it's ever been before—but we've got to find it and bring it back in at any cost. In the meanwhile, do whatever you can to locate Goodthunder. I'm sure someone's got to have a lead."

17

Reggie Goodthunder sat motionless in his friend's living room. A wry smile tugged at the corners of his lips—not Goodthunder's grin, but that of the entity controlling him.

"I'm not fooling around," Atreyu said. "And it ain't paranoia from this crappy ditch weed they grow out in this part of the country." He inhaled deep and tossed the half-smoked joint into the empty pizza box resting atop his second-hand coffee table. "I swear, I heard something outside," he choked the words, still holding in the drag.

Goodthunder cocked his head and pretended he was listening. "And I'm telling you that it's nothing. Probably just the wind or a stray cat."

Atreyu shrugged and exhaled a bluish vapor, coughing on the garbage smoke. Waving the air to dispel the cloud he asked, "Tell me why you suddenly showed up outta nowhere, man? It's been forever since I seen you last. I mean, you're welcome to crash here for as long as you need, but I'd like to hear something about your life—I still hang with some of the old crew from the Rez and I'm sure they'd love to hear bout what you been up to since they put you into that hoity-toity military school and you ghosted on us."

"Let me show you a magic trick," Goodthunder said instead.

His friend rocked back on his heels a little bit. "Um. Okay," he acquiesced to the odd and sudden request.

Still in his military garb, Goodthunder tossed his belt and sidearm onto the table before standing and unpocketing two pairs of handcuffs. Goodthunder squatted against the old, cast-iron radiator in his friend's apartment. He handcuffed one wrist to the far side, slid down to his butt so his back rested against the metal, and nodded his head to the other side in a request for assistance.

"What's this? Some kind of escape artist trick?" Atreyu mused as he clicked the second restraint tightly in place.

"Something like that," Goodthunder replied.

Atreyu tilted his head. "There it is again. I'm telling you, I keep hearing something!"

"Ignore that," Goodthunder said quietly, drawing him closer. "I've got to tell you something."

He turned to look at his friend with their faces only a foot apart. The door burst open and a team of government agents poured through the door wielding both guns and entity capture tech.

In full view of the ECT Goodthunder spat in Atreyu's eyes, sending the man reeling and screaming. A split second later, the unrestrained civilian jolted to his feet with a maniacal chortle.

Before the ECT could react, Atreyu leapt over the couch and snatched up Goodthunder's handgun. Goodthunder screamed and pulled at his restraints. The team brought their arms to bear against his friend while he remained helpless to act!

The point-man in riot gear pointed his carbine at Atreyu while another man dropped to a knee and aimed a himt with a Baconator. Atreyu stumbled out of the way and continued cackling. He raised his forty-five and put two rounds into the chest of the team-member wielding the GB. The point-man fired six times and put six holes in Atreyu's torso.

Goodthunder wailed and protested. The shooter lifted his helmet-shield to show himself to the shackled ECT member. Goodthunder calmed slightly to see Agent Scofield's face.

Seeing the recognition on his face, Scofield turned his attention to their fallen teammate who groaned as he rolled him over. Anders groaned as the Sergeant helped him up.

Scofield tapped the man's body armor. "Additional precautions," he stated. "We knew that Little Satan is a devious little bugger—we thought he might try something like that."

"Indeed," Goodthunder replied.

"What happened here?" Scofield asked as Rodriguez entered the room, carrying a handheld EMF scanner and another touch-screen tracking device that the military science team had designed to track their seven modified entities as part of Hermes.

"I don't quite know," Goodthunder said. "We were on that mission and then I was suddenly here," he rubbed his wrists as Scofield unlocked his cuffs and nodded to his teammates. "Let me do it."

Rodriguez retrieved Anders' GB and surrendered it to Goodthunder who demanded it with an open palm. Cursing through his grief, Goodthunder shined the laser field around his friend's corpse until it caught a lock on the entity and pulled it out like a swirling ball of ether. The indicator marked that a capture was complete, and he tossed the containment cell back to Rodriguez

"I remember right before the capture operation to retrieve Little Satan at that campus. A pizza delivery guy jumped me and—then boom—I was afflicted. Must've been another entity. They planned this. I'm telling you, these things are smart! They've learned from us." Goodthunder nodded to Rodriguez. "You guys used that thing to find me?"

Rodriguez nodded and held up the scanner. Hermes was new tech, even to them. "We can track our seven assets anywhere our satellites can see. Accurate to within twenty-five feet—but it sure gives the little critters a nasty sting in order to generate a read on the network."

He handed it to Goodthunder who took a look at it. The released ECT member rubbed his wrists and looked over the equipment which was barely more than a glorified, three-dimensional radar scanner.

Scofield, gripping his carbine tightly asked, "Is Little Satan here? I mean, the afflicted person the demon is driving?"

Goodthunder nodded to his friend's corpse. "Whatever was in me is over there. In… in Atreyu. Or what's left of him." He switched off the Hermes unit.

Scofield raised an eyebrow. "How is that possible? Our Seven can't leave their hosts or multi-afflict."

He shrugged. "I don't know how it managed it. Evil little genius somehow figured out how to bypass the host-lock those metaphysicists rigged up. You guys busted through the door, and all of the sudden my mind was free… Atreyu went nuts… and then he was dead. I think the entity wanted to kill a friend—and wanted me to watch… maybe to make me think it could get to me… that it could hurt those close to me."

Rodriguez checked his screen. "We're definitely in the right place. Target is in this room." He swapped for the EMF reader and pointed it towards the deceased. "Goodthunder's right. We have another reading." He pulled out his own GB and harvested another entity with the capture tech.

Rodriguez checked the corpse with his EMF reader again. It registered as clear.

Anders, finally on his feet, took the first ECP unit from and slapped a label on the containment cell. He scrawled on both cells with a felt pen, *Little Satan,* and put both of them inside his satchel as they returned to ECHQ. They could scan the containers later to determine which of the units held the little bastard.

#

Swag frowned as he walked the brightly lit halls of Ark I with Hank. He needed a few hours to cool off after Jonas held him hostage until Braff arrived. The general had let him go, as expected, and had a private conversation with Jonas— presumably about pulling a gun on Braff's prized civilian asset.

He and Hank had just come from a massive control area for the electrical network; many identical rooms throughout the bunker managed the massive power grids which operated primarily on solar power and geothermal systems. A mechanical drone zipped past them to perform an automated diagnostics check. It easily navigated through the spacious rows of equipment.

"I've got a feeling you didn't come all the way up here to look at my progress, impressive as it may be."

Swag shrugged. "I don't know how you got the light grid up so soon. Man, do you ever go home?"

"I got my orders and a tight timeline," Hank replied without making eye contact. "Braff wants it operational—at least at minimal capacity by the end of the year. It's too big of a project to just walk away from it every night, plus it's easy to lose track of time when there is no darkness. So yeah… I moved in."

"*Braff,*" Swag muttered as if the name were a curse.

"Trouble outside the Ark?"

Shaking his head, "I'd normally talk about this sort of thing with my friend, Raymond…" Swag trailed off.

"The guy you did your research with, Raymond Lems?" Hank asked.

"Yeah. He and Braff have a long-standing feud." Swag sighed. Knowing he was about to spew all his frustrations on his new friend. He hoped the results wouldn't prove too gruesome; Swag was running out of friends.

"I just... I can hardly believe that the General expects me to make quality choices and do my job when he doesn't let me in on all the details. I know there are some things that I'll never get access to because I'm not military—but I think he's been playing my knowledge gaps against moral interests, and I don't like that. It's exactly what Raymond warned me about.

"I mean, I know it's all in the interest of a greater good, but still. It makes me wonder what else Raymond could've been right about."

"So why don't you ask him?" Hank asked as he looked over a diagnostic panel.

"Because he won't talk to me, now. He thinks I threw him under the bus in order to move up the chain of command. It feels kinda like Braff has been trying to drive a wedge between us—maybe he has been all along."

Hank nodded. "I agree that General Braff can be as slippery as they come. But I also believe that he sees things that nobody else does."

Swag cocked his head inquisitively.

"Not like in a prognosticative way," Hank clarified. "But I think he has a certain kind of understanding of people and of how the world works. He sees what is coming and he knows who to appoint to certain positions in order to keep the world—his world—balanced. He's no prophet and he's not infallible, but when he moves someone into a position or job, he's got a pretty good reason for it. By the same token, if he *doesn't* offer someone a job or fill a position... well, he might have a reason for that, too. I generally trust his judgement."

They walked through a large warehouse-like storage room filled with sealed food containers and other basic resources. "I have a lot of talents—but I'm not incredibly unique in that." He held out his hands as if to emphasize the grandeur of the stored loot. "My parents were, are still, huge preppers. They were even featured on one of those apocalypse prepping television shows. Background history, passion, and skillsets: Braff knows who will succeed in their areas of talent."

Swag swallowed Hank's opinion bitterly. "So you think he might see some flaw in Raymond and he's doing this for the greater good?"

Hank shrugged. "Maybe. Or maybe Braff is just being an egotistical turd and is engaged with his own personality conflict. That sort of thing isn't beyond any of us—and I know there are certain things that can set him off. But as for me, I play with all my cards on the table. Come on," Hank waved him forward and handed him a thick, bound manuscript.

Swag leafed through it and followed Hank deeper into the facility. He realized he'd never been down some of these particular hallways. "What is this, and where are we going?"

"I'll show you everything—the heart of Ark I. That booklet is the complete dossier for the guest-list. One thing I will say about Braff is that he knows how to pick people. Check out the first tier of people in that list." Hank flipped a few pages open. "These are people who are 'Must Haves' aboard the Ark when and if the world falls apart. It's full of experts in their field; Tier One individuals aren't beyond being kidnapped for the greater good of humanity if it comes to that and if we have enough time to make such extractions."

Swag gave him a skeptical look, but that melted away as he thought about it logically. "Braff does like to wield his 'good-of-the-many' argument."

Hank grinned and flashed Swag a Vulcan hand signal to show he understood the Mr. Spock inference. He flipped a few more pages and showed Swag that his name appeared in Tier One. "Here's proof of what he thinks of you, and for what it's worth, look at this." Hank tapped the footnote at the bottom page.

Swag followed the page number and entry under his dossier entry. It led him to a list of persons in "Tier Three: nonessential personnel *necessary* to Tier One." He scanned down the page until he located the numeric entry from his footnote. Raymond and Jessica were both listed. The general knew that Swag's friends were important enough that they he couldn't function without them.

"It's quite a guest-list," Swag agreed.

Hank Chu bobbed his head agreeably. "Well, it's a work in progress."

Jonas, Hansen, Frey, and Jindal looked up from the joint project in the ECHQ lab when Scofield returned. He triumphantly raised a pair of ECP units and the four very relieved looking scientists gave hearty applause.

Frey took the units and hooked them up to perform a quick diagnostic scan as Jindal congratulated Scofield on the successful hunt. "Did you let the kid, Nathaniel Tower, know that all is well?"

Scofield winked in response. "I told Goodthunder to do it before he took some much-needed R and R." He'd already briefed the science team on the incident—all except for Swaggart who remained out of the info loop after his recent confidentiality snafu, although they all fully expected to see him again soon. Braff would probably fix the protocol issue by increasing the scientist's clearance level again, which would likely irk Jonas further.

"Sounds like quite an exciting ordeal," Hansen stated blithely. None of the scientists envied the helter skelter that the ECTs endured in the field.

Frey called out and requested assistance. "Can you all verify what I'm seeing?" He switched the diagnostic readouts to the main viewing screens mounted on the walls of the lab. Jindal joined him and double-checked Frey's work.

"What? What am I seeing?" A nervous Scofield watched the scientists thoughtfully rub their chins as they looked over the readouts. "Have you figured out how Little Satan was able to jump out of the body he was supposed to be locked in?"

Jindal shook his head negatively without taking his eyes off of the data. "You said that Goodthunder had two entities afflicting him, another safeguard Little Satan overcame—you said it was Little Satan and another low-level one—he transferred them both to another person?" He pointed to the two ECPs with glowing indicator lights.

Scofield nodded, still confused about where this was going.

Jonas followed up the questioning. "The suspected terrorist who originally carried the body-locked Little Satan was dealt with according to normal procedure?"

Pointing two fingers at the side of his head, Scofield mimicked a gunshot to the head and nodded. "Of course. So what are we looking at?"

"Goodthunder didn't tell you the full truth," Jonas replied. "He spat two entities into his friend and you collected them—but neither of them was Little Satan." He pointed to the screens numeric field under the entity 'label' entry that their system generated in order to tag and track their data. "That is essentially a 'power ranking' for the entities we capture. It's both an estimate of these things' intelligence and abilities as well as a unique identifier, the equivalent of an entity's fingerprint."

"We call it the 'Jonas Scale,'" Jindal noted of the man who devised it.

Scofield looked at the two recent acquisitions' numbers. Both were just breaking into the upper three-digit range. "What's Little Satan's power level?"

"It's over nine-thousand."

The impressed sergeant kept a blank face as he put connected the dots. "There were three demons all along, then, and Little Satan is still controlling Goodthunder!" he finally spat, looking for confirmation on his logic.

All four of the scientists nodded agreements. Jonas, always a stickler for protocol, mumbled a barely audible correction. "Entity... not a demon. Demons are myths."

Scofield cursed and whirled around. "Turn up that tracking system you eggheads invented—Hermes—turn Hermes back on," he called over his shoulder. Scofield pulled out his mobile phone and dialed Braff. This particular creature seemed to get more devious at every turn.

Hank led Swag through a large room in the central promenade near the primary living quarters. A rounded, pillar-like facility sat at the center, giving every angle he looked out from an atrium-like impression.

He typed in an entry on a keypad to the main door of the central control hub and didn't even bother to hide the code which Swag obviously learned by now. The shared knowledge didn't bother the programmer.

"Welcome to Operations," Hank said as they entered the room which looked more like the command bridge of a spaceship as seen in any number of bad sci-fi movies. Computer consoles, screens, and dedicated control stations had been strategically laid out for some future command crew to control the entire facility with ease.

An alcove built into one wall contained desks and work stations. One had been faithfully arranged to mirror General Braff's office complete with live grenade paperweight and a hermetically sealed package of cigars. The engraved nameplate read Gen. R. Braff. Swag's eyebrows rose. If Braff was tucked out of the way in the central operations station, then who ranked high enough to be in charge of this place?

Noticing Swag's awe, Hank tapped a few keystrokes to take the screens off standby and nodded to the main console. A whole network of streams came alive and revealed software connections and links to high level government systems, satellite feeds, and other government programs and databases.

Slack-jawed with wonder, Swag asked, "Are you inside the CIA and FBI mainframes right now?"

"Some of their systems we have only *limited* access to." He winked, "Franklin Cuthbert is very well connected. The EC has a kind of a global watchdog authority; they've got secret influence in many areas."

Hank pulled up a blinking, red command window that asked for a confirmation code to proceed. "This here is the master command and control authorization window. It can slave everything to Ark I's Operations center. If it goes active, every single government system could be monitored, accessed, or controlled from this seat."

"Every system?"

Hank nodded. "Everything from welfare vouchers to tactical, nuclear cruise missiles."

Swag pursed his lips to whistle, but his mouth had gone dry in awe.

"You know what that means?"

The scientist stared at him blankly.

"Whoever knows the codes to access this room is the most powerful man in the world," Hank stated.

Swag was cautious to only touch things carefully, like when he'd held a gun for the first time. His fear of accidentally unleashing nuclear winter was apparent. Hank grinned at him and led them away from the room which sealed behind them, resetting the lock automatically.

"That must've taken some serious string-pulling to accomplish."

"That's what the EC does, Swag. They pull the serious strings. There are major events and powers shifting in the world right now—things influenced by a world that *you* uncovered. Are you going to lend your voice to guide our destiny, or do we leave it up to the lawyers, politicians, and soldiers?"

Something in Hank's tone resonated within him. "Then what do I do?"

"Just do what you do best," Hank said. "It's the same way I cope with my own failings and inadequacies: do the work you were made to do."

Swag shot him an irked look.

"Sorry," Hank corrected. "Do the job you evolved to be best capable of. Your specialty is researching the entities—what's the most pressing concern that the EC has regarding them?"

"Right now it's storage. We definitely need a long-term solution."

"Then find that solution. *It's what you were meant to do.* You'll probably understand how to fix all of your personal issues while you work with the things that you *are* capable of controlling. I find that doing mundane things brings me my greatest epiphanies."

Swag nodded. "But what do I do about all my ethical objections—how do I handle those?"

Hank shrugged. "Just do your job. Ethics are not your burden to bear. You only have to worry about solving the problem with the resources at hand."

The scientist stared off in deep thought. It was true that Pandora would become a reality with or without him: it had become an absolute necessity of the times they found themselves living in. Swag knew he needed to focus more on his job and it was possible his personal issues might even sort themselves out independent of him.

"Thanks," Swag said after a long, introspective moment. "I think I know what I ought to do—I just hope I can match your madcap work ethic. Maybe I'll get Cyborg-3 completed before you finish Ark I."

"I'll bet you a bottle of that old Glenfiddich that you're wrong," Hank challenged and they both laughed. The bet was struck and ideas for a containment unit already swirled around Swag's mind.

Scofield finished briefing Omega Team, *his team*, inside the mobile base. They'd parked at the edge of a college campus where they'd traced the signal to—Little Satan could run, but not hide from Hermes.

Compared to the other ECTs, Omega had less entity capture experience or familiarity with the Baconators. They'd performed operations under the supervision of other well-trained capture teams; Omega's members had other skills and were selected for past experience in more traditional subterfuge.

The sergeant bit his lip and hoped that he hadn't scared Tower, the greenest recruit on the team, when he reminded Omega about the entities' ability to swap bodies. Their ability to learn from the memories and talents of the afflicted and enable them with superhuman strength and resistance were never forgotten once seen in person.

His other four members of his covert ops team, Rodriguez, Jones, Baker, and Schwartz had all been on a few missions, temporarily replacing members of the Chi Team in order to acquire additional training. Chi Team, or ECT-X, was Goodthunder's team—the original Entity Capture Team formed by the Eidolon Commission before they began secretly training additional, clandestine groups.

"Remember," Scofield urged, "If you get caught in a dark area you could be susceptible to them, so make sure you use the UV flashlight feature on your Baconator and watch your EMF readers." He tapped his wrist-mounted reader to reinforce his comment.

Minutes later, Omega's agents moved in formation through the campus, heading towards the men's dormitory over the noon-hour, careful to use the cover of the sun to help keep down the chances of a body-jump. Students who noticed the agents dressed in SWAT gear quickly turned and fled as years of cultural reaction to university terror attacks had trained them to do.

Fixated on the transponder from the Hermes tracker, they'd pinpointed the location inside a dorm room. Members of the six-man team converged on the location from different angles. Suddenly the little blip disappeared from the display.

The team halted in their tracks and checked in with the mobile base. Mobile HQ reported the same thing.

"What's going on here," Rodriguez also asked via earpiece. "I'm blind."

Schwartz clicked his PTT button to open a channel. "Same here. Can they do that? That should be impossible—he can't get away from Hermes?"

"Unknown," Scofield reported.

The mobile base scrambled to narrow it down, but they had no ideas. Their equipment showed no failures in Hermes.

Scofield urged action. "We still have our location set; ETA is two minutes or less. Keep your GBs hot and ready. Move in, team."

Quickening their pace, the team converged on the door. The hallways had been otherwise empty. Word must've traveled quickly via text that some kind of military or police force had stormed the campus.

Jones kicked in the door and the men poured into a room barely big enough to contain them. Two bloody bodies lay in mangled repose. One belonged to Goodthunder, the other was a college student.

Tower grabbed a couple photos off the block wall where they'd been taped as Scofield spun a slow arc, analyzing the disturbing scene. All walls had been covered in theoretical equations spanning floor to ceiling. The sharpie markings might as well have been in a foreign language to the soldiers.

"Rigor mortis is set in on Goodthunder's body," Rodriguez reported. "He's been dead a while, and someone twisted this kid's neck like a pretzel."

Tower requested data from Mobile HQ; they had hacked into the university records as soon as they hit the grounds. "Who resided in this room?" He stared at the photo and got the student profiles in his earpiece. One was a business major and attending on a football scholarship. "That must be him," Tower pointed to the student with the broken spine where he lay slumped over a ratty lounge chair. "Tell me about the roommate?"

"Cross country distance runner. Name is Jeremiah Higgins, listed in our who's-who database of promising people to watch. Kid's a math prodigy and has been studying theoretical physics. The EC nearly approached him, but research on his torrent download history showed he might have had earlier contact with Cerberus in high school—so he posed a security risk and the brass declined to pursue him." Mobile HQ's broadcast crackled and ended.

"Great," Scofield muttered as he sent four members of Omega out to check their perimeter and try to get eyes on Higgins. "Patch me through to ECHQ. Get me a link established with our science team."

A few seconds later, Frey's voice broke the line. "We are here, Agent Scofield. We can see the entire scene through your body cameras."

Scofield leaned over and gave an evil eye to the camera. "What's going on, guys? Hermes is down—Little Satan slipped off the reader. EMF is blank, too. Goodthunder is dead and the entity is afflicting a math-genius college student." He briefly explained Higgins' background to them.

Jindal asked Scofield to pan the camera over a section of the computations. He complied. A moment later Jindal moaned, "Oh no." The scientists chattered amongst themselves for a moment.

"What is it?" Scofield demanded.

"He's figured out how to disable the tagging component. Little Satan can no longer be tracked by Hermes—it has… he's altered himself, evolved beyond it," Jindal stated. Worry permeated his voice.

Scofield bit his tongue and cursed. Things got more complicated by the minute.

###

Raymond scratched his stubbly chin and leaned over the half-empty bottle of Southern Comfort. He hadn't responded to the hails from any of his so-called friends. He was pretty sure, however, that he was being watched by government operatives. He was sure he'd seen movement or light artifacts in the apartment across the street which he knew had been vacant for weeks now.

An alert on his phone informed him that he had another email in his inbox. "Probably another rejection," he muttered. Raymond felt confident that Braff was behind his failure to secure work anywhere else. He hadn't needed to make a resume in years, but he was quite certain that he was over qualified for any of the positions he'd applied for. He'd even been turned down for a job teaching math at a community college!

He wiped the bleary edges away from his vision and opened his email account. "God, I've got to get out of this hole."

The new email claimed to be from himself: Raymond Lems. He nearly clicked delete out of habit, thinking a spammer had gotten past his filter. Then Raymond noticed the subject line: *The three Headed Dog Sees You.*

He connected it to Cerberus and opened it immediately. His palms began sweating; Raymond's stomach soured with grim accusation even as he read the message.

We are going to blow the lid off of E.C. New proof that O.H. was murdered, along with others. We know much: the general implanted innocent people in order to politically motivate D.H.S. sanctioned assassinations.

We know much but need more evidence. You can help. Find me on your anniversary. We will wait where you were supposed meet with O.H.

"How do they know about my anniversary?" he muttered aloud. He shrugged. It was Cerberus… who knew how much information they could dig up. The date was months away yet, and nobody intercepting this message could know either that date or where Oswald Harrison had instructed the scientist to meet him. Not even Swaggart could know *both*.

18

Bleary-eyed, Swag stared at the circuit board and forced his eyes to refocus on the issue at hand. He identified his problem as a poor solder, reached into the machine, and reattached the shoddily connected wire lead to the Cyborg-3 circuitry.

Sitting back on his haunches, he rechecked the diagnostics display and sighed with relief. Everything mechanical worked up to his current checkpoint. Swag rubbed his tired eyes, leaned his weight up against the exterior housing of the apparatus, and stumbled to his feet.

He'd been working exclusively on Cyborg-3 for several weeks on end—or had it been months, now? He'd been given full control and oversight of the hardware aspect of Project Pandora: a full-scale entity detention facility. Swag rubbed his eyes again, and *thought* it had been only weeks—but he couldn't be sure. He'd spent so much time on the machine that the days and hours had blurred together. He didn't even remember when he'd last left ECHQ—maybe a week ago when he'd gone up to play chess and walk the halls of Ark I with Hank. Swag had finally begun to realize what his friend had been talking about when he'd relocated and flung himself into his job with such singular focus.

Hank had made even more progress in developing Ark I since Swag plunged into developing the new Cyborg model.

The friendly competition helped take off the edge of the dull monotony of their tasks.

Swag glanced at his coworkers. *Speaking of dull monotony*, he thought, assessing their personalities. He really did miss Raymond. Swag wished he could at least insert Jessica into the crew, but Braff feared that the female dynamic might slow their process at best and distract the other men, at worst. A smile tugged at the edge of Swag's lips... *she really was a firecracker*, he thought. Maybe Braff was right.

Jessica had been given a different role, in the meanwhile, and continued as the research head collecting data at their original, downtown facility. He knew how much she hated it and he wondered if she continued in the hope that Raymond might still return to the project. Swag certainly didn't think it was because of any lingering dedication to the project. She was brilliant in her own way, but she'd always seemed more dedicated to the people that she worked with than to a specific field of research.

His phone vibrated in his pocket and Swag reached for it. Jessica had sent him a text. Even though they hadn't communicated in a while, they were still connected deeply enough that it didn't feel at all out-of-the-blue.

Lunch at that crappy gyro cart downtown? We need to catch up.

Swag looked from face to face of the men he shared his lab with and reminded himself how long he'd been in relative isolation. He deserved at least a little respite from the doldrums. Just reading the short message sparked his mind and body back to life.

He checked his watch and estimated the travel time. *Meet you there at 12:30?*

#

"Truthfully, I thought you would've quit," Swag told Jessica as they stood outside of the greasy food-trailer which reeked of old oil and Greek spices.

Swag's hands were full. He held a brown cardboard box with ventilation holes in his hands.

Jessica nodded and accepted the foil-wrapped packages that closely resembled a meal from the olive-skinned entrepreneur and dropped her spare change in his tip jar. "I thought I might've, too," she agreed and handed him one of the gyros. They sat on the concrete edge of a raised garden bed that girded up a bank of urban shrubbery.

"I went on a couple weeks' vacation instead. I tried to decide what I was going to do." She spoke the words as if they tasted bad.

Swag stared at her for a moment. Her usual spunk and that glimmer in her eyes seemed to have died—or dulled at the very least.

She sighed and continued, "I really don't enjoy what I'm doing... but I know that it serves a huge need and is for the greater good. But every day I feel a little bit like I trade pieces of my soul for empirical data. Luckily, we've finally ruled out *young* children as viable carriers for the entities—so at least that's some good news. No more experiments on kids under eleven or the mentally disabled... entities can't seem to afflict either of them—and probably for the same reasons... but *innocence* isn't scientific and it's too hard to quantify or qualify ."

Neither took a bite of their meal.

"Raymond still hasn't contacted you?" he finally asked after a moment of shared silence.

"No. I'd hoped that you might have some information. I'm worried about him, Swag."

"Has anybody checked on him to, you know... to make sure he's still alive and well, at least?"

Jessica nodded. "I've tried to drop by a couple times. His mail is being taken care of and his recycling gets set out—although it's mostly empty booze bottles at this point."

"You know, if there was anything that I could do to help, I would do it, right?" He glanced away from her yearning gaze and stared into the shadowy area beneath the foliage nearest them. The whispering started to call from the back of his mind.

Jessica nodded. "I think he feels like you abandoned him—chose Braff over your friendship. I know it's a very unmacho way of thinking, but from a lady's point of view, I would probably feel the same if I were in his shoes."

He skootched away from the darkness slightly and tried to push the ethereal murmurs out of his mind. Swag suddenly remembered why he didn't often leave the HQ very often; everywhere he looked he spotted shadowy areas—vulnerable places where light didn't reach. He forced himself to ignore it and concentrated on his lunch date.

"Do you feel that way, too, Jessica? Does it feel like I chose the EC over us?"

She shrugged in response, but did not look him in the eye. It was as good as any "yes" she might give him.

He placed a hand over top of hers. "Hey. I'm sorry. I never meant for you to feel like I'd thrown you under the bus."

She shuddered slightly and relaxed. Her shoulders slumped as she released her pent-up frustration in one heavy breath.

"I'll talk to General Braff and see if there's anything we can do." He corrected himself, "I'll make sure I do something to fix this."

Jessica nodded and kept her face taught to make sure she didn't lose any tears.

"Is there anything I can do in the meanwhile?"

She forced herself to be a little more cheerful. "You can tell me what's in the box."

Swag handed it to her. "It's a gift... an old friend, really."

Jessica lifted the lid and spotted Horton who inquisitively raised his nose to sniff her. She stuck her hand in to pet the aged, mostly senile rodent and squinted to hold back the saline emotions threatening to escape her tear ducts.

"I remembered how much you always loved him and that you used to have a pet rat as a kid. We've pretty much moved past any animal testing at this phase, so I thought you'd like to have him."

Jessica leaned against him and bumped shoulders playfully. It was a good gift.

He pointed towards an ice-cream vendor setting up down the block and blazed a trail towards another questionable gastro-intestinal decision. With people around, he kept his voice low but gave her a quick summary of the work he'd been up to at the EC and gave her a basic outline of the Ark Project.

"Because of your importance, you and Raymond were always on the list to get in," he stretched the truth only slightly. "With the current state of things I think it's important that you know about it." He nearly trailed off again to listen to the ethereal voices coming from another bank of shadows. Swag shook away the distraction and resumed the conversation. "Something about the way things have shaped up at the EC gives me a bad feeling—like something terrible is coming for the human race."

Jessica took his comments in stride but lightened the mood with an elbow to her friend's ribcage. "Don't tell me you're getting all religious on me all of the sudden. I thought destiny and prophecy and all that were for people like your parents?"

Swag forced a playful smile and changed the subject. "You know it's a long drive to the other facility and you'll probably need to *finally* accept that company car, right?" he teased back, making her wrinkle her nose in pixy-like fashion. Her disdain for driving was well-established.

They finished their street-food and parted ways. Swag felt better, though they both still shared concern for their mutual friend.

Swag dialed Braff's number as his car pulled out of his parking spot. "I've got a request," he told the general, though his tone of voice made it clear that it was more of a demand.

"What can I do for you, Swag?"

"General, I need Jessica Hiddleston on my team." He intentionally used *need* instead of *want*.

"She is doing important work downtown..."

Swag cut him off. He didn't plan to take no for an answer. "Important work that I think we ought to have readily available to us on a moment's notice."

"Oh, I agree with you there. But I recall that we discussed some earlier concerns and how convenient it is to have someone we can trust running the secondary research facility in our metro location."

"I hear you, General. But I'm telling you that I *need* her."

Braff held the line for a moment, mulling it over. He wasn't oblivious to his Swag's past; he always operated best with a partner to keep him motivated and focused. With Raymond absent, Swag ran the risk of emotionally floundering. Swag was important, and Braff had to weigh any risks against the scientist's productivity and well-being.

"I agree with you," Braff finally acquiesced. "She's certainly become the leading expert in her field of entity attachment and affliction transmission."

"So, you can transfer her to ECHQ?"

"I'll work out the details over the next couple of days and I'll get her the necessary clearance. I should be able to make it happen within a week or so."

"Thank you, General."

"Don't mention it. You just do me a favor and get that containment unit operational... and soon. I hear there's a wager over whether you or Chu will complete your magnum opus projects first and I bet on you... wagered my finest cigars against a bottle of that fancy scotch he likes so much."

###

Scofield waved an obligatory greeting at Swag as the scientist entered the main hallway at ECHQ. Swag definitely walked with a bounce in his step. Something had lightened his spirits over midday.

"Come with me, Doctor Swaggart," Scofield motioned him over.

Swag gave him an apprehensive glance.

"General Braff wanted me to show you a few things," he responded. "He's bringing you in the loop on stuff you hadn't been cleared for until now." The agent swiped his key card at a terminal and a door hissed open. It led to an area Swag had never been to before. "Braff said something about a bottle of whiskey hanging in the balance, whatever that means."

Swag grinned; his eyes captured every detail of the unfamiliar terrain as they walked. "I've never been here before." A large stairwell yawned open before them and led downward. "I didn't even know there was a basement."

At the bottom Scofield threw an electrical lever and several banks of lights turned on. A huge platform with electrical terminals and welded reinforcements extending deep into the foundation of the building had been built in the far corner.

Fully completed pieces of the Cyborg-3 platform had already been moved into position for the live-demo they planned to initiate in the near future. The polished, metal restraint chamber stood in stark contrast to the warehouse-like environment that surrounded it. A machine gleamed silver like some kind of space-aged sarcophagus—the box meant to hold the legion-afflicted Joshua Brady as soon as they initiated Pandora.

Tracing the walls with his eyes, Swag found hundreds of the ECP cells hooked up to an electrical grid. They glowed with a dim light as they lined rack after rack of the enormous basement. Further down the line, many of the original containment cells had also been connected hearkening back to the time before they'd upgraded to the BCnTR devices.

"What is this place?"

"The future home of Cyborg-3. It's where we plan to keep the containment unit you're working on."

Swag tried to count the ECPs and settled for an estimate that hovered well beyond two thousand. He tried to guess at the scope of the Eidolon Commissions secret projects "How many? How long has the EC been capturing, afflicting, and running side projects with the entities?"

"A lot… and since the beginning," Scofield replied. "We've been collecting them all along, since the early days when the Eidolon Commission first formed and got government sanctioning—well *unofficial clearance,* anyways."

"But how? There are so many."

"There are actually *ten* Entity Capture Teams responsible for various parts of the country, each working capture missions. You can see that we're already running out of capacity. We could keep racking them up this way, but the other geeks in the science wing say it's going to run out far too soon, plus this system is far too vulnerable."

Swag walked along a wall and ran his finger along a laden shelf. "That's obvious."

"You can see why we need Pandora completed as soon as possible," Scofield continued. "The General wants me to help get you anything you might need to stay on schedule."

"Tell me about these teams," Swag asked.

"There are three on each coast and another three in the central states… and then another one."

"Omega Team?"

He nodded, thin-lipped. "They each cover a pretty large geographic area. Except Omega, it's the special ops one."

Swag crossed his arms. "And which one are you a part of?"

Scofield gave him a cagey look.

"I assume you lead your own team. Omega Team, right?"

Scofield nodded measuredly. "Correct."

"I've known there had to be multiple teams for a while, now. But information is hard to come by. Some of the dots were easy to connect even though the hard data had been limited."

"What are you getting at?"

"I'm just trying to figure out the big picture," Swag admitted. "Raymond always balanced me out with his skepticism. He was a kind of a compass for me, you might say."

Scofield shrugged, but hid his nervousness at the suggestion they'd been too easy to figure out. Hacktivists were already sniffing too close for his comfort.

"How is Omega Team connected to the Sinister Six?"

The question rocked Scofield back with surprise. It might as well have been a slap to the cheek.

"I don't understand why you would ask that?"

"Research material is very limited, as I mentioned, so I did lots of searches on the names of afflicted people our teams interacted with—names pulled from reports. There aren't too many specific names mentioned except for when there's been a fatality. Outside of Chi Team, the ECT I worked with before they upgraded me to ECHQ, the only other team to log deaths in the field was Omega Team—I've known of at least those two teams for months now because of the fatalities."

Swag continued, "Chi had the incident with Goodthunder and also the one where you shot that guy in the head, setting Raymond off. And then there was the mishap when we lost Ripley and Gifford. In two of those three incidents, by the way, you were there. Do you know how many deaths Omega has been responsible for?"

"Tell me," Scofield said.

"More than two dozen. You haven't had a single loss to Omega team. But what is interesting about the names of the dead, beyond the isolated incidents where something went terribly wrong, is that every fatality is some sort of blood relation to a member of the Sinister Six, the domestic terrorists rotting in prison right now. So tell me about the Sinister Six."

Scofield grinned. "You're very observant, Doctor. But I'm afraid that I cannot talk about that. It's just not relevant to the project. I can level with you this much to satisfy your curiosity though: that connection is real, but it has nothing to do with any global impact the Entity Capture Teams are having."

"Global impact?"

"Here's what I mean," Scofield stated, "I believe in the project, the whole thing—but maybe 'National Impact' is a better phrase; I just assume that other governments will follow suit once we establish a history of results attributed to our work. Did you know that the national crime rate has dropped by almost four percent since we started capturing these entities—mostly as a reduction in violent crime categories? Entities must be responsible for at least some of the malice and malevolence in this world. The Six were just a part of that whole thing. And besides, it's not my place to talk about it. I'm sure the General will fill you in on it at some point in time—for now, let's focus on this entity storage system."

###

Hank Chu drove the electric cart while General Braff rode shotgun. Tires squeaked slightly as they toured through the hallways.

"As you can see, General, Ark I is almost fully operational."

"It's remarkable," Braff stated.

"You know, I'm sure that you're a very busy man, Roddy. I'm quite certain you could have gotten all of this information in my regular reports."

"I know that," he said. "But sometimes it pays to get outside the office and actually put your boots on the ground and spend some time where it counts—with the people who count. So tell me," Braff said amiably, "how is your family situation?"

Hank winked at the officer. "This wouldn't have anything to do with that bottle of whiskey you think I'm gonna owe you, does it?"

Braff laughed, "Maybe. But Swaggart and the team are running preliminary tests on Cyborg-3 as we speak." He grinned, but knew the competition wasn't really close by a true measure of scales. The general handed him a gift—his neatly wrapped cigar humidor.

Hank looked at Braff and was genuinely concerned for him, even if they made light of the situation. They'd known each other long enough to understand what things each other valued, and Hank understood that family was an open wound for Braff.

He tore the wrapping paper off and grinned.

"I always knew you'd finish first. Let me know when you're done smoking those and I'll take my box back."

Hank nodded and sighed, reflecting on his own family. "Shelly and the kids are doing okay... well enough in my absence," he said.

Braff shrugged with understanding. "That's all well and good. Are they doing as well as they ought to? Are they better off without a husband, a father?"

Hank shot his boss a pained look. He bristled defensively for a moment, and then his hackles quelled. "They've been on my mind a lot, lately."

"If there's one thing I can guarantee," Braff said, "It's that you are on *their* mind, too. I never talk a lot about it…" he trailed off. "How Wanda was taken from me." The general swallowed almost audibly. "If I've learned anything since those dirty ragheads took my wife it's how important family is. It is everything."

Hank stared at the dash of the cart. He knew too intimately how Braff's wife had been beaten, raped, and murdered by the Sinister Six. Wanda was more than Braff's wife, she'd been family; Shelly and Wanda had been as close as sisters could be prior to leaving for opposite coasts for college.

No one ever brought up Wanda and Braff rarely discussed it.

Hank sighed, "I admit I've been thinking long and hard about them. I know Shelly and I had a lot of problems—but who doesn't right?"

Braff slapped him on the back. "Ain't that the truth."

"The work on the Ark is nearly complete. I wasn't going to mention it until later, but I intend on taking some time off as soon as I hit the initial benchmarks to make sure the station is fully operational."

"You gonna go home and make things right?"

Hank nodded. He'd only recently made the decision, and hadn't really come to grips with it until now. "Yes sir."

"Then take all the time you need when you go," he said. "I'll be glad to lose a box of cigars to you for that. And tell Shelly 'hello' from me. It's been too long since we all got together."

Hank agreed, but knew the reasons behind it. Braff had avoided the extended family get-togethers ever since a falling out with his son.

Both men nodded.

Ark I was so far ahead of schedule that it either attested to Hank's insane work ethic or to the efficiency of the droid work crew he'd programmed. Hank accomplished what no other man could have done in such little time.

"I hope you can put just as much effort into *her*, now, as you did into *this place*. A good woman is…" Braff trailed off, lost in thought and obviously doing his best to contain the emotion his memories brought up. "Trust me. Don't let Shelly go if you can hold on."

Hank rubbed the tightness from his face. "Thanks, Roddy. I think I'll be out of here by tomorrow night."

###

"I hear there is a bet between you and Chu," Jindal joked over the noise.

Swag shrugged. "Yeah, but I'm pretty sure we've already lost. I think the Ark has been basically functional for days, now, and we've still got some diagnostics to tweak on our end." He grimaced and tried to ignore the nearby, shrieking noises.

Jonas rolled his eyes and stood to adjust the gag that had slipped free from Joshua Brady's mouth. He was rarely the one to encourage the things that normal humans found enjoyable—even if those things were great motivators.

"I also heard of another member doctor joining our team," Jindal asked with a lecherous tone. "I heard she is quite pretty—even cuter than Jonas."

Jonas shook his head and scowled playfully, trying best to act as if he hadn't heard the barb.

The civilian scientist grinned. He could hardly wait for Jessica to arrive—even if he'd hope to spare her from the sort of work he was engaged in at the moment.

Swag looked up and noticed the security cameras panning back and forth across the grounds and recording them for posterity. He frowned and wondered how history would remember him. He hoped future generations wouldn't judge him too harshly.

Giving the signal to Jindal, Swag ordered the unit sealed. They all stood aside and watched the heavy plates as they slowly enclosed the edges of the shiny, steel sarcophagus. With a resolute click they sealed shut, hiding the thrashing, snarling body of Joshua Brady within the tomb-like enclosure of Cyborg-3.

#

"Throw your leader out the window!"

Scofield smirked as the middle easterners obeyed and threw Sharif off the sixth story balcony. It would be more accurate to say that the entities threw the man over. They were the ones in control of the suspected terrorist cell members—and Omega Team was in control of them.

Despite the loss of the Little Satan, the other six entities operated perfectly and had even become more compliant in recent weeks. *Maybe these things can be trained... like dogs,* Scofield wondered as Sharif plummeted towards the ground, spinning clumsy arcs.

Sharif landed on the concrete with a sickening, wet thud that snapped his neck. Half of Omega Team waited near the rear entrance where the body had fallen. They didn't worry about any entities inside the obliterated victim; Scofield knew all along that Sharif had been unafflicted.

The sergeant smugly chuckled at the mangled corpse on the sidewalk and gave a hand-signal to his team before raising his megaphone. Braff would be pleased with another tally mark against his enemies—Sharif had been a cousin to one of the Sinister Six, but an oath is an oath.

Scofield felt confident that the operation would go as planned—another big win for Department of Homeland

Security. He knew his men in Omega stood ready to scan and capture as needed. The team could rush in should their six subservient assets refuse any order—Hermes had helped bring the entities under heel. None of the privatized demons wanted the EC to activate the Hermes system.

Hermes inflicted some kind of trauma on whatever passed for their supernatural physiology and had become one more tool in their arsenal. In human terms it could only be understood as "pain."

"Omega and DHS teams, standby," Scofield ordered through the radio.

"Acknowledged."

"Acknowledged."

Scofield triggered the megaphone. "All operatives working with EC division of Homeland Security are ordered to exit at the rear of the building. The rest of you will exit at the front and be taken into custody. You will be given a fair trial. You have five minutes to comply before we enter the building and use lethal force."

He knew that they'd gathered enough evidence over the last few days that any case against them would be open and shut. After introducing their six entities into the suspected cell, they'd tried to engineer human genocide within the controlled environment. The entities did exactly what they were designed to do: incite violence, death, and chaos—and all under the direct observation of government recording equipment.

Omega Team did what they do best: push suspected terrorists over the brink by afflicting them. In the end they would acquire concrete terrorism evidence and arrest their prey. No lawyers dared represent suspects with such overwhelming proof if they could manage otherwise. The EC and DHS partnership created a revolving door for domestic terror suspects.

Eidolon Commission brass used the ends to justify the means. According to the data, domestic terror numbers were down—and that was all that mattered.

Scofield smiled as the back door swung open. He didn't need to consult his EMF meter even though it went wild with elevated readings.

A bedraggled Middle Eastern man exited, He fixed the sergeant with the hollow, cold eyes of a murderer.

"Abbadon," Scofield stated with a curt nod, recognizing the body-locked, ethereal asset by the face they'd confined it to.

Agent Schwartz harvested Abbadon with his Baconator.

Agent Tower clicked handcuffs onto the confused human as he emerged from the fog of the affliction. "What? Where am I?" He demanded answers that wouldn't come. Tower shoved the man to the ground where he would wait for DHS to arrive after Omega finished reclaiming the remaining assets.

"Leviathan, Mephistopheles, Samael, Asmodeus, Belphegor," Scofield ticked them off as they emerged single-file and into the waiting hands and ECPs of their handlers. As Schwartz harvested Belphegor, Scofield recalled the other members of Omega Team who waited by the front entrance in case any tried to make a break for it. One of the support staff from the Mobile HQ collected the filled ECPs into a tote and ferried them back. He would return them to the Cuthbert Research Center under armed guard.

Tower looked up as he slapped the shackles around the last prisoner. "Sergeant Scofield? Am I seeing this right? Is that kid filming us?"

Scofield stood stiff with shock and dropped a string of profanity.

Tower recognized him and snapped his fingers for a moment, trying to remember the name. "Jeremiah Higgins—that's the kid from Goodthunder's murder!"

"Little Satan," Scofield hissed.

Higgins stood there defiantly. He'd filmed the entire capture operation and his camera still rolled. Higgins sneered a challenge to Omega Leader.

"Omega Team! On me," Scofield barked as Rodriguez, Jones, and Baker rounded the corner. They immediately understood the situation and all six charged after the afflicted college student. Higgins turned and fled with the speed and agility of a startled gazelle.

"Watch yourself!" the sergeant yelled right before they turned into the alley where the enemy escaped.

Thirteen afflicted humans, all homeless by the looks of them, whirled around to face the six-man team. They stuttered and jerked with the graceless, unhuman movements typical of bottom-level entities according to the Jonas Scale. The humans became beasts of only one mode—physical violence.

The wall of enemies snarled and steeled itself to pounce.

"We don't have time for this." Beyond the afflicted, a door to an adjacent warehouse hung wide open; a weak hydraulic door assist struggled to close the entry. Scofield raised his carbine and flooded the alley with a spray of bullets. The thirteen bodies hit the floor and Scofield slammed another magazine into his weapon before clipping his Baconator to the rail-mounted attachment on his gun's muzzle.

His team followed suit and they charged forward into the warehouse, hot on Little Satan's tail. The lights suddenly went black and the team flipped on the UV lights on the Baconators. Any of the remaining, natural light went out when the door finally clicked shut behind them.

"Scanners!" the sergeant called. The EMF display couldn't be fooled; it registered one strong reading deep in the middle of the warehouse which contained simple construction supplies. It was just Omega Team versus Little Satan.

Scofield smirked; he'd read the devious little miscreant correctly. "Fan out! Lights at max," he ordered from the blackness. If any of the doors or escape routes opened they'd know exactly where Higgins escaped to. "We've got him, now."

The team spread out, goose stepping through the darkness and waving their illumination beams in wide swaths as they followed the strong EMF signature that blipped in front of them on their directional navigation grid. Suddenly, a thousand identical blips showed up everywhere!

Omega team spun circles as they cursed and called out, searching for the afflicted. Copper wire-wrapped rods of rebar pulled stray nails and metal shavings across the ground to where the make-shift electromagnets lay scattered at regular intervals.

"It's a trick!" Schwartz howled, understanding exactly how the entity had created the fake signatures in the electromagnetic field.

"I've got him! I've got him!" Tower screamed in the darkness nearby. The nearby members sprinted to the location where Tower had his carbine-mounted GB shoved into Higgins' face as he triggered the Baconator's harvesting field.

"Don't shoot! Don't shoot!" Jeremiah Higgins screamed. His face was streaked with tears and he pleaded for his life. "Please! I have no idea how I got here!"

The college student broke down, bawling. Hot snot flowed from his nose as he begged. "The last thing I remember is some military guy named Goodthunder coming to my dorm room and ordering me to turn out the lights! Please—oh God! I don't want to die!"

Tower cussed and slapped his Baconator. "Something's wrong! The stupid thing isn't reading a capture. My ECP is empty!"

Schwartz leaned over and glanced at the LED readout. It hadn't switched over. A moment of dawning recognition punched through his mind as he glanced at Higgins. "The entity's not in the boy!"

He whirled his light around just in time to catch sight of Scofield emerging from the shadows—his eyes burned with hellfire and malice. Scofield snapped his weapon to his shoulders and mowed down his team before any could react.

"Oh God, oh God, oh God, oh God…" Higgins chanted the mantra as the red-eyed madman bent low to stare him in the face.

The afflicted Scofield snatched the college student's mobile phone out of his shaking hands. "God cannot help you now," he hissed with an otherworldly voice filled with hatred and vitriol. Scofield put the carbine's barrel against Jeremiah Higgin's head and pulled the trigger.

19

Braff leaned across the steel table and glowered at the dark-skinned man whose wrists were shackled to the mount at its middle. Three security guards stood behind the foreigner.

The man in his late twenties refused to make eye contact with the General.

"Glad to see you're happy, healthy, and fed, Uqbah," Braff said sarcastically as he spread a small stack of photos across the table. Men bearing a striking familial similarity to the prisoner lay dead with their bloody, mangled reposes captured by film. "I'm sure you recognize some of these men like Sharif and Khalid al-Kassab. Just think, if it wasn't for the American justice system intervening, the other inmates would've beaten you and your friends to death a long time ago."

Uqbah al-Kassab did not look up, but he did see the photos. He tried to remain stoic, but his tear ducts refused to cooperate and sprang a slight leak. Salty drops fell and splattered onto the pictures.

"Look at me," Braff demanded.

Uqbah ignored him.

Braff leapt across the table and grabbed Uqbah by the hair, wrenching his head up to meet his wild gaze. "I said look at me!"

"You got to let him go, General," one of the guards cried out. He pointed up to the cameras. "You know the rules—they record everything now for the safety of minority inmates."

Braff released him and sank back, but he had Uqbah's attention. The prisoner sat back in his chair and faced his adversary.

"I made you a promise before they pulled you out of gen pop and gave you and your friends special treatment—special food and privileges, even visitation. *Where is my visitation?* You know what you took from me—and what I've pledged to take from *you!*" He growled, glancing down to the photos.

Braff stood, leaving the solemn Uqbah shackled to the table. He retrieved the next stack of pictures from his jacket pocket. "I've got to leave you, now, but I expect I'll see you again next year... I've got five other visits to make."

The guard at the door stopped him momentarily. "Your photos, sir?" He pointed back to the table where Uqbah fingered them sorrowfully.

"Make sure he gets them back to his cell. Everyone should remember family." He stepped through the door when his cellphone chirped. He looked at the message and his face fell. Something even more important than his annual meeting came up—and that meant something had gone horribly wrong at the EC.

The brilliant LED screen burned Braff's eyes with a message meaning it was all about to hit the fan. *Media has Joshua footage. Security breach—threat level black.*

General Braff tucked his packet of grisly photos back into his pocket and hurried back to his car.

#

Knowing that Jessica's credentials were finally in the works, Swag tried to salvage his relationship with his longtime partner. Surely Raymond still respected their time-honored tradition of celebrating their initial discovery.

Holding a boxed cake—a store-bought *Happy Anniversary* cake from the area grocer—he took a deep breath and rapped on the door. Nobody responded. Swag knocked again. Still no response. He set the cake down on the floor of the hallway and knocked again. And again.

Finally, he slumped down to the floor and sat leaning in the hall. He banged on the door behind him.

"Come on, Raymond. You've got to talk to me *some time!*" He pounded on the door with a closed fist. "Raymond? Come on man! I'll stay out here all day! I'm sorry alright? Open up!"

A door down the hallway opened up and an elderly Hispanic woman stuck her head out. The air from her apartment escaped, coloring the corridor air with the faint smell of cumin, cooking lard, and cheap laundry soap. "He's not there! Quiet down! I can't hear my T.V."

Swag scowled at the irony. Before knocking, the only noise in the hall had been the muffled sounds from her television which blasted at maximum volume. "I'm sorry Mrs. Martinez." He remembered her name at the last second. Swag scooped up his cake and walked towards her door. "Do you know when he'll be back?"

He winced at the loud volume of the Latino news network's broadcast as he drew nearer.

"Never, probably. He moved out days ago."

Frowning, Swag stepped up to her doorway, sighed, and handed her the cake. He wouldn't feel right eating it without Raymond, not even if he shared it with Jessica.

Mrs. Martinez accepted the cake and stared at him quizzically.

Swag glanced past her shoulder and caught a glimpse of her TV. His jaw dropped at the sight. The news broadcast showed video footage of Joshua Brady struggling against the heavy, steel binders that affixed him to the Cybrog-3 machine as scientists pumped him full of injection after injection and further afflicted him with the contents of the old ECP cells.

Swag's eyes widened like dinner plates. He spotted himself on screen as he turned to supervise the initial tests. He didn't understand the words of the newscast, but he recognized the footage from a couple of days ago—it had been pulled from the security cameras at ECHQ. *This is a huge security leak!* The scene cut away to footage of an Ark I loading dock receiving massive supply shipments; the graphic overlay seemed to indicate an enormous tax conspiracy.

In a breakout picture footage showed local riots. A cop car burned as people held up signs claiming that the "end was near."

Whirling around, Swag ran down the hallway. He stumbled, groping for his keys and cellphone at the same time. Tripping towards his car, he pressed a thumb on the lock scanner and checked the phone. There was already a text message from Braff.

Get back to HQ NOW!

Swag slid into the driver's seat and hit the ignition. The radio blasted him as soon as the key turned. He dialed into a news network and the breaking story was all they discussed.

"No, no, no!" he cursed as he merged into traffic. Roads were clogged with traffic; the situation was made worse with double parked cars jamming the roads as people loaded vehicles with basic supplies. More than a few people openly carried guns and Swag did a double take at the militia-style members standing vigil on their sidewalk as other people prepared to bug out. Further down the street he saw the reason for their armed presence.

On the next block down a riot had started. A Molotov cocktail burst against one of the cars stuck in traffic. A chorus of horns erupted. Swag cut a hard turn and hopped a cub in order to get onto a side-street.

"What do you want to talk about first?" the news personality asked. "What is obviously a top-secret government apocalypse bunker being loaded with food and supplies even while our nation fails in the war against hunger, or the fact that Joshua Brady—who was supposedly executed by lethal injection months ago—appears alive and well… or as well as a private citizen being tortured by government scientists can be? Our guests are Johan Barminsky, conspiracy theory expert, and Reverend Michael Severson of the Pillar of Fire Church."

"It's not a church, exactly," the reverend interrupted. "We're more of a movement."

"With adherents."

"That's correct."

Barminsky broke in. "I think the Joshua video is just one of a few interesting pieces Cerberus leaked to the media—I'd most like to talk about these 'entities' that they loaded Brady up with."

Swag wheeled around a corner, looking for a break in the panicked traffic.

"You don't think that the source, a clandestine hacker group, lends suspicion against the credibility of the footage?"

"Absolutely not! Maybe if we only had the one piece, but when you add it all together, this is a slam dunk argument. The government has been infecting citizens with demonic creatures in some cases and has been ghost-busting them in others."

"That sounds crazy," the host stated, "except that there is proof. Where does science begin, and religion take over? I mean—these are two radically different worlds, aren't they?"

"No. And they never have been," Severson stated. "It's always been just one big…"

"I expected *you* to say that," the host interrupted.

"But there was proof released by Cerberus. Eight years ago there was a paper published by one Doctor Jimmy

Swaggart which hypothesized a metaphysical link between the supernatural and the natural. His math seemed to add up, but nobody took this guy seriously and he was never funded. The paper was never made available except by the info dump dropped by Cerberus. It looks like someone tried to cover this discovery up."

"That sounds like some crazy conspiracy-level stuff. Anybody can write something, however. That doesn't make it credible… thanks to the self-publishing industry *anybody* can write nowadays."

"Yes, but the paper actually made it into the *American Journal of Physics'* Quantum Mechanics issue. Swaggart essentially pioneered study on Zenotian Para-Existential Fields—which *nobody* is studying—but here's the thing: the whole issue was scrapped at the last minute and released late. His paper never saw daylight—ironic since the article suggested that darkness was the only state to release the 'supernatural' entities from the quantum zeno effect—a state of binding paralysis.

"The publisher's parent company is owned by Franklin Cuthbert and we only now have the article because Cerberus provided the original draft of the journal before it was delayed. The released issue replaced that content with a fluff piece about collegiate studies."

"So some crack-pot fringe doctor predicted demons in the dark nearly a decade ago, but he never did anything with it?"

Barminsky interrupted again. "He tried, and probably assumed he'd been laughed off by the science community. Two years ago Swaggart essentially disappeared, but the hackers show that he was suddenly funded by Franklin Cuthbert's Eidolon Commission. He's still out there; Cerberus provided payroll records listing Swaggart as a beneficiary of their healthcare policy."

"Oh my God," the host was suddenly convinced of the vast conspiracy. "So you're saying that…"

"That demons do exist," the reverend stated breathily, "And they live in the darkness.

"I've been saying this for years. According to my research, demonic activity has been on the rise in recent years—and has spiked for multi-year periods every millennium. I could cite source after source, but it's moot. Now, though, *science finally agrees*: demons really could be hiding behind every bush!"

Swag cranked the wheel again and found himself plowing through another clogged street. "Entities, you moron," he whispered and turned the volume down, looking for a way through traffic. *"They're not demons, they're entities."*

He swerved away from a picketing group of protestors in front of a police department. They carried signs demanding *Justice for Joshua*. Another piece of tag board had the ghost-buster's logo with a second, opposite slash-run calling for "no ghost-busters." Swag snatched his ringing phone up as he passed a group of arm-band-wearing activists as they burned down a grove of trees; their matching t-shirts read "Diggleton's Army."

"It's Braff," the general barked.

"Yeah! I'm here, General," he swerved out of the way of another car driving the wrong way down his street.

"Did you see the Joshua Video?"

"Part of it, General. In Spanish."

"Listen. I've got about a million fires to put out right now. Some network just put the ECHQ address out for its viewing audience. Things are going to get worse before they get better. Get here as soon as possible—I've got to put everything on lockdown. I'm giving you full security clearance. I need you—and I need you *here*. Now."

"I understand." Swag stepped on the accelerator.

"I'm just saying that I heard the Pope was involved—this conspiracy goes all the way to the top!"

Swag's radio continued puking bad news as the public radio announcers interviewed locals and took calls from its listeners.

"If there're demons under every bush, then I say we burn down everything that grows," one redneck caller drawled. "I don't believe the super-zition, though, that the gov'mint was using some special demon task-force to make people act like terrorists so they could take em out. Everyone knows terrorists already got demons in em—all Muslims do, so the gov'mint don't got no need for it."

As Swag's car crawled through traffic, another mob roved through the street. A handful of young men threw large stones at a bank of stained glass windows on an old Lutheran Church. They shouted obscenities meant for the Pope as if he could somehow hear them—as if the Pope were remotely related to the wholly different denomination. Swag shook his head disgustedly as the men dispersed, looking for whatever other trouble they might be able to cause while they raged against facts they were fully ignorant of.

The dark whispers began to creep through his mind again as he watched them. Their chants grew louder as the rioters drew closer.

Protestors began opening the doors of any vehicles moving slow enough for them to access. One of the men waved a handgun to coerce the occupants into giving up valuables. Traffic crawled to a stop and one of the men tapped menacingly on Swag's window with a rock, demanding his attention. Swag refused to meet his gaze. The whispering reached peak loudness as the stone-wielding man waited just outside his door.

"Hey! Open up!" the man screamed obscenities and Swag tuned his face only enough to trade glances.

Dawning recognition spread on the guys face. "You! You were the guy on the Joshua Video!" The man screamed for his friends. "This is one of those guys from the Eidolon

Committee or whatever!" He turned back and spewed a string of curse words. "Open up—right now!"

Swag shook his head in refusal and the assailant tried to smash the window in with his stone. The window held fast, and his friend came over and pointed the muzzle of his pistol at the window. Swag screamed as the man opened fire. The glass held, but lost some of its transparency as it deflected the bullets. A ricochet sliced a bloody streak across a bystander's neck.

The scientist cranked his wheel and gunned the engine. Diving for cover, members of the mob leapt out of the way as Swag's car plowed right through the mass, no longer caring who he might hit.

NPR broadcast a cacophony of noise as they went live from the site of a riot. Someone with a megaphone cried out with a list of demands and a call for fellow insurrectionists to overthrow the government. The person on the microphone kept insisting one thing. "They should have told us. We've been walking in the dark all this time and *they knew*—that's why I joined Diggleton's Army. It's why I'm down with the militia movement: *they should have told us!*"

#

Jones, the front-end security chief at ECHQ escorted Swag into the packed conference room. Swag arrived late because of the riots. He and Jones both took seats at the meeting for high-ranking personnel which had already begun. The Eidolon Commission's chief officers sat at the front of the room.

Braff nodded as the two found seats. With no small talk the General launched directly into his briefing. "This is bad, folks. Someone committed the highest level of treason by stealing and leaking that footage. Most of it revolves around general ECT operations and Pandora. The Ark project has also been outed, although the facility is currently closed up and set to standby. Director Chu finished it and left for some much-needed R and R a few days ago; he left things set slaved into automated mode. His last words were literally 'Don't worry—the droids can take care of any issues—what could go wrong? It's not like the world's gonna end in the next couple days.'"

The general chuckled incredulously. "But he probably made the right choice—he's logged too many hours without a break and deserves his time off. And we all know this media nightmare isn't going to be anything more than a temporary snafu, right?"

A murmur of assent rippled through the crowd.

Henry Winger stood and addressed them group. "Listen, folks. We've made plans for exactly this sort of thing just in case word got out to the public prematurely. We've planned for mass hysteria and panic—that's why ECHQ was refurbished the way that it was. We're remote, our systems are self-contained—yes even our network, and the building is virtually bomb proof. Not even Cerberus can get in here. We've just got to stick to the plan." The sociologist shrugged. "Our models show that within a few weeks everyone's going to go back to worrying over politics and celebrity divorces." He took his seat again.

Braff nodded his agreement. "To that end, we've kicked Pandora into full active mode. It was already operational, and we've got our techs working to dump the rest of the entities into the containment unit since we heard the news break this morning. That will free up a crap-ton of ECP cells in case worst-case scenarios start to evolve. Jones guarantees that the scanners at the front are fully operational now, even if they've been acting glitchy over this last week."

Jones, seated next to Swag, raised an arm to give a reassuring thumbs-up to that info.

"If any of them things tries to get in here we'll have them stuck inside Cyborg-3 before they even know what hit em!"

The men and women nearly cheered at his promise.

"We've still got quite a crisis, though. We need to identify the security leak and I need to bring some of you in on more details to help us shoulder the burden. As of right now, if your security clearance was below level four consider it elevated. If you did not know the extent of our operations, this means I'm trusting you with high-level government secrets. Some of what we do here is unsavory, but we do it in the interests of protecting our loved ones and the innocent.

"The EC has been working with DHS operatives since our inception in order to cultivate a set of entity assets that could be either weaponized or used as a tool for manipulation. I admit this only under the strictest confidence. We have successfully deployed these assets in a number of missions and thwarted several attempted terror plots by putting murderers behind bars *before* they committed crimes instead of *after*."

He didn't disclose all of the facts—he didn't need to. All of their security footage and log entries from the last few days had been erased. Most staffers could glean that information from the context of the briefing. It was enough, however, to simply reveal their breach of confidentiality. With self-contained systems the footage could not be hacked—there was no remote access. Someone intentionally stole data and gave it to the press.

Donna Loebel raised her hand. "Have you looked into the other civilian scientist, Raymond Lems, as the possible security leak?"

Swag's heart sank at the accusation. He knew it couldn't have been Raymond, but he also knew that Raymond was stuck outside in the anarchy that brewed in the city streets. If he'd been revealed as having any connection to the EC, he would have a target on his head for the Pillar of Fire adherents and whatever Diggleton's Army was.

Braff shook his head. "He never had the clearance allowing him access to this sort of information. Research division did regular, remote scans of all his accounts. He turns up clean, though we know Cerberus made attempts to contact him throughout the last year and pump him for data. We can't determine that he's ever actually given up any classified information, but if he has, it's certainly not related to this." Braff turned his attention back to the crowd.

"My current concern is that Omega Team may have been compromised. Perhaps one of them were turned against us for some reason." He cast a sympathetic gaze at Jones. The security chief's brother was a member of Omega. "The team has also failed to check in for a briefing and has been AWOL now for days which makes them suspect."

Franklin Cuthbert shook his head. "That timing doesn't make sense," he said. "Their last mission concluded successfully, and their absence began days before the stolen Joshua Video took place."

Loebel chimed in, "He's right, General. Your report stated that Brady was enroute here from the Black-Stone facility at the same time as Omega Team's mission. DHS records verify timestamps as we transferred him for the last time."

Braff nodded definitively. "So Omega Team is cleared, of this, at least. If we can spare the resources, we ought to attempt a search in the middle of this PR nightmare. Something happened to them and they're all gone... dead or worse."

Jones raised a hand. "Sir? You're incorrect."

The room fell deathly silent as Braff fixed him in his gaze. "Explain?"

"Agent Scofield came in... several days ago, the evening after the mission you were just talking about."

"You're *sure*?" he asked as he yanked out a tablet and typed in a few commands.

"Absolutely. I remember because it bothered me the next day when I found out that the rest of my brother's team hadn't reported in—I thought Scofield must've been an exception."

Braff nodded, flicking his finger across the touchscreen. "I believe you." He growled, not taking his eyes off the screen, "but I'm not finding any record of Scofield's keycard being swiped at any locks. The system would have logged him if he'd used it anywhere—and to steal that kind of data, he *would have needed it* in order to gain access."

The general continued his scowl. "I'll look into it personally," he vowed. It was their strongest lead. Braff clicked a button and a slide projected onto the screen showing a photo of a man, lips bent into a shouting shape.

"Next order of business, we've got to do something about this lunatic." His fiery eyes attributed to his crazy vibe; his pudgy frame and balding head made him look more like a washed-up weekend warrior than anything else. "If you guys thought that Pillar of Fire group was radical, get a load of Jethro Diggleton, a leader of some kind of religious militia whose even more zealous than the POF guys. He's gone viral and he's bad news."

Raymond paced in his tiny efficiency apartment as the television broadcast the chaos and anarchy as it unfolded. On the one hand, it terrified him to see the backlash as the information leaked about the human tests that the EC had conducted. They also revealed some of the more nasty ethical violations that had been performed on Joshua Brady. On the other hand, this was exactly what megalomaniacal organizations like the EC deserved.

The Eidolon Commission had wormed its way through so many sensitive areas that *some* crumbling of the culture and infrastructure was inevitable. That kind of clandestine influence couldn't be ripped out without some kind of social erosion.

Footage from an online video showed the crazy preacher Jethro Diggleton waving a bible through the air and riling up dissent. He screamed at a crowd of people, "There's a devil in the darkness and hiding in each shadow. There's a demon under every bush—like they are transmitted via trees! You people listen: the child army of almighty God must rise up and defeat this great evil!" Diggleton began shotgunning scripture quotes taken grossly out of context and twisted them to fit his meaning.

The news piece showed a variety of social media memes branded with a Diggleton's Army watermark. Some showed dangerous, homemade ways to create chemical defoliants including a poor-man's Agent Orange. Others called for rallies and protests at specific locations and times for specific purposes—chiefly civil disobedience meant to cripple government facilities and stymie any peace-keeping response.

A marginalized segment showed the Islamic backlash anywhere that significant populations existed. Muslim communities demanded retribution from the government forces and flames lit the backdrop of every scene they broadcast.

Hysteria continued to mount, but didn't look to level off any time soon. Raymond heard the sound of chainsaws outside and the distinct cracking sounds of felling trees.

He felt certain that some kind of grand correction had come at last. Perhaps a civilian oversight council could take over the EC's work. He didn't know what the future would bring or exactly what was needed to fix the problem—but there certainly needed to be less control in the hands of power mongers like Roderick Braff.

Raymond's cell chimed. A text message read, *Cerberus: 2 hours.*

He wondered for a moment what Cerberus could still want with him now that they had given so much information via the media. He only had access to information far less damning than the stuff they had already released to the news networks. Perhaps they intended to interview him and get a first-person account of working with the Eidolon Commission? That might further verify the findings they'd already pushed out on a worldwide scale.

    Raymond shrugged and grabbed his coat. They'd set the date and place weeks ago and he intended to see this thing through.

20

A disgruntled Roderick Braff poured over the surveillance feeds from ECHQ building. He gently rubbed the tender spot he suspected might be a developing ulcer and scanned the view screens which played recently recorded events in super-fast mode. Facial recognition software that the EC plied from various social networking companies catalogued everything and everyone on the feeds.

Braff didn't trust anyone else for this particular task. The EC had a leak somewhere and the General only knew that it wasn't him. He didn't want to alert the rest of the team—and potentially the spy—that he alone possessed a top-secret collection of data backups that Hank Chu installed. Not even the computer running their software and recording systems knew that the covert recording software backed everything up on a remote drive; only Franklin Cuthbert and Roderick Braff knew it existed. The general said a silent thank-you to Cuthbert's paranoia.

The running time stamp scrolled by at lightning speed and the data bank listed everyone by name, title, and ID badge number as the software crunched the raw data of facial symmetry, brow ridge, hairlines, nose size, etc. A name suddenly popped up on the index and caught Braff's attention.

He tapped a hotkey and the recordings slowed to normal time. Braff rewound slightly and watched Sergeant Darren

Scofield walk through the main entry doors to ECHQ. Techs had the scanners broken apart for maintenance at the second checkpoint as they tried to repair them. They'd been going off randomly reporting entity detections when not in use and reading false positives.

Scofield nodded to Jones at the front gate and walked through nonchalantly, almost unnoticeably, sidestepping around the maintenance detail. He momentarily disappeared before another monitor caught him. From the rear, only, the recognition software bounced a polygonal halo around his form, searching for data, and then reverted to the digital ID marking tag that overlaid his form and labeled him as Scofield.

The Sergeant walked up the stairs. A new camera acquired an identity confirmation in the stairwell. Scofield swiped his access card on the top floor where the computer control room housed their data hub. He slipped inside the nexus of the ECHQ which typically remained unstaffed.

High clearance level was needed to get into the control center, and it needed to be accessed so infrequently that it didn't require wasting resources with direct human oversight. It had really been a testament to Chu's skill.

A single surveillance camera watched over the infiltrator as he toggled on a security terminal, hacked the system, and located the bank of video feeds. He inserted a cable and downloaded a massive amount of data, including the Cyborg-3 test videos, to a portable drive and then began deleting huge swaths of data.

That must've been the missing surveillance records and keycard logs. Braff rubbed his chin and watched Scofield exit the room wearing a grin unlike anything he'd ever seen. He was unaware that the sergeant possessed even rudimentary hacking skills.

As the general took one final look at the screen he realized he didn't know if Scofield was afflicted or was a genuine traitor. Perhaps he was working with an activist group such as Cerberus had this been a long gambit? Braff momentarily questioned everything. He only knew that Scofield had been compromised. The time stamp on the feed read approximately ten hours prior to the Joshua Video breaking on the news networks and the internet.

Raymond took a seat in the café and casually picked up the newspaper. He didn't have a mobile device with him again; Raymond remained as paranoid as ever about the government's ability to track him and he'd been careful to drive all around the town in order to establish odd patterns of behavior prior to this meeting.

He looked at the date atop the paper's runner. Today was the day: the anniversary of when they'd made their big breakthrough and gotten their first entity to attach to a lab rat.

After flipping sheets of newsprint back and forth a few moments, he tossed it aside. The papers had been printed too early and they hadn't had anything new to report on regarding the Eidolon Commission; the Joshua Brady Video was still breaking news and they hadn't peeled deeply enough into the onion that was this conspiracy. Journalists unraveled and proved all of Raymond's wild speculations about the EC's villainy as true.

Raymond sighed. Today had been a long day and his evening was likely to get worse. The news networks earlier speculated that martial law might be enforced but the riots and looting seemed to quell as the sun crept closer to the horizon.

The café had mostly emptied as the evening drew nigh, even though a conglomeration of UV grow lamps had been cobbled together in the seating area. A barista made a crude attempt to ward off any entity transmission in the mom-and-pop cafe.

Raymond grinned. The low-tech solution would probably work, for the most part. He assumed the nervous-looking man at the counter was the owner who'd filled in for a wait staff too afraid to stay on the job past dark.

Hearing the shuffle of feet behind him, Raymond turned. His heart plummeted. *I thought I'd been so careful!* He recognized the EC agent who approached and took the seat directly across from the former scientist.

"Happy Anniversary," Agent Scofield said as he leaned forward.

Raymond visibly slumped in defeat. "Are you going to arrest me? How did you find me—how did you know?"

Scofield chuckled. "We made this appointment many weeks ago. As for how I knew the date... that's a whole different story."

Still apprehensive and not wanting to accidentally misread the situation and incriminate himself, Raymond led him, "So you're..."

"Cerberus," Scofield confirmed as he set six gel-cap pills on the table in a neat line.

Raymond was still nervous, but went with it. "I'm not sure what it is that I can provide to you—especially if someone like *you* is already with them. Surely you've got access to a far higher level of clearance than anything I could secure."

"Agreed." He slid a handheld tablet across the table and then picked up a fork. He pierced the coating of each pill so that their contents could be more quickly absorbed. The substance within the capsules oozed out the punctures.

The video and data stolen from ECHQ looped on the device he passed—the same footage played all day by the press. "Who do you think leaked the Joshua Video." Scofield winked. "But you know something about hate and about mutual enemies... like General Braff."

As he spat the word "enemies," Raymond caught something in his eyes—a wild shot of red energy streaked his iris.

"*You're one of them!* Who *are* you?"

Scofield tossed back the ruptured pills and chased them with a glass of water. His voice dropped an octave and took on animalistic traits. "An intelligence far beyond what you can comprehend, mortal. My brothers and I are capable of learning, overcoming handicaps, much like how I defeated the limitations your pitiful engineers devised with Hermes!"

Raymond sat back aghast. He'd worked extensively with the entities, but he'd never sat and had a conversation with one until now! "What do you mean? Did the government use you?"

"They tried—your Eidolon Commission invented a body-trapping field which confined us to hosts of their choosing." Scofield leaned in again. "You must understand, human, we've been here since the beginning—since before the age of man—and we bow to no power but our own."

"What do you want, then, freedom? I cannot help you by allowing you to afflict other people. I don't know anything about their body-lock, or about Hermes; I wouldn't know how to disable it even if I was willing."

"My brothers' plight is moot, and I can leave this body whenever I want—I've evolved past such pitiable concerns. No. I am here to *teach you*." Scofield handed over a file which included nuclear codes, timed satellite strikes, planned defoliant bombs, and new types of bioagents which could attack and kill the oceanic phytoplankton responsible for over half the earth's oxygen.

He scanned the data briefly. "What is this supposed to teach me?"

"Through many thousands of years I've learned something: for my kind to survive—for it to thrive—it requires the eradication of your species. You are going to help me accomplish that."

Raymond looked at him wild-eyed, still fixated on the fact that his hands had acquired nuclear codes and a planet-ending blueprint resilient enough to make a Bond-villain jealous. "I don't understand. You know I won't help you—why give me these?"

Scofield grinned evilly. "Sometimes it is difficult to retain *all* memories, thoughts and skills during a transfer—it weakens with every jump and this data is far too valuable to forget."

With dawning recognition, Raymond leapt to his feet, attempting escape. With lightning-fast reflexes, Scofield snatched the terrified scientist's wrist and refused to let him go. "I'm going to take away everything your partner has ever loved," he hissed. "I too have enemies whom I hate! I will destroy your partner, the one who broke into our world with his terrible, flattening energies!"

Raymond grunted with pain and horror. *"Who are you?"* he asked, suddenly realizing exactly how the entity knew the date of the anniversary. This was no coincidence—his eyes widened in terror.

"You called me *Little Satan*." Scofield wrenched the scientist's hand forward and bit it hard enough to draw blood.

Raymond stood straight and then dusted himself off, shaking the flowing blood from his wounded limb.

A very confused Darren Scofield demanded to know where he was and how he'd gotten there. Raymond merely stared at the agent who grabbed his churning, pained abdomen. No longer possessing the entities super-human resilience, Scofield coughed and then doubled over, spasming violently as he hacked up blood and foam.

Raymond turned and exited the café as the poisoned man screamed with weakening rage, demanding to know what it had done to him.

Braff unstoppered the cork of an old bottle of single-malt and poured a glass of scotch as he picked up the telephone receiver. He briefly shuffled some papers in search of a cigar and remembered that he'd handed it to Chu. Braff sighed uneasily and then dialed the number for his son.

The General waited for the pulsing tones of the dial signal to subside. His son's prerecorded voice invited him to leave a message. Braff had expected that; it had been a long time since his son had returned a call or answered any ring from a government line or restricted number.

Fingering the family photograph he kept on his desk—dating back to when Wanda remained alive—he tossed back a swig of his drink. "Jason. Listen up. I know you don't want to talk to me—but this is important. You need to get up here immediately. Drop everything else and get up here now. The news reports are… it's all much worse than it looks. Hell is about to let loose all over the world; I need you to get into the underground shelter that we've prepared." He briefly ran down the details of Ark I and left instructions on how to avoid the apocalypse. "I know it's been too long since we've spoken… I heard that Sheri left with the kids. This is serious enough that you need to bring them with. Convince them. Force them. Do what you need to." He paused. "I want you to know that… I mean, if you… listen, Jason. Just get up here."

Braff severed the line and hoped that his son would listen to his message in time. He fingered in a code that let him broadcast all throughout the ECHQ building.

"This is General Braff. Until further notice, all personnel are confined to the premises. Call your loved ones and give them directions to the ARK facility if it eases your mind, but until further notice, all persons are to remain on-site. We've got a messed-up planet to fix."

Jessica heard the sharp rapping on her door and stole a glance through her peephole. "Oh my God—Raymond!" she flung the door open to him. "You look like hell," she ribbed him as she leaned in for a long-overdue hug.

Raymond stiffly returned her embrace, almost like a robot.

"What is it? Why are you doing here—not that I'm unhappy to see you, but I thought you'd completely walked out of our lives?"

"I've had…" he searched for the right words as he meandered through her apartment, "a change of heart." Raymond spotted a lanyard and Jessica's crisp, new ECHQ identity card lying on her kitchen table. He lifted it up and dangled it almost accusingly.

"Yeah," she stated sheepishly. "It just came by courier this morning… right in time for the planet to hit the crapper. Can you believe it?"

"Yes."

Jessica sighed; she turned away from him for just a moment and tapped a few keys on her computer. A status bar began loading across the screen as her laptop transferred the encrypted data to the ECHQ database. Most of the data except for her final findings had been sent ahead of her already via a sophisticated, data replicating physical drive that allowed the secondary research team downtown to get their data to ECHQ despite their closed system. It was a one-way street for data transmission, but that hadn't ever mattered. The Cuthbert Research Center didn't share info with the beta facility—it only took it.

"I've got to finish uploading all of my latest research, so I can get it over to the new facility before I relocate." She turned back to her guest as the task processed in the background.

"I don't know *how I feel* about working for them either—not after seeing that video. I don't know if I really want to follow through and work for the company—maybe you've been right all along."

"I'm rarely wrong," he agreed coldly.

"But on the other hand," she digressed, "it's not like I've been doing anything different in the downtown lab's experiments on human subjects."

Raymond wandered through her apartment while Jessica continued rambling on about her thoughts and feelings. He spotted the nearby cage where Horton shuddered and fluffed his cedar shavings.

"I guess, going back to the first hand, if you were still serious, maybe I'd finally have a real reason not to head up to the ECHQ. That is, if your offer to grab a drink still stands? I know it might be unfair to Swag, but it feels like I might already have everything I need right here. Do you still feel the same way?"

Raymond nodded and stepped in towards Jessica. "I do feel that way. Everything I need is right here." His eyes flashed red, shot through with demonic malice. He turned his head so that she couldn't notice.

Jessica stepped forward to embrace Raymond as he slipped the lanyard around her neck and tightened it like a garrote. He snapped it tight as Jessica struggled, choking as she tried to scream with surprise.

She flailed and kicked, trying futilely to call for help. Coldly, Raymond squeezed, trying to snuff the light from her eyes.

Jessica centered herself, pushed the terror far from her mind, and rammed her hip into his midsection. She used it as a fulcrum and judo-flipped him over her body and onto the floor. He snarled with that same afflicted roar she'd heard so any times in her experiments and she realized that Raymond was no longer in control.

Raymond righted himself and launched towards her as she ran for her kitchenette where her cellphone hung in a charging cradle. She reached for it, but her assailant knocked her to the ground.

With the upper hand, Raymond snatched a serrated knife from the butcher block and plunged it into Jessica's midsection. She screamed in torment.

Raymond stabbed her again, and again. He cackled with demonic glee as his repeated efforts splattered long arcs of crimson, macabre art all over the white cabinets. He only stopped once she finally fell still and let her afflicted friend have his murderous way with her.

Covered in blood, Raymond left her limp form crumpled into a heap upon the floor. He pocketed her access card and then stepped over her body to scoop Horton up from his cage.

As if picking up their conversation, Raymond casually repeated, "Everything I need is right here."

21

Swag finally appreciated the security measures Cuthbert demanded for his cars as he parked haphazardly on the curb near Jessica's place. A band of protesters had set a nearby convenience store on fire down the street.

He locked his car and sprinted up the steps to his friend's apartment, careful not to step in the trail of not-so-fresh blood that painted the hallway and stairs of the building. His guts twisted into a knot when he crested the landing and followed the crimson trail back to Jessica's door.

After knocking futilely for minutes a nearby burst of gunfire sent him back to his car. Hoping against hope, Swag followed the trail back outside with every intention of following it.

More gunfire rang in the air as he slid into his drivers' seat and started the car. A barefoot, screaming woman with torn clothing sprinted down the sidewalk as five teens chased her, shouting threats, and grabbing their crotches like stymied characters from A Clockwork Orange.

Swag checked his mirror in order to spin a U-turn and follow the trail when he caught sight of an ambulance speeding down the street with its lights flashing. Another trio of ruffians took aim and shot out the wheels of the passing ambulance; it veered to the side, hit a median, and overturned. The vehicle skidded to a stop and two of the brutes ran after it, guns in hand. Its cache of drugs was their most likely target.

The third gunman looked up and made eye contact with Swag who gripped the wheel. Swag noticed the thug check his ammo and grin.

He bit his lip and put the car in gear. Swag headed back to ECHQ quite certain that there was nothing he could do to help his friend save hope that the blood trail did not belong to her.

#

Doctor Jonas paced through the room and rubbed his chin. The Eidolon Commission's science team sat in the "think tank" and poured over the high points of the data summaries that Jessica Hiddleston had uploaded to their system late last night.

Until very recently, the bulk of their time and efforts in human experiments had been focused on completing Pandora. Hiddleston's findings raised eyebrows.

"Very interesting results," agreed Frey as they poured over the data summaries.

Jonas nodded his head. "The numbers of those with immunity are higher than we thought, but there is still so much more to be learned. Is there any correlation between the morality or religious choices and those who seem to have an acquired immunity? And what about those who seem immune by their nature: those test subjects with genetic, mental deficiencies—where is the line…" Jonas fumbled through the reports. "Genetic mental retardation. What about conditions like onset dementia or Alzheimer's?"

Frey nodded, "Much more research is needed. We will have to ask the researcher."

"We are at least in agreement on that point," Jindal said. "Some people, for reasons not yet known, cannot be afflicted."

"Where is this Hiddleston, anyway?" Hansen asked, slightly irritated. He looked at his watch. The entire team had anxiously waited to meet her.

Jindal piped up, "She should be on her way. I spoke with Swaggart this morning. With the civil unrest and with the rest of the facility on lock-down, he went to pick her up... he insisted it was him since he'd lobbied to bring her on staff."

Hansen blinked as if his brain had just blown a vessel. "What? But he can't do that!"

Jonas merely shook his head. "I thought we'd already established that Swaggart played by different rules than everybody else?"

Everyone knew that Jonas didn't appreciate the civilian's disregard.

Hansen agreed with Jonas. "Swaggart and Hiddleston are assets—valuable ones at that! We can't allow them to go gallivanting out and about while the world descends into some kind of Mad-Max-like setting. Did he take an escort at least?"

Frey shook his head. "His handler was Scofield..." he trailed off. Everyone knew the Sergeant had gone dark.

Hansen muttered a string of colorful profanities in several languages. "They'd better get back here safely," he finally said, as if the alternative would somehow earn them an extra dose of ire. "The world is falling apart out there according to yesterday's reports. By all accounts, it's going to show up on our doorstep at any minute if we don't find a solution. If we can find the common denominator perhaps we can engineer some kind of vaccination. The world needs saving—it needs men like us right now more than it needs Scofields and Braffs."

As if in response to his observation, General Braff's voice boomed over the loudspeaker. "All personnel, please report to your duty stations. We've got incoming civilian protesters. I do believe it's finally hit the fan. Avoid using deadly force, but keep these people *out of our facility*. Cyborg-3 is the most secure location on-site, but we cannot let it be compromised."

The scientists traded glances with each other. Hansen snatched the remote control and activated the flat panel television while Braff continued issuing orders.

He flipped through the news networks which broadcast scenes from the previous night and morning: the world had gone insane. Men wearing crudely spray-painted Diggleton's Army insignias set fire to a forest on the west coast where the arid climate had fanned it with wild abandon; groups overseas overthrew a chemical manufacturing plant and gained access to enough dioxin to wipe out massive swaths of rainforest in the interest of eliminating demonic threats.

A talk-show personality interviewed a guest who claimed to be filled with thousands of demons. Straight-faced, she insisted that humankind was meant to bond with the ethereal beings and everyone needed to partner with the entities and accept their inhabitation as if it was a positive thing. The church of Scientology decried the entities as an example of evil-causing Thetans and purchased large blocks of advertising across various networks.

Another shaky video recording captured a group of protestors demanding the release of Joshua Brady. A mob from Diggleton's Army started a street fight and an entire city block erupted in violence.

Hansen's eyes widened with panic.

Through the intercom, Braff addressed the non-combatant residents of the building. "Non-military personnel, ensure that the loading of Cyborg-3 continues unchecked. We cannot allow the many thousand entities we've managed to confine to be released back into the world—some of the people at our doorstep want nothing less than that! You have one hour: get those things locked away inside Pandora's Box!"

Hansen stopped surfing channels when a network broadcast a helicopter's view of an amassing crowd outside of the familiar surroundings. Protestors surrounded their headquarters. None of the scientists dared utter a word—they'd obviously lost sight of current events while they'd consumed the data within Hiddleston's reports.

The screen switched to a reporter on the ground who interviewed a shirtless man with wild hair and a scraggly beard. A peace-sign hung from his hemp necklace. Although he was far too young to be a hippie and looked more like a liberal arts major, he'd obviously made an attempt to enculturate himself in one faction of the protest movement. "So tell me why you're here?"

Folks in the background held up signs with slogans such as "Entities are people too!" and "EveryTHING deserves the right to live." Others condemned Diggleton and other people on the other edge of the extremist fringes such as the Pillar of Fire.

"You know, man. I just, like, think that everything should be given the chance to live. I mean, come on, man. These things evolved too. Everything in nature is necessary. Like, we all need to just get along."

Another person in the tumultuous crowd leaned forward and hollered into the microphone, "Live and let live! Wooo!" He marched off through the crowd and shouted as if he'd somehow just achieved a mighty victory for humankind.

"You do realize that you're marching against a military base?" The reporter's gaze was as pointed as her question.

"I don't know, man," the student shrugged. "I feel that this is like, a peaceful protest, so I just don't think that the military should do anything about it." The cameraman zoomed in on a guard in the distance as he clutched his rifle with white knuckles.

Hansen turned back to his men and checked his wristwatch. "I think we have a very big problem... and where the heck is Swaggart?"

#

With blank, dead eyes Jessica moved mechanically, methodically. She half-crawled, half-dragged herself along the sidewalk. One hand clutched her bloody midsection and the other propped herself up on her hip. Since sun-up she had managed to slowly inch-worm herself through the hall, down the stairs, and several blocks away from her apartment complex.

Nobody would stop to help. Phone lines were down, which didn't matter because the hospitals had closed, anyway. She grimaced and shuddered with pain as she moved so slowly. Two blocks behind her, an overturned ambulance had been abandoned; it was of no use. A wave of looters had luckily ignored her. So much of mankind had slipped into some kind of corporate, Neanderthalic mind; fortunately for her, raping someone in her bloody and crippled condition still remained distasteful.

Jessica was thankful for that, at least, although she watched more than one woman flee packs of slavering men. She glanced backward to see that the sun had barely risen. Her rust-colored blood trail indicated how slow her pace had been.

A lady walked hurriedly past and Jessica croaked a plea for help, barely able to hold her belly together. The pedestrian ignored her and kept her eyes ahead as if showing compassion might somehow harm her chances of survival as the world descended further into madness. Jessica wanted to cry, but she knew she had to keep it together: every remaining drop of fluid was precious, and she'd already lost too much.

She continued crawling forward—praying for some kind of rescue... wishing that she'd have done a million things differently in her life. Jessica wasn't quite sure where she could even go except to look for Swag. She kept crawling, four inches at a time; each thrust made her relive the knife strokes that nearly killed her last night.

A bus pulled up ahead and emptied its contents onto the corner before resuming its route. Jessica held out hope that the planet struggled to maintain itself in the face of such anarchy. *If the bus lines are running, other things have to still be running, too, right? What's a better sign of order and infrastructure than buses running on schedule?*

Footsteps stomped up ahead. Jessica's head was full of dense fog and pain, but a large man and a small girl ran towards her. She could barely make sense of it all through her failing senses. Suffering through her stupor, Jessica tried to tell them everything that happened to her, pushing words through her bruised and damaged throat. Her shaky, low voice was unfamiliar to even her and she felt quite certain she rambled like a drunk. Jessica's internal filter seemed to have switched off amid the pain.

Her addled brain barely registered the words, "I'm a doctor. I can help."

Oddly enough, it was the little girl who peeled back the bloody, tattered shirt that stuck to her gelled and dirty midsection. She grimaced, but the big man helped lift her up and bore Jessica's weight.

"The hospitals are all closed," the girl said. "We just came from one... more like escaped from it. They actually chained the doors shut—everything was overwhelmed and so overrun that they've just closed up shop to any new patients. We got out this morning, but someone jacked our car."

"I like the bus," the big guy stated.

"It's crazy that they're still running, even, but the mayor is trying to bolster confidence by keeping public transit going."

Jessica stared at them as if dazed, but mostly followed the conversation. She groggily nodded along. "My friend is at the EC. He told me they had doctors and a big shelter—an end of the world bunker. If you can get me there, he won't turn us away..." she trailed off for a few moments like she'd slipped out of consciousness.

Another bus rolled up to the corner where they waited with a small crowd of people. It halted, hissed its air brakes, and the doors parted.

Jessica groaned and frowned as the people jostled and bumped against her, but her saviors did their best to get her aboard and into a seat. "Tell us more about this apocalypse bunker," the girl said in an effort to keep Jessica conscious and communicating.

Rambling on about what she'd heard about the place from Swag, she told them as much as she could remember during waxing bouts of lucidity. "He called it the Ark... like from the Bible story," Jessica smiled. "That's a pretty cute story—as far as children's' apocalypse fables go."

The girl continued asking Jessica questions as they rode. They traveled for quite a while and answers came less and less frequently. The girl did her best to treat and dress the wounds on Jessica's stomach. Her wounds needed serious treatment before they could get the bleeding scientist to her friends.

"At least the bus is headed in the right general direction," Jessica roused and said, slurring her words. "Are you a praying man?" she asked the guy. Jessica was sure they'd introduced themselves by name, but she couldn't find that information in her pain-wracked memory.

"I can pray," he said, looking up from his book. Ironically, the young girl seemed to be the one in charge of the duo. She laid the back of her tiny hand on Jessica's forehead to check her temperature and scowled at the result.

Jessica blinked slowly. "Pray for me? Pray that we get everything we need to survive. I think... I think it's all ending."

"Yes, ma'am," he promised her as she slid into silence. The bus rumbled to a stop at a covered pavilion near the edge of the city.

A young man wearing unkempt hair and a Diggleton's Army t-shirt boarded. He bent low near the driver and held a quiet but animated argument with him. Finally, he yanked an automatic pistol from his duffel bag. He sprayed a quick burst of bullets through the ceiling and took command of the bus.

People screamed and cowered in their seats. They shrank back as the wild-eyed man shouted orders. "We're going to the protest!" he screamed. "Driver, take us to that EC place on the news or I'll start shooting hostages! I swear to Jesus I'll do it!" He leveled his barrel at the seats.

Nodding, but watching the man in his large mirror, the driver complied.

"If you all join the protest, nothing bad will happen to you. But we're not stopping until we get there and we're not going to quit until those species-traitors protesting outside the Eidolon Commission get what's coming to em!"

#

Swag honked his horn and aggressively goosed his gas pedal threatening the throngs of people with car-on-human violence if they didn't make way for him. At the rear of the crowd, the two shirtless twenty-somethings in cargo shorts and Birkenstocks turned and raised their middle fingers nonchalantly as if an offensive gesture could provide some kind of magical barrier of cockiness to protect them from the front bumper of a Volkswagen.

They grinned defiantly as Swag honked his horn. The smugness fell off of their faces as Swag laid off the horn and stepped on the pedal. Eyes wide with sudden gravity they yelped and dove aside, prompting a mass parting of the crowd as the car roared through, clipping one of the cocky youth's leg.

The crowd cursed as he plowed through it; Swag didn't care. He only wanted to get back to ECHQ. He'd left at daybreak when there had only been a large gathering of idiots protesting outside the building. By the time he got back it looked like the entire Burning Man Festival had assembled at the front of the structure.

Protestors' vehicles lined the large parking lot; they'd parked strategically in order to create a bottleneck where they could block traffic at their discretion. Only one road remained on the main route which would allow Swag to park on-site.

Swag seethed; he'd failed to find Jessica. He could only hope the best for her, but his gut assumed the worst: one of his last friends on this planet probably lay dead in the aftermath of the chaos caused by the Joshua Video.

Despite the conditions, Swag drove too fast, letting his emotions dictate the throttle. He reveled slightly in his base human instincts, watching people scatter away from his car as they feared for their safety. A woman with long dreadlocks and flowing clothes refused to move. She stared Swag down as he roared closer. She held her cardboard sign high and accusatorily. "Humans are the real monsters," it read.

She'll move, he thought, charging forward. Swag locked eyes with her as the car shot forward—he suddenly realized that the woman would not move: she was prepared to die on this hill, all for some idiotic pseudo-moral stand. Swag wasn't prepared to kill her for it, and He slammed on his brakes, but too late.

Swag's car screeched and skidded to a halt a couple feet overdue. His front end slammed into the martyr and knocked her backward. She screamed in pain and toppled backwards on broken legs. An angry crowd immediately surrounded her and began throwing bottles, stones, and whatever else they could find towards the scientist's car.

He performed a quick three point turn and plowed across an empty grassy berm and onto a gravel side-road which led to the backup parking lot and helipad a short ways up the hillside—a leftover from the building's days as a hospital. A few of the more rabid protestors chased after Swag for a hundred feet, shaking their fists as the car departed via a less congested route.

Swag slid the transmission into park and scanned the area before exiting. He caught sight of a large crowd of angry men and women approaching on foot in his rear-view mirror. Down the slope near the headquarters, the crowd was thick. As he watched the pulsing crowd below and the approaching group that he'd nearly run over, his mind drummed rhythmically; the dark whisperings that long plagued him vied for attention with an otherworldly gibbering.

The scientist feared he might be unable to get through without incident and, so he fired off a quick text to headquarters—he'd snuck out earlier, but he knew he was too important for the military to abandon over an act of disobedience. Swag hung his head for the long minutes he'd have to wait helplessly. He composed another text—this one to Jessica.

Hope you are OK. Tried stopping by to get you. Come to ECHO if you can. Swag didn't know if civilian networks still operated. His mobile ran on a more efficient military network that Chu promised could still work even in the wake of an EMP burst. The text was meant more for Swag's catharsis than anything else, though, and he knew it.

He sighed, nearly overcome by his raw nerves as he thought of the bloody scene at Jessica's. In desperation, he very nearly stooped to prayer. Instead, he merely whispered, "please be okay," hoping his good thoughts and intentions might somehow influence any potential higher powers and energies that dictated the universe. Swag bit back his emotions and tightening gut; he repeated that same mantra for Raymond, too—still hoping that his friend and partner might somehow come to his senses in the wake of tragedy. Perhaps together they could devise some kind of clever solution and allow Braff and the EC to defuse the panicking public.

A few moments later an armored personnel carrier left the rear of the ECHQ and rumbled towards his position. It kicked up a thick trail of dust as it moved; the crowd gave the armed military vehicle more respect than it did for Swag's Volkswagen.

It parked next to the scientist's car which was surrounded by protesters who hurled insults and threats at his windows. Swag was glad once again for the additional security.

Jones, riding atop the APC, pointed the fifty-caliber roof-mounted gun at the crowd nearest the driver's side door. They grudgingly dispersed and allowed Swag a cushion just large enough to exit the door without threat.

"Good to see you, Doctor," Jones said as Swag closed the locked door behind him. "The General would freak out if he knew you'd gone off the reservation despite such explicit orders last night." He nodded at the civilian, indicating he should get onboard. "Did you at least get what you needed?"

"No," Swag frowned. "I was too late. And I'm running out of friends."

"Understood, Doc. It'll be our secret."

Swag nodded and hopped aboard the APC. Jones barked an order and the vehicle turned a tight circle and returned to base. The crowd of "peaceful protestors" had swelled exponentially. Glancing back to the approach, more buses arrived dumping loads of humanity. A group in the distance sprayed the tree-line with defoliants; behind them, the flora they'd obviously gotten too already had wilted and turned a sickly combination of brown and yellow.

"Diggleton," Jones hissed.

A minute later, their APC pulled past a razor-wire fence behind the building and into the motor-pool. The heavy door slid shut and sealed them in.

# # #

General Braff paced in his second-story office and kept the phone to his ear. A collection of televisions on the far wall each displayed different news networks. Any of those not showing the mass pandemonium around the world instead displayed live feeds of the growing crowd on the EC's doorstep. A mini-window showed looped clips from the Joshua Video, villainizing the Eidolon Commission by showing the worst parts of the afflictions they exposed the criminal to—the narrative played heavily on the accusation that the government somehow controlled the entities and was directly responsible for any number of worldwide ills.

"I really need you here, Hank," the General said.

"I know—I know," Hank said via encrypted phone. "I'm trying to get my family together, so we can weather this storm in the Ark. I just want to wait a couple days in case the chaos dies down, first."

"Nonsense!" Braff promised, "The roads might not be safe, but I'll send a chopper for you in the morning."

"Um, it's not the trip that worries me," Hank Chu hedged. "I'm more concerned with bringing them straight into the powder keg that has developed outside ECHQ."

"I understand," Braff assured him. "But we really do have the situation under control."

"I'm sure you do. We'll come straight away if the fervor dulls any. In the meantime, Ark I should be fully operational. The supplies are all onsite, even if unorganized, and the drones should be mostly up to task; there're just a few little glitches to work out of the automation. Even with just a skeleton crew the Ark should be functional and self-sufficient… it's up to you and the EC whether or not to enact the preservation protocols and call in the 'guest-list.'"

"Yeah," Braff rhythmically drummed his fingers on his desk as he thought deeply on the matter. "That's the quandary right now…" he trailed off and watched live feeds of a world caught on fire.

A knock on the door interrupted the reverie. Braff looked up. "Give me a moment, Hank." Braff pressed a button to mute the line.

"Can I help you, Lieutenant Jonas? Is everything alright with Pandora?" a chord of worry rang in the general's his voice.

"No sir," the enlisted scientist replied stiffly. "I just thought it was my duty to report in on Doctor Swaggart."

"What's wrong with Swag?" Worry permeated his voice.

"I'm concerned," Jonas said, trying ineffectively to not sound like a tattletale. "He broke the rules and left HQ this morning but hasn't reported back yet. May I come in?"

#

"Thanks again, guys," Swag stated as they arrived at the front end of the security check-point area where Jones was stationed. "I really owe you one."

He looked up at the crowded mass that pressed against the glassine wall. A line of military enforcers stood posted every ten feet behind barricades. They held their weapons at the ready.

Swag's eyes caught sight of the familiar face. He and Raymond locked eyes, acknowledging each other.

Raymond waved a security badge in front of the first wave of over-taxed soldiers as he glowered at the scientist and Agent Jones. The sentries motioned him forward and let him scan his card at the door which unlocked and allowed him entry.

"I know him," Swag confirmed to Jones as Raymond walked ahead towards the second checkpoint: a set of scanning posts with built-in EMF detection sensors.

"That's funny," Jones mumbled as he glanced at the security screen. "I always thought Jessica was a girl's name."

"What?" Swag exclaimed even as Raymond stepped brazenly through the scanner area. Amber lights strobed on their posts and shrill klaxons erupted in the entry hall.

Sentries who stood guard nearby whirled around and leveled their rifles as Raymond continued his purposed, intentional walk, still staring at Swag. His eyes had contracted to pinpricks with bloodshot edges wrought with malevolence and hate.

Raymond sneered at Swag as the dawning recognition set upon the scientist's face. The afflicted scientist growled at the guards who rushed towards him and rammed an arm inside his jacket pocket threateningly as if he had a concealed weapon on his body.

"No!" Swag screamed, even as the security officers opened fire on his afflicted friend. Shot after shot rang out as each bullet from the highly-trained officers found their mark in Swag's friend.

Raymond's torso erupted with gore and carnage; bloody holes riddled his body which collapsed to the floor. Swag fell to his knees as the ammunition tore his friend's body apart.

The crowd outside pounded on the windows and hurled accusations. Mobile phones held high above captured the incident and the dissenters surged forward. The protest reached a fever pitch and verged on becoming a riot as word of the event rippled through the crowd.

Tearfully, Swag looked up just in time to spot the lab rat crawl out of Raymond's pant-leg and hurried away. "It's him! The entity," he yelled as the response team rushed to Raymond's corpse with drawn GBs and an EMF scanner.

The first agent on the scene shook his head in disagreement as he scanned around the body searching for entity signatures. "Afraid you're wrong, doctor. There's no sign of an entity anywhere in here."

"No! In the rat—he's in Horton!" he yelled, crawling to his knees and forcing his way into the bloody scene, but the rat was nowhere to be found and the surging crowd began overwhelming the blockades, demanding the team's attention.

The agent shrugged, discreetly scanning Swag, just in case. "Sorry, Doc. I don't know what you saw, but there's nothing here."

Both men jumped to attention as a loud crack echoed at the doorway. Someone had thrown a lawn-chair against the glassine window. "Murderers!" someone in the crowd cried.

An officer bent over Raymond's body and pressed two fingers against his carotid artery. "Someone get this man up to the infirmary!"

"My god," another gasped. Blood coated the floor around the body. "Nobody could have lived through this—his will to live must be…"

The drums and voices began again between Swag's ears; they overrode the concern that he felt for his friend—maybe his only friend left in the world. "Listen to me," Swag interrupted as two men hurried over with a stretcher. "We've got to find and collect that entity!" He reached out his hand and beckoned for the soldier's Baconator.

#

"I'm sorry Hank," Braff said. "I'm going to have to call you back." He hung up and turned his attention to Jonas.

The scientist lifted his hand, just about to launch into some kind of report against Swag when he shrieked with pain. Hopping on one leg he shook off the rodent that had latched onto his ankle with its teeth, flinging the blood-stained white rat into the corner of the office.

Jonas turned and grinned maniacally at Braff. He growled with a monstrous, guttural rumble.

Braff narrowed his eyes to slits at the afflicted scientist. "There you are!" he murmured, snatching his GB from his waistband. "Now I've got you!"

Jonas leapt backwards and out of the range of the device. He scooped up a chair and hurled it towards the General, knocking the capture equipment from his hand. The afflicted scientist charged forward and tried to tackle him.

Braff caught him in a headlock while splaying his legs for support. The old dog threw a flurry of blows and rained fists onto the scientist's head before finally thrusting a knee upward into Jonas's face.

With a busted nose, the possessed scientist careened backwards into the wall. He stumbled to his feet and wiped the stream of blood from his upper lip as Braff hurried closer to where his GB had landed. Before he could bend down to retrieve it, the enemy snarled and made a second attempt.

Again Braff caught him. He relentlessly beat the scientist's face for the second time when the crack of a handgun erupted; intense pain tore through Braff's body. He stiffened and staggered backwards, releasing his headlock.

While the General snatched his enemy, Jonas used the vantage to seize Braff's sidearm and shoot him in the belly. The afflicted scientist fired two more shots into the industrial window. At the close distance, the bullets proved force enough to shatter the thick panes, but barely.

Jonas snatched Braff's security ID and keys and then unceremoniously kicked him out the window where the General plummeted to ground below. Stepping out and into the hallway, Jonas, under Little Satan's guidance, found the maintenance closet and snatched a can of spray paint and a sheet-sized drop cloth.

With a grin he spray-painted a message to the unwitting troops below on the sheet. "Help us—we're held against our will!" The demoniac hung the banner from the second-story window bank even as his human ears picked up the sounds of the zealous protestors taking up a call for action when they spotted it.

He scooped up the old rat from the office floor and departed. Turning a corner into the hallway, Little Satan flipped Braff's security card between his fingers with excitement. He swiped the access card to the control nexus where he'd recently visited as the late Agent Scofield.

Pulling the wheeled chair over to a station in the central hub he cracked his knuckles and dug deep within himself to find the snippets of past lives he had stolen from previous victims. He keyed in a bunch of keystrokes and hacked into Chu's system for a second time.

With a Grinch-like grin and a violent tap of the Enter button he deactivated every electronic lock and security gate within the Cuthbert Research Center. He tapped on the keys and entered more commands.

Moments later a cascade of tiles opened into the most sensitive parts of the US government's operations. He typed with uncanny precision and summoned the stolen nuclear secrets with eidetic recall.

A few deft keystrokes later, the computer screens flickered with red warnings. Banks of screens around the control nexus switched to targeting maps and trajectory arcs as nuclear missiles surged from their underground, automated berths, and launched skyward where they raced towards targets across the globe.

Nukes belched from the ground. Bombs fell from satellites. Experimental lasers and death technology from every country's most brilliant and viciously destructive minds surged into activation all at once.

The beast grinned. Soon, atomic fire and fallout would scrape the bulk of Earth's oxygen-creating vegetation clean from the map. Low flying missiles detonated over oceanic swaths of phytoplankton promising to sterilize the waters of their presence for years. Nuclear fire raced towards massive tracts of rain forest which would soon burn unchecked.

Jonas—Little Satan—kicked the chair backwards and stroked the little rodent's head. Horton perched on the mad scientist's shoulder, riding atop of the white lab coat splattered with blood stains from both the General and from Jonas. The afflicted scientist headed towards his next objective.

###

Camera crews broadcasting via satellite uplinks streamed in alongside the protestors who pushed their way inside the EC building. With panicked looks, the soldiers pointed their weapons at protester after protester, unsure of what to do. They remembered Braff's last briefing when he instructed them to avoid civilian casualties.

"Stand down! Stand down!" Jones shouted to the men as he dropped the impotent phone receiver. Unable to reach Braff, he was in charge now, but he intended to minimize the damage if possible. Live video footage of a US military force mowing down protesters would not reflect well on the EC.

"Fall back and protect the containment area," he barked, knowing that it would remain secure. Its doors were held shut by old-fashioned mechanical locks instead of the fancy electronic systems which had just failed and opened to the general public.

The amber lights and warning klaxons from the entity detector intermittently signaled the presence of afflicted humans amid the throngs of protestors as they poured through the gates. With so many people, it was difficult to identify which ones were carriers and it was impossible to do anything about it.

"You've got to find the rat—Little Satan!" Swag still screamed at Jones as he pushed his way through the crowd. "He's the one behind all of this!"

Jones shoved his way forward and pressed a handgun into Swag's palm. He grabbed his own weapon and backpedaled towards the lower level access doors. "I've got too much going on right now to worry about one missing entity!" He pointed to the GB in Swag's other hand. "You've gotta figure it out on your own, doc."

22

Michelle looked over at Ricky. He stared down into his joke book and focused on the print as if this were any normal bus-ride rather than a trip into the mouth of hell; Ricky's lips moved as he read the words silently. Her brother sat next to the window where he held the wounded blonde, Jessica Hiddleston, in the crook of his arm. A puddle of blood had dripped and pooled beneath their seats.

Ricky caught sight of her watching him from the corner of his eyes. "What? Take a picture. It will last longer," he laughed.

She smiled blandly and gave him a courtesy chuckle. Michelle almost had to stand in order to see over the top of the seats and glimpse their kidnapper. She quickly sank back down when he turned to look at his passengers. "Ricky. I want you to make sure that you stay by my side all the time, okay? Even if things get really scary, I want you to follow me."

"But what if they get *too* scary?" Ricky speculated. "Like, worse than PG-13 scary?"

"Even then. Promise me. If we're not moving, you can read your book, but if I go you've got to close your book and follow right behind me. Understand?"

Ricky nodded. "Okay. I promise." He offered his little finger for her to commit him to a "pinky swear."

Michelle hooked her finger around his and shook it. She leaned over Jessica and gave him a quick hug and then took the woman's wrist and searched for a pulse. There was none, as she'd guessed. Michelle frowned—Jessica must've bled out.

"Here's our plan, Ricky," she whispered as the gun toting maniac stood to brace himself against the sharp corner the bus rounded as it entered the EC grounds; someone had vandalized the sign on the corner which labeled the area as *Private Property – Cuthbert Research Center* with vulgar graffiti. "As soon as we can get off of this bus we are going to make a run for the shelter that the nice lady told us about, okay? It's the only place where we can be safe."

"Is she coming with us?" Ricky asked in his most concerned voice. His volume matched his sister's whisper.

"No, Ricky, I'm sorry. She fell asleep and didn't want us to wake her. She'll come when she's ready, okay?"

Ricky looked at her as if she'd talked down to him. "I know what it means when someone is dead, Michelle. If she died you can tell me."

Michelle looked him in the eyes and her face softened. She'd never realized how grown up he really was. She bit her lip, "You're right. I'm sorry."

"So she's dead?"

Michelle nodded.

Ricky's face looked pained. He curled up his book and set it on the free space at his lap. Gently brushing the hair from her face, he leaned down and gently kissed her forehead. "It'll be okay. She's in Heaven now."

With a melancholy smile Michelle squeezed her brother's hand.

He stared off into the distance for several long moments and Michelle rested her head on his shoulder, enjoying the moment. "Michelle?"

"Yes, Ricky?"

"I think I want to be an archaeologist. You know, for a job... like Indiana Jones."

She grinned at his constant optimism. Michelle had just introduced her brother to the film a few days prior. He'd obviously been enamored. "You'd make a fine archaeologist, Ricky."

The bus decelerated as it crested a hilltop and overlooked the burgeoning crowd at the end of the long driveway. "Faster," their captor in the Diggleton's Army shirt commanded. He prodded the driver's back with the gun's muzzle to emphasize the point.

Slipping over the edge of the fulcrum point in the road the bus picked up speed and careened towards the parking lot. In the distance, a set of tire tracks tore up the grass where some idiot had veered off the road, up a hill, and cut around the parking lot.

Their captor picked up the handheld controller for the PA speaker. "Ladies and gentlemen, we've arrived at our final destination and are about to make a point! These traitors to the species need to be taught a lesson. If you're not with humanity, then you're against it—and there's only one punishment for treason!"

The driver took his foot off the accelerator as they approached the bottleneck. The crowd ahead seemed to move as one, trickling towards the building at the base of the hill, pushing its way inside.

"I didn't tell you to slow down. I said to gun it!" He jabbed his weapon into the driver's back.

"But we'll hit them."

"That's the point! Either you ram them and take out as many as you can, or I'll shoot you in the back of your little, bald head!"

The driver looked up and into the faces of each passenger on his bus, speeding up as he did so, buying just enough time to say goodbye with his eyes and apologize for what he planned to do. "I won't have any part in this madness!" He slammed on his brakes just before they arrived at the edge of the crowd.

Enraged, their captor blasted a round through the rear of the driver's skull. He slumped over and fell aside, hooking the wheel with his limp arm. The dead weight of the body pushed on the accelerator and the long vehicle raced ahead while turning a sharp, elliptic arc.

The gunman cackled with glee. Passengers screamed, and the crowd outside shrieked in terror as the deathbus mowed protestors down from behind.

Finally, at the apex of the terrible ride, the tires gave out under the jackknife turn; the bus toppled and rolled, crushing demonstrators even as they fled for their lives. The murderer at the front of the bus fell forward as the transit vehicle bucked and jerked. His head crashed through the window and crushed like a grape when the tipping vehicle rolled over on it.

The vehicle skidded to a stop and Michelle righted herself while she tugged on Ricky's hand. He struggled to get to his feet. Abject terror was evident in his eyes and blood trickled down his forehead, but he grabbed his joke-book and followed obediently. Her eyes spotted a worn path leading up the steep slope of the hillside. "Come on! We've got to get out of here!"

Gasping for breath where he lay busted on the curb below his office window Roderick Braff stared up into the sky as he returned to consciousness with a ragged cough and a splutter of blood. The edges of his vision spotted the billowing, skyward streaks of nukes launching from silos on the horizon. He knew there were missiles stored about ninety miles west of ECHQ.

Braff's ragged breath came in deep, unhealthy chortles. It took all of his mental energy for the slightest movements. He suspected he had a broken back and likely a punctured lung; every move risked paralysis, but the risks were necessary.

He crawled into a seated position as the glass crunched under his body; the crowd moved slowly past him and into the building as the general pulled his cracked cellphone from a pocket. Miraculously, it still worked. With great pain he thumbed in the code he'd committed to memory.

It dialed and then connected to an open line. On the other end he heard screaming and pandemonium.

"Hello?" he coughed. "Hello? This is General Roderick Braff, confirmation code eight, seven, one, zero, alpha. We have to order full evacuation and institute the Ark I protocols immediately! The entities have launched our nukes. Mister President?" Only silence greeted him, though Braff had the dread sense that someone still listened on the other end of the channel.

"Hello?" He asked again. "Is someone there? Who's there?"

A few tense seconds of silence followed. Finally, a raspy, low voice hissed a response. "We are Legion." The afflicted person severed the line.

Braff's heart sank for a few moments as his mind entered a tailspin of despair. His heart hardened in his broken body when he thought of Wanda and Jason, their only son. He had to throw down this threat *for them*—he had to do it so his son's world could survive.

With steely resolve he tapped a few new commands into his barely working mobile device and opened a specialized app Hank Chu had built for him. Logging in with the thumbprint scanner General Braff took over the national Emergency Broadcast System.

He identified himself to the listening public: whoever remained alive enough out there to hear it and respond. "You may have seen the news about the Eidolon Commission. As one of the chairmen, I promise you that we only intended good for the world. You may have also seen the parts about a massive shelter we built in the mountainside: all of that is true. The bunker is real. We call it the Ark and I urge you to get to it as soon as possible. The main gate has a filtration system: it scans residents for the presence of entities and it can automatically quarantine the infected. If you're driving a bus, in a car, or can somehow get to the Ark, I urge you to do so—and do it now!"

Braff paused long enough to lick his lips. "I don't know if you've looked to the sky. I don't know if anyone out there is listening or if the news is still even broadcasting, but America's nuclear arsenal has just been fired by enemies. The President and Joint Chiefs have been compromised by entities. Get to the bunkers. Don't let today be humanity's Extinction Day.

"This is General Roderick Braff signing off. And Jason— my son, if you're listening to this, please know that I'm sorry... for everything." One thought gave him slight consolation: if this was the end, at least it would finally destroy every rag-headed Jihadi-John on the planet and his wife would finally be avenged.

His finger slipped off the digital button and the shrill emergency broadcast tone took over to signal the end of the alert. Braff coughed up a bloody wad of phlegm and let the busted phone fall from his grasp.

#

Jonas, steered by Little Satan walked a lazy path through the hallway while humming the melody to Sinatra's *My Way*. He twirled the keys he'd stolen from Braff on his index finger and rammed one into a door that led to the second-floor armory.

The doors opened, and two banks of the massive arsenal spread before the puppet master. Rifles, pistols, grenades, and all manner of military-grade weaponry covered one wall. The opposite wall sported hanging hooks to stow the EC's stock of BCnTRs; a cubby-holed wall contained a bulk supply of ECP cells meant for imprisoning Little Satan and his brothers.

He sneered at the weapons of their warfare and snatched a handful of C4 charges. After stabbing the detonators into the explosive lumps the devious shadow lord exited the room and renewed his tune. Little Satan kicked his way through the doors to the stairwell and began to descend towards the sounds of the writhing masses involved in the protest.

Jamming another key into the large door, Little Satan peered through the tiny window at Agent Jones who desperately tried to maintain control of the situation on the other side of the locked door. With a deviant grin he twisted the key and then busted it off inside the lock's tumblers, rendering it permanently unlocked. He flung the doors wide and led the slow descent towards the basement level.

Braff's voice crackled on the loudspeaker, but the thrumming, chanting protest songs of the crowd easily drowned it out. Nobody could hear his announcement. As the crowd pulsed forward, sweeping Jones and the other forces along in its tide, Little Satan squeezed the trigger button on his detonator. Shaking the building violently, the entity capture equipment melted into slag in the room above. The lights flickered, and the speaker system shorted out, silencing the General's plea for evacuation.

The crowd continued moving, following Jonas downward without hesitation, taking up a protest-chant in time with the marching rhythm. Little Satan smiled at the irony of it. The demonic pied-piper was like a new Moses leading humanity's new, fallen Exodus.

He steered them every step of the way until they arrived at the bottom stair. With a final shove, he pushed open the doors to Pandora's Box: Cyborg-3. The containment system sat alone in the basement as a bastion of human arrogance-- an unbroken Ozymandian monument.

The afflicted doctor grinned as the remaining military tried vainly to get ahead of the crowd. He would not be denied—they would never guess that Jonas had been compromised.

General Braff's emergency message kicked in on the ECHQ's loudspeakers. The crowd ignored it wholesale, as if they couldn't even hear the pleading tone in his voice. Swag had never heard his voice take quite such a quality.

Half-way through the announcement the building shook and the speakers failed.

The scientist pushed against the crowd and managed to squeeze between a number of idiots with their cell-phones out and switched to video capture mode. Swag scowled at them and their all-consuming interest in recording the moments they created while refusing to think of the repercussions made at the expense of lives lived via social media.

Maybe we deserve for this to happen! He thought. Darwin might have agreed, but it still felt wrong according to the morals his parents had so diligently instilled within him.

Swag slipped past another crowd. The amber lights flashed behind him and the warning klaxons indicated more afflicted persons slipping through with the crowd. Swag's hand grasped his Gadarene Baconator, but there was nothing he could do at this point except to follow Braff's evacuation order. Ark I was the best hope for the species at this point.

Busting free from the flow of the human traffic, the scientist scrambled to the edge of the building and sprinted towards an abandoned UTV cart. The derelict had been covered in spray-painted, anti-government slogans and curse words. He tried to slip into the driver's seat when a snarling, slobbering madman clubbed him from behind.

Swag whirled and rolled across the ground, barely managing to evade another pounce by the afflicted man who swung a gnarled tree-branch. He shook off the pain and ducked under another potential clubbing when he recognized the man. Swag had seen him countless times in photographs.

Jason Braff chucked the branch at Swag who he reached for his GB with one hand and pistol with another. His stick clubbed the scientist in the face.

Swag's nose sprang a bloody leak; the GB and pistol both fell from his hands as Jason followed the blow up and tackled him. As the afflicted man tried to grab and choke the life from Swag's body, the scientist reached vainly for the loose Baconator. His fingers clutched nothing but dirt wherever he reached.

The strong fingers of the afflicted one finally found Swag's throat and clamped down like a vise. Swag groaned and gasped; his eyes swam with black and his hand continued searching for the lost GB. *Dear God—let me find the damned thing!* his mental boycott slipped as the demoniac very nearly choked the remaining life from his body.

Suddenly, his hand closed around the weapon. Swag snatched it up and clicked the activator button. The electronic field ripped the entity from Jason Braff and confined it within the ECP.

Jason fell over, exhausted and disoriented. Swag gasped for air and scrambled backwards. He tossed the device aside; it was useless without a fresh ECP and he didn't know where he'd be able to find one.

Huffing and puffing, Jason thanked Swag. He tried to explain. "I got a call from my father, the General. I came when I heard how worried he was… I came even though my estranged wife refused to come with the kids. I don't know what happened, but as soon as I got here a protestor spat in my eyes—and then I woke up and was choking you to death! I'm sorry—I don't understand what's happening!"

Swag waived his apology off. "Don't worry about it right now. I worked closely with your father." He pointed to the cart. "Get in. He'd kill me if I left you behind."

They little cart wormed its way up the hills on the back route to the Ark. They passed a large number of strangers listening to General Braff's repeating audio loop playing on emergency radios. The cart zipped by and Swag pointed to the stragglers making the climb. "They're all heading the wrong way! The doors are on the other side."

"Will they make it all the way around if we tell them where to go?"

Swag mulled it over in his mind "No," he finally said. After skirting the steep edge of the sheer cliff face that plummeted into a ravine the vehicle rolled to a stop. He pushed the handgun into Jason's grip. "Do you know how to use that?"

"Are you kidding me? Roderick Braff was my father; of course I do."

"Good," he swung his legs out of the cart and moved towards the back service doors to Ark I. "You need to check their eyes. You'll be able to tell when one of them isn't right. Only let them come one at a time. Shoot them if you have to—there're no sensors on these doors and only I have the access code."

"Shoot them for disobedience?"

Swag nodded solemnly. He kept his voice low, "If they riot it's all over."

They leapt out of the cart and Jason nodded an acknowledgment. Swag ran and accessed rear door thirteen where he punched in Chu's secret, numeric password and slipped inside the airlock. He could let individuals access the Ark as he double checked the refugees.

The first person met up with Jason. At his command, she pulled down her eyelids, so he could better look at them.

Jason waved her forward and she approached the Ark's back door as quickly as her legs carried her.

23

Swag peered into the Asian woman's eyes and looked for some kind of sign that she might be afflicted. Finally, he let the nervous woman pass. As the hatch hissed and unsealed the lock released. Swag tapped a few commands on a nearby service droid that had been powered-down. It came off standby and followed Swag's orders. Its input screen switched over to display mode.

The door cycled and admitted another person as the automaton's feeds connected to both the ECHQ's security system and the cameras near the front entry of Ark I. A handful of soldiers hurried towards the mouth of the great facility and set up a guard station; the General's broad call would undoubtedly attract both good and bad attention.

A small wave of humanity rushed forward and into the open bay doors. Guide rails split people up individually and separated them like cattle. Automated EMF scanners performed an analysis on each and then either opened to release the person into the Ark or detained them. In the few seconds since the system powered up Swag hadn't seen the alert system detect any afflicted, but he knew what would happen if it did; the pen would lock down and the floor would open, ejecting them down a large, steep chute which eventually dumped into the ravine bed far away.

The scientist checked the next prospect at the door. His video switched from a large man and small girl grudgingly releasing clasped hands in order to enter the sensor pens. The Cuthbert Center's basement came onscreen showing Cyborg-3 surrounded by protestors.

Swag looked back to Jason and saw him trying to keep the snaking line of people composed in an orderly fashion. The line kiltered at an askew angle as people tried to get a view of how close they remained from the front.

Jason dealt with the anxious commotion at the front of the line and couldn't see the trouble coming. Swag banged on the door and yelled, but he couldn't get his partner's attention—he could only watch as a man ran up the hill at a full sprint and headed directly towards Jason Braff.

With wild, flailing motions so often associated with the movements of people afflicted by low ranking entities on the Jonas Scale, he came. The wild-man plowed through a middle-aged couple and clobbered Jason with a ramming shoulder.

The line erupted in a frenzy and every man and woman bolted for the door, clogging it up and prohibiting Swag from opening the door to help his friend's son. He could barely see over the clamoring throng as they crushed themselves against the door and beat their fists upon the locked portal.

Jason fired a burst of rounds into his attacker; the gunshots spurred the crowd to even more urgency. The afflicted one shrugged off the non-vital wounds and wrestled the gun from the general's son.

Swag crawled halfway atop the wheeled automaton, so he could see above the crowd. He gained just enough elevation to spot the attacker hurling Jason's bloodied body over the edge of the cliff before whirling to fix the helpless, trapped multitude in his gaze.

Turning away, Swag took a firmer grip on the droid and ordered it to report in at the Ark's operational hub at top speed. Passing the dozen or so refugees he'd been able to admit into the facility, his robotic ferry zipped away. Swag couldn't bring himself to look backwards.

#

Little Satan drew upon the knowledge embedded within his host and meandered towards the Cyborg-3 control kiosk while still maintaining the disguise that was Jonas's body. He'd taken his host mostly out of convenience but reveled in the man's insecurities, knowledge, and deeply-rooted jealous ambition.

Jonas stepped between the huddled protestors who'd begun seating themselves cross-legged and chanting, "Peace for Joshua. Peace for Joshua." The gleaming, stainless steel container towered over the mass of bodies like a gleaming idol of some entombed god. Its surface was only marred by the ruddy, Krylon tag, "C3."

Still, people trickled in and found seats on the floor, eager to be a part of what they rightly assumed would be a historically momentous occasion. The faint glow of cellphone LCD screens lit the floor-sitters like decorative Christmas lights marking the coming of some new messiah.

The only ones who remained standing were the actual, legitimate newscasters who broadcast the scene live. Commentators tried providing reverently whispered observations promoting their specific brand of social justice as if they'd somehow done the entire world a favor by televising the events.

All eyes seemed to turn to the scientist with his blood splattered lab coat. They quickened the mantra and increased their volume as if they somehow influenced the EC scientist to do their bidding. "Peace for Joshua! Peace for Joshua!"

#

After activating the central systems hub in the operations center, Swag powered up the main console and input his—Hank's—passcode. A popup box opened and asked if the user wanted to activate the Proclamation Network. Swag had no idea what that was and exited out of it while pulling up the main OS.

A litany of feeds from all across the media networks and from the private cameras posted around the EC's properties came online, feeding the operations hub with data. The enormous banks of television displays reacted to the viewer. Swag toggled the audio controls to determine which channel's sound played.

Several channels had gone offline. Many of the smaller networks looped the same pirate feed: Jethro Diggleton screaming hateful rhetoric into his microphone. An anchor for the BBC reported on the worldwide attack by Cerberus. The clandestine group of hackers were systematically taking down media broadcasts and replacing it with video or audio of Diggleton. Even internet podcasts and news services were overrun by software that rewrote and replaced the original ensuring that everybody heard the preacher's message.

Swag scowled—he already knew enough about Diggleton to dislike him. The man was an idiot, and not for the usual arguments Swag had against religious figures.

A regional newscast flickered on screen and the Diggleton's feed replaced it. "We've got to do everything we can to rise up as one species, as one army, and show these demonic creatures who is boss. There are no Republicans, no Democrats, no Methodists or Lutherans—there is only Diggleton's Army!"

The crowd surrounding him at the rally cheered and he launched into a diatribe on how the outbreak of demonization was God's punishment upon the Earth for its willingness to turn its back upon all the prophets who had come before, including Diggleton who had heard the voice of God: and it told him to raise up an army to throw down everything he called wicked—to lay waste to any known Muslims or so-called women's health centers.

Swag glanced to the side where another news service reported on the hackers' feed. An inset video showed a burning abortion center followed by the execution of a local Imam by men wearing Diggleton's Army shirts.

Jethro Diggleton whirled and turned with his microphone as charismatic as a snake oil salesman. Spit flecked off of his microphone and the camera panned to catch a quick shot of Diggleton's secretary seated nearest him.

Swag frowned when he saw her. He knew just enough about the controversial preacher to have heard about the scandals, cover-ups, and rumors involving infidelity with the secretary and multi-level financial scams.

She was a gorgeous specimen by any account—but Swag wasn't looking at her manicured and sculpted body. He was looking at her eyes. They glinted just enough and for only a moment, but Swag was an expert in his field. He knew that the woman was afflicted.

The world had gone mad—and the entities had engineered it from the beginning.

#

With a grin, Little Satan took his place at the console and typed in Jonas's access code. The gleaming containment unit billowed steam and split down the middle. The C and 3 parted like a divide in the Red Sea. It slowly separated, and the pod opened to reveal the condemned Joshua Brady bound and gagged in corded, steel restraints. To counteract the massive strength boost the affliction imbued in him, his hands had been bolted to the interior frame. A metal plate pierced his hands and feet to hold him within like some kind of futuristic crucifix machine devised by mad science.

A collective gasp rippled through the audience, followed by a cathartic wave of accomplishment. Newscasters gushed about the protestors' accomplishment in the EC basement. A falsely positive emotion spread through the crowd like a contagion.

Little Satan turned his head and surveyed the scene. And then Joshua Brady's head snapped to attention. Even through his plastic face shield the crowd could see his baleful, burning eyes.

The front row gasped as the prisoner glared at them. His mouth-gag muffled a pained roar as he pushed against the restraints. Brady began to thrash and tear against them. The newscasters fell silent as the human component of Cyborg-3 twisted his head and bit a hole through his own cheek in order free his demonic snarl. The banshee shriek filled the room and the protesters shifted nervously. Some at the back crept to their feet.

In a feat of superhuman strength, Joshua Brady tore one arm free. Steel cables frayed and snapped. Flesh tore free from the human body and Brady burst out of the holding chamber, leaving a severed left hand still bolted within.

He ripped the spit-proof face gear off of his head and freed his body of the final restraints. Brady took one look at the silenced, expectant crowd and then pounced into it.

A hemp-sandaled college student shrieked as the bloody, monstrous creature snapped him up and peeled the man's lower mandible from his face like it was nothing. Brady vomited down his victim's throat hole, filling him with demons before flinging him aside.

Brady swung his bloody stump-arm like a club, flinging hot blood into the stupefied faces of the front row. Wherever the blood met mucus membranes those persons began to growl, afflicted by the legions.

The front line turned on the men and women behind them. They ripped apart their human peers with tooth and claw, snapping through bone and skin with predatory ease.

Bodily fluids sprayed everywhere. The first, jawless victim staggered to his feet with contorted movements and launched himself at the human crowd.

Little Satan watched over the scene with eager, hungry eyes. Finally, the dread recognition of what had happened set in on the crowd and it turned to flee. The congested hallway remained stuffed with bodies; protesters still pushed forward, trying to get downstairs and witness the promised historical hallmark.

The raging, ecstatic violence of afflicted legions overwhelmed the middle ground and the infected ones quickly overtook those with enough sense to flee. Screams echoed through the EC halls, but still an oncoming horde moved towards the danger with crushing force, as if grapes slowly pushed through a winepress.

As the orgy of violence spilled up the clogged stairwell and into the main level, chaos and anarchy ruled supreme. Blood and gore splattered the hallways as demonic foot-soldiers tore flesh and joint from torso and limb.

Like a startled school of fish, the mass of humanity which pushed forward into the Eidolon Commission's building turned about face and fled the deadly monsters from below the stairwell. Pandora's Box had been flung wide and the few armed military forces still at ground level were quickly overwhelmed. The pulsing horde either eviscerated them or turned each into afflicted beasts in their own right.

Suddenly, every man and woman who'd earlier been deaf to Braff's warning message heard it loud and clear. Each one made a mad dash for the slope towards the front of the mountain which promised salvation in Ark I.

#

A multitude of screens fed Swag video data as he watched within the heart of Ark I. He ignored the Cerberus feeds and concentrated instead on the ones providing him actual information.

Jonas released Joshua Brady and the beast took over, butchering the deceived and the well-intentioned. Blood ran thick as a slaughterhouse in the lowest level of the containment facility.

Camera feeds from inside ECHQ fed him the gory details as Swag observed the horror overtake well-intentioned men and women gathered down the mountain.

The single, operational camera in the parking lot showed people scattering as they fled the violence as it spilled out of the building they'd earlier clamored to get inside.

Inside the operations hub Swag saw everything—and not just at their site. The news networks that still remained broadcasted scenes from around the globe. Gone was the concern for Diggleton and Cerberus. New and live footage showed images of burning forests; black skies roiled where everything turned to flame and ash. Half of the eastern Chinese and Russian territories had been nuked. The only remaining pieces of Japan were the crumbling chunks of Mount Fuji that slowly slid into the Pacific.

Swag could feel tremors underfoot. He looked up at a news feed that crackled with electromagnetic static. The cameraman captured a nuclear detonation inside the mouth of Mount Nyiragongo in the Congo. Lava spewed into the air and the feed winked out of existence. The scientist searched the bank of news screens—an eruption in the Congo was too far away to feel! Other feeds showed different eruptions; the entities' nuclear targets included the world's largest volcanoes. Their ash alone could blot out the sun and enhance any nuclear winter the entities had orchestrated.

Just as soon as Swag thought he'd determined their attack plan—to starve humanity of their necessary oxygen—he watched a nuclear blast wave tear apart Phoenix Arizona. The channel switched to a test pattern and Swag flipped the screen to a CCTV feed of refugees storming the arrival gate. People cycled through the entrance protocols as fast as they could—still too slow.

Two charter buses pulled up to the main gate and belched its contents into the swelling crowd. A strobing alarm went off as the first of the entity-carrying guests caught in the system were trapped in a self-contained box and flushed through the drop-tube which emptied two miles away.

One of the bus drivers scrambled from the large vehicle and barely got ahead of the crowd by sprinting up the hill. The violence-loving symbionts snatched men and women from the crowd, shredding them along the mountainside or infecting them with vestiges of their own legionic horde. A twisted fiend jumped a super-human distance and landed upon the bus driver's spine; he used his teeth to tear out the human's neck, splattering his hopes and dreams all across the edge of the gravel approach mere feet from the door to salvation.

Swag's knees bounced anxiously as he watched the military try and deal with the threat. Ravenous beasts in human bodies poured forward like a wave. Muzzle flashes erupted time and time again as the soldiers grudgingly fired into the familiar faces of American civilization, snarling though they were.

One by one the soldiers at the perimeter ran out of ammo and were caught by the afflicted chargers. Swag watched the few remaining military personnel scramble towards the entrance bay in horror, realizing that they had no way to shut out the overwhelming horde that approached.

The scientist flipped open the case protecting the big, red button he knew he needed to push, and soon. Just beyond those doors a huge crowd clamored for the entry. It had grown to several thousand strong and they squeezed into a space meant for less than a quarter as many.

Coming over the ridge Swag spotted Joshua Brady, drenched head to foot in human viscera and fluids. Brady rushed ahead and began to rip humans apart in as gruesome a manner possible. Swag tried to look away when the last of the news networks blinked out of existence in a burst of nuclear static.

People at the front of the entrance began jamming multiple candidates into the processing machine which caused false positives. Innocent and unafflicted people were forcefully plunged down the evacuation tubes. Other people tried to bypass the system causing it to lock up and shut down sections, stranding others in malfunctioning gates.

Still, the officers inside the entrance looked for a way to close the doors. Jonas, obviously afflicted, walked slowly over the top of the ridge and approached. Brady and his army of devils continued to dismember the screaming, cornered innocents who sought admittance inside the Ark.

Swag's heart groaned and something deep inside him broke as he stared at the big red button. His ears pounded with the thumping and cacophonous whispers that taunted the remotest parts of his mind. He slapped the switch and activated it. A warning flashed, demanding those in the entry back up. The massive, bay doors at the entrance suddenly slid shut with uncanny speed, catching half a dozen people inside its path, crunching them with mechanical ease.

Swag stared at the blank screens from around the globe. He looked to the exterior camera showing the last of the outsiders pounding on the door. They wailed for help, begging the operator to open it just a crack.

Despondent, Swag turned and stared at the exit door to the operations hub and then glanced over to a locked, emergency compartment where he knew a self-destruct system and a loaded three-fifty-seven were kept. He closed his eyes. His ambitious life flashed before him, reminding him of his curiosity and the drive to disprove his hyper-spiritual parents' beliefs. That drive played directly into the creation of Extinction Day. The world was dead, and deep-down Jimmy Swaggart knew that he had been the one to kill it.

#

Roderick Braff clutched the seeping wound in his midsection as he shifted the commandeered sedan into park outside of the main entry to Ark I. The gunshot wound had sapped too much strength for him to make the journey on foot.

Just before hooking his thumb in the door handle to exit the car he spotted Joshua Brady and his minions attack a group of helpless refugees trying to gain entry into the Ark. Too late—he watched as the door lights began a three second closure warning and then slam shut. Braff didn't know who operated the controls, but he applauded that person in his heart. He knew he or she had made the right tactical choice, though it must've been painful to watch the slaughter of those who had arrived mere seconds too late to be saved—just as Braff had done. He or she would have to listen to the latecomers as they pound helplessly on the door.

Braff put the car into gear and turned the vehicle around. On the horizon he saw the sky begin taking on an ochre tint as the oxygen burned off with nuclear and volcanic fire. Before the ravenous beasts could shift too much focus from their prey and give him chase, Braff piloted the car down the steep, rock-strewn paths. He locked eyes with Jonas who stroked his pet rat as he sped out of the gravel approach. Braff flashed him an obscene gesture and then accelerated away from the area.

Pot-holes jarred him fiercely despite the vehicle's shocks. Braff grimaced against the sour pain radiating from the gut-shot.

Veering off of the main path, he gunned the motor as his car climbed the steep incline, heading towards the bank of rear-access doors. Of all the things General Braff was, a person without a plan rarely described him.

Braff kept the accelerator pressed hard in order to keep his momentum. He piloted the craft precariously close to the steep drop into the ravine off to his left. Far ahead, he recognized the blood-drenched figure of an afflicted man standing in the glorious wreckage of the human form. Macabre smears of entrails and gore stained the grass ahead.

The beast locked eyes with the general. Braff reached for his hip and wrapped fingers around his GB. He relaxed his grip and thought of a better plan which could keep his last ECP freed up for emergency use.

Braff's jaw set, and he screamed as he steered the front-end towards his enemy as if the sedan was a missile. Just as he rammed the bumper into the afflicted person's gut, Braff threw the door open and tumbled from the automobile. His car careened over the edge, taking the snarling demoniac down to the bottom with it.

Crumpled on the ground, Braff groaned and held his stomach. The clots had broken free and fresh blood poured from the wound. He half-stood and half crouched, resting on his laurels. Braff thought that he'd lost his Baconator; try as he might, he couldn't spot it anywhere on the rocky mountain-side. Finally, nearly giving up on hope, he spotted the device and clipped it firmly to his belt before crawling towards a higher elevation. The air grew ever-more thin as the general pushed ahead.

He ground his teeth against the pain and crawled up the side of the mountain. Braff didn't have the access code for the rear doors; Chu hadn't yet sent him a special passcode since leaving. However, he *did know* of a sensitive point in the exhaust network which he could access.

Along the stony ridge above the service doors the general found his mark. Braff kicked free an air circulation vent and crawled into the ducting. Eventually, he found what he was searching for and pulled himself through a laser-filtered segment of the system. The lasers were harmless, but would prevent free-floating entities from accessing the unlit duct system. It was an exhaust port and so the pressurized air that flowed out from the hole would keep any other, natural threats from entering.

He crawled inch by painful inch until the narrowing passage snagged and crimped down on his midsection. Spitting dust from his mouth and flinching against the UV lasers that scanned his face Braff groaned and pulled himself free, snapping his belt and nearly tearing his pants off in the process.

Braff kept moving forward and suddenly fell through a high ceiling duct that gave way. He landed on a tall stack of crates in a storage bay near the C block. Still bleeding, he crawled down to the ground and searched until he found a long pole lying along the edge of the room: fifteen feet of plumbing drainage pipe.

The general crawled back up to where he'd fallen into the storage facility and used every inch of the pipe's reach. Over and over he rammed the blunt end of the rod into the ceiling where the ducting passed overhead and crumpling it closed with less than two inches of clearance; he ensured that none could follow his exploit.

Satisfied, he finally rolled himself back down to the ground level, exhausted. He staggered through the room, drunk on blood loss. Braff silently congratulated himself on keeping a backdoor contingency active rather than having Chu close the loop because of the potential security weakness.

Braff meandered towards the exit door. He felt a presence behind him, as if he was being watched. In the distance, pacing him, he spotted the white lab rat that had bit Jonas before he'd turned—it still had blood on its muzzle. Braff slowly reached towards his waist and grabbed only shredded fabric where his Baconator had been hung—*it must've torn free inside the ventilation shaft!*

The general drew his sidearm instead and fired every round at the rodent. It hopped and skipped with super speed and agility.

Intense pain shot through Braff's midsection and he dropped a hand to his mid-section. Chunky, black blood pulsed from the massive wound and he knew his chances of survival plummeted.

Braff's thoughts turned inward. He still held out hope against all odds that Jason had heeded his warning and somehow made it inside the Ark. He didn't want to risk his son's safety by potentially exposing him or the population of survivors to this tiny deviant.

He leaned against the wall nearest the door controls, leaving a bright, bloody print next to the panel. Braff pushed the magazine release and dropped the spent container from the grip of his pistol before loading his spare and racking the slide.

Staggering back to his feet, Braff unloaded a full mag's worth of ammo into the control panel, obliterating it and trapping him inside with the carrier rat. The General dropped his sidearm to the floor and then slumped against the wall; he slid to the floor nearest the destroyed console and held his aching belly.

Braff squeezed his eyes shut and wandered through his memories, reliving his favorites: his marriage to Wanda, the birth of Jason, his promotion to general. He lost control of the mental stream and was forced to relive the aftermath of Wanda's rape and murder by the Sinister Six, a group of pompous foreigners on student visas; they had possible ties to radical Islam, but it couldn't be verified. Braff tried to course correct—to dwell on Jason's sixth Christmas when he'd given the boy his first BB gun, though he never turned out to be much of a crack shot.

He could not pick and choose the moments. Braff relived the imagined assault by those cursed ragheads and his promise to avenge her—a threat he'd personally delivered to the Six while they languished broken and beaten in the prison hospital. *I will kill each and every member of your family who sets foot on American soil!* Braff re-experienced the cancerous disconnect as vengeance displaced his bond with Jason—the distance drove a wedge in his son's late teenage years—that growing apathy was the *real* reason his son didn't complete the humidor… he always knew as much but could never admit it to himself—until now.

Braff squeezed his eyes shut. Tears came anyway.

Outside, the world burned. He'd miscalculated the potency of the asset entities he'd tried to wield. Braff tilted his head back to rest against the wall. Using the entities might have literally amounted to a deal with the devil—one that cost everything. He'd done it all for Wanda, and he'd probably do it all again if given another chance.

He'd commissioned the Ark for Jason and his grandchildren; but he could only hope and pray that they'd made it in.

"The best laid plans of mice and men," he started. "*Rats and men…*" He touched his leaking midsection and used the sticky fluid to write a simple warning on the wall.

Feeling his life leak away through the hole in his guts, General Braff's hard heart cursed the world and claimed one final victory against any humans or ideologies related to the torment which had ended the life of Wanda Braff.

"It was worth it," Braff whispered, pushing as much vitriol into his last breath as possible. Roderick Braff hung his head and died.

# # #

Jimmy Swaggart unlocked and opened the access panel. He stared at the self-destruct system with dispirited eyes; it resembled a credit card machine and Swag knew the sliding activation key was locked in an adjacent compartment.

He reached in and hefted the Colt Python that lay alongside the device. Swag reached for the revolver with cold, hard resolve. Guilt weighed too heavily on him; it crushed his very soul.

Swag's arm trembled as he held the heavy .357 magnum. *Did he have a soul? What would suicide mean if he pulled that trigger?* He cursed his parents for so deeply programming their religious propaganda into his brain—but even that reflection became difficult. His mind had become so clouded by the incessant whispers that he could barely think.

He needed to stop it—had to end the otherworldly chattering before it drove him into the throes of madness! Swag jammed the barrel of the handgun into his mouth. Cold steel clinked against his teeth like a hammer on porcelain.

Swag hesitated.

He willed himself to pull the trigger, but his finger refused to move.

He was a coward. The murderer of planet Earth deserved self-imposed execution!

Still, his finger refused to grant him the release of death.

Bleary eyed, he lowered the gun. Swag sobbed and threw the pistol back into the compartment; the lock clicked automatically. He looked up as the first wave of humanity's remnants filtered into the central promenade area. Conviction and shame overtook the scientist who felt the crawling ache of innocent blood staining his hands.

Slipping past the door, he slinked around a corner and wandered out of sight. The operations center closed of its own accord and Swag darted down the bright corridor in exile, unable to die—but feeling too much guilt to remain among the survivors.

PART III.

THE DEVIL INSIDE

1,298 Days Post Extinction-Day

24

Jimmy lay on his mattress and waited for his parents to come and tuck the nine-year old into bed. A lamp on his nightstand lit the room and revealed the opened pages of the Bible passage his parents had instructed him to read before sleeping: a text from First Corinthians. He'd already done that; Jimmy was a good reader and he only waited for his parents to return.

After a short time lying on his side, the odd voices came to him, pounding in his ear like some ancient war-drum. After a few minutes, it began sounding more like an ominous voice, the other-worldly whisper of something demonic. The shadows from below his bed-skirt seemed to loom all the larger.

This wasn't the first time he heard the voices and Jimmy was convinced that the Devil sometimes hid under his bed—just waiting for him to drop his feet over the edge in the event that he'd forgotten to say his prayers. His parents had always told Jimmy that God had an immense destiny for him and had called him by name, like Samuel in the Old Testament. Jimmy felt certain that Satan waited to snatch him by the feet and drag him into the abyss at the first possible moment in order to prevent whatever mystical destiny awaited the child. Jimmy always said his prayers, but he never hung his feet over the edge.

Melinda Swaggart finally came into the room to put her son to bed for the evening. "Did you read your Bible tonight, Jimmy?"

He shook his head yes.

"What did you think of First Corinthians chapter eleven?"

Jimmy's reluctant eyes said everything. "I'm not sure I understood it." A hint of fear warbled in his voice.

"What's not to understand?"

"The part about drinking Jesus's blood."

He continued speaking, but his mother seemed caught off guard—as if she'd quite forgotten what was in there. She leaned over to examine the Scripture as her son continued speaking.

"It says if someone's not worthy when they take communion they are guilty and will receive damnation."

Melinda nodded along as she read the open text and confirmed his words. "But it's not like that, Jimmy."

"So, when God made people sick and die because of that in verse thirty, that didn't happen?"

His mother bit her lower lip and shrugged. "Sometimes you've just got to have faith, sweetie."

Jimmy knew that phrase was her go-to answer when she didn't know something. He also knew better than to say as much, but his fear overrode his common sense. "I took communion. Was I worthy enough for that? I don't want to go to Hell."

Melinda hugged the boy. "Don't worry about that," she squeezed. "You're special and God has a plan for you—just like Samuel the prophet. Remember how God touched his feet and called his name as a boy? Hell is for other people, bad people who don't believe like we do. I'm sure you'll figure it out—you can ask Pastor Walt next time you seen him."

Jimmy shook his head and accepted that answer. He didn't want to think about *anything* grabbing his feet—friend or foe.

Melinda stood to leave for the night.

"Can I stay up and read tonight?"

She nodded her head. "I suppose so—but not too late," she warned.

"Um. Can you hand me my encyclopedia? I don't want to get out of bed; I'm already comfortable." His eyes quickly glanced down at the dark floor where those scaly arms might have waited for him. Jimmy trusted his mother, but he wasn't entirely certain she could beat Satan in a fistfight.

Melinda replied with a sympathetic smile. "Which one?"

"Letter E please."

His mother pulled the volume off of the shelf and passed the children's encyclopedia to Jimmy before kissing his forehead and departing. He flipped the pages and curiously fingered the section near the rear where the swath of pages of forbidden knowledge had been ripped out. Jimmy knew it was the section on evolution because of the notes in the rear appendix.

He flipped back towards the front and leafed through a section on the human ear. The text explained that odd sounds could be caused by pulsatile tinnitus—the sound of his heartbeat or blood flow. Dust, ear wax, a misaligned hair or other foreign body touching the eardrum could cause exactly the sort of sounds Jimmy heard in his head.

His eyes ravenously scanned the pages, devouring the information. Jimmy suddenly realized that the whispering in his mind wasn't demons at all—it was entirely natural. For the first time in his life he doubted the existence of God, or at least the accuracy of his faith in Him.

What if angels and demons never existed? What if all the prophets and stuff never heard the voice of God, but just had goofy hairs in their ears or high blood pressure making them hear stuff? That's possible I guess… I never heard the voice of God—maybe none of its real?

A few minutes of deep rumination passed with the boy's head on the pillow and that blood-induced whisper returned. Jimmy paused mid-thought—not certain he liked where his thoughts took him. Upsetting the Almighty was a terrifying prospect for a child, and he still hadn't said his prayers for the night.

Jimmy glanced at the darkness below his bed. Tonight he prayed differently than he was used to. He didn't pray for safety or the poor children of Nicaragua that his missionary uncle had been sent to teach—he didn't pray for forgiveness of sins or daily bread. *Lord, if you've really got some big destiny or something for my life then call me by name. Make me hear your voice.*

As if in response Jimmy immediately heard his name through the pounding of his pulse in his head. *Swag! Swag!*

It cut through the fog that permeated his mind. Confused, Jimmy's heart leapt. *This wasn't how this memory happened! I prayed and nobody answered… and my name's Jimmy, not—*

#

Swag's eyelids fluttered, and he felt a powerful pair of arms scoop him up in the oxygenless environment. The feeling of weightlessness tethered his body to his mind as it struggled against the whelming blackness that tried to extinguish the scientist's life.

Choking on the void, his eyes focused just enough to recognize a terrified looking Ricky wearing the improperly donned environmental suit. His savior's outfit wasn't sealed and leaked air as the large man tried his best to run through the darkness with only a handheld flashlight to guide him.

Swag's chest heaved and felt like it had collapsed as he tried to suck in air.

Ricky screamed the entire distance from the access door to where he'd hefted his breathless friend. Twenty feet into the return journey, he whirled around, looking for something.

Swag's purple face beckoned Ricky to sprint back inside where he could breathe again. Then he saw it! Ricky's light beam caught the folded and rolled form of his joke book where it lay in the distance.

Ricky looked back for a second, and then down to his asphyxiating friend. Ricky ducked his head and went back to the Ark, leaving behind his last link to his pre-E-day life. He screamed the whole way back and didn't calm down until the airlock pressurized.

Coughing and clamoring for breath, Swag hacked and wheezed until he puked all over his damaged suit. Once he got a hold of his bearings, Ricky clapped him in a big, worried hug. He cried, "I don't know what we're gonna do!"

The big guy rocked for a few moments under the comparatively bright beam of an emergency light. Several banks of the backup units remained lit through the long tunnels.

Leaning against the wall and bleeding from a nasty looking gut shot, Swag spotted Janet. Her bloody handprint on the airlock controls suggested she had been the one to let Ricky out and then back in via the locked chamber. Her eyelids fluttered excruciatingly as she tried to stand and finally gave up, slouching back to the floor. Dark, tainted blood had spilled out from the ragged edges of her wounded midsection.

Nearby, Ricky paced nervously and looked through the door's tiny porthole. Somewhere in the darkness beyond laid his book. He fretted under his breath, "I have to start wearing a backpack like Janet. She's always been smart like that."

Swag wrinkled his nose at the foul odor wafting off from Janet. He didn't know much about medical science, but even he recognized that the bullet must've torn up her digestive system and was slowly, painfully poisoning her.

"You can fix her, right Swag?" Ricky pleaded. "She saved me. Edward tried to kill me, but she shot at him and scared him off. We ran away."

Swag crawled over to the injured woman. Their eyes locked and they shared a moment. Both knew that she didn't have long.

Janet waved her handgun like a drunken person. "Do you think I could've really killed that thing with this?"

"Probably not," Swag admitted. "Not unless you hit it in the head or maybe the heart and used hollow-point rounds or something. It would do such massive damage to Edward's body that he'd bleed out right away—but the entity wouldn't be harmed. These things are completely immune to shock and some of the other things that affect humans. It makes them appear tougher and stronger."

"It figures," Janet muttered. "But at least I saved him," she nodded towards Ricky.

Swag cocked his head inquisitively.

She gritted her teeth through the pain and then continued. "As soon as you left, Edward returned. He took out Bart and chased Gordon out the airlock—he had a broken light."

"It's not Edward," Swag assured her. "It's an entity named Little Satan."

This time it was Janet's turn to look inquisitive.

"It was the first entity discovered by my research team several years ago—one of seven experiments that we named."

The information didn't help her understand.

"Never mind, it's a long story."

She nodded and continued her account. "Gordon got possessed... afflicted. He must be near door number thirteen still."

"He's at the bottom of the ravine," he told her.

Janet waggled her head and winced. "When Edward came back and got inside—they opened the doors to circulate some oxygen—he began taking out anybody that was a threat to him first. By the time I got back to the main level, I found him shrieking 'Immune! Immune!' He was stabbing Father over and over. Then he started chasing Ricky, screaming the same thing."

"Percy and Andrew?" Swag asked.

She shrugged. "I didn't see them. I don't know. I just figured if that thing thought Ricky was a threat I'd better protect him."

Swag squeezed her hand. "You did good." He held up his Mark I capture device for her to see. "This here is the earliest version of the Entity Capture Tech that the Eidolon Commission used to free afflicted people."

Janet smiled and waved her handgun again. "Better than this?"

Swag nodded. "It's like kryptonite for Little Satan."

"Good," she grimaced. "I've only got one bullet left anyway." She put the weapon in Swag's hand. Her eyes pleaded for him to understand her subtle request.

His eyes understood, but Swag glanced apprehensively at Ricky.

She caught his apprehension and grimaced through thin lips. They both knew they couldn't abandon Ricky, even momentarily, to do what needed to be done for Janet. "You're sure you got this?"

Swag nodded.

"Give him hell with whatever your kryptonite thingy is, Doc," she said and took her gun back. Skootching forward and wincing at the blinding pain she slipped her backpack off and motioned for Ricky to take it. "I think you need this more than I do."

Ricky took it, but didn't seem so sure about smiling. Plus, it was heavy.

"You can go ahead and empty it out and put your things in it," she said.

He nodded.

"Come on, Ricky," Swag put an arm around him. "We've got to get back and finish this."

Ricky looked nervous as he wringed his hands. He didn't know quite how to deal with his stress without his joke book to leaf through. "Is Janet coming?"

Swag shook his head. "She's going to stay here for now," he said softly.

"Okay," Ricky said as he reluctantly shuffled his feet towards the community.

The walked ahead for several minutes, eyes always forward. In the distance behind them a single gunshot rang out and echoed through the hall.

Swag nervously held the Mark I in his hand as he and Ricky walked through the halls, passing by a bloody, abandoned electric cart. They didn't know where Edward had gone, or if Little Satan still used him as a host body.

Drawing ever closer to the promenade section, a voice shouted behind them. Ricky clammed up and Swag whirled to face the threat, capture device held out like a Star Trek tricorder.

"Ricky!" Michelle exclaimed with relief from the door she'd cracked open. "Get in here, you guys."

The two hustled over to the infirmary where she'd locked herself inside. She sealed the entry behind them.

They spotted Father immediately. He lay unconscious, hooked up to machines and intravenous fluid lines. Michelle had done her best to bandage his stab wounds.

"Is he…"

Michelle shook her head. "He's unconscious, but his vitals seem strong. We'll have to wait and see." She waited through a moment of silence. "Janet? As soon as she lured Edward away I got Father out of there on the cart."

Swag shook his head. "She's gone. Percy and Andrew?"

Michelle shook her head. "As soon as he took them out, he unloaded every bullet they had into whoever he could find. Luckily Edward had very little experience with guns. He didn't hit anybody else before he found a knife and caught Father."

"I think Little Satan was trying to take out the greatest threats first, that's why he's gone after who he did as soon as he did." Swag paused and then held up his device, offering a glimmer of hope. "I got it. It was in my car, right where I left it."

"Will that thing really help us capture this thing?"

Swag nodded enthusiastically. "We've just got to find it, first."

Michelle shrank back uneasily. "You remember what happened the last time you went looking for it in the hallways? We need to do some recon before we go rushing blindly into some kind of trap."

They paused in the thoughtful silence that followed. "I have an idea," Swag finally said. "Would you say that Edward is mostly a software guy or a mechanical one?"

Michelle shrugged, not seeing the difference. "He can work on either—he's pretty talented and has taught himself a lot of things."

Swag waved that away. "Entities mainly imprint on natural talents first and education secondarily." He waved around at all the emergency lights which had dimmed a couple lumens in the time since he'd left.

"First, I need to figure out how he turned the lights off—he's disabled either the hardware or the programming." He turned to Michelle on a hunch. "I think the lights can be brought back up. Is Edward more likely to work on an old car or code a video game?"

"Definitely video games."

"Perfect. That's what I'd hoped for." He rummaged through the drawers and cabinets until he found a screwdriver in a small utility box he'd dumped out. Poking his head out the door, Swag scanned the hallway and then darted out and into the wide passageway.

Swag unscrewed just enough of the protective plate which shielded the light emitters. He reached his screwdriver into the gap and rammed it into the light panel. It flashed and went dark, and then he returned to the safety of the locked door and watched through the small port hole to wait.

"What are you doing?" Michelle finally asked.

"Here it comes," Swag said as the robotic repair droid whizzed through the hallway and followed its programming. He stepped outside the door and let it repair the damaged illuminator before typing in a command on the touchpad. The command shut the machine down. Using his screwdriver he wedged the tablet free of its mounting bracket and slipped back inside the infirmary.

Swag grinned as his fingers flew. He walked through the operating system how Hank had taught him years ago. "I've got Hank's codes," he said. "I can control things no one else knows exist, including Edward." He toggled the systems and found a piece of software that had been disabled. He tapped the light controller and the banks switched back on. Swag grinned.

He reactivated the air cyclers next and then pulled up the security cameras inside the main living area and turned the screen to Michelle.

Edward hissed at the lights and airflow. He stood in the main commons area and tried to access the control center. Edward tried random codes on the keypad and pried on the barrier when those methods failed.

"I've got a plan," Swag said.

###

Swag crept through the edge of the promenade and got as close as he dared to the afflicted teen who vainly tried to open the central operations door. Tablet in hand, he'd passed by a number of frightened humans who cowered in hiding, ready to bolt at the first sign of attack.

He fixed his eyes on the madman. If Little Satan got inside that room, the human race would be lost for sure.

Tense and fearful, Swag double checked his screen one final time and then shouted at the beast. "Hey you!"

Afflicted Edward whirled to face him.

The scientist stood tall and brazen. He pumped false hubris into his voice. "I bet you thought you got rid of me outside, didn't you?"

Little Satan snarled and sprinted towards him.

Swag's eyes widened in terror and he spun on his heels, headed for the labyrinth of residential halls. He rounded a corner to one block and dashed inside the apartment zone that had been set up on a grid pattern.

Little Satan slid around the corner, slobbering with rage.

The scientist tapped the screen and a door-to-ceiling fire barrier slid down to section off the hall behind them, trapping them in the bottled section of the maze. Swag raced towards an intersection, hoping to seal the beast within. He hurried past and heard a woman scream behind him.

Spinning to face his enemy, Swag held his finger over the control to seal the zone behind him and lock up the beast when he saw a pregnant woman rushing down the hall. He recognized the Asian lady as she hurried, cradling her swollen belly—he remembered admitting her on E-day. He only knew that her name was Janessa.

Janessa had slipped out of an apartment just behind the scientist and found herself in hot pursuit by the afflicted person. Tears streamed down her face as she tried to run from the coldly nonchalant pursuit.

Forty feet past the intersection, Swag bit his lip and watched the woman struggle to reach the intersection ahead of the enemy. His finger hovered over the button. Suddenly sure that the woman wouldn't make it he reached inside his pocket and drew the Mark I.

Little Satan reached the intersection at the same time as the woman. Janessa collapsed to all fours in terror as the beast caught up to her. Little Satan ignored her and instead locked his eyes on Swag as the shrieking, sobbing woman crawled away from the possessed Edward.

The scientist held his gaze, daring the enemy to approach. With his hand Swag beckoned the woman to continue crawling to the next section of tunnel so he could seal it, too.

The beast narrowed his eyes. By reaching the intersection, he'd already escaped the human's trap; Little Satan glanced down at the Mark I device and growled. With murder in his eyes, he sauntered towards the woman who clawed for distance.

Janessa spotted him behind and wailed, quickening her pace. Little Satan reached out to grab her. Just before he could seize her, the woman's foot cleared the safe zone and Swag hit the switch. A fire door clamped down immediately, sealing it off and saving the woman and her unborn child. A moment later he snapped the other two zones shut before running to her aide.

Once he got her calmed down and locked in a safe room Swag returned to the sealed cell. He opened it and rushed in, Mark I blazing and whirling in every direction, hoping he'd been quick enough to catch his prey.

The area was clear.

Little Satan predicted his actions and used her as a ruse, knowing Swag would save her before closing the gates. The misdirection helped him escape before the firewalls could imprison his host.

Swag cursed. The entity was free again, only now the scientist didn't know where it had gone. Little Satan had gained the upper hand and they'd lost the element of surprise.

25

Michelle jabbed her finger into Swag's chest as best as she was able. "Listen. If we're going to stand any chance at surviving, you've got to level with me about how you know what you know. How you can do the things you can do?"

Swag nodded thoughtfully while he accessed the network of systems from the portable tablet he'd taken off of the maintenance drone. Members of the community stood sentry over the doors and watched for the afflicted Edward. Swag had begun sealing doors as the community gathered in the promenade area.

"I knew the person who built this facility," he admitted as they headed back to collect Father from the infirmary. The main medical bay lay just beyond the residential hub. "The builder was actually a relative of both Father Ackley and the dead soldier we found in the storage sections. I'd guess that's why Father has an access code and it's probably what brought him here in the first place—but he must not have full access, otherwise you guys would've been able to get the electric carts before I got here."

As they walked to retrieve their fallen comrade Swag told her everything: the fact of the master code, his ability to open the main control room, and how his presence inside Ark I had been more than random luck.

"Really," she broke the tension. "You wrote the combination inside a paper duck?"

Swag smirked. "I had to put it somewhere—but you must make sure that you don't know the code. Knowing it makes you a high priority to this vindictive entity."

"Don't worry. I won't steal your precious ducks," Michelle said in a terrible Lord of the Rings Gollum impression.

He knew Michelle had her own code which gave her access to the room Little Satan so desperately sought, but if Sam and Frodo could erase the code from Swag's mind, he might consider it.

Moments later, they arrived at the medical area and regrouped with Ricky who had nervously folded an entire army of origami birds and placed them around the body of the unconscious minister as if they could protect him from the evil one if it came down to it.

Ricky leapt to his feet and embraced them both. "I knew you'd come back!" he said. "Did you get it; did you catch the shadow-monster?"

Michelle shook her head and Swag grimaced. Crestfallen, Ricky sank back into his seat.

Swag looked down at Father's wounds. Michelle changed out his bandages for fresh ones.

Biting his lip, Swag wondered if the entities could force their hosts to remain conscious during take-over. Could it force Edward to remain conscious during the affliction, so he'd be forced to watch helplessly through his eyes while the beast controlled him and repeatedly stabbed his mentor before attacking poor, simple Ricky?

A memory clicked into place inside of Swag's mind. Right before E-day Jessica had been preparing to share data regarding types of people who were immune to affliction. *What are the similarities between Ricky and Father? Why did Little Satan consider them threats?*

Together, they got Father's gurney prepared for transport to the community. Swag pulled Michelle out of earshot from Ricky. "Promise me something," he asked.

Michelle noticed the serious in his voice and gave him her full attention.

He hedged for a moment. "No one else will be able to access the main control room, right?"

"Jack has a code, but I don't believe he's ever been inside, even," she trailed off. "Why? What are you saying?"

"My code controls everything. If I'm ever in danger of becoming afflicted... my knowledge is too dangerous to give it to Little Satan... If the entity ever takes me..." He trailed off.

Michelle's eyes pierced through him, making him use his words.

"I'm saying that I'm too dangerous to be taken alive. Don't risk the remnant's safety for me."

He paused, and Michelle could tell something was processing deep within her friend's thoughts. Finally, Swag confided in her, "The code is hidden in my room, just in case you have to... you know. I had to hide it somewhere in case I'm ever gone when it is needed. But you have to promise you won't go looking for it."

Michelle raised a curious eyebrow and glanced down to the sidearm holstered at her friend's side. She nodded. "Okay, but don't do anything foolish and throw your life away."

###

Swag pushed the gurney through the door of the smaller medical bay located inside the community where Michelle could set up a workstation. The smaller clinician's room was too close to hide in during Edward's earlier attack and not nearly as well stocked with supplies and equipment.

Victims of the violence lined up against the walls on either side as the scientist exited and noted the wide variety of injuries. Some had been grazed by bullets or boasted other moderate wounds.

He shook his head. Disabled people would make easy targets for an entity—or worse, if another entity somehow got into one of these barely-functioning people it would ignore the damage and instantly become a death machine cloaked in human flesh. Swag thought of the Legion that burst out of Joshua during the E-day; those memories remained all too fresh in his mind. Mankind could not afford to allow another entity inside of Ark I.

While Swag knew he had to push the other afflicted carrier, Gordon, off a cliff to prevent a second attacker, he also knew that entities could leave a host and freely move during the darkness. Once daylight ended beyond those airlocks, the fiend inside of Gordon's corpse could find its way back to the threshold of their shelter and Little Satan could let it inside and increase in power by also joining with the teen.

Swag caught sight of Jack and flagged him down. The man ambled through the crowd before closing the distance with the scientist. He didn't seem like he had much of a purpose beyond trying to come to grips with the destruction wrought inside the dwindling group.

"I need you to call a town-hall kind of meeting in a little while. Just give Michelle enough time to patch these people up, first."

Jack's eyes glinted for a moment as if he resented the newcomer giving him an order; Jack was higher on the chain of command than Swag after all. Something softened and he recognized the pettiness of his response. Jack nodded his head and turned to make the arrangements.

"Before you go," Swag caught him one last time as he scanned the disheveled crowd for anyone else who might have had a military background, "do you have keys to the weapon locker?"

Jack nodded, reluctant to admit it. Since the deaths of Percy and Andrew, nobody else had the keys to the weapons room. It operated on a physical tumbler-style code or a physical key. Not even Swag could open it without one of those.

"Good. Make sure you lock away anything that can do mass damage to our people. We can't afford another massive loss of life."

Swag turned his attention back to the problem of the entities outside and the fact that they'd lost any idea of where their enemy had went. Keying in Hank's override code, Swag double checked that none of the exits had been used since Ricky's daring rescue.

He locked down the airlock cycle feeds. Nothing was getting inside or out of Ark I unless they knew Hank's code and entered an override command.

Shouldering his backpack, Ricky paced anxiously. People assembled nearby and his sister diligently applied bandages to the wounded. He kept checking on her as the fast-paced work wound down.

Jack and Swag stood together, but before either could address the crowd a much-panicked Jennifer stood to address them. Agitation flooded her voice. "This is it," she wailed. "Finally, it's come to the end of the human race!"

Tears streamed down her face, crisscrossing the jagged, red claw marks where the entity made her cut herself during the first affliction in the Ark. "Don't you all get it? We're going to die in here!"

Jack tried to calm her down by escorting her to the back of the crowd.

"No!" she shoved away from him. "We're all doomed. It's the end!"

Jack and Swag traded nervous glances as the woman pushed the crowd's emotions to the brink of despair. Swag had no idea what to do, but noticed Michelle's diminutive form darken the doorway as Jack tried to grab her again.

"Get off of me! Don't touch me! You're all going to die, and these people are going to let it happen!" She thrust Jack away again, harder this time. He tumbled past Michelle who stormed past him.

Jennifer turned to the tiny woman just in time to find the small doctor swing her fist. Her roundhouse caught the unhinged woman's jaw and knocked Jennifer flat on her back. She collapsed like a sack of laundry with tiny Michelle towering over her.

"Do not get up until I say so," Michelle commanded. "We've had enough out of you for a while." She balled her fists threateningly and searched for a response.

Jennifer held her throbbing jaw but nodded.

"Good." Michelle shut down the crowd's anxiety with a call to action. "Listen up everybody and pay attention or I'll do the same to you." She stepped back and muttered to Jennifer, "Find me after this and I'll get you an ice pack for your jaw."

Swag stepped forward into the vacuum Michelle left for him. "We're not done-for yet," he assured the people. "I've analyzed as much information as we can get and I'm confident that we're still only facing one entity—not an entire legion as we did at E-day. I've taken steps to lock the Ark down so that no more can get in. At least we won't have any more of these things taking us by surprise."

He held up his sidearm and waived it in the air. "Just in case any of you have weapons and ammunition but haven't yet had them collected, please see Jack Carrington." Blood splatters still stained the floor and walls nearby and Swag motioned to the grisly mess. "We don't want a scene like this happening again. The fewer lethal weapons floating around out there, especially anything with a full-auto mode, the more likely we'll be able to reduce casualties."

"So this thing will kill us one by one, instead," a voice rose from the gathering.

Another voice yelled, "If we can't fight back we don't stand a chance!"

Swag held both of his hands up in order to calm the group and prevent any more objections. "I do have a weapon," he yelled. He held up the Mark I. "I was able to retrieve the device I left the Ark to find. If I can get close enough to it, I will be able to force it out of Edward and into the light where it will be trapped. And I understand your concerns, but this device is the only thing left on the planet that can hurt this thing."

News of his plan calmed them slightly.

"We have to be diligent—I don't know where it's gone, but we *do* know what it wants." He pointed across the way to the central hub where the battered doors to the control center stood stalwart. "If it gets inside the main operations room it will be able to kill us all with a few flips of a switch."

"Then what do we do?" The pregnant lady Swag had earlier saved looked ready to help in whatever way possible, even if she wore the terror of it so evidently upon her face.

Swag looked at his watch and calculated the time since his last sleep. "We make plans—Janessa—plans to endure and survive. We *will* beat this thing. Right now, we rest and regroup. Those of you who are healthy enough should talk to Jack. We need as many eyes as we can get on our camera feeds or watching the doors as sentries; we've got to locate this thing, first of all, then we can get it out of Edward."

A chorus of assents and many nods agreed with him.

"Right now we're playing defense. Once we have a location we can form a plan on how best to proceed. One thing is certain: this thing *will* come back at some point. We're ready for that; we just need to make sure we see it coming. We can open some doors to bait it, but the entity knows we are hunting it and slipping through a guarded door plays more into *our* hand than *its*."

Slowly, the individuals made their way to Jack to set up a duty schedule and make sure that someone watched security feeds at all times. Michelle watched Jennifer. Even she stepped forward, albeit reluctantly, to take a shift.

Michelle asked Swag, "Are you really going to rest?"

He cursed and rubbed his bloodshot eyes. "I'm so tired that I don't care if I even wake up." He paused at the morbid joke and corrected himself. "Yes—I haven't been this tired in years."

She studied his weary face for several seconds. In that moment she was convinced he had no intention of choking back one of those horrible pills to help him sleep. "Sleep well," she said, opting against the awkwardness of a hug as he staggered towards the nearest pillow. "You deserve it."

A loud slapping noise jolted Swag from his sleep. He groaned and rolled to his side. How long had he been asleep? He checked the clock—not long, but longer than he intended.

More banging on his door… pounding fists and a voice. "Doctor Swag—er, Swaggart. They said to wake you! We found him—we have Edward."

He leapt to his feet as he grabbed his tablet and sprang for the door. Throwing it open he found Eunice, a mousey lady he'd spoken with only in passing. "Where is he?" Swag asked.

"Right outside the main door," she said worriedly.

Swag stared at her incredulously and wondered if it could be so simple. *Of course not*, he thought and then activated his camera feeds on the tablet. Edward paced outside the main gate, occasionally stopping to pound on the thick door. He could see the boy yelled intermittently; swag toggled the audio control.

"Come on! Let me in, guys. I don't know what's happening and I'm so scared. I'm covered in blood and I don't think it's mine."

After barking orders Swag assembled a squad of people at the door. They wore facemasks and covered their skin, prepared to help subdue the boy in case this was some sort of trick. Swag clutched the Mark I ECT unit as the door hissed open.

"Stay right where you are!" Jack leaned forward, leading with his handgun so that the boy didn't rush inside.

Edward's hands shot into the air in surrender and he sank to his knees. "Please don't shoot me! I have no idea what's happening—I just woke up a little while ago in a work room," he pointed down the long hallway. "I have no idea how I got there."

Brandishing the Mark I, Swag crept forward and kept an eye on the youth. He thumbed the activator a few times while Edward stood well inside its effective range, but it produced no effect. Finally, he slipped it inside his pocket and grabbed Edward by the head.

Swag checked him all over, especially his eyes, before declaring him clear. "He's free. He's not afflicted."

Jack, with his gun still trained on the boy asked, "Are you sure?"

"Of course I'm sure."

Jack's gun didn't waiver as he watched Edward with set face and stern jaw.

"Do you want to shoot him just in case?" Swag asked.

Jack shook his head and holstered the gun.

As they escorted him inside and closed the doors a barrage of questions hit the teen. Where did you wake up at? Are you sure you can't remember? What did it feel like?

Swag didn't pay any attention to those things. He stepped out of the group and wandered with his arms and hands out like a kid catching raindrops. He pulled up his tablet and worked furiously for a few moments before scowling sourly.

Michelle watched him curiously for a few seconds. "What's wrong?"

He tore his gaze away from the vent shafts and looked at her with a grave face. Finally, he spat profanity in short bursts. "There's no air circulating in here."

26

"It just died," Swag shot over his shoulder as Michelle and Jack followed him into the control hub. Ricky trailed after the party almost as an afterthought.

The group walked through the high-tech office which resembled every war-room they had ever seen in the movies. Swag threw himself into a wheeled office chair and tapped a few keys to wake up the main computer. His companions shadowed him.

Swag's despair broke momentarily when he saw their expressions. Michelle and Jack had seen inside this room before, but Ricky? The simple man looked around the room with wonder as the computer systems came online flooding the room with LEDs that blinked like swarms of fireflies.

He entered his master code to access the powerful switchboard and pulled up the oxygen cycling systems and found the toggle grayed out. Swag tried to switch it, but nothing happened. He bit his lip and cursed.

Jack leaned forward. "What've we got?" He hadn't yet heard what the problem was but had followed the others when he saw the panic plastered to their faces.

Ignoring him, Swag concentrated on the computer system as he scrolled through the data and looked for system alerts. Michelle filled Jack in on the oxygen problem. Jack leaned back and spat a string of exasperated profanity.

"You took the words right out of my mouth," Swag agreed as he stopped scrolling. "Got it!" He pointed to a highlighted yellow line with exclamation marks bordering the status note. Opening the data packet he back-traced the diagnostic alert; they had cycled into unsafe levels. Within a few seconds Swag had reverse engineered the problem and found the root cause: a setting intentionally changed well beyond operating parameters that burned out a piece of hardware.

"How did that thing know how to do this?" Ricky asked as he adjusted the straps on his backpack.

"Whatever Edward knew how to do; the entity could do after Little Satan took him over. It's how they learn and work—they retain some skills and memories from their hosts when they hop bodies," he said matter-of-factly, remembering that entities' capabilities weren't common knowledge to those without ties to the EC. "We don't know their retention level is, but they have limits. Skills and memories must somehow atrophy over time."

"So he can just hack into any system to screw with us now?" Jack cried.

"No," Swag said as he pulled up the community roster Father had saved to the desktop. "But that reminds me that I needed to talk to you about something." He stood and motioned Michelle to take the chair. "Can you update this list for me while Jack and I have a quick chat? I need to verify who is still alive and account for everyone inside our doors… With Edward returned, I think Little Satan has gone bodiless, which means it must be hiding in the dark somewhere." He bit his lip, not wanting to even speculate that the adaptive Little Satan who evolved beyond Hermes' control might've learned a way around the light.

Michelle gulped against the lump in her throat but nodded and complied.

"I want to help," said Ricky.

Swag gave the big man an awkward hug-shoulder-pat hybrid. "I know you do," he said. I'll let you know as soon as I've got something I can put you in charge of."

"Okay," he said hesitantly, like he didn't quite believe him. "I really can help, you know."

"I know you can," Swag agreed, looking at his friend with soft eyes. "You saved my life once already—nobody knows what you're capable of as much as I do."

Ricky nodded, fully assured this time.

Jack took a few steps away to chat with Swag. He had noticed how the man had seemingly transformed into a wholly different person since his trip outside of Ark I. "What's up?"

"Now you understand how these things work." Swag tapped his temple with an index finger. "You and I are the last two people with the information that this thing really craves."

Father's number two man stared at Swag for a few seconds until he figured it out. "The code to get into this room?"

"Exactly."

"I have a code," Jack admitted, "but I honestly don't know the first thing to do with all of this," he gestured to the computers and consoles that surrounded them. "I was an English teacher. Outside of word processing, I'm not much good in here. I could barely run my email software, in all honesty."

"We can't know what Little Satan retained from Edward's or any others' minds," Swag said. "But if he could've hacked those doors he would've done it already. He needs the code and that puts the two largest targets on our heads. We have to be extremely careful—this thing is clever, *and it wants in.*"

Terror creased lines at his eyes and Jack nodded measuredly. "So what, then?"

"You may not be good with computers, but I need you to stick close to this room. At least I have some experience combatting these things..." He pulled out the Mark I and waved it momentarily.

"That's all well and good," Jack sighed, "but that won't help us if we all asphyxiate."

Swag nodded. "I do know what's wrong. It's a failed circuit board."

"You know electronics?"

"No. But I was there when Hank warned the General that he needed to have them all replaced because of this possibility." With a few keystrokes he brought up a real-time diagnostic that showed air pressure, oxygen levels, and systems performance stats. See that?"

"What am I looking at?"

"The system isn't just failing to recycle and oxygenate our air supply, it's actively venting the oxygen—pumping out our breathable atmosphere. We won't be able to survive for days—we've only got hours... General Braff's crew was supposed to swap them out. If they did, they must've missed one—but luckily..." he trailed off, recognizing that none of these people had any idea who Braff or Chu were.

"But luckily?"

"I know where they kept the spare parts," Swag finished. "The replacements had a built-in surge protector to prevent hardware failures like this."

Michelle interrupted them. "Everyone is accounted for." She hopped out of the chair. "What's next?"

Scowling, Swag muttered, "*Triage.*"

She gave him a wry look.

"You might not want to know." He lapped Ricky on the shoulder. "I need my best friend with me, Ricky. You can come with me."

###

Ricky looked around behind him and checked to make sure nobody had watched him slip away; he was not in his room. He felt guilty about that, but he needed something before he went on a short trip. Opening the door to Swag's room, Ricky tiptoed inside.

Ignoring the guilt in his gut, Ricky goose-stepped quickly. He had told Swag he needed five minutes before they left, and his stomach soured at the thought he might get caught—but he knew he needed to risk it. Ricky wasn't stupid—he just had Down syndrome—but apparently, he was the only one of his friends who knew their own limits. He understood how scary a mission with Swag might become and Ricky needed the one thing that might help him overcome his fears.

He scanned the ledge that encircled the room. Most of it had been filled up with the origami figures they'd made together. Most of them were ducks. Maybe it was the simple design and lines, or maybe it was because Ricky liked ducks. Regardless, he found that they were the easiest animals to fold.

Taking a freshly folded duck from his pocket Ricky approached the most special duck in the world. He didn't want Swag to think he had taken back his present. It would be awful if Swag thought he didn't want to be friends anymore.

But Ricky knew he needed that last remaining page from his joke book. If Swag was taking him on a mission, Ricky knew he'd need it. Something in his gut insisted he was right...despite the guilt. He just hoped that Swag wouldn't notice it had disappeared if he replaced it.

He stood in front of the prize and swapped the replacement duck from hand to hand much like he'd seen Indian Jones do with a sack of sand. Finally, he made the switch as quickly as possible, holding his breath the whole time. Once he finally exhaled he looked around, half expecting a giant boulder might chase him from the room.

Ricky put the most special duck in the world into his backpack and walked away from the room. He turned a corner and spotted Swag and a few others heading through the hallway. They waved him over and he trotted ahead.

With a little distance between himself and the crime, Ricky felt only *slightly* guilty. He'd replaced the duck, after all.

#

Triage, Swag thought as he signaled his crew to follow. He held a rolled-up tarp under one arm. Mankind was an endangered species and Swag needed to protect it as best as possible. Distasteful as it seemed, he needed to quietly assign values to every person in the community and risk only those with the lowest value. He knew he couldn't tell them, but those people made up his crew.

Jack and Michelle remained in contact by radio. Swag left them in the control room while he led the mission, bringing along Bud and Eunice. They were a much older couple who'd been on the same bus that brought Michelle and Ricky to the doors of Ark I. They were well past their prime and couldn't contribute to any future repopulation efforts once this whole debacle concluded. *Triage*.

Ricky followed them closely as well. Michelle hadn't been happy about his inclusion, but his enthusiasm at being picked for a team with such an important mission helped Swag calm her nerves about it.

Swag anxiously bit his lip as they walked. He'd promised to keep Ricky safe and she'd believed him—he hadn't explained the reasoning: Ricky was his *Plan B*.

When he'd first met her brother Swag hadn't really know what to think. Few people are ever prepared to embrace the disabled at first meeting. But now, after what they'd been through, Swag knew his affection for the man went far beyond surface appearances. That fact made it harder to lie to Michelle. A ball of dread formed in the pit of his gut and made the scientist suspect he would have to violate that trust. He had to give Ricky a job that only *he* could do. A bad job.

Pressing towards the airlock, Swag held his Mark I device at the ready and had instructed each of his teammates how to use it if he somehow fell under Little Satan's thrall. He knew how the entities worked—and he knew *this one* especially. Something devious waited for them; from the deep parts of Swag's mind, warnings screeched.

It didn't take them long to arrive at the airlock of door thirteen. They reported the location to their friends via radio. Swag left Ricky and Eunice at a distance while he scouted ahead. Dried gore and blood splattered the wall-mounted illumination panels, dimming them only slightly. Swag turned over Bart's body and found where the afflicted Edward had torn out the man's throat; what looked like teeth marks scraped the skin near the open wound.

Swag and Bud quickly wrapped the body in the tarp both in respect for the fallen and so that they wouldn't panic Ricky. They couldn't do anything about the blood splatters or the crimson tire tracks from where the afflicted Edward had earlier commandeered the cart that carried Gordon before the wounded soldier had been thrown outside and turned into Swag's adversary on the mountain trail.

"I was afraid of this," Swag spat after he turned to examine the environmental suits.

"What is it?" Bud asked in his warm baritone, not entirely understanding what he was seeing.

"The light rigs are gone," Swag stated into his handheld radio. "It must've either hidden them or destroyed them."

A brief blurt of static and then Michelle's voice came through, overpowering the muted curses flowing from Jack's mouth. "All of them? What about the spares at the motor pool?"

"Good call," he replied, already in motion.

The foursome regrouped and headed towards the hangar where Swag had earlier taken an electric vehicle to show Michelle the gardens. The stop at door thirteen had been on the way to retrieve the spare circuit boards needed for repairs, anyway.

As they neared the large door to the motor pool Swag spotted the familiar bend in the tunnel. He knew that around the corner they'd find the dark hallway. A whisper crept into his ears, trying to begin those dark drums, but Swag turned his face and rejected the sound, expelling it from his mind. They turned and went into the garage.

Just inside the large, corrugated door Bud found a rack of hanging environmental suits. "Where are the lights?" he asked while sorting through the rubberized outfits.

Swag, Eunice, and even Ricky joined him in rummaging through the items. Swag found some of the metal pieces used to construct and repair the harnesses and held up an adjustment tool. "It's the right spot, Bud. They were here, but *it took them too.*"

A pall of doom loomed over them until Swag dispelled it with a stroke of hope. "Airlock eight!" He cast a sidelong look to Ricky, but Ricky didn't understand what he'd referred to: the door where Ricky had rescued him from certain death.

"Can you and Eunice take one of these electric cars over to number eight? There should be a light harness there."

"If I knew where it was," Bud stated.

Swag spotted a stack of laminated, card-sized maps resting on a nearby desk which had never been used. He snatched a card and a spare walkie from the desktop, checked the battery, and handed them to the older man.

Ricky followed them over and curiously looked over the maps. He liked maps, and these were smaller than the ones he and Swag had drawn. Ricky didn't know whether or not

Indiana Jones would've used one of the laminated cards if he had the option.

As soon as Bud and Eunice got seated in the cart Swag handed them another tarp. "Janet," he said softly.

Eunice nodded and hid the tarp away.

"Let me know when you've found it. We'll go grab the QSM boards from storage."

As the other couple pulled out in one of the vehicles, Swag waved to Ricky. The big man looked the map over inquisitively. It had more detailed information than the larger maps he and Swag had drawn. Ricky decided the map was okay and slipped it into his backpack before loping over. He crawled into the passenger seat. "We're gonna go fix it now?"

"In a little bit," Swag said sniffing the air. It already smelled different—somehow thinner. "We're going to go get the parts quickly and hope that the others will have a light harness for me when we get back."

"Okay." He grinned. "Can I drive?"

Swag chuckled. "Not this time." They pulled out and went the opposite direction as the others. "Maybe once this is all sorted out I will teach you."

Ricky snorted as they zipped along. "Okay. But it sure seems like Mariokart to me, and I already know about that."

Moments later Swag stopped the cart next to a dark, rubber skid mark. He clambered out and looked over the wheel marks. They pointed straight at the intersection ahead. He hadn't noticed them when they passed this way earlier.

"It looks like a burnout, except that these things don't have that kind of takeoff power." He swallowed the lump in his throat—they must've been left intentionally; only driving at fast speed and slamming on the brakes would lay down enough rubber.

Ricky joined him at the black streaks. He looked up and pointed straight ahead and into the darkness of the unlit corridor. A red taillight reflector barely caught enough light to glint through the darkness.

Nervous, Swag led Ricky to the edge of the cursed hall and squinted, trying to look into the unlit distance, but he couldn't see well enough through the void.

Taking off his backpack Ricky pulled out a bright flashlight. The beam cut through the black and shone brightly enough that Swag had to squint against the rear reflectors.

"What all have you got in there?" Swag looked at Ricky and his backpack.

"Just… stuff I find."

Swag nodded and let Ricky keep his privacy.

"Can you shine the light up a little higher?"

Ricky complied, happy to help. The light revealed a pile of light harnesses heaped upon the flatbed on the rear of the cart.

Swag's eyes scanned the threatening darkness and wondered if this was some kind of elaborate trap. Still in thought, he nearly jumped to yell when Ricky took a nervous step into the darkness. His frightened fists clutched the jittering beam of light.

"Ricky! What are you doing?"

"Y-you said it couldn't hurt me or Father cuz we were special. Right?"

"I *think* so, yes. Ricky, come out of there!"

"And we really need those lights?" He took three more steps through the dark.

Swag bit his lower lip, even though his friend voluntarily played the part he suspected he might need him for all along. "Yes, if I'm going to go outside and fix that last circuit board."

Ricky gave a kind of squeal as he steeled himself and then he dashed towards the light rigs. He yelped as he ran as if he'd waded through a cold pond. The light flipped around, and Ricky's flashing beam momentarily blinded the scientist. Out of breath, Ricky laid the contraptions at Swag's feet.

"You did good, Ricky," he said as he picked up the harness. Swag sighed as he looked it over. All of the light panels were cracked and busted. None of them would work.

Ricky spotted the disappointed look on Swag's face. "You need me to get some others?"

"No," he replied. He knew Little Satan toyed with him; undoubtedly the others had also been damaged. "Let's go get the parts. It should only take us a few minutes."

As soon as they got into the cart the radio crackled and Bud's voice chirped through the tinny speaker. "Everything's here except for the light rigs. We found a couple envirosuits... also some skid marks like someone came in too hot and slammed on the brakes."

"Copy that." Swag said, trying not to curse and give Ricky a bad impression of him. The skids confirmed his thoughts: Little Satan destroyed all of the light rigs, so they couldn't safely go outside. "We'll meet at your door in about twenty minutes." Swag exhaled his resignation and zoomed away to retrieve the QSM circuit boards. He dreaded the part that he knew came next.

#

Standing several feet away from the corpse encapsulated within the tarp Eunice flashed Swag a disapproving look as the group stood at airlock eight. "No. you can't ask him to do that," she insisted.

Swag ignored her and walked towards Ricky who stood close to the door. Eunice glared at his back, but Bud stayed her with a hand on her shoulder.

"Ricky, you know how you wanted to help, earlier?"

Ricky sighed, drooping his shoulders. He was decidedly less enthusiastic about it, now. "You want me to go outside again, don't you?"

Grimacing, Swag nodded slowly.

"I don't like the dark."

"I know."

An awkward, heavy moment lingered between them.

"You don't have to do this, Ricky," Eunice called.

"Yes, I do," Ricky said.

Swag glared at Eunice. Ricky was right—it had to be him.

"It's not right," Eunice insisted.

"I never said it was right," Swag snapped at her. "But right now, Ricky is the only one who stands a chance of saving the human race and I can say from personal experience that he's better suited to it than anyone else inside Ark I."

Eunice glowered while Ricky beamed at the remark. "You really think so?"

"Buddy, I know so. And I know it's scary, but all heroes get scared at times."

Ricky nodded and fidgeted with the QSM board Swag had given him. "Will it be hard?"

"No. It only goes in one way and it will be easy to install. Just pull the one with the red light out of its socket, and plug this new one in; the light will turn green and the machine will reset and work properly."

Swag showed him where the malfunctioning unit could be reached on a map. Following a service trail beyond this door would take him there with relative ease. "The light rig is busted, but you've got your flashlight and we will be with you every step of the way. There's a camera on your helmet and I'll be able to talk to you through it on the microphone and earpiece."

He'd begun showing Ricky how to properly don the outfit, something his friend hadn't done last time. Behind him Eunice snorted and scowled. Finally, she went back to the electric cart and sat with a huff. Stewing a few seconds longer in the cab, she picked up the radio and called for Michelle.

"Michelle, did you know that Doctor Swaggart is sending your brother outside into the dark with no light?"

Swag's radio picked up the broadcast from the unit clipped to his belt. He fixed her with a deadly glare.

Michelle's shouts rattled the tiny speaker. "He did what!"

Slowly, methodically, Swag walked with measured steps towards the woman while she jawed over the radio like Swag's perpetually disappointed grandmother at bridge.

"Yeah. He's got the poor boy dressed in that space suit and is about to send him outside with nothing but a flashlight and a microchip thingy. I tried to tell him it's a bad idea, but he insisted that poor Ricky goes outside."

Swag took his wild eyes off of the woman for a second and levied them against Bud who'd stepped between him and Eunice, anticipating trouble. Bud stood back when he saw Swag's rage held in check by the man's willpower.

Leaning forward into the cart Swag plucked the radio from her hands. She tried to snatch it back, but the intensity of his gaze pushed her back into the seat.

"Listen to me and listen well," he hissed quietly enough that Ricky couldn't hear. "The entire species is resting on the shoulders of that man right there. I will only say this once: this is not a democracy and I will not let his sister, Father, and every other person back in the community choke to death because someone failed to make hard choices. This is not the good-old days in the U S of A, and the only thing keeping me from slapping the insubordination out of you and throwing you through that airlock right now is knowing how it might distract Ricky when I need him focused. *Might* distract Ricky. One more peep from you and I swear that this tarp will have *two* bodies in it. *Do you understand?*" His question remained far from hypothetical and demanded an answer.

Blanched white from his dire warning Eunice nodded.

"Good. That was your only strike." Swag tossed the radio to Bud and fixed him with an intense gaze; he'd been close enough to hear. He wouldn't need a similar pep-talk.

Bud nodded in response to Swag's questioning look which demanded a similar answer.

The radios continued to squawk. Michelle demanded that someone respond. Finally Swag held the unit to his mouth. "Michelle?"

A burst of angrily squelched words flooded the airwaves.

"Michelle, calm down," he insisted.

"Don't you dare tell me to calm down!" Another barrage of angry words. Finally, the channel clicked slightly, ending her transmission.

Swag let the silence play out for a couple seconds, giving her a few moments to process the difficult news. "Michelle, do you trust me? I know this sounds hard and I don't have time to explain what's actually happening over here, but do you trust me?"

It was her turn to leave a few seconds of contemplative silence in the transmission's wake.

Ricky beckoned for the radio. Swag handed it over.

"It's the only way," Ricky said into the walkie.

Michelle responded, "I love you Ricky. Be careful."

"I will." He gave it back to Swag who gave the big guy a hug. Ricky readily returned it. "Keep my sister safe," he whispered.

"I will."

Swag motioned for Bud and Eunice to approach. "You guys help him get ready and make sure his air supply is on. I need to get back to the main control room in order to unlock this door. I'll radio when you can let him out." He climbed behind the wheel of the other vehicle and looked at them with serious eyes. "You will let him out."

They nodded, and Swag sped back towards the promenade.

###

The door hissed, and Ricky stepped outside, tiptoeing nervously through the cold air. He walked up the trail at a steady pace, following the laminated map card from the motor-pool. Swag had drawn the general route in black sharpie and labeled a few crudely drawn landmarks to keep him on target.

Swag, Jack, and a bleary-eyed Michelle watched the real-time video feed from the large screen in the central console of the operations room. The indicator readings from Ricky's HUD had mirrored on their screen. Aside from his pulse being understandably high, everything looked fine.

"You're doing good," Michelle encouraged him as he huffed along, scanning the beam of light around in broad swaths.

Swag grinned as Ricky deviated course slightly to the place where he'd rescued Swag once before. A beam from the flashlight scanned the footpath until it locked on the old copy of *1001 Jokes and Puns*. He quickly bent and retrieved the lost book. Ricky stuffed the book into his backpack before wordlessly resuming his mission.

Despite the directions Swag had given him, landmarks proved difficult to spot in the terrain and Ricky hadn't understood all of the instructions. He'd gotten twisted around a few times, but eventually he climbed a steep embankment and found the control box jutting up from the jagged rock.

After figuring out how the access hatch released, Ricky exposed the face of the maintenance panel. Rows and rows of similar looking boards jutted out from their installation ports on the main bank. Each one had an indicator light glowing with a dim emerald hue—all but the solitary bright LED that shone red.

"This is it?" Ricky asked as he set the repair board on the ledge just inside the hatch.

"That's the one," Swag confirmed.

"Is this the one? Guys? Swag—Michelle?" The line garbled with static.

"Ricky can you hear us?"

On the screen Ricky paused and then finally rushed to remove the damaged unit. Working too hastily he didn't quite get the new board seated fully. The light next to the port remained red.

"What's that noise?" Fear bled into Ricky's voice and the camera blurred as he whipped his head one way and another. He screamed and then the camera spun as Ricky's footing gave away. The video and tilted skyward for a second before switching to static and then going black. The information supplied from the HUD had also winked out. Its data switched from an actual reading to an estimated number based on the rate Ricky had been using the suit's resources.

"Ricky?" Michelle shouted into the receiver. "Ricky!"

Swag hung his head as the seconds stretched into a couple minutes. Nothing but dead air came back over the severed connection. Pain hung thick between the crew in the operations room… and then the air cyclers suddenly powered up.

"Ricky? Ricky, it's Michelle," she said frantically, but try as she might, no reply came.

Michelle couldn't tear her eyes away from the screen. Her raw emotions threatened to undo her with every new second that slipped by.

Minutes stretched out piling onto each other until an hour had passed, and then another. As Ark I's oxygen readings on the main diagnostic console crawled north of ninety percent, Ricky's O2 estimates languished.

Swag finally took the radio and said heavy-heartedly, "Bud. Eunice. You two can come back now." He slumped dejectedly into his chair and hung his head.

Even though the air had come back on it still felt like a defeat.

Michelle, broken hearted only moments ago, stood and wiped her eyes. She smoothed her clothes with a sudden, unnerving tranquility. Everything about her calm composure indicated that something inside her had just died. Wordlessly she turned and left the control center. Neither Swag nor Jack dared stop her.

27

Michelle wandered back and forth in the promenade. She aimlessly paced the distance between the main water station and the door to the central control hub. Unsure how much time had passed or how many laps she'd fretfully walked; her anxiety rendered time meaningless.

Upon measured steps she tried to calm the burgeoning emotions that threatened to overwhelm her mind. Reaching the fountain station in the main court she paused for a drink. Michelle's mind threatened to tear itself apart over fear that her brother lay on the mountain slope choking on his depleted air tank. On a return lap Michelle's mind convinced her that Ricky lived and waited for someone to open one of the lesser known airlocks that dotted Ark I.

Her mind fixated on the hope and conviction that Ricky was somehow fine. She felt the communal eyes upon her, pitying her and judging her all at once as news of her loss began spreading, mostly thanks to Eunice, the disgruntled busybody.

Checking in on Father didn't alleviate her mind. He'd improved much, and his progress pleased her, but her mind wouldn't give up the thoughts that she needed to strike out and rescue Ricky.

Michelle slipped out and into the hallway nearest the entry to Ark I's tunnel network. She knew on some deep level that Swag would do everything in his power to bring

Ricky home—but *he was her brother*. If anybody could—or should—be there for him, it was her.

Finally, her nerves got the better of her. Michelle hastily jotted down a few notes and hung them on a clipboard at the foot of Father's bed... just in case. *Not that anything could go wrong,* she assured herself despite noting her patient's detailed care plan.

With hardened resolve she left her infirmary, turned towards the endless hallways, and struck out at a brisk pace.

###

Swag scanned the crowd and tried to locate Michelle. Enough time had passed that he hoped she might've cooled down enough to talk. He was sure the loss of her brother would eat her up inside... and he wasn't doing much better himself at the moment.

He stood on his toes to try and get a better angle to help him spot the tiny woman. Swag made a circuit around the promenade and checked in at the infirmary but didn't see her anywhere. Concern growing, he returned to the community.

Others noticed his search; his face wore a look of confused disquiet. As Swag began another, more urgent circuit, Jack spotted him from his post near the operations door. Jack read his concern and sent Edward to see what the matter was.

Swag closed the gap, glad Jack took his warning to stay near the operations room seriously. He linked shoulders with Edward. "Have you seen Michelle?"

Edward shook his head negatively and waved to Bud and Eunice; they stood at the nearby fountain and filled their water jugs. Bud raised his eyebrows inquisitively at them, but Eunice bristled when she saw Swag.

As they approached, Swag and Edward stepped around the dark stains which had seeped into the floor at the subterranean hatch's edges, marring the surface with bloodlines. They marked the access to the below-decks utilities where the afflicted Debra emerged to terrorize the community and overtake Jennifer before Debra's body succumbed to its wounds. Jennifer had barely ventured beyond her cabin doors since.

"Have you seen Michelle?" Swag asked them, trying to keep his voice down.

Eunice crossed her arms and looked away.

Bud pointed to the distance. "I saw her heading that way about an hour ago. I expected she went to see Father. How's he doing, anyway?"

"He's doing better. You're sure she went to see him?"

"Well, no," Bud responded. "I just assumed so."

Eunice sighed loudly, inserting herself without speaking.

Swag wasn't prepared to stomach any of her passive aggressive games. "Do you have something to contribute, Eunice?"

She played coy at first, but finally turned to face him. "You sure don't seem to get it, Mister Swaggart." She rolled her eyes like a teenage diva. "If you can't see it then I just don't know that you can be helped."

Swag bit his lip and let her vent for a second, hoping she could provide him with something useful. He momentarily longed for the days of his solitary lifestyle—just so long as it didn't include people like Eunice. Of all the aspects of human companionship provided by the remnant, attitudes like this were his least favorite. He glanced at Edward who stood still as a board, trying to avoid Eunice's scrutiny.

"You sent her brother out there to die and then you just left him there," she spat accusingly. "Michelle obviously went in search of him. She's probably put on the tiniest enviro-suit those EC monsters left in this godforsaken place and now she's wandering around outside looking for Ricky." She glanced at a digital clock on the distant wall and noted that the sun wouldn't be up quite yet. "In the dark," she added insidiously.

"You know that for sure?" Swag kept his tone even.

"Well, no. But it's what any person with a scrap of decency or an ounce of humanity would do. If she's not with Father, you can mark my words that she's outside."

Eunice raised her finger and started wagging it to further chastise him, but Swag had already turned to leave with Edward in tow. Instead, she called after him, "This is your fault, you know!"

"Is she for real?" Edward asked under his breath as they made a line for Jack.

"I'm afraid so." Swag pulled Jack aside as he picked up a radio. "I'm taking Edward with me to look for Michelle. Keep me up to date on anything important."

Jack looked worried. He whispered, "Do you think she went outside?"

"God, I hope not," Swag muttered as he pulled up the operations' screen and double-checked the door logs. "Nothing in or out since Ricky left." He rubbed the frustrated grimace from his face and hovered his cursor over the lockdown sequence; the doors had been made operational again in order to let Ricky depart, but now…

Jack stood behind him, watching him hesitate. After a few seconds he said, "You have to do it Swag. It sucks, but you have to lock the doors. If Ricky was capable of getting back to a door, he would've done it by now. You said it yourself, Michelle is essential personnel. We can't let her out where these… things, can take her."

Swag tried to look at it from another point of view. "Ricky has *maybe* an hour or so worth of oxygen. He *could* still be alive."

"And two hours more of darkness," Jack said, dispelling Swag's hope. "I know you see what I see."

Swag stood, vexed and frustrated; he grabbed a handful of his own hair and growled through his anger. Finally, he turned and kicked the office chair across the room. "Damn it!" he screamed at whatever fate or forces above might be in control—condemning his friends to such torment turned his stomach.

His mind cycled through snippets of all the times in his life his friends had been doomed by his own hand or his unfortunate timing: Raymond, Jessica, and now Ricky. Finally he hung his head and clicked the door lock command, sealing out all remaining hope of Ricky's reentry.

Jack let him vent his rage for a few moments longer before he dared say anything. "You did the right thing. We both know it."

Swag sighed. He keyed in another command and then typed Hank's master code in to verify and override Michelle's key and lock her out of the central operations hub for the next twenty-four hours as a precaution. He looked away and glanced at the General's desk tucked into the alcove beyond them. Swag wasn't about to risk Ricky's sacrifice to clumsy administrative oversight—that was the one thing Braff *had* taught him.

With a frown the scientist turned and left the room. He grabbed Edward as he left and the two took off in an electric cart.

A few minutes later they checked in at the infirmary. Edward spotted the care plan Michelle had clipped to Father's chart. "Why would she leave such a detailed message behind unless she anticipated something drastic?"

Cursing again, Swag turned and left the room with Edward hot on his heels. They clambered into the vehicle and zipped down the hallway in search of any clues for Michelle's whereabouts.

###

Ricky crawled to his knees. Howling fearfully, he blinked back the hot tears which kept blurring his vision. He kept forgetting that he wore a helmet and, out of habit, tried to wipe them from his face to no avail.

Even without the tears getting in the way he couldn't find his bearings in the dark. Nothing but blackness existed beyond his helmet's face shield.

Some kind of beeping in his helmet finally distracted Ricky and an unfamiliar icon lit up on the edge of his helmet's HUD. He didn't know what it meant, and the interference made him tangle his sometimes-clumsy feet.

Get up! Get up, he told himself. *What would Indiana Jones do? What would Swag do?* He finally mustered the internal fortitude to push the terror out of his mind and think clearly about his next step. Ricky got to his feet.

Earlier on the ridge, he'd lost his footing and slipped down the slope, only barely catching the edge of the mechanical service box that he'd opened in order to make repairs. When he fell, the video and microphone had gotten disconnected or broken—Ricky wasn't sure which. While he'd managed to pull his way up just enough to switch on the QSM board and help his sister and his friends, he eventually slid over the edge and into a gully. Ricky had so completely lost his bearings in the fall that he'd become hopelessly lost. He even dropped the map Swag gave him along with his flashlight; neither were anywhere to be found.

Ricky looked for the way back, but it did him no good. The ravine was some kind of a deep, bowl-shaped pock in the mountainside and he wasn't sure which way he'd even tumbled down.

After finding the easiest way up the embankment he tripped on the silver handle of his flashlight. He nearly began crying again just to have light again—however dim. The all-consuming darkness of the morning strangled the beam of light as Ricky wandered for over an hour, looking for any familiar landmarks.

He wished his friends could come get him. *Even if they had light suits, they wouldn't know where I am... I don't know where I am.*

The whelming fear crept into his mind again and he countered by thinking about positive memories. He liked his times folding origami with Swag the best... sometimes they'd also drawn maps of the Ark. Ricky suddenly remembered that he had their hand-made map in his trusty backpack. He liked his backpack, but he was pretty sure Debra had died right after giving it to him.

Ricky pushed those thoughts away and concentrated on the map.

He studied the hand drawn papers for a few seconds under the dimming power of his flashlight. It shone less brightly than it did an hour ago, but there was enough light to make out the familiar icons on the map that Swag had drawn for him. Ricky felt pretty sure that some of the rugged, silhouette forms on the ridge were the long-range communications array. He didn't know exactly what that meant, but he'd also heard about that kind of thing in the movies and recognized the shape of a satellite-dish shape and got excited. It wasn't on the map, but Swag had referenced its general area when they'd drawn the map.

Trying to calm his breathing, Ricky plotted a course back to the airlock doors, though his heart felt a sinking feeling that either his air or flashlight might fail first. Death scared him incredibly. Ricky tried not to cry, but he really didn't want to die, and the flicker of his light beam suddenly convinced him that would happen. People around him always talked as if he didn't understand, but Ricky understood perfectly well when people talked about how horrible it would be to run out of oxygen—and he knew that it was his likely fate.

Blinking back more tears he came to the edge of a rocky overhang. He leaned up against a mechanical housing unit to rest for a moment while trying to make sense of the new beeping in his HUD. Ricky was pretty sure the oxygen indicator's flashing between orange and red was a bad thing.

He felt ever more certain that he needed to control his breathing.

Ricky looked down the ridgeline as the steel shell below his frame hummed with some kind of activity. He scanned what lay below the edge with his flashlight. Some kind of old road or trail stretched below him and into the distance.

A glint of light reflected off something nearby. His flashlight caught the rearview mirror of a car parked on the road. His heart leapt into his throat with joy and he hoped an airlock might be nearby. He took out his map again only to find that it was quite a distance before the next airlock. He hoped that the unmarked road would get him to an airlock before the oxygen expired.

No sooner did he put his map back in his pack than his flashlight sputtered twice and then died.

Panic set in. He tapped the device hoping it could come back on at least long enough to help him over the dangerous ledge and onto the road. He felt the tears welling up deep inside. The dead batteries refused.

Ricky crept towards the edge in pitch blackness and soon discovered the lip of the cliff. Turning backwards he dangled his feet over the edge and into nothingness where he could not see. He knew it was maybe a ten foot drop at most, but the all-encompassing darkness enveloped him in a blanket of fear. He crawled back and tried a different route.

On all fours, Ricky tried to navigate the stony edge. His breath came in ragged, gasps, consuming more and more precious oxygen. Finally, the darkness won his heart and Ricky curled into a weeping, bawling heap.

He let out a long moan of dread, wishing he'd never tried to be brave, wishing none of this had ever happened, wishing he had enough light to read his joke book by. As his sob ran out of breath and he paused to suck in another despairing gulp of air, he heard the wail of a warning alert inside his helmet. Ricky noticed the red oxygen alert on his HUD as it switched to black.

Rocking himself slightly Ricky recited the few jokes that came to mind as he tried to distract himself from his dire situation. "How does NASA throw a birthday party? First, they have to planet. What's the difference between a guitar and a fish? You can't tune a fish." Ricky's resolve finally broke for good. Snot ran down his nose and tears flowed. He wasn't able to wipe away either. Through his ragged breaths and cries he was barely able to ask, "Why did the belt go to jail?"

His eyes suddenly fixed on a light source. It barely glowed in the darkness and pixelated like crystals through his tear drenched eyes. A dim light hid within the machinery he'd rested against. Beyond a heavy, hinged gate the metal housing pulsed from the inside with a dim light. Ricky crawled to it and opened the grate—it was surprisingly easy to remove—he peered a few feet ahead. As his eyes further adjusted he moved in deeper and his breathing calmed enough to answer his own joke, "Because it held up a pair of pants."

The opening appeared to be a metal shaft of some kind. He pushed his backpack ahead of him so that he could move through without getting stuck. Ricky found the source of the light: a very dim network of moving lasers that crisscrossed the ducting. Ricky didn't know what they were, but they didn't hurt him when he put a hand in the field of beams and, so he kept going. Several feet beyond, he spotted some kind of flashlight and grabbed it up. He hadn't seen one exactly like this before, but he hoped it would be super bright.

Ricky thumbed it on, but it didn't light up, though an LED glowed, so it had power. He stuffed it inside his backpack next to his other, drained flashlight. "Maybe I can swap bulbs or batteries later?" he wondered aloud.

He pushed a few more feet ahead. The beeping continued, and his HUD warned him that the oxygen was all but gone. In the distance he spotted a light shining through a crimped and broken section of ductwork.

With eyes swimming from the oxygen-starved environment of his suit, Ricky peered through the hole. A huge warehouse sprawled below. "Just like the end of Indiana Jones," he croaked.

Ricky struggled to get his arms into position and he took his helmet off. He took a deep draught of thin, but oxygenated air which flowed around him as it bled out and into the void behind him. Ricky smiled, finally latching onto a small shred of hope. And then the ducting hardware suddenly broke free and Ricky plummeted towards the ground.

They hadn't even made it to the first set of airlock doors on their search when Swag's radio crackled. Jack asked, "Swag, are you there?"

Edward grabbed it and responded. "He's driving. This is Edward. We read you."

"Michelle is here."

"Oh good," Swag said with relief as he slowed the cart.

"She sure must be ticked off at Swag, though. She's in his room, trashing it like a little Tasmanian devil... well, she's trashing parts of it."

Swag snatched the radio as soon as he'd turned the cart and pointed it back towards home. "Wait. What do you mean by that?"

"She's ripping each of your little paper ducks apart," Jack said. "I thought I heard her trying to get into Operations, but you locked her out. I guess that must've really sent her over the edge."

"*The most special duck in the world*," Swag gasped. "Jack! Jack, you've got to keep yourself locked inside the control room, but you've also got stop her from getting those ducks!"

Confusion permeated Jack's voice. "What are you talking about?"

Punching the throttle as high as it would go he yelled into the receiver, "It's Little Satan! Michelle knew that I hid my secret, the master access code, inside one of the ducks—it will let the entity into the operations room and kill everyone!"

Jack's voice came back huffing and puffing as if he'd sprung into movement. "I'm on it!"

Swag's speed made the wheels squeal as they rounded a couple sharp corners. Coming up to the final straightaway the scientist tapped his code into the tablet and tossed it to Edward.

"We're going to come in hot. Get those main doors opened or else we're toast." Swag fumbled at his belt to make sure the Mark I device was still clipped and easily accessible. "If it comes down to it you know how to use this thing, right?"

Edward finished tapping in a few commands on the tablet and tried to ignore the butterflies running amok in his gut. "Got the door opening, now." He nodded to the Mark I, "Just point and click."

"Basically, yes, and watch out for vomit backsplash."

The long corridor began straightening out for the final approach and the slowly opening door moved along its hydraulic rail. Swag bit his lip and hugged the light panels nearest the wall so that he could "thread the needle" as the huge doors opened with reluctant speed.

Edward squirmed and hugged his knees as they shot towards the opening sliver of space that granted them entry. He groaned anxiously as they shot through.

Swag barked the next order, "As soon as you can, cycle it back so it closes again. We can't let the entity get away!

We've got to capture it while we can—as long as it hasn't found my duck."

Far down the promenade they spotted a throng of people flailing with enough commotion to look like NFL teams at the line of scrimmage. The shoving intensified as the cart drew closer and Edward tapped the door commands as quickly as he could. A huge group of people had captured tiny Michelle who fought them with superhuman strength.

"Hold her! Hold Her!" Swag shouted. "I've got the capture device ready!"

Michelle busted free and charged away like a rushing linebacker. She grabbed a handful of Eunice's hair and flung the bystander clear across the room before the diminutive doctor collapsed. Swag leapt from the vehicle with the Mark I pointed at his friend; he jammed his finger against the switch.

She crawled to all fours but remained crouched over, trying to collect her breathe in great heaving grasps. Swag, confused, kept pressing the activator button over and over, but it had no effect on her.

Finally, Michelle looked up and into Swag's eyes. "I'm so sorry," she said, seeming more childlike than ever before. "I'm sorry I left."

Swag spotted the thick dribble and chunks of vomit streaking down her chin. He whirled around and found the old woman Michelle had flung in her final act of desperation. A slimy pool of barf marked the spot where Eunice had slid to a stop before leaping to her feet and escaping.

The older lady sprinted at an Olympic pace and easily slid between the closing aperture and the wall while Swag remained helpless to act except for glaring daggers at the door as it hissed shut.

"I'm so sorry," Michelle said again, bawling hot tears as she crawled to her feet and stood before her friend: helpless, exhausted, and humiliated. "I don't know how it happened. I don't remember any darkness; I bent over to get a drink and then I was falling down, and I was here."

Swag pulled her into a hug and let tears of his own boil over. "I'm just glad I didn't lose you, too. I don't think I can take another one."

28

Jack joined the cluster of people who'd gathered outside the door to Swag's apartment. The danger seemed to have finally passed. He motioned to Swag and silently asked if it was safe for him to approach.

Swag nodded and resumed helping provide first aid. None in the mob that tried to capture the afflicted Michelle seemed too badly injured; the worst injury was a dislocated shoulder. Michelle sheepishly joined the first aid efforts, but her eyes remained distant and remorseful.

"I'm so sorry," Jack said guiltily as he walked among the injured.

"No," Swag insisted. "You did the right thing. The entity didn't get what it wanted. I looked through the mess. I didn't see the duck anywhere. It was on a very specific piece of paper. I couldn't find it, but neither did Little Satan."

After they finished treating the last of the hurt ones, Swag shook Michelle out of her growing fugue. While the smaller clinic within the promenade had a cache of supplies, they'd gone through a significant amount of them. "Do you think we ought to restock from the infirmary?" The larger sickbay connected to the medical storage cache.

Michelle turned and stared at the huge door which sealed the remnant off from the tunnel system—the main infirmary was located about a quarter mile down the hall on the other side of the barricade. A light of dawning terror lit in her eyes and she grabbed Swag.

"The demon might know my code—it can get to Father!"

Swag sprang into action with Edward hot on his heels. A palpable tension rippled through the crowd of mixed wounded and healthy people; Edward got the door to begin opening as Swag pulled the cart up. Edward and Michelle leapt aboard even as the vehicle still moved. It peeled away and hurried towards the massive gate.

Michelle ventured, "Maybe we should risk a facilities change and move Father closer—back to the smaller facility?"

Swag nodded his agreement as he piloted the craft through the tight opening which crawled ajar at what seemed an infinitesimally sluggish pace. Loping towards them at her top speed, Eunice charged them from a distance, running with a fierce limp.

Reaching for his Mark I Swag asked a question without taking his eyes from the approaching woman. "Didn't she seem a lot faster when she ran away earlier?"

Michelle nodded.

"Much faster," Edward agreed.

Swag stopped the cart and disembarked. Holding the device at the ready, Eunice remained undeterred. The scientist activated the Mark I anyways as soon as she'd come into range, just to be safe.

Her face had reddened from the jog and pain creased the old woman's face as she limped towards the group. Sweat stains ringed her armpits and framed the puke splotches which stretched from her midsection to collar. Tear streaks crisscrossed her face.

Swag turned to his comrades and asked with worry in his voice, "Guys? Where did Little Satan go?"

Father grimaced as they loaded him onto the back of the electric cart. He whistled sharply and sucked air through his teeth while he gritted through the pain.

Swag tried to be more gentle as he helped the man lie back. He'd slipped between conscious and unconscious three times since they'd arrived on the heels of discovering Eunice. The fact that he was conscious at all was a miracle.

Blood seeped from the man's chest where the afflicted Eunice had used a scalpel to cut the lines of a satanic pentagram across his torso. Little Satan could have killed the remnant leader but chose instead to taunt them.

"You don't understand," Father insisted, grunting through the pain as he faded in and out of cognizance. "Only faith can beat this creature."

Swag nodded and helped get Father situated, presuming the man's rambling was connected to his barely lucid state. Edward followed Michelle from the storage section with an armload of supplies.

"Power will soon fade," Father croaked as his eyes rolled back in his head. His breaths became ragged and labored as he continued trying to get his message across. "Every one thousand years it happens… have to have faith."

Michelle got close and put a hand on Father's head.

His eyes suddenly jolted open and he tried to sit up, but couldn't. "My journal! My notes—they explain everything," e insisted, and then collapsed back into unconsciousness.

"Wait. What do you mean?" Edward asked him, but the seemed more permanent this time. "He was trying to omething," the youth insisted.

ded like religious rambling to me," Swag said, dom thoughts strung together."

time with him," Edward insisted. "He kept search on the history of demons early happened. It may be just 'religious rambling,' but do you really want to take that chance?"

"I already know I can preclude the idea of faith and religion," Swag insisted. "I know what I *can* prove and operate only on the empiric. Faith has no place in science."

Edward frowned at him. "Maybe we can at least check out his journal… just in case it has something useful?"

Swag shrugged and left it in the realm of possibility. They pulled the cart around and returned to the promenade, leaving the door opened behind them since all persons were presently accounted for and quick access to the main infirmary might become a high priority if anything else went wrong.

#

Swag led Eunice towards his ransacked cabin. His door remained open despite the automatic closing feature in the door's mechanics; debris and random items had jammed the door's runner.

His quarters overlooked the main court. The scientist locked eyes with Jack who stood on the far side of the chamber making small talk with a few other men. They nodded to each other, signaling *all clear* to each other without words.

Eunice slumped wearily into a chair in Swag's quarters. She rubbed the aching knee that had been causing her limp. "I really don't know what else I can tell you," she insisted. "I really don't remember anything, just like everyone else wh[o] ever got possessed."

"Think," Swag insisted. "Did you feel anything, ha[ve] lasting impressions beyond the 'grossness' of it al[l? We've] got to get all the details we can in order to beat t[his."]

She shook her head repeatedly. "No. [It was] like blacking out on a tequila bender [and I] found puke as I suddenly, slowly

Father grimaced as they loaded him onto the back of the electric cart. He whistled sharply and sucked air through his teeth while he gritted through the pain.

Swag tried to be more gentle as he helped the man lie back. He'd slipped between conscious and unconscious three times since they'd arrived on the heels of discovering Eunice. The fact that he was conscious at all was a miracle.

Blood seeped from the man's chest where the afflicted Eunice had used a scalpel to cut the lines of a satanic pentagram across his torso. Little Satan could have killed the remnant leader but chose instead to taunt them.

"You don't understand," Father insisted, grunting through the pain as he faded in and out of cognizance. "Only faith can beat this creature."

Swag nodded and helped get Father situated, presuming the man's rambling was connected to his barely lucid state. Edward followed Michelle from the storage section with an armload of supplies.

"Power will soon fade," Father croaked as his eyes rolled back in his head. His breaths became ragged and labored as he continued trying to get his message across. "Every one thousand years it happens… have to have faith."

Michelle got close and put a hand on Father's head.

His eyes suddenly jolted open and he tried to sit up, but couldn't. "My journal! My notes—they explain everything," he insisted, and then collapsed back into unconsciousness.

"Wait. What do you mean?" Edward asked him, but the coma seemed more permanent this time. "He was trying to tell us something," the youth insisted.

"It sounded like religious rambling to me," Swag said, "maybe just random thoughts strung together."

"I spent lots of time with him," Edward insisted. "He kept a journal and did lots of research on the history of demons and all of the apocalypses that *nearly* happened. It may be just 'religious rambling,' but do you really want to take that chance?"

"I already know I can preclude the idea of faith and religion," Swag insisted. "I know what I *can* prove and operate only on the empiric. Faith has no place in science."

Edward frowned at him. "Maybe we can at least check out his journal… just in case it has something useful?"

Swag shrugged and left it in the realm of possibility. They pulled the cart around and returned to the promenade, leaving the door opened behind them since all persons were presently accounted for and quick access to the main infirmary might become a high priority if anything else went wrong.

###

Swag led Eunice towards his ransacked cabin. His door remained open despite the automatic closing feature in the door's mechanics; debris and random items had jammed the door's runner.

His quarters overlooked the main court. The scientist locked eyes with Jack who stood on the far side of the chamber making small talk with a few other men. They nodded to each other, signaling *all clear* to each other without words.

Eunice slumped wearily into a chair in Swag's quarters. She rubbed the aching knee that had been causing her limp. "I really don't know what else I can tell you," she insisted. "I really don't remember anything, just like everyone else who ever got possessed."

"Think," Swag insisted. "Did you feel anything, have any lasting impressions beyond the 'grossness' of it all? We've got to get all the details we can in order to beat this thing."

She shook her head repeatedly. "No. Nothing—it was like blacking out on a tequila bender, except in reverse. I found puke as I suddenly, slowly woke up and became me again. I remember dropping the knife and washing the blood off my hands right away."

"Wait," Swag pounced on the detail. "The blood on your hands was still wet?"

Eunice nodded.

"Where were you when came back to consciousness? Was it a knife or a scalpel?"

"A scalpel, I suppose, but what difference does it make?"

"You were in the infirmary when you awoke?"

She nodded again. "Like I said: Tequila bender, hunched over the puke pot. Well, the sink in this case… it was one of those scrub sinks like the doctors used in all of the old hospital dramas."

Swag rubbed his chin thoughtfully. "This is important. Do you remember vomiting in the sink? Like, did the waste go down the drain or into an incineration or waste bin?"

"I remember puking in the *sink*. Retching all over the drain was the first thing I recall. Then I shut the water off and ran to find help."

"Did *you* turn the water on, or was it already on?"

She thought carefully about it before replying. "It was already on. I just turned it off."

Swag leapt to his feet and lost all interest in the witness. "I know where Little Satan has gone!" He dashed out and into the courtyard area, haunted by his deduction: *there were no lights* inside *of the water reclamation systems—it was inside the pipes. The plumbing network provided an infrastructure that could take the entity almost anywhere!*

He arrived in the main area where Janessa, the pregnant woman he'd saved earlier, hunched over the drinking fountain at the main water hub. She suddenly stiffened and contorted. Her slender fingers gnarled into knobby, greedy claws and she snapped her head around to stare directly at Jack, fixing him with predatory eyes.

Swag's heart plunged sickeningly into his gut. Little Satan must've remembered from Michelle's mind that Jack had Operations access.

She launched towards Jack as if the fetus her body carried did nothing to encumber her.

"Affliction! Affliction," Swag screamed as he sprinted towards the fray.

Jack whirled to face the source of the warning. His eyes widened in dawning terror as he recognized what happened. He whirled around clumsily and made a dash for the safety of the control room door.

Janessa outpaced Swag easily. His Mark I would never come to range before Little Satan had the chance to claim Jack, access the room, and doom them all. A small crowd parted like a Red Sea of bystanders as they fled before the pregnant, afflicted woman. Jack cursed, struggling to correctly enter his entry code under such duress.

"Jaaaack!" Swag howled, urging him to do better.

"Yargh!" Jack screamed as he repeatedly miskeyed the code in his haste. Bud and Edward stepped up to try and shield Father's second-in-command. They knew that the beast would tear through them in no time at all.

Swag made a split-second decision with only a seconds remaining before Little Satan would have its prize. He planted his feet, drew the sidearm from his hip, exhaled an aiming breath, and fired in one instinctive move that would have made Agent Scofield jealous.

The pregnant woman spun and flopped to the ground as the bullet tore through her; she skidded to a stop in a bloody mess at the feet of the surprised trio. Jack collapsed to his knees in a heap of fear and failure, thinking that the ringing gunfire had been the demoniac's attack.

"Nobody touch her," Swag screamed as he ran onto the scene. He asked in passing, "Are you guys all okay?"

Edward, Bud, and Jack stood rooted to the ground, completely taken by the shock of Swag gunning down a pregnant woman. "I finally got you," Swag muttered a bunch of curses on his invisible enemy.

He barked orders that nobody heard through the initial fog. Swag shouted them again. "Edward! Edward," he snapped his fingers to get the youth's attention. "Get to the clinic and wipe that blood off of your skin. Do not get it on any wounds or let it get inside your mouth or in your eyes—none of it did, right?"

Edward had gotten the worst of the spray; the rest seemed to have splattered to the floor nearby. He looked at the scientist blankly for a second and then shook off the shock. "No. I—I don't think so."

Swag grabbed him and checked his eyes. There was no change in them. He clapped Edward on the shoulder. "Put your bloody clothes and any rags or wipes you use someplace safe and under direct light. We will worry about containment later. Bud?"

The older gentleman seemed as cool and collected as ever. He gave Swag his attention.

"You didn't get splattered, did you?"

He shook his head in the negative, only slightly less affected by the shock, but he hadn't been quite as close as Edward had been.

"Cordon off this area with tape or rope or whatever you can find. Nobody gets close; no one touches anything nearby. Get a bright UV lamp on the area too, just in case."

Bud nodded and trotted off to find the supplies and carry out his task.

Michelle was already jogging over when Swag waved her off. "Extra precautions! Go back and get some kind of protective barrier. This thing can only travel through bodily fluids with these lights, so we've got to be super careful."

"But Janessa… the baby—every second we waste means we might not be able to save them."

"Exactly," he said commandingly and pointed back to the clinical room. "The longer we argue, the less time she has. Double layer yourself just to be safe."

She glared at him for a second and then turned and sprinted back to get supplies and returned moments later as Swag checked over Jack. He did an eye check and ordered him to remain inside the control room until things got sorted. He'd just pulled the shell-shocked Jack sheepishly to his feet when Michelle shouted her findings.

"I've got a pulse! It's weak, but Janessa is still alive."

People begin poking their heads back into the promenade area, curious about the situation.

"Somebody, help me get her over to the clinic," Michelle called for an assistant.

Swag overrode her. "First, they've got to get protection on," he pointed to the room.

Edward stepped closer. "I'll help. I'm already covered in blood, so what does it matter?"

They both looked at Swag. Swag could feel everyone's eyes on him. He nodded, measuredly.

Swag kept his voice low. "We've just got to be safe. We can't take any chances. And first, turn her head." He leveled the Mark I at her as Michelle pivoted her face to the side.

He pushed the trigger. Nothing happened. He pushed it again, hoping she'd vomit.

Michelle motioned Edward to help her lift.

"Hang on a sec," Swag insisted. "Something's not quite right." He tapped the Mark I against his palm and tried again. He didn't know for sure if it could force a comatose patient to expel the entity, but he assumed it would. There were so many variables that the EC had never actually field tested.

"You'll have to fix the thing later or find a way to test those fluids already on the ground," Michelle took charge as the medical authority. "My only concern right now is keeping Janessa and her baby alive." She held Swag's gaze, "Right now, *you're getting in the way of that.*" This time he was on *her* turf.

He reluctantly nodded and began fidgeting with his device, trying to troubleshoot on the fly while the others worked to save the pregnant woman.

Michelle and Edward hoisted Janessa onto a sheet of plastic so they could contain any possible contaminants. Just as they began to drag her body towards the medical area Bud arrived with a portable, high-intensity light rig. He set up the freestanding tripod scaffolds and erected a quarantine zone.

"You're a good man, Bud." Swag nodded to him briefly, and then left him to do the work. He followed Michelle at a distance, still playing with the Mark I.

29

Swag looked to his right and spotted the remnant holding vigil beyond the windows of Michelle's medical bay. He glanced left, past Father's still body, and to the thin, hanging sheet which separated them from Michelle and her two volunteers who had some cursory medical training. They worked feverishly to save the life of the unborn child and Janessa.

Scowling, Swag felt the weight of the gun at his side. He remembered saving Janessa's life on E-day only to put a bullet into her years later.

He turned the last few screws into the Mark I device he had built so many years ago and sighed. This was the same tech he'd built a decade ago and repeatedly tested on Horton and Little Satan. Swag *knew* this machine, and by all accounts it should've functioned. Swag had hooked up electronics testers and checked battery life. He hoped that cleaning the internals of the unit might do the trick, but he wouldn't be able to get beyond the sheet and try it on Janessa until they'd finished operating on her gunshot wound.

He swallowed the lump in his throat. If Swag tried it again and it failed to expel the entity it meant that the alternative diagnosis could be more dire… unless he'd made a grievous mistake in the promenade, earlier.

Sinking the last screw, he heard Father groan at his left. Swag put down his newly repaired device and leaned in to listen.

"Did... did you get my journal?" Father's eyes barely opened as slits, but he pointed as best as he was able to the work tray near Swag's chair. The Mark I and Father's tattered, old Bible both rested upon it.

"I'm sorry. Not yet. But I thought if I read some Scripture to you it might help give you hope. I never really knew if people could hear things or not when they were in a coma, but I figured we could use all the hope and help we can get—even if I'm not sold on the premise, I know you are."

Father groaned in response. The growl carried a note of disappointment.

"I've mostly been running things in your absence. Well, Jack and I. Michelle's helped a lot, too."

"It will be harder for *you* to accept," he said in his slow, matter-of-fact voice. "Blind is the man who views science and religion as polar opposites rather than different hands of the same body. *Faith is the only salvation for the human race.*"

Swag looked at him. "You said that before. What do you mean by it?"

Father coughed, "You already know... deep down." He coughed again. "Read... read my notes. It will make sense." His eyes rolled back and Father stiffened slightly, exhaled a long and raspy wheeze, and then relaxed. The monitors hooked up to him screeched.

Panicking Swag looked back through the window. No-one outside holding vigil could see what was happening.

"You hold that here! You hold that one there," Michelle barked orders to her helpers on the other side of the drapes before finally bursting through. "Start CPR," she ordered Swag.

Dutifully he began chest compressions on Father. Michelle pulled out an AED and began a charging cycle.

"Clear," she yelled.

Swag pulled off and Michelle hit Father with five hundred volts. His heart immediately began to blip on the monitor again.

They both waited tensely to make sure that his condition stabilized. Finally Michelle said, "I know you mean well and that you want to stick close, Swag, but you've got to go somewhere else. I don't want you to take this the wrong way, but you've got to stop killing my patients."

Nodding, Swag collected his refurbished device and Father's Bible. "I understand," he said truthfully. "Sorry."

Michelle nodded, though her face glowed softer than her stern demeanor. "I've got this—it's *my* specialty. You go figure out a solution to our *other* problems… like that." She pointed to the pile of bloody rags and clothes Edward had deposited in a biohazard bucket.

Swag shook his head again and left. He knew she was right: he would be more useful elsewhere.

On his way out the door Swag stated, "I have a short-range EMF sensor I pulled from the Ark's main gate a little while back; it can be retrofitted to a battery pack. It is bulky and only accurate to within a few feet and with a direct field range, but it should work."

She stared at him, beckoning for an explanation while snapping on a fresh set of latex gloves.

"I built an entity detector; if it's trapped under the light or inside of a citizen I'll be able to find the little bugger. Those clothes are fine—I already checked them. They can be cleaned or destroyed safely." He scowled. "The blood in the promenade court also registers as clear."

They locked eyes for a few seconds. Swag hoped that she would suggest that he test the patient currently bleeding behind the curtain, but she didn't break her resolve to help Janessa first, and play ghostbuster afterwards.

Michelle shrugged and returned to the other patient who urgently needed her. "I wish I could help—but you're going to have to figure this one out on your own."

Edward looked up guiltily.

Swag walked in on him rummaging through Father's belongings. Swag cocked his head in disapproval for a second, and then shrugged as he slid into the recliner in the priest's office.

When Swag didn't say anything Edward assumed he should continue his search. "I'm looking for Father's journal," he explained.

"I figured as much."

He continued digging through the piles of materials, binders, and books. Edward shot Swag a few curious glances. "So Michelle kicked you out, huh?"

"Yup."

Edward smirked. "Sounds about right." He slumped down into Father's office chair and looked around the room while Swag toyed with the Mark I unit. "Does that thing even work?"

He sighed. "I'm *certain* that it does. Everything tests fine, but…"

"But what?"

"But I can't find any trace of Little Satan."

"In the clothes or blood?"

"Neither," said Swag with a frown.

"Could it be flattened, you know, trapped under the light panels? Would it still register on the sensors if it's airborne?"

Swag rubbed his chin. "I suppose it's possible. We'd have to make a grid and run the EMF sensor over every square foot of the courtyard between the fountains and the control room. I mean, the sensor would still find it, but blood spray or mist can be almost microscopic—I guess that I could've missed it."

"Well, if it's not in Janessa or in the blood splatters, then it's got to be somewhere nearby, right? Otherwise we'd all be dead by now." Edward stared at the scientist for a few seconds. "So what's the hold up?"

"I haven't actually scanned Janessa yet."

"But you tried the Mark I on her."

Nodding apprehensively Swag admitted, "Yes. And I *think* it was working when I did it."

"But you don't know for sure?"

"Exactly," Swag said with Father's words ringing in his ears. "But believing something worked with no result is a far cry from empirical certainty... and I'm not ready to rule out that variable just yet."

Edward chuckled, "But Michelle won't let you in the med-bay, will she?"

"No," Swag merely mouthed the word. "I am a little scared by the other wild card variables. There are so many things we still don't know about the entities."

Edward raised an eyebrow and let the scientist work through his thoughts.

"Janessa just recently started her third trimester. We never had any kind of data on how these things work in that kind of situation." Swag pinched the bridge of his nose and tried to recall anything Jessica Hiddleston might have said about testing children in her research.

"An old, um, colleague of mine was doing experiments with the Eidolon Commission to gather data on entity-host-takeovers and was about to release her research to us. Some of it involved children and special interest groups that had some sort of apparent immunity to affliction, but I never actually got the data. We also never worked with pregnant women because of certain ethical concerns and, well, fear of lawsuits. I'm sure the EC was looking into a way around it though…"

Swag caught the incredulous look on Edward's face at the admission. Swag shut his mouth, trying not to look as monstrous as Little Satan.

"And people like Ricky?"

Tightlipped, Swag nodded. "It's why I suspected he had immunity all along. Other clues confirmed it… well, Ricky confirmed it."

Edward shook his head in dismay. He was entitled to his disgust but knew first-hand how vital the information was to the success of the human species.

They sat in silence for a few more seconds. Swag, still trying to work through his thoughts, ventured another.

"Could the entity get into the fetus? I mean, if I try to expel it from Janessa, could it instead be in her womb—and if I *could* expel it from the fetus, where would it go? If the baby is immune, could the entity hide in the amniotic fluid?"

"I thought kids were immune."

"I *think* but I don't *know* anything about the matter." He grabbed a handful of his hair and tried to ride out the whelming frustration.

"Won't it be a moot point once you can scan both Janessa *and* the fetus with the EMF sensor after she's stable and resting?"

Swag raised a finger to disagree with him, but then snapped his jaw shut. "You're right."

Edward shrugged. "Just relax for a few seconds, man. Have a little patience."

He nodded his agreement and then pointed behind Edward. "There's the journal."

Swiveling in the chair, Edward cursed. "I must've looked right at it six times and missed it every time."

Swag puffed a resentful burst of air. "Yeah, I feel you on that one."

As Edward flopped Father's journal open on the desk a ripple of excitement ran through the voices in the promenade where the crowd held its vigil. Swag turned his attention outside.

He couldn't tell what had caused the enthusiasm and it seemed like it had been too long since anything positive had happened. Something definitely stirred up the crowd. Swag stepped outside and Edward, ever curious, followed him.

Finally Swag spotted it, a head taller than everyone else, Ricky strode into the promenade. Dirty, tattered, and bruised he waved as he walked through the large door they'd left open.

Ricky grinned lopsidedly, unabashedly receiving the hero's welcome. He scanned the crowd and then finally locked eyes with Swag.

The scientist's jaw dropped. He suddenly didn't know what to think anymore. Swag could only join the rest and applaud.

30

The crowd enthusiastically embraced Ricky as the gentle giant walked through them and nursed a slight limp. Men and women slapped him on the back and thanked him for his bravery; they nearly toppled the injured man with their accolades.

It all seemed to suddenly stop when Swag approached. Those who had gathered for the vigil sensed the emotional turmoil rolling off of the scientist.

Ricky ran towards Swag and the friends collapsed into a tight hug. "I'm so sorry I asked you to go outside," Swag said.

"I know. You had to. And I'm not afraid anymore."

"You saved us all, you know that, Ricky?"

"I know." Ricky smiled. "And thank you; I'm brave now."

Swag squeezed tighter, refusing to quit the embrace. He suddenly recognized exactly how much hell the remnant had been through since Ricky's presumed loss. He also realized that a part of him had been lost since sealing those doors. In the hours since then he'd managed to anger Michelle, nearly kill Father, shoot a pregnant woman, and nearly lose his mind in the pursuit of his ethereal enemy.

After rubbing tears away from his eyes Swag clapped Ricky on the back. "I have no idea how you—"

The door behind them opened as Michelle emerged to give the vigil holders a progress update. "Ricky?" Her voice brimmed with schoolgirl delight and she threw herself into her big brother's arms. "How did you survive? Oh Lord, look at you! You need to let me look at those bruises right now."

Michelle turned to look at the too-crowded medical facility. Her volunteers remained monitoring the two patients. "Maybe we can just go to our apartment to do that?" Michelle began to lead Ricky away when a voice called out asking after her patients.

"How are Father and Janessa?"

Michelle turned to answer Jennifer. Even she had emerged again despite facial cuts that had begun healing as tender, pink lines in the flesh. Her return from solitude was a good sign. "They are both stable but will need rest and continued observation." The crowd murmured their gratitude, and no one asked the primary question they all wondered about.

Swag caught Edward's cautionary glance from the edge of the crowd, and then fell under Michelle's gaze. "Michelle," he hunched his shoulders with sorrow, bending closer to her level. "I'm so sorry. Ricky's back, but still… that doesn't…"

She nodded as if she accepted it and then looked back at the clinic. "She's strapped down for now. Do what you have to do, Swag, but do it quietly… after the crowd has left. We can talk later."

Swag swallowed the lump in his throat and nodded. "I'll see you soon, Ricky," he promised. He motioned to Edward that he should follow.

Ricky waved, and they parted ways. A few members of the crowd remained in the court, but they kept silent as the two men slipped silently inside the clinic; the people knew his purpose.

Only minutes later, Edward held the bucket and Swag scanned her with the Mark I hoping to make her vomit. Nothing happened. They checked her eyes but couldn't detect any signs of affliction.

Swag cursed. Desperate for data he and Edward set up the clunky EMF scanner they'd pirated from Ark I's intake area. They set it up meticulously, checking and double checking the connections.

Janessa registered as clean. They worked in silence and rescanned her half a dozen different ways including invasive scans of her womb, but the data was conclusive: Janessa did not hide Little Satan.

Edward finally broke the silence which grew more uncomfortable with each failed attempt. "Are we even sure that she was even afflicted? Could it all have been just..."

Swag shook his head. Not only was he certain, but the alternative was unfathomable. "No. Little Satan took her. I *saw* it." He refused to believe he'd shot a pregnant woman with false cause.

His assistant merely nodded. Edward had also seen the whole thing and believed the scientist, but they had nearly run out of options.

Sighing, Swag said, "We've got to scan that entire area. Go see if Bud can help set up a search grid. It's going to be a long night... day... rest cycle? I don't even know how to say that anymore."

Edward nodded, but replied, "I don't know either. I'll cut you a deal, though. You read through Father's journal like he asked you to and I'll do the scanning with Bud."

Swag's mouth tightened as if sour.

"Hey," insisted Edward, "you're getting off easy. Bud's gotten weirder than normal since you shot Janessa right in front of him."

"You think everyone older than twenty-five is weird, and Bud's the oldest person in the Ark."

"Fair enough," admitted the youth, "but I think PTSD is pretty likely—I'm going to have to babysit him while we scan every square inch of the promenade floor." He paused and stared off into space for a moment. "I've just got a bad feeling about everything, still, and we can use every bit of help we can get. I think Father might have some insight to share—even though he's in a coma."

Swag nodded reluctantly. "Okay. But be thorough… and let me know as soon as you find anything."

"We will."

"And take this. You know how to use it." He handed Edward the Mark I. "If it's disembodied you might come closer to it than I and you should have every tool necessary available to protect the Ark."

Edward nodded.

Swag turned to leave, but then held up a finger as if he remembered one more thing.

"I'll be *fine*!" Edward insisted. "Now you're just stalling."

Busted, Swag nodded. He left for Father's office.

###

Swag sat in the office chair and stared at the two books on the desk. One was Father's journal; the other was his Bible. He swiveled anxiously in the seat, not enthusiastic about the task at hand.

He sighed, then spun a couple circles and swiveled again. Finally, after looking around the room for any ready distraction and finding nothing else to hold his attention, Swag reached out and flipped open Father's journal. The first few pages hooked his interest with ornate, hand-drawn symbols and correlating charts. A few pages deeper, Father's scrawls indicated an explanation of the contained Gematria, a Kabbalistic numerology sometimes used to try and predict the future.

The preacher's words on the topic were not kind and Father's vitriol against the gnostic soothsaying made Swag laugh. Father opposed the practice as vehemently as Swag resisted religious thought.

Still, for all of the scholar's fury, serious effort had been given over many pages to record and interpret the cyphers and charts from different sources. Detailed methods for decoding Equidistant Letter Spacing filled the margins along with many of Father's personal notes… ELS met with mostly skeptical observations from the minister except for his notes on rabbinic wisdom where it was clearly intentional by the original authors.

Is he warming up to some of this nonsense? Swag asked himself. *This is the sort of stuff my parents would have loved.*

Stuffed between pages, a photocopied page unfolded into a copy of an ancient manuscript. At the top, someone had written a title for the work: *The Counsel of Elymas.*

Swag's mind regurgitated information drilled into him by his parents. *Elymas was a sorcerer who fought against the disciples.*

The lines of Father's journal faithfully reproduced the ancient text and the gematriatic numbers; many of them were circled in blue ink. Swag scanned the leaf for clues before realizing it was an ELS sequence from some third party he wasn't familiar with. Another line was written below it: the translation.

Ending every millennium the bonds of Hell soften three, break seven, and heal three. Father wrote in the margin, "3+7+3=13!" Swag flipped back a couple pages to a variety of numerical codex lists indicating special meanings for numbers. Some omitted the number entirely, one did not. It read *13. Depravity and Rebellion.*

Something uneasy twisted in his gut. He turned another page.

A horizontal line spanned two date ranges list of date ranges on a rough timeline. The far left read 970 BC, the next was dated 33AD with a scribbled crucifix under it. The next two marks were 1033 AD and the date of Father's journaling with a parenthetical reference as "(Now)".

Below each marked date he had listed a litany of major world events in tiny print. Swag squinted in order to read the script.

980-960 BC. Solomon becomes king. Pseudepigraphal/Kabbalistic books with partial truth to demonic activities? Keys and Testament of Solomon. Solomon eventually subdues Beelzebub and demonic activity quiets for a period. Great earthquakes and destruction of major cities Dor and Megiddo. Chinese Anthropocene efforts at the River of Sorrow kill millions—were the perpetrators demonized?

†. Resurgence of demonic activity in texts surrounding time of Christ. Many exorcisms in Bible and other historical and extra-biblical texts. Significant increase in apocalyptic literature. Son of Perdition indwelt and possessed by Beelzebub, "Prince of Demons." Murder of Jesus orchestrated by demonic forces and conspiracy by "children/followers of the Devil" from Jn.8:44. Resurrection shatters their power, sends demons back to torment of the Abyss ("waterless wandering"—temp. inability to take a human host?)

Rise of Caligula, collapse of Rome as demons try to wipe out humanity… a shadow of the apocalypse—or an attempt to kick-start it?

Fear gripped Swag and he slapped the journal shut and smoothed the goosebumps that formed on his arms when he read the line "take a human host." Cautiously and skeptically he peeled the cover open again and scanned the inside liner for Father's mark. He'd written his name, the topic of his research, and a date range of a couple years. The scientist's gut plummeted in freefall. The dates ran parallel to his original research with Raymond... their findings, albeit from vastly different perspectives, coincided and collided with empirical certainty! He turned back to Father's timeline.

>   *960-990 AD.* Mass panics about coming apocalypse and rise of Antichrist.
>
>   *1000 AD.* Beginning of famines, plagues, mortality rate. Abbo of Fleury preaches the coming end. Otto III institutes renovatio imperii romani in order to create barrier against coming forces of Hell. Outbreaks of heresies. Glaber predicts unleashing of Satan.
>
>   *1025AD.* Instances of blood rain, sun goes dark 3 days, Apocalyptic visions in monasteries, accusations and burnings of "heretics" carried out.
>
>   *1033 AD.* Major earthquakes and civil uprisings with heretical bents. European famines. Mass pilgrimages to Jerusalem and recommitments before respite begins—possible satanic incarnation via Yosef ibn Naghrela who incites Berbers to massacre Jews—was eventually crucified.
>
>   *Modern era.* Natural disasters, wars and rumors of war, disease, civil unrest, rise of severe mental health defects. Cultural acceptance and expectation of spirit of Belial/Matanbuchus.
>
>   * *Each cycle grows in intensity—are we on the cusp? How soon?*

Swag turned one more page. Two items slid out from between the pages. An obituary for Wanda Ackley-Braff, the victim murdered by the Sinister Six so many years ago. It listed her surviving family as her brother Sam Ackley, husband Roderick Braff, and Son Jason Braff. The second item was a photo print of Swag and Raymond shaking hands with General Braff, Franklin Cuthbert, and a few other members of the EC brass who'd been cropped out of the photo.

Flipping it over, Swag recognized Braff's distinct handwriting. *You may have been on to something, Sam. Keep your eyes on these two.*

Swag stared long and hard at the materials in his hands. A shadow darkening his doorway startled him. He jumped and reflexively snapped the journal shut.

Ricky stood in the doorway, clearly amused by his friend's fright. He sat opposite of Father's desk and put his backpack on his knees.

Clutching his chest as if that could calm his racing heart Swag admitted, "You scared me."

"I know." Ricky smiled and quickly changed the subject. "You should see some of the neat stuff I found."

Swag looked at his friend quizzically.

"First I have to say I'm sorry. I took something without your permission." Ricky pulled the most special duck in the world from his backpack and handed it over while removing the joke book from his bag. "Sorry. But I needed it to help me be brave when I went outside. I also found this really neat, new flashlight."

Swag waved him off as he greedily took the paper duck. "That's okay, Ricky, really it is," he insisted as he searched Father's desk for a sharpie. He momentarily lost all interest in whatever else had brought Ricky by.

With a sigh of relief Swag jotted a series of random numbers on either side of the hidden combination and then added a line of numbers above and below that string in the hopes that he could add at least one more layer of protection by obfuscating the master code.

Ricky watched him work, but didn't ask any questions.

"You did really good, Ricky. You probably don't know it, but you might have saved mankind, again, by borrowing this."

Blushing at the praise, Ricky gratefully accepted the duck back into his possession when Swag gave it to him saying, "You keep it, my friend. It might be too powerful for anyone else to hold. You're kind of the resident hero around here, nowadays."

Ricky put it back into his pack.

Swag leaned back in the chair and sighed with relief. Knowing the duck's fate was one less burden on his taxed brain.

"Is something on your mind, Swag?"

The scientist looked into Ricky's eyes. They brimmed with pure empathy and the desire to help—he spotted something else there: an oft discounted, raw intelligence—a logic unbiased by personal desire, past experiences, or ulterior motives. He instinctively knew that Ricky's advice might be the most honest he could ever get.

"Yeah," Swag chuckled. "All kinds of things on my mind." As if the floodgates had opened, he poured out all his thoughts to his friend: his struggle against the beliefs of his upbringing, all of the arguments for his atheism, his inability to find a comfortable theodicy, his struggles with morality and the Eidolon Commission, his failure to pinpoint the location of Little Satan and the guilt he carried for shooting Janessa, the knowledge bomb dropped by Father's Journal, even his feelings of inadequacy when he compared himself to the remnant's long-time leader. "Father's insistence that 'Faith is the only salvation for the human race' is absurd! I mean, I discovered these things with *science*—why change what's been working for me up 'til now?"

Ricky nodded along, trying to catch as much of what he could as it came at him. He never broke eye contact as his friend shotgunned him with topics and stream-of-consciousness struggles as fast as he could reload.

"I'm just so angry at everything," Swag admitted, slumping further into the chair. He took a deep breath as Ricky studied him from across the desk. "I think I can recognize that I've got too many problems to deal with—too many irons in the fire—I need to deal with some of them before I can try and tackle Father's challenge for faith. I've got to get through everything else, first… right? Right. I can't take on one more thing."

Once convinced, he finally relaxed. Ricky leaned forward.

"That's pretty stupid," was all he said.

Swag blinked like he'd just been slapped.

"All that other stuff you're trying to do is for everyone else. As soon as someone challenges you to work on your own problems, you refuse." Ricky shook his head, confused why Swag couldn't see it.

"Once, when I lived at a group home for other people like me, a mean boy at a park did this." Ricky stood and put an arm out wide and wiggled his hand until Swag turned to look at it. "When I looked at it he kicked me in the family jewels and ran away laughing with his friends. Now do you know what I mean?"

Swag's very confused look gave him away.

"It's what you're doing, dummy." Ricky said with exasperation. He shook his hand again. "You're doing this hand thing so that you have to look at that instead of dealing with the important stuff."

"Misdirection," Michelle said. She stepped through the door where she'd been eavesdropping and took a seat next to her brother.

"Yes! Thank you," Ricky said.

Swag swallowed and nodded. "Maybe you're right," he said quietly. "I've just got a hard time dealing with faith. I've never seen it actually fix anyone's situation—more often than not it's just heaped on more badness."

Michelle shrugged. "I'm not exactly someone that could be called a 'person of faith,'" she admitted with air quotes, "but I don't think faith is something that is results-oriented. It's not about fixing your problems; it's about surrendering them to something or someone else. At least, that's what my mother always said."

A melancholy moment washed over them. Swag, still weakly attempting to avoid his internal struggle, asked Ricky to tell him more about how he got back into the Ark. Ricky was glad to share.

"I told you I found a cool flashlight, but I didn't tell you about when I fell through the ceiling and broke a crate. I found something magic inside." He teased them with the description, drawing in his suspenseful audience.

Finally he exclaimed, "I found a giant box of Twinkies!" He excitedly retrieved them from his backpack and pulled a few of the shrink-wrapped spongy treats from their wrappings and gave one to each of his friends before stuffing another into his own mouth. Through the crumbs he told them about finding Braff's body, prying the malfunctioning door open, and wandering the halls until he found his way back.

31

Bud knocked gently on the door of Father's office where he heard Swag's voice. He'd never been a very bold or daring man and he didn't dare intrude on a conversation of significant importance. Bud hovered in the doorway before finally knocking and interrupting the conversation between Swag, Michelle, and Ricky.

Swag looked up at the older gentleman and pushed away the two big books before him on the desk. He looked relieved for a distraction, as if the topic of conversation had been awkward for him.

"Can I ask you something… in private?" Bud asked.

Swag nodded. They stepped outside around a corner where a hallway wrapped just around the bend from the promenade. "What's up, Bud? I thought you were helping Edward with the scanners?"

Bud's composure broke, and his eyes welled up. "Swag, I can't remember anything! I think I'm afflicted. Oh Lord-this is how it happens, isn't it?"

Swag grabbed him by the shoulders. "What are you talking about? Have you blacked out? When did you wake up? What's the last thing you remember?"

The senior man wiped the tears from his eyes and then the moisture at the corner of his lips. It left a thin and faint red streak across his cheek. Blood.

"Wait. That's blood."

"I'm not bleeding," Bud said with a shaky voice. "The last thing I remember was the loud bang of the gunshot and Janessa falling—and then *nothing*. Well, except a few moments ago; I suddenly started remembering again, er, thinking again.

"I was at the water station in the Promenade and Jack was there. He was laughing… laughing and bleeding from his neck. I didn't understand why until I realized I could be afflicted. I came straight to you—I thought that maybe your gadget can fix me."

Swag shattered his hope. "That's not how it works at all!" He cursed Little Satan's cleverness at hiding in the man—even performing Bud's regular duties—until he had the chance to take a host with control center access.

The scientist reached for his Mark I where he kept it clipped to his hip, but then remembered that Edward had it. A scream pierced the air around the bend, coming from the Promenade.

Swag whirled and sprinted for the main courtyard.

Swag burst into the main opening and spotted Edward, struggling to crawl on his side. His eyes had glossed over with the distinct look of shellshock. The smashed sensor lay scattered across the floor, adhering to the sticky smears of Edward's blood the beast had splattered across the tiles. Three other men lay crumpled in heaps nearby, each in similar or worse condition. Bodies littered the path between Edward and the control room.

With his neck leaking blood from the nasty wound, Jack finished pressing the button sequence and then turned to face Swag. His black, empty sockets radiated hatred and his smile twisted with perverse glee. The entity had done it; Little Satan won.

Swag's ears pounded and grew hot. Dark whispers threatened to creep into his mind and crowd out his vision.

He felt suddenly lightheaded, anxious, nauseous, and terrified all at once. Doom sank into his soul—there was no way to stop Little Satan from accessing the sensitive chamber, now.

In his hand the afflicted man held up the Mark I device for the scientist to see. They locked eyes and with a sneer of disgust Little Satan crushed the apparatus. He stepped backwards through the door so that the last thing Swag could see was his devious smile. The entry shut and locked with Jack inside.

Seconds later, the lights went out. Shrieks of terror rose up all around the promenade: desperate wails of dread.

A low and growling voice flooded Ark I via the intercom system. "I always knew it would come down to you and I, Mister Swaggart." His words dripped with evil that punctuated his plosive syllables.

The whirring hum of the battery backups vibrated momentarily, and the emergency lights came up once again. Swag felt each and every eye upon him as if those luminaries had been spotlights.

"I have long wondered if you knew that *it was me* under your bed as a child. Do you remember that, little Jimmy?" The demon had certainly mastered condescension. "I think I might enjoy watching the final hopes of the human race fade and die alongside the dwindling energy supply. These millennia have taught me the little joys found within the virtue of patience."

It spat a final challenge before dropping the microphone and severing the line with a sharp pop. "Tell me Mister Swaggart, where is your science now?"

32

Not many minutes had passed before the entire remnant gathered in an all-too familiar formation in the main court. There, the battery powered luminaries burned brightest. They trembled as a single cluster beneath the pall of despair.

Ricky and Michelle jogged towards the group from Father's office. Ricky, with his backpack slung over his shoulder, clutched three books to his massive chest: *1001 Jokes and Puns, The Holy Bible,* and Father's private journal.

As they closed the distance Swag caught the murmuring voices. He did a double take and saw Jennifer speaking—but many repeated her comments.

"I hear voices in the dark… pounding like drums."

"I hear them too."

"Whispers—taunting me from the shadows."

Swag turned to Jennifer. "What did you say?"

"Don't you hear them? It's like a dark voice in my head—pulsating in my mind."

The scientist noted that the final vestiges of humanity could easily be wiped off the map if the people panicked. He glanced at the control center door; Swag didn't have a plan for the creature yet, but he knew they stood no chance if the group panicked.

"Everyone listen! Everybody look at me," he shouted. "The whispers are not real! They're just nonsense sounds called tinnitus. Michelle can tell you, too—it's just the fear making blood rush across your eardrum—that's the sound you're hearing, and I can prove it."

A hopeful sentiment rumbled through the mass. They looked to him to verify their trust.

He knew that there were no words—just the muted rhythm of each person's heartbeats—it was pure physiology. "Okay. Everybody close your eyes and concentrate on the 'voices' you're hearing for ten seconds. I'll count them down—after I say 'one' you all shout out what you heard the voices say! Ready? Go."

Swag ticked off the seconds aloud, quiet at first. The dark cacophony niggled at the edge of his own consciousness, too, but he paid it no mind. He already knew focusing on it would yield nothing but the fwump fwump of his own circulatory system. It should be the same for each person gathered.

He finished his countdown. "Three. Two. One!"

A resounding chorus of fearful voices proclaimed all at once, "I'm coming for you!"

Swag's eyes widened in terror and he realized they were right. He could suddenly make out those words now, too!

Nearly a dozen people in the crowd sprinted into the darkness and beyond, shrieking in madness. One of the pregnant women in her late second trimester gripped her belly in anguish and collapsed to the floor as the abject terror caught up with her body. Michelle ran to her aid, bull-rushing her way through the terrified crowd.

Swag's mind reeled, and his mind swam like he'd been locked for hours in a sauna. He staggered over to where Michelle knelt with the woman in distress. His eyes had trouble focusing, but he felt every eye upon him and heard the fright permeating the words anyone nearby.

His ears picked up snippets of conversations as some huddled together to die.

"This is the end."

"Somebody's got to do something. Why can't anybody do something?"

"If only Father was conscious."

"How can Swaggart do nothing?"

He turned to face the doorway that separated the people from Little Satan. It loomed menacingly on the edge of the courtyard.

One voice rose above the chaos… Ricky's. "I'll do it. I will go."

The purity of his voice silenced the crowd.

"No, Ricky! You can't go," Michelle insisted as she pressed inquisitively on her patient's abdomen.

"I have to go. Don't worry. I'm brave now." He held up his backpack and stuffed the joke book inside the bag and held the Bible. "Besides, I've got all of this stuff to help me. I'm prepared for anything."

With wet eyes Swag watched his friend volunteer to lay down his life on a fool's errand.

An overwhelming sense of conviction washed over him. *This started with me and it ought to end with me*, he thought.

Swag turned to his friend as the finer details of a plan came together in his mind. He gently took the bible from Ricky's arms. "I have a plan. Do you have the duck?"

Ricky nodded vigorously and began to dig through his pouch for it.

"You won't need it yet," he promised, "but it will be a necessity soon."

Ricky cocked his head. Michelle, nearby, understood that it held the access code—though she would need Ricky's help to narrow down the actual numeric string.

"You've been brave enough, my friend. It's my time to finally put Little Satan down for good." He stared down at Father's dog-eared bible, not quite certain how he would be able to use the book to do that. "I will beat this demon or die trying." Swag's mind raced with all of the options available to him: his holstered sidearm, the magnum locked in the safe box, the grenade on Braff's never-used desk.

"I'm coming with you," Ricky insisted.

"I'm sorry, Ricky. You can't. This is something I have to do alone—just like you had to go outside alone. If I don't, I'll never be brave like you."

Ricky stared at his friend, tight-lipped.

"You can come *after* me," he promised. Swag knew that it would be necessary given his plan—the scientist knew that only one course of action would work.

Swag kissed Michelle on the forehead. She grabbed his shirt and forced him to move lower, so she could kiss his lips instead. When they pulled apart they knew each other's thoughts. *That moment might have been the only chance either would ever have for a kiss—Swag didn't expect to survive the next few minutes.*

Throwing his arms around Ricky's meaty frame, Swag said, "I will see you soon, buddy."

Ricky squeezed him momentarily and then let him go.

Swag faced the door in the distance and took the first step towards his assumed destiny. The scientist had a date with a grenade and a bear-hug. He held the Bible by the spine and let the tome plop open wherever it may, and he uttered the first prayer he'd offered in decades.

"Dear God, you'd better have something in here that works."

#

Swag glanced down as he walked towards his doom. His eyes caught the preacher's highlights in Psalm 23. *Yea, though I walk through the valley of the shadow of death, I will fear no evil: for thou art with me; thy rod and thy staff they comfort me.*

Immediately, his spirit bristled at the notion of God's presence. Ricky's words rang in his mind and chastised him. "That's pretty stupid." Swag's cheeks flushed, and he thought of Michelle's advice, "It's about surrendering to something or someone else."

Is it really as simple as all that... is faith just surrender without needing answers to those questions? How can it be as simple as just believing and trusting in a higher power? How can I really do that without knowing what comes next?

Swag stood in front of the door and shifted nervously on his feet. He methodically pushed all the numbers except for the last one. Life within Ark I had not been ideal, but he still wanted to savor the last few moments he had left.

Turning his head, he heard the approaching, heavy footsteps. "You can't come, Ricky. I told you."

"I know, but you should let me—I'm brave now. Besides, you need this," he rummaged through his backpack, trying to locate something. "I know it will help."

"Sorry Ricky. Even the most special duck in the world can't help me. I've got to be brave like you." He pressed the final key and the door slid apart. It quickly shut behind him and locked Ricky out, where it was still safe… for now.

33

As soon as the door locked shut Little Satan had Jimmy Swaggart in his sights!

Swag whirled just in time to block the fiend who swung a broken chair leg like a club. Father's bible flew out of his hands and skittered across the floor where it broke open and split the binding. It lay in two halves.

Yanking his gun to bear, Swag fired two shots too early. He howled with rage as he jerked on the trigger until his magazine emptied.

The demoniac leapt and dodged with uncanny agility and speed. Even if Swag had been a marksman he might've fared no better.

He threw the useless weapon at the enemy who easily sidestepped it. Swag turned to run for the rear wall, but the fiend caught him in seconds and spun him around.

A baleful, empty flame smoldered in Jack's eyes. It had burned away everything that remained of the former English teacher—only demonic hate remained.

Swag lashed out at his attacker, throwing his fists clumsily. He missed widely on all accounts, but blocked the counter-attack with his face. Swag's head rocked back, and he saw flashes like stars as he staggered backwards.

Little Satan cackled gleefully as the scientist stumbled upon his feet. He charged ahead with super-human speed and slugged him so hard that Swag flew across the room. His body smashed a video panel and he crumpled to the floor.

Gasping for breath that wouldn't seem to fill his traitorous lungs, Swag looked over his shoulder. If he could only will his body to move he might still survive. The locked panel within arm's reach concealed another handgun. Swag finally stumbled to his feet and leaned against the wall, punching his combination into the keypad.

The demon shambled forward slowly, arrogantly. His growling breaths rumbled like a stalking lion that neared his prey.

"All those years you thought you were studying me, human. But I studied you—and you were not my first. I've watched your kind for millennia."

The hatch on the wall clicked open and Swag snatched the heavy pistol from its resting place. Whirling, he jammed the Colt Python into Jack's face and pulled the trigger. *He couldn't miss!* Click.

With eyebrows raised in surprise, the afflicted man took one step back and laughed.

Swag pulled the trigger again and again. Click. Click. The revolver had never been loaded.

Swag panicked and dropped the piece; he sprinted towards the alcove. Little Satan snarled; with one scooping motion he snared a nearby chair and flung it at the scientist. The furniture struck him with incredible force and knocked him off his feet. Swag scrambled off his knees and tried to get to Braff's desk.

Little Satan took three quick steps and kicked the human with all his fury. Swag felt his body leave the ground—felt ribs break with the impact and then again when he landed in the nook.

The demon taunted him again as Swag slumped off the desk and anxiously searched for the final, explosive weapon. "I called out to you for so many years, Jimmy." His sinister voice dripped with false compassion. "You heard the drumming of my voice as I cooed your real name in the dark: 'faithless one' my brothers and I called you." He sneered as he approached the crawling scientist who scrambled across the steel desk and snatched the explosive device before retreating and cowering below.

Swag scurried from under the shelter and slithered away as Little Satan hurled the metal frame onto its side. The attacker leapt across the distance and tackled the human who pulled the pin on the grenade.

Screaming with everything he had left, Swag lunged for the demonized Jack.

Quick and too clever, Little Satan sidestepped the charge, snatched Swag by the wrist, and spun him around. The demon had no understanding of the device Swag held; it looked very little like modern grenades and so Little Satan paid it no mind.

With the live round still clutched in his hand, the demoniac pinned Swag against the rear wall. The beast grinned at the presumptuous savoir of the human species. "You still think you can win," the monster glibbed, hissing into his prey's face.

Swag smiled through the bloody saliva that reddened his teeth. "That's because I know how to count," the scientist's mind counted down to the end.

Those cold, vacant eyes fixed on Swag and suddenly recognized the Type 91 for what it was. "Five. Six. Seven…" As the scientist's heart sank into his gut, Little Satan knocked the grenade from his hand and sealed it inside the safe, slamming shut the locking door Swag had just pulled the .357 from. A split second later the wall rumbled with concussive force.

With his free hand, Swag pulled free an old-style corded telephone and smashed its bulk across the surprised face of the afflicted. Swag scrambled across the floor in an effort to escape, but Little Satan pounced on him with predatory instinct. He wrapped the coiled telephone cord around his victim's neck and squeezed.

Gagging and choking, Swag's face reddened and he could feel the crawling blackness crowd his vision. His eyes wanted to roll back in his head and he saw sparkling glimmers like gold dust floating in the creeping void.

"Oh no you don't," Little Satan threatened. "You don't get to die so easily, not until after I take your body and use it to rend flesh and sinew from each person in this pitiful Ark." He loosened the cord only enough so that Swag could not die.

"When I'm done with the others," he growled, "I will take my time with your friends and peel them like Canaanite grapes before steering your body outside and into the wasteland. There, I hear my brothers whisper of the others who still live—others whom I will also destroy!"

A spark of hope lodged in Swag's heart at the demon's admission. But still, despite the slackened cord, Swag's body momentarily lost consciousness.

Little Jimmy felt like he'd been choking but he ignored the odd sensation. He sat cross-legged on his bed where he read from the book of Revelation. His parents hadn't assigned the passage; it was extra reading he'd done out of dogged curiosity. He possessed a morbid interest in the apocalyptic.

Then I saw a great white throne and him who was seated on it. The earth and heavens fled from his presence...

The boy stared at the text. He didn't understand—why would everyone abandon the God who had done so much for them? "Even the angels?" he whispered, remembering the passage from Matthew which *had* been his given reading... *the heavens and the earth would pass away but the Word would remain.*

A rivulet of fear trickled through him and he shuddered. *Not me, God,* he prayerfully promised. *Everyone else can leave you and flee—but not me. I will stay. I won't abandon you.*

Swag's mind reeled back to the present. Sucking in a gasp of air, he teared up at the memory. He'd felt that promise so deeply—his child-self had so fervently believed. Little Jimmy hadn't needed proof or evidence—he *knew* God. He didn't care if God was big and scary or that he couldn't understand and relate to Him... as a child, everything and everyone had felt like that.

With wet eyes Swag desperately wished that he was nine again, that he could be a child—have that kind of faith. Returning from the visionary lapse in consciousness, he gagged against the telephone cord as it bit into his neck.

Swag didn't care about the evidence anymore. All he wanted was to have such a heavenly confidence again—that feeling of connection to a higher power. If it meant surrendering everything he thought and held to be accurate, then fine! None of that mattered in the final seconds he had left of his life, anyway. Only a few seconds remained to him and Swag decided to give it back to the God of his youth.

I may flee like everyone and everything else, but take me as I am, Lord. I'm sorry that it took me so long to come around—give me faith again.

Little Satan hissed as he leaned forward and hovered above Swag. Drooling hot saliva, he whispered into his captive's ear. "The time of man has ended, little Jimmy Swaggart. The day for *my* kind has finally arrived."

The demoniac cackled and sank his teeth into Swag's neck. Thick blood bubbled up through the punctured skin and Little Satan shook his maw like a junkyard dog on a bone.

Swag screamed.

A mouthful of flesh muffled Jack's growl as he maintained his clamped jaws for several seconds. The guttural rumbling turned confused and frustrated as three entire seconds passed.

The demon can't take me! Am I immune? The fervor of righteous indignation welled up deep within him.

Little Satan reared back and roared. He attempted another bite on the nape of the scientist's neck, but the suddenly catalyzed Swag jerked his head backwards and head-butted his captor, breaking Jack's face open.

Gasping for air, Swag scrambled forwards while Jack tried to rub the shock out of his bleary eyes. Swag snatched the Colt Python by the barrel and pistol whipped the reeling man. The butt cracked Jack's temple with a sickening thud.

Swinging wildly, Little Satan's clumsy but powerful strike knocked Swag over, more like a push than a punch. The gun-that-was-a-club fell from his hand and the wielder slid to a stop ten feet away.

Swag reached for the broken chair leg. Just as he laid hands on it, Little Satan was on him. The scientist struggled against the beast who tried to grab ahold of him by the neck. Finally, he kicked the afflicted man off of him and sprang to his feet.

With his best homerun swing he smacked Little Satan across the torso with the makeshift club. The demoniac didn't budge—even though the force of the impact busted bone and dented Jack's torso like an empty tin can.

Little Satan snarled defiantly as two of Jack's ribs punctured through the skin. He glared at the scientist.

Swag swung again, smashing the weapon across his enemy's face, turning the beast's head to the side. He took a step back from seemingly impervious monster. The demoniac smiled deviously; blood spilled from his split lips.

With violent force he unleashed a series of hellish blows. Fist after fist connected, pummeling the poor scientist's face, spinning him, and knocking him backwards.

Swag feebly tried to take the offensive, but his punches fell aside limply as the enemy easily batted them away before slugging him in the gut. The follow-up strike knocked the staggered scientist flat on his back.

Little Satan grabbed Swag by a leg and flung him into the center of the room where he collapsed near Father's broken bible. Swag's eyes caught a highlighted passage in Acts 16. He mouthed the words silently—and when the afflicted reached down to seize him again, he instinctively read the verse aloud. "I command you in the name of Jesus Christ to come out!"

The demoniac bristled and snapped erect. It hissed and snarled at the sudden convert's words.

Swag struggled to his feet while the demoniac remained mere few feet away, stalking him with sidesteps meant to keep the reluctant prey in its sight. Swag read it again with more confidence this time. "I command you in the name of Jesus Christ to come out."

It shuddered and batted at its ears as if the words caused physical pain. He seethed, "Jesus Christ I know… you I do not."

"You'd better get real familiar with me and real quick, then," he spat. "My name is Jimmy Swaggart and I command you in the name of Jesus Christ to come out of him!"

The demoniac writhed and shrieked with an ear-piercing scream. He stepped forward aggressively.

"I said to come out in the name of Jesus Christ!"

Little Satan's resolve broke; he pivoted on the balls of Jack's feet and sprinted for the door. Just as the routed fiend got to the exit it opened from the outside.

He skidded to a halt just as surprised as Swag was by the turn of events. A very astonished Ricky stood in the doorway holding the unfolded duck in one hand and a Gadarene Baconator in the other.

Reacting on instinct alone the big man triggered the GB even as he flinched in surprise. "Flashlight!" Ricky yelled, identifying the device he'd found in the air duct.

Jack shrieked as the device ripped the ethereal Little Satan from the man's battered body. The human host collapsed in an abused heap as the LED on the Entity Containment Device flipped colors to indicate a completed capture.

Hot on Ricky's heels, Michelle burst into the room and tried to help Jack whose breaths came in ragged gasps. Blood leaked from his swollen chest wound; it bubbled bright pink indicating lung damage.

Ricky rushed towards Swag who took one wobbly step towards his friends and then collapsed in a pile of his own. "I'm sorry, Swag. I know you told me to wait, but I heard a bomb and Michelle said I was a hero."

Swag futilely tried to get to his feet again and then resigned himself to receiving assistance. "It's okay. You did good, Ricky. You saved us again." He coughed and winced through the pain that wracked his body. "Do me a favor and go over to that computer over there?"

Ricky complied, and Swag walked him through what buttons to click so that power to all of Ark I's systems restored. The lights came back on in full.

Swag's eyelids fluttered, and he lost consciousness.

34

Normalcy—or whatever passed for that within Ark I, had almost resumed.

Ricky pushed Father Ackley's wheelchair toward the door to the control room. Despite a nasty limp, Swag pushed Jack's. He pushed his luck even though Michelle had just cleared Swag to be on his feet again after Little Satan's attack a week ago.

Their reluctant doctor couldn't keep the anxious men in her medical bay any longer. Michelle knew she probably couldn't stop them and she couldn't monitor them every minute of the day; she'd scheduled an exam for Janessa and several other swollen women who neared their due dates. Both Janessa and her baby had shown much improvement. Their prognosis was good.

The guys had slipped out of sickbay without Michelle's permission as soon as the doctor began Janessa's procedure.

"I still think we ought to race," Ricky laughed, trying to bait his friends.

"I think that would be a terrible idea," Father said, though not without humor. "Besides, Ricky, I need you to take me to my office before we join Swag and Jack in Operations."

"Okie-dokie." Ricky turned sharply and loped away with the minister who begged for his pilot to slow down.

Swag accessed the control room door and wheeled Jack inside. Nobody had been inside it since the attack. The room remained trashed and smeared with blood, now long dried.

Jack, feeling his salt, thought he might try to leave the wheelchair, groaned, and suddenly thought better of it. He painfully laughed through lips that had been stitched back together with black medical thread. "I think I'll stay put."

Swag patted him on the shoulder and then walked gingerly into the middle of the room where he bent to retrieve the two halves of Father's Bible. It took several seconds to accomplish such a simple task. Stiffly and with labored effort he finally stood straight again.

The door opened, startling both men.

"Oh. I thought you might've been Michelle coming to scold us," a relieved Jack admitted.

Father chuckled. "No. But I assume it won't be long before she finds us." A thick binder rested on his lap and Ricky pushed the man towards the main operations console.

Swag met him halfway and returned the man's Bible.

"You keep it," Father told him with a wink. "I'm sure I can find another somewhere in storage."

Swag nodded gratefully and Ricky maneuvered Father's chair to the keyboard.

Father peered at the frame of the flat-panel monitor hanging on the wall and traced a thin crack back to a bullet hole; luckily, the breach was an inch away from the screen and it hadn't cause any functional damage. He glanced at Swag.

Swag shrugged.

Father returned to his work and opened the binder to a few pages marked by index tabs. "You might have noticed how Hank barely got this place fully operational before all hell broke loose," he said as he scanned a tree of commands in the binder. "But not *everything* is fully functional, yet."

"What do you mean?"

Father winked at him again. "Enter Hank's master code and get me into this console."

As Swag complied Father asked, "What do you think about when you hear the name Ark I?"

"I don't know," Swag guessed, "Noah… floods?"

Father shook his head to the contrary. "What about Ark II or Ark III? Where is everyone else?"

"I always figured that this was a prototype and they'd never gotten around to building any others," Swag guessed.

Interrupting them, the door opened behind them revealing Michelle.

"Uh-oh," Ricky laughed nervously.

Swag grinned sheepishly, but Michelle didn't seem all that angry.

"I'm just surprised I was able to keep you guys on bedrest for as long as I did," she smirked.

Father motioned to the binder on his lap. "I've known for a long time that there were other Arks. But I don't know if anyone else actually got to safety on E-day. You're right, though. Ark I was a kind of prototype according to Hank's notes, but it was also more than that. Each of the Ark shelters served a special kind of purpose beyond mere preservation of the human race."

Recognizing the quizzical look, Father explained. "Ark V is located in Colorado, hidden underground near the Denver airport—it's basically a giant zoo meant to preserve as many species of animals as possible. Ark I is the communications and operational spearhead—without Ark I active, nothing else works quite like it should. Humanity should be able to coordinate any other rebuilding efforts with our resources. Except that the communication systems were never brought online.

"I'm pretty sure Hank died on E-day, but luckily he left a way to put it all back together."

After a few vigorous keystrokes a login box popped up onscreen asking to activate something called the Proclamation Network. The box asked for login credentials—just an empty input field. Father turned to Swag with raised eyebrows.

Swag sighed, seeing how fate had tied everything together and interwoven throughout his life. He chuckled to himself how he suddenly believed in things like fate. "Twenty-seven. Sixteen. Fifteen."

Father pressed enter and long-dark screens all over the operations room sprang to life—even monitors that had never been active before. Sensor readouts scrolled, and automated satellites fed their data to Ark I. An image of the spinning globe took over the main screen.

Dots lit up five of the seven continents and indicator labels marked them as a worldwide network of Ark facilities. Messages logged and held in queue from leaders of the other Arks, each checking in and awaiting contact like the feed of an abandoned email account. A number glowed beneath each tag to indicate the number of survivors at each one.

The people in the control room traded hopeful glances.

Jack watched a sensor display from the oceans. "Guys? This might be significant." He pointed to the screen which showed an elevation in oceanic plant life. A rolling percentage indicator detailed the estimated date before photosynthesis from the aquatic flora returned the planet's oxygen to minimally livable levels.

Data continued pouring in and confirmed that the world had begun a steady healing process. "Two more years," said Michelle. "In just two years we can go outside again."

"Will the demons be gone by then?" Jack asked.

"They will never *really* be gone," Father stated. "They've always been here, hiding… chiefly in the darkness of mans' hearts." He turned his attention to the new, incoming messages from the other Arks whose systems had also begun lighting up once the Proclamation Network had gone live and linked the systems together.

"Then what now?" asked Michelle.

Jack noted any reluctance to jump for joy. "If these things are still out there, what does that mean? There's darkness in the world and we can't change that—we'll never truly be safe."

Jimmy Swaggart also bobbed his head thoughtfully. He tapped the old book Father had given him. "It simply means that we must always take care to walk within the light."

THE END.

About the author:

Christopher D. Schmitz is author of both Sci-Fi/Fantasy Fiction and Nonfiction books and has been published in both traditional and independent outlets. If you've looked into indie writers of the upper midwest you may have heard his name whispered in dark alleys with an equal mix of respect and disdain. He has been featured on television broadcasts, podcasts, and runs a blog for indie authors... but you've still probably never heard of him.

As an avid consumer of comic books, movies, cartoons, and books (especially sci-fi and fantasy) this child of the 80s basically lived out Stranger Things, but shadowy government agencies won't let him say more than that. He lives in rural Minnesota with his family where he drinks unsafe amounts of coffee; the caffeine shakes keeps the cold from killing them. In his off-time he plays haunted bagpipes in places of low repute, but that's a story for another time.

Schmitz also holds a Master's Degree and freelances for local newspapers. He is available for speaking engagements, interviews, etc. via the contact form and links on his website or via social media.

Help!

Thank you for reading my book!

Would you please take a moment to leave me a review online? Amazon, Goodreads, or anyplace else you use is an awesome start. You can also share this title with your friends on social media and requesting it via your local library will also help.

Reviews and recommendations help more than anything else out there to help spread awareness about artists and authors. I sincerely hope my stories are worth sharing with the rest of the world!

And as always, check me out online at:
www.AuthorChristopherDSchmitz.com.

Thanks for reading and sharing!

Christopher D Schmitz

SPECIAL OFFER:

Thank you so much for checking out my book! As a special bonus for you, I'd like to invite you download the prequel story for free. *The Dark Veil Opens* tells the story of Swag and Raymond, before the Eidolon Commission got involved, and their first meeting with Jessica... and their introduction to Little Satan.

To get your free exclusive, simply visit this link:

https://www.subscribepage.com/shadowless

Enter your email address and then collect your book. It's that simple and you'll get the story right away!

EIDOLON COMMISION

Discover Fiction Series by Christopher D Schmitz

The Esfah Sagas

Adjudicator

The Hidden Rings of Myrddin the Cambion

Dekker's Dozen

Wolves of the Tesseract

50 Shades of Worf

The Kakos Realm

Anthologies

Faith in Fiction

Please Visit
http://www.authorchristopherdschmitz.com
Sign-up on the mailing list for exclusives and extras

Other ways to connect with me:
Follow me on Twitter: https://twitter.com/cylonbagpiper

Follow me on Goodreads:
www.goodreads.com/author/show/129258.Christopher_Schmitz

Like/Friend me on Facebook:
https://www.facebook.com/authorchristopherdschmitz

Subscribe to my blog:
https://authorchristopherdschmitz.wordpress.com

Favorite me at Smashwords:
www.smashwords.com/profile/view/authorchristopherdschmitz

My Amazon Author Profile:
https://amazon.com/author/christopherdschmitz

Follow me at Bookbub:
www.bookbub.com/authors/christopher-d-schmitz

Made in the USA
Monee, IL
21 July 2023